HUNGRY HEART

SLATER SIBLINGS SERIES

MISSY WALKER

For all the Rosie West's in the world that keep dreaming.

1

ROSIE

Have you ever felt that warm, tingly sensation that washes over you when you listen to your favorite song or watch your favorite movie?

It's the moment when emotion takes over your senses, and you're left with a scattering of goose bumps splintering across your skin or a deep exhalation after holding your breath without even knowing. Sometimes, it is a fluttery sensation in the depths of your stomach or a slash of heat across your chest. It's a feeling that permeates through you, transcending worries or fears, exciting you while also cloaking you with an unexplainable sense of calm. And at that moment, nothing else seems to matter. Even as the world around you crumbles to ashes, your focus remains solely on that *one* feeling.

I imagine that's what love is.

I *imagine* because the truth is, I have absolutely no clue.

I'm twenty-two and still a virgin.

Yes. Seriously.

After my mom's death in a car crash just after my high school graduation, love and sex took a back seat. My focus shifted to learning how to survive. As a result, my experience with love is limited to a string of unsuccessful relationships that never lasted more than a few weeks. Yet, every time I read Darcy or Brontë, I have *that* feeling. I'm guessing that's what love feels like, and I'm clinging to that hope with both hands.

My roommates, Sara and Ethan, like to call me a pathetic romantic and a foxy bitch. But honestly, I don't mind it because they always keep it real with me. Yeah, I know I'm a sucker for a fairy-tale ending, but I also know it's not always going to be rainbows and butterflies. Still, a girl can dream, right?

As a die-hard romance novel enthusiast, I spend most of my free time lost in the intricate world of love. However, Sara's suggestion to check out some 'recreational' websites made me realize the need to expand my knowledge beyond the realm of idealistic love stories.

Let's be real here—I don't want to be clueless when it comes to satisfying my future partner. So, I ventured into the uncharted territory of *those* websites. Mr. Darcy certainly wasn't offering his secrets on pay-per-view, so I took the initiative and did some research. I'm not willing to sleep with just anyone to improve my skills, but I want to have some basic expertise in the matter. Sleeping around? That's not who I am, although you wouldn't know it if you saw me now.

I place my hands on the smooth, cool surface of the marble vanity and lift my head to meet my gaze in the bathroom mirror. As I stand here, the pervasive bass of the music resonates through every inch of my being. The vibrations are so strong that they seem to penetrate even the most intimate parts of my body, heightening my sense of awareness and drawing me further into the moment.

With my hands still resting on the cool marble and my eyes fixed on my reflection, I allow myself to be fully immersed in the pulsing rhythm of the music, feeling its energy and power course through my veins.

It's two weeks before the January semester returns, and my senior internship begins. I should be reading up on my final subjects and not pulling double shifts at the Vanilla Club, the exclusive gentlemen's club where I work.

Fortunately, I'm able to get by with studying less, thanks to my scholarship and decent intellect.

I twist the ends of my blonde wig and adjust the tight black lace bustier trying to cover my barely encased large breasts. It doesn't leave much to the imagination, nor does the leather pleated mini-skirt that barely covers my bottom. My needle-thin black patent pumps lengthen my legs and round out my slutty and hopefully tip-worthy uniform.

I pick up the perfume bottle and depress the nozzle. A fine cool mist scatters along my collarbone as the scent of orchids fills the space. At the same time, the bathroom door flies open, hitting the tiled wall with a thud.

"Rosie, hurry up!" Kara tosses me an impatient scowl.

Naturally blonde and stunning, Kara has worked at the Vanilla Club for years, showing me the ropes when I started just three months ago. Her eyes lower to my outfit, and her scowl morphs into a dark smile.

"That bustier is fucking hot. Hello, tips!" She snaps her fingers above her head, and I exhale through a smile.

Damn, I hope so.

My gaze drifts back to the mirror where a long blond wig hides my thick brown hair pinned up in a chignon underneath. Layers of mascara coat my long lashes and frame my hazel eyes. My signature Venetian-red lipstick outlines my cupid bow and makes me feel like Marilyn fucking Monroe. I need that boost of confidence when I'm here, feigning my existence. It's not easy strutting around pretending you are some sort of sex-kitten to VIPs when in reality, the closest thing you've done is kiss a few boys and get groped on prom night.

But that's irrelevant because I'd pretend to be Donald Duck as long as the tips continue to roll in.

Manhattan's Vanilla Club is an exclusive invitation-only nightclub. Based on limited membership and word-of-mouth, it is home to business moguls, entrepreneurs, and celebrities. The exclusive membership is an eye-watering sum of a hundred grand a year, and the owner, Dante Blade, prides himself on the exclusivity of his clubs that have grown legendary. Scattered up and down the East Coast in only the most exclusive sites, Dante is a multimillionaire and is now a celebrity in his own right. His lavish lifestyle and business achievements have earned him a prominent place among the elite social circles that populate these high-end locations.

None of that matters to me. I only work here because I need a lot of money in a short amount of time, all because my brother, Gabriel, is in trouble again. He put my name on a deal with the loan shark, and now, if he doesn't pay it back in time, they can come after me too.

Yes, I should be angry. I was three months ago when Gabriel confessed it all to me. I was fucking livid. But being that way now will not help me. And it certainly will not expedite paying back his debt.

Goodbye, librarian, and hello, lingerie waitress.

I'm the first to admit the odd change of employment, but all I care about is my brother's happiness. That and the priceless possessions my mother left me. There is no way in hell the sheriff's department will confiscate them to pay back a debt.

"I haven't got all day!" Kara taps her palm against the wooden door, and her gold bangle clangs from the impact.

"I'm coming!" I huff out and quickly set the perfume bottle back. I inhale deeply, which is difficult considering my waist is bound tighter than my own...

Well, you know.

I follow behind her and quickly fall into step down the long, dark corridor.

"The guys at table six are so drunk. I bet they won't know how many Benjamins they slip you. As your VC bestie, I'm gifting table six to you."

I give her a knowing look. "That's because I gave you the billionaires from Brooklyn last week," I counter.

Laughter rolls off her size zero frame. Unlike me, Kara would bed a guy just for another mojito. No judgment here. That's just how she rolls.

"Oh yes, my new Louis Vuitton thanks you too."

My laughter echoes around the corridor as light gives way to dark, and the unpredictability of inebriated men awaits us.

I strut across the club's herringbone floor, the sound of my heels clicking being drowned out by the dark and sexy beat of the music. The club spans two levels with private areas upstairs. Anything goes up there—or so I'm told.

Down here, where I work, there is a strict no-touch policy. But up on the second floor, different rules apply. There, the beautiful women dance to the loud music and walk around in lingerie, submitting to the whims of their wealthy patrons, whatever they may be. It's said that many ruthless deals were made here, even with political and underworld alliances.

With money, one could have anonymity, and any desires these men have could be fulfilled. Although sex is banned in the club, it isn't uncommon. Rumors even fly around that a prominent congressman was on the receiving end of fellatio in one of the ten private suites upstairs. The story never made it to the media, but that didn't stop his wife from filing for divorce a week later.

I stick to down here because A, I'm a virgin and like to think I'm waiting for Mr. Right, and B, at least down here, there are rules guests need to obey.

Kara heads toward her group of tables and gestures toward table six with a jut of her chin. Seated around the velvet lounges is a group of six men, all in expensive suits and in various states of inebriation.

I inhale a deep breath to steady my nerves, and with my shoulders straight, ramrod back, and chin tilted to the ceiling, I smile broadly as I saunter toward them.

"Well, fuck, aren't you something." A voice beside me draws my attention, and I look down to see eyes fixated on my breasts.

Subtle.

My smile is near breaking point, but I take in the men at the table. Gold shiny watches reflect in the dim lighting while tailored suits and expensive cologne invade my senses. Maybe this is the break I've been waiting for.

"Good evening, gentlemen. Welcome to the Vanilla Club," I purr in a silky voice.

Voices moan and whistle in appreciation as I take each of them in, one by one until I reach the head of the table.

Green eyes land on mine. Dark, like perfect emeralds, they send a tingle of heat up my spine. I roll my lips inward, and my smile brightens.

Perhaps tonight won't be that bad.

"Can I start you off with some scotch?" I pull my gaze from the heart-throb with the sharp jaw and perfectly coiffed dark-brown hair.

"Scotch and a blow job?" a voice asks, and the group erupts into husky laughter. The sound reverberates through the room, causing me to flinch momentarily before quickly regaining my composure.

I shift my attention back to the piercing green eyes staring at me. He's assessing me, and a smirk slowly curls on his lips. Irritation prickles over my skin as I try to maintain eye contact with him.

Why did I think he would be any different from the rest of them?

"*Pathetic romantic.*" The voices of my roommates, Ethan and Sara, ring true in my ears.

I dig my stiletto into the wooden floor and force out a smile and turn toward the crude voice. "I'm sorry, sir, but this is not that kind of establishment," I say through gritted teeth, determined to assert my boundaries. "I'll be with you shortly to bring your order of scotch," I add politely, not waiting for a reply before turning on my heel and making my way toward the bar.

Despite the patron's inappropriate request, I maintain my professionalism and composure, not letting the encounter shake me or affect the quality of my service. But as I walk toward the bar, my pulse races from the interaction, and I take a deep breath, steeling myself for whatever else the night may bring.

Jesse leans over the bar and tosses me a wink, his smile widening as he greets me or any of the other waitresses who work here, for that matter. "This place is like a second home to you, Rosie," he remarks.

"Sure is." I let out a sigh. "How's it going, Jesse?"

"You all right?" He polishes the marble to a diamond shine and stares past me, his gaze settling on the table I just came from.

"Admirers of yours?" he asks as his brow arches into a question.

Turning around, I find piercing dark green eyes staring back at me. Leaning against the cold brass bar, a wave of heat ripples across my skin as his gaze lingers on me.

Immediately, I turn back around to face Jesse. I'm used to guys checking me out, but this attraction is different—a strange and unsettling allure with a hint of danger that my body responded to. It's like the pull of a dark star, irresistible and potentially destructive.

"Ah... lucky me," I stammer nervously. "Let's just hope they tip well."

"What will it be?"

"Scotch, thanks."

He selects the bottle of scotch, then fills the six tumblers with ice. "Well, you certainly are looking fine tonight, Rosie." His gaze drops to my chest, then his mouth curves into a wide, mischievous smile.

I roll my eyes. "You say that every night you see me strutting round here."

He puts his hand to his chest and feigns a look of offense. "Not true!"

"Such a flirt." I tsk.

He shrugs. "Okay, why deny it?" He carefully eases the tray toward me. "Just flaunt that delicious ass of yours, and you'll be fine." Jesse smirks. "They're drunk, rich, and ready to party. It's just a regular night at the VC."

Nervous laughter escapes my mouth, melting into the music. He's right. I'm sure he is right. I am just paranoid, overtired, and nervous about my final interview for my summer internship on Monday.

I'm sure that's all it is.

"Thanks, Jesse." I cautiously lift the silver tray and hold it securely in the palm of my hand. The tray's coldness seeps through my hand as my fingertips provide the right support to keep it steady. Not an easy feat in needle-thin stilettos, mind you, but three months in on the job, and I haven't dropped a tray yet.

I breeze past the oversized ornate gold gilded cages where beautiful women dressed in the finest lingerie move seductively to the music.

When I arrive at the table, I carefully set down the tumblers full of ice and pour their drinks. One after another, they graze my hand or pretend not to see me by accidentally touching me.

Typical.

All except him.

When I move around to him and lean across his broad shoulders, he makes no attempt to touch me accidentally.

I remove my hand from the tumbler and catch a whiff of his scent. The spice and woody oak hits the base of my nose and threatens to overtake all my senses.

His gaze travels up my arm slowly until his eyes reach mine, burning a hole through my panties. "I don't want this."

It takes me a moment to realize he's talking about the drink.

"No, sir?"

"That brand tastes like chewed-out ass."

"And you'd know what that tastes like?" The words slip out of my mouth before I can reign them back in. I can't help but mock the rich prick. Usually, I smile sweetly and take any requests, but something about this guy is rubbing me the wrong way.

He narrows his eyes, and a furtive glint catches my attention—an alluring heat that seems to intensify the frisson of electricity already surging between us.

Is he enjoying toying with me?

Regardless, I can't be that cavalier. I need this job. "What is it you'd like?" I ask, quickly correcting myself and smiling sweetly.

His gaze drifts from my eyes to my lips, tracing deathly slow along the column of my neck to my breasts spilling from my bustier. Like a sultry embrace, a seductive warmth envelops my body as the heat circles its way around my thighs. It's as if the temperature has been turned up, causing my skin to flush and my breath to quicken with every passing moment. The sensation is thrilling and unnerving, leaving me feeling vulnerable yet exhilarated at the same time.

His eyes quickly dart back to meet mine. With a stern expression, he declares, "There's nothing you can give me."

"Excuse me?" Heat gone, incoming hate, and an invisible hand that slaps him across the face. Damn, he is handsome, but a girl has some level of self-respect.

Ignoring my question, he continues, "Macallan. A glass of Macallan."

He turns, ignoring me completely, and a new level of anger slides down my shoulders.

I roll my tongue against my bottom lip and set the tray down on the ledge, determined not to let this man in my head.

"Stop stealing our girl, Vin," a drunken voice calls over the raucous table chatter.

"She's not my type," he replies without hesitation.

Asshole.

What was his deal?

Vin. So he has a name. Now all I need is a voodoo doll and a wheel of needles.

"Come on, we're getting thirsty over here," a voice calls.

"Coming." I smile and start pouring the rich amber liquid, filling one glass after the next.

"How I'd like to make that a reality." A man sitting directly below me and beside Vin whisper shouts, and it's met with overzealous laughter.

Oh, for fuck's sake.

Everyone but Vin is laughing and high-fiving each other like a typical frat party.

Vin looks me up and down with a distasteful expression and remarks, "You couldn't even make a cucumber come, Dylan, let alone her."

What is his deal?

Vin steeples his perfectly manicured fingers together on the marble tabletop, a wicked smirk spreading across his thick lips. "Something tells me she's not easily satisfied," he says, his tone dripping with condescension.

My jaw drops open as frustration and anger start to well up inside me, and I can feel the heat rising in my neck.

"I'll take that drink now," he demands.

Oh my God.

I am only halfway through pouring the drinks when he raises his eyebrows impatiently.

Fine.

I set the bottle down with a thud in the middle of the table.

It's obvious that Vin is the big shot here, and if I want a big tip, I'll have to play nice.

Can I do that?

I'm not entirely sure.

As his velvety eyes roam over me, I feel a confusing mix of arousal and hatred. It's as if I'm caught between two extremes, and my patience is slowly slipping away. All I want is to escape from his intense gaze, but I force myself to maintain my bitter restraint.

"Of course, sir," I reply through gritted teeth.

2

VINCENT

I have a secret.

I am not just here because my brother, Julius, asked me to leave the London office for six weeks and mentor a group of interns here in New York. I'm here for pure vengeance.

However, as I sit here, I find myself no longer consumed with thoughts of retribution or caring about appeasing our business partners. Instead, my focus has shifted to a tall, shapely blonde with stunning cleavage and a sharp tongue that I want to quiet with my thick dick.

The thought of seeing those crimson lips sealed shut is incredibly arousing, as is the idea of giving her a firm spanking over my knee. My dick twinges as I picture it in my mind.

She turns abruptly and steamrolls toward the bar. The sway of her curve with each step is captivating, and if it weren't for that sharp mouth, maybe I'd consider.

No.

What the fuck am I thinking?

Normal women can't handle my needs. All women

want more—large house in the country, picket fence, and two-point-four children.

Not.

A.

Chance.

She informs the bartender of my preference, and he immediately reaches for the top-shelf selection.

Good girl.

Lingerie waitresses are a dime a dozen, but this one piques my interest for some reason. When I'm not running one of the most successful venture capitalist firms in America and England, it's rare for anything to arouse my interest. Yet, there's something about her. It's almost like she doesn't belong here.

I fix my gaze on her as she leans against the copper bar, her long legs drawing my attention. I find myself yearning to run my hand up those legs, to lift her skirt and show her how to behave.

"Vin, tell me, where are we at with the board?"

My eyes snap back to the table, where five pairs of bloodshot eyes stare back at me, waiting for an answer.

"Charles, I think you should worry about getting your dick sucked and let me worry about the board," I respond, not nearly in the mood to talk business with drunk and disorderly clients. Cackles of laughter fill the thick cigar-laden air.

He curls a wiry smirk before asking, "At Slater Corp's expense?" he asks.

"You have the full buffet at your disposal," I reply curtly, wanting to distance myself from these fuckers as soon as possible.

"How's the missus?" Stewart asks. "About to drop any day?" he adds, bemused.

Charles turns to Stewart, and his face fills purple with rage. "Why the fuck did you bring that up, Stew?" Charles pierces his colleague with a stare, and he shrivels into the back of his velvet chair.

Charles glances back in my direction, almost seeking my approval. He's weak as fuck and a liability waiting to happen. If it weren't for his company's massive portfolio, Slater Corp would have steered clear of them completely.

"I don't give a fuck what you do," I retort, and it was the truth. A long time ago, I learned that this life is ours for the taking. Emotions land you in trouble. They are a liability, and in business, showing weakness is like blood in the water for a shark.

My emotions were stripped from me the summer afternoon when my brother was murdered.

A pair of long, smooth thighs appear before me, pulling me out of my darkened thoughts. I gaze up and pierce her hazel eyes with a stare.

"Your Macallan, sir," she sneers, her white teeth bright under the shade of red lipstick. "It's the best we have here," she adds with a sarcastic drawl that makes my dick pulse.

The balls on her.

As she places the tumbler in front of me, I notice a brief flash of a scowl on her delicate features, though it quickly vanishes, leaving me to wonder if I imagined it.

I can't help myself when I say, "About time."

Never said I wasn't a jerk, and toying with her was the best part of my day so far. I watch for a reaction, and she doesn't disappoint. With a sudden movement, she jolts upright and stands next to me, firmly planting one hand on her hip.

"What is your problem?" she demands, loud enough for Charles next to me to hear.

Well, that's a first. The gall on this pretty little thing. I contain my amusement, trying to keep a straight face.

Charles chimes in, "Do you know who you are talking to, sweetheart?"

As if I require his support.

She glances at Charles momentarily. Then her wide green-brown eyes lock onto mine, her pale skin flushing with anger.

I dismiss Charles with a flick of my hand. He shrugs, then turns to rejoin the conversation with the others.

"Who are you then?" She shrugs. "Everyone is equally important here."

I curl my index finger, signaling for her to come closer. As she draws near, an incredible aroma invades my senses, as if the very essence of a thousand blooming flowers has been distilled into a single fragrance. I find myself utterly captivated by her scent. For a fleeting moment, I am almost transported elsewhere, lost in the hypnotic spell of her intoxicating allure.

"I'm no one," I whisper darkly, holding her gaze as a charged energy swirls between us. I observe her chest heaving with rapid breaths, and I can't help but drag my sight to the curve of her breasts before quickly snapping out of it.

No, I stick with women who can handle my dominant needs. I like it rough. Hard. Void of any emotion. I have an agency that takes care of my needs here in Manhattan and back home in London.

How old was she, anyway? She looks barely twenty.

"Hi, no one." She's mocking me, and on some level, I like her defiance. If it were anyone else, though, they'd be punished.

"Hey, sexy..." Charles grabs her wrist, and I flinch.

She quickly snaps her hand away and glances up at the security guards near the entrance. She shakes her head their way, a signal she is okay.

"It's Rosie, and sir, we have a strict no-touching policy."

Her eyes dart to mine briefly as frustration grips my throat.

That fucker.

Charles is so unpredictable, and I don't like unpredictable. It isn't the first time he's skirted the line, and my brother, Julius, and I agree he is damn close to being fired from his own company.

Consequences be damned. We'd figure the rest out. We always did.

"Cigars. I will return with cigars," she utters nervously, sensing the tension, then smiles sweetly, but underneath that exterior is a woman who is uncomfortable.

Like a predator, I watch every stiletto step she makes along the wooden floors toward the bar. The bartender beams brightly when she approaches. He's done it with the other waitresses too, but he is extra touchy and flirty with her.

Why can he touch?

And why do I suddenly want to feel the smoothness of her skin?

It's because you can't.

That's all.

Slowly, she peers over her shoulder, her gaze landing on mine immediately. She flicks out her blonde hair, and her jaw tenses when she sees me.

She despises me. Good, take a number, little one. I don't pretend to be anything else.

The bartender says something to her and circles her

wrist. She doesn't shake away, and I wonder if she's sleeping with him.

My nostrils flare at the thought. Yet, even though I choose to be this way, I can't help the jealousy burn in my throat.

Even so, I'm not going there. Plus, I doubt my friend and owner of the Vanilla Club, Dante Blade, will appreciate me sleeping with one of his girls.

Tell my dick that. It has other ideas. I have women in each city I stay in, so it's time I called up one of them because this beauty was getting my dick harder than a steel rod with her sass and sinful curves.

On her next round, she approaches from the opposite end, expertly distributing cigars and snipping tips for each man. She moves in the background slowly, like a hovering panther. As she approaches Charles, the asshole is already eye-fucking her like a new Bugatti driving down Route 66. But she doesn't falter, deftly removing a cigar from the packet while effortlessly balancing the tray.

She stands further away from his chair, and I notice she's careful not to get caught up in the same situation again.

Good girl, intelligent to steer away from danger.

Charles pulls out his chair closer to her. Startled, she flinches, causing the tray to wobble and the remaining cigars to fall onto the floor.

"Shit!" She exhales before quickly recovering. "I mean, I'm so sorry. Sir, let me get you some new ones."

"Shouldn't you pick those up first?" Charles asks, locking eyes with her while arching a salt-and-pepper eyebrow.

That fucking snake.

"Of course." She rolls her lips inward, then bends over, revealing her lace panties.

Fuck.

Her bare back is laced up by black rope, zig-zagging down her back. Soft notes of cinnamon and vanilla hit the base of my nostrils. In my vision, Charles smirks at me. I can't stop what's coming. His hand extends and swings to her curvaceous behind.

What happens next is clear as fucking daylight and too quick for me to intervene.

His eye crinkles into a suggestive wink just as he slides his hand up and underneath her skirt. She lets out a sharp yelp and abruptly stands, hitting her head on the table as she rises.

A surge of outrage pulses through me. How could he have done that to her?

"What the fuck?" She spins around with a look of pure rage in her eyes, directing it at me. Then, before I can even react, she grabs the tumbler of whisky and hurls the entire contents onto my Brioni shirt, drenching it completely.

"Fuck!" My white shirt was now slick with candy-amber liquid.

With a sudden outburst of vitriol, I push my chair back and stand. As I step toward her, my anger and frustration mingle with a strange sense of arousal, and an indescribable energy seems to crackle between us as we stand here, touching. Fiery eyes shoot back at me. Smokey and mysterious, they are huge and hypnotizing, momentarily catching me off guard.

Her hazel eyes narrow as she stares at me, and her pupils dilate, betraying the anger coursing through her veins.

"Vincent, I'm... er..." I overhear Charles' shriveled pin-dick voice beside me, but without taking my gaze off her, I urge out a response.

"I'll deal with you later, Charles," I add with a furious acidity.

She blinks, breaking the moment as confusion swipes over her face at our exchange.

"What's going on here?" Two big security guards appear, and she steps back. I scrape my lower lip with my teeth, barely able to control myself.

She exhales and replies, "Nothing, Angus."

She needs this job.

Interesting.

I narrow my eyes at her, trying to understand why this little kitten is so interesting to me. "This isn't nothing, little one." I point to my now-stained shirt, sticking to the contours of my chest. The shirt I don't give two fucks about.

I'm fucking irate with Charles, but even more so with her. He assaulted her, and she isn't going to do a damn thing about it.

Well, if she won't, I will.

"Sir, would you like to make a complaint to management about your waitress, Rosie?"

I look at her. Vulnerability flashes across her hazel eyes and sullen face, then as quickly as it came, it went, replaced by a scowl and a dare that just wills me to rile her up even more.

Well, you asked for it, sweetheart.

"Yes, I think I would."

"Come with me, sir," the security guard says.

"No, I don't think that's necessary." I lift my phone off the table.

Caught in the crossfire of amber liquid, I shake off the excess droplets and pull up a number I have on speed dial.

I then turn my screen to show her who I'm calling. Her face pales when she recognizes the name.

Dante.

"I can make the complaint myself," I say, doing her a favor because she doesn't want to be here.

If looks could kill, hers were thunderous. As I press the 'send' button on my phone, she abruptly spins on her heel, causing her frilly leather skirt to flutter and reveal the curve of her backside.

Her sudden movement catches my attention, and my eyes follow the swish of her skirt, settling on her enticing ass— annoyance and desire war within me.

Adieu, Rosie. You were a delightful diversion.

3

ROSIE

The sunlight filters through the curtains, transforming the darkness into light.

What time is it?

I open my eyes and squint as I adjust to the brightness. Suddenly, the events of the previous night flood back, abruptly jolting me awake.

Vanilla Club.

Green eyes and a sharp tongue.

Assault.

Drink throwing.

Asshole.

I didn't know if I had a job anymore at the Vanilla Club after his conversation with the owner Dante. Chances are, I was out on my ass.

Fuck. That's all I need.

I roll onto my pillow and let out a stifling groan.

What the hell would I do now? I earned barely half the money working at the university library compared to what I make working at the Vanilla Club.

No, I would crawl my way back, tail between my legs, and beg for my job back. I had to.

How did things get so fucked up?

One minute I was handing out Cuban cigars, and the next, I was tossing a drink on Vin and his designer shirt. It didn't matter how chiseled his body was or how his wet shirt hugged his muscles. It was all overshadowed by his ruthless exterior.

He had clawed underneath my skin and baited me all night. But I was still at a loss. Was it he who reached up and underneath my skirt, grabbing my bare ass with his clumsy fingers? I just assumed it was. Yet, something told me there was nothing clumsy about Vin.

He had an undeniable air of confidence and grace. Everything about him reeked of precision and skill, making me think that every action he took and every word he spoke was deliberate and purposeful.

Perhaps, I'd made a terrible mistake, especially when it sounded as though his friend was apologizing.

So what? I snap. I envy Kara's ability to tolerate lewd advances, insufferable arrogance, and inappropriate touches. I've been able to ignore it until now.

The Vanilla Club is no stranger to incidents of women being touched, even with their strict policy, and it certainly wouldn't be the last.

If I want to keep the money coming in, I have to tolerate it as much as it disgusts me to do so.

But last night was different. *He* was different.

My mind swirls back to the intoxicating hit of his expensive cologne, a scent that enveloped my senses and held me captive, just as his overbearing confidence and intense gaze kept me from falling apart at the seams.

It is so unlike me to lose it, but something about him flicked a switch inside me.

"Ugh!" I let out a frustrated sigh and ball my fists into cleavers at my sides.

I roll back over and yank the covers up, seeking warmth from my heavy duvet, my oversized Guns and Roses T-shirt not enough.

The sounds of plates clashing and pans banging in the kitchen let me know it's still morning, and I haven't wasted the entire morning sleeping.

When I turn my alarm clock to face me, the red digits indicate it's nine twenty-seven, and I pick up my phone off the wooden nightstand. Two missed calls from Kara and one from an unknown number.

I'll deal with Kara later.

She cornered me before I fled last night, asking what had happened. I just left, unable to string a sentence together, let alone try to explain that I'd just been groped and the asshole who supposedly, although probably, didn't grope me was now on the phone with Dante and firing my ass.

The strange thing is, I had no missed calls from my manager at the Vanilla Club, giving me a slice of hope that my job is still intact.

A text message from my brother lights up my screen, interrupting my thoughts.

Gabriel: *Tips?*

My heart sinks for him. I hadn't stayed long enough to get a single cent last night, and chances were I was out, but I wasn't going to worry him with that. He had bigger things to worry about, like saving his own ass.

Me: *Four hundred.*

I lie, but it is much easier to fib when you aren't face-to-face.

I'll beg, borrow, and steal if that's what it takes to get my brother out of trouble.

Gabriel: *Thanks, sis. I got another two hundred yesterday... don't ask.*

"Fuck!" I let out a frustrated sigh while my fingers quickly type out a reply.

Me: *How did you get that, Gabe?*

Gabriel: *I said, don't ask.*

Me: *The reason we're in this mess is because of you not asking enough questions.*

He would have never taken the money if he had known about the exorbitant interest rates and harsh payment terms the loan sharks demanded.

He needed money for a new car, then repairs to fix it, which still hasn't been done, then money for a scheme he invested in with some friends of his. The list goes on, and now we're here in this shit heap of a mess. Honestly, he's older than me by only three years, but most of the time, I feel like I'm the one who's got it together. It's low-key draining.

The three dots appear immediately, and I click my fingers impatiently on the screen, waiting for a response.

Gabriel: *Rosie. I know. I'm sorry. I'm trying to sort this mess out.*

I let out an audible sigh. Maybe I'm being too hard on him.

Me: *I know you are. Listen, we will get the money.*

A few moments pass before the dots appear again.

Gabriel: *I don't know. They have given me until March.*

March?

Oh no.

I click over his name, and he picks up on the first ring. "March? What happened to July?" I ask, my frustration seeping through the receiver as I press it even closer to my ear, desperately waiting for his response.

"Apparently, they were being nice, allowing me the extension until July, but my loan conditions specifically state March. I guess the devil's in the details."

My stomach twists into a ball of knots. "But there's no way we can pay back forty-eight thousand dollars in that time frame. We've barely paid anything as it is, and it's January already. "

"Please don't say that," he says, sounding panicked.

"Gabe, what the hell are we supposed to do?" My voice is trembling.

"I'll think of something," he reassures, trying to remove the fear that threatened to spill over into a full-blown panic attack. Then it comes to me.

"I can quit my internship and pick up more shifts at the club," I say in a lightbulb moment.

If I'm still employed, that is.

"I've told you before, and I'll say it again. If you do that, I will never speak to you again. There is no way I'm going to fuck up your life like I have mine."

"But, Gabe—"

"Rosie." His voice booms down the line, scaring me into silence.

I shake off the fear and straighten. "Well, I'm not giving up. I will do everything I can to clear the debt."

"This isn't your burden to bear, sis."

"Well, without Mom here, all we have is each other."

Silence fills the line before he speaks again.

"I love you, sis."

I let out an exhalation. "Love you too."

"I have to go. I'll speak to you next week."

The line goes dead, and like clockwork, I know I can expect his call next week. I just wish it was to catch up. I miss the days when Gabe rang me to see how I was doing rather than how much I made from tips.

I fling off my quilt and leap out of bed, immediately feeling dizzy. I stagger and grab for something to steady myself, accidentally causing Brontë's *Wuthering Heights* to tumble off my nightstand. It hits the ground with a loud thud, and a cloud of dust sparkles in the stream of light. Damn, I don't like feeling like this.

I need to sleep more.

"Rosie, you up?" Sara's voice filters through the door crack.

I focus on the gray building outside my window, and the dizziness slowly dissipates enough for me to walk.

"I'm up," I yell back. I open the door, spotting my two roommates in the kitchen before doing a double take.

What in the actual?

I watch as Sara pours milk from head height into a bowl of cereal while Ethan tilts his head and flicks his tongue in and out at the speed of light, trying to lick the milk with his tongue.

"What the fuck are you two doing?"

He swallows when he sees me and stands, then swats away at his long blond hair just as a broad grin lifts into his cheeks. Sara chuckles as she tilts the milk carton and seals it shut with the lid.

Ethan's face flashes with mischief as he says, "Trying to build up my tongue muscles." He rakes a hand through his hair as he wipes the back of his other hand on his boxer briefs.

We've been roommates in New Jersey since college started, living in Saddle Hills just outside of the campus. Sara and Ethan already knew each other from mutual friends, so when they let me join in as the third roommate, it felt like we had all been lifelong friends.

Sara is the closest thing I have to a best friend, and Ethan, well, he is the dose of humor we crave in our lives.

Especially back then, when my mom had just passed away, and I had no one to guide me.

"He is persistent." Sara flicks a strand of long blonde hair from her face, humoring the man-slut we lived with.

"Show me you're a master at fellatio without showing me you're a master at fellatio," he says with a toothy grin.

"You're not actually serious!" I walk over and shove a sponge in his chest. "Wipe the drops of milk on your tank top, Fabio."

He grabs it from me, then says, "Well, how can one please a woman if they don't try? It's like resistance training. Except this time, it's with my tongue against their..."

"Got it!" I hold my hand up. "I really don't need to know the ins and outs of what you do with your tongue, Ethan."

Oh, dear God. Wrong choice of words.

Peals of laughter erupt, reverberating through the living area and bouncing off the thin walls.

"Just hand me that goddamn coffee, would you?" I say, shoving him out of the way.

Sara chuckles as she hands me the coffee from underneath the percolator. Searing hot, it matches the shade of my now crimson skin.

Sara takes her bowl of extra milky Frosted Flakes and sits beside me while Ethan's phone buzzes. He disappears down the hall to take it.

"You were home early last night, weren't you?" Still in her satin pajamas, I wonder what time she got in to realize I had come home early.

"There was a bit of an incident," I admit into my coffee cup.

She sets her spoon down, and it clangs on the countertop. "What kind of incident? Are you okay?"

I sip the black liquid. Piping hot, it burns the back of my

throat as I swallow it down. The taste of the familiar coffee, although the packet stuff, is the caffeine hit I need.

I set the mug down. "I dropped something at the VC, and then when I went to bend over and pick it up, some rich asshole had his hand up my skirt."

"What the hell? I don't know why you work there. Honestly, Rosie!"

"It's fine." I wave her concerns away, even though it is anything but fine.

"So what happened?"

"I threw a drink on the asshole."

Midway through another spoonful, she laughs out loud, causing the milk to spray over the counter. She wipes it up with her napkin, then turns to face me. "Seriously?"

I nod, quite impressed with myself for a nanosecond before reality rears up and squashes my bravado.

"You badass." She tilts into my shoulder, nudging me with her body weight.

"Yeah, I'm so badass... I might be out of a job."

"No."

"Yes. Turns out the guy is some big shot and was on speed dial with Dante, making a formal complaint about me when I turned and left."

"As in Dante, owner of the Vanilla Club Dante? Why would he have his number?"

I shrug. "Something tells me he has the president's number. He just gave off this powerful vibe." My mind drifts to his emerald eyes as a scattering of goose bumps erupts up my arms.

"Sounds like someone's crushing..."

"You can't be serious. He was an asshole of all assholes."

She shovels in mouthful after mouthful, and the sound

of her masticating her food puts me on edge. Then she pauses midspoonful. "Well, I say, forget about it. Let's enjoy this week until the final semester starts."

"Ugh, and I have to prepare for my internship."

"Well, knowing you, you'll ace it."

If I didn't know Sara, I'd say she sounded jealous. But she has nothing to be jealous about. Coming from a family of doctors and surgeons, she's studying for her medical degree.

Ethan reenters the room, eagerly asking, "What did I miss?"

Sara recounts my story so I don't have to relive it, and I sip my coffee, listening to the recap.

"Fuckwit. You're the one who should complain. He goddamn assaulted you!" Ethan spits out in disgust.

"Yeah, well. I'm no one." I remember his words to me last night said in a haunting tone that stirred something within me.

"Imagine if he knew you were a virgin," Ethan offers, popping a brow as the thought settles low in my belly.

"Oh, my," Sara agrees, and they exchange knowing glances.

Okay, so my two roommates know I haven't lost my V-card. I'm like the sideshow act on a never-ending door of shameless one-night stands and drunken college sex. Sara and Ethan are equal in that department, but they also are pretty cool with my decision to wait for someone special.

"What the hell has that got to do with anything?" I ask, taking my coffee to my lips and inhaling it, thinking about how Mr. No One could take me.

A blush creeps in, burning the tips of my ears.

"I just find it so strange. At night you're a vixen in

lingerie, and come daylight, you're a prude tighter than a nun's hole."

"Ethan!" I yell while half laughing at my roommate, yet the irony isn't lost on me. "I'm no prude," I retort, trying to mask the annoyance in my voice.

Sara stands and empties her bowl into the sink. She glances over her shoulder and adds, "He's right. If any of the guys at Trinity University knew, I swear they'd be hunting you down."

"Phew, not me. Too much responsibility." Ethan slinks down beside me. Taking Sara's seat at the counter, he unscrews the cookie jar and pops a homemade cookie in his mouth.

"Responsibility?" I question, not that I'd ever go there with Ethan. He's cute and all, but seriously not a stable-relationship guy. My first guy is going to be tall, dark, and handsome. Mr. Darcy, on steroids, will do just fine.

"You're gorgeous, Rosie, but I don't want to start a foot-ball team with you."

Sara lets out a snort of laughter while scrubbing her dish in the sink.

"What's that supposed to mean?" I level back at them. It seems they outnumber me two against one.

"Rosie. Look. Eventually, a man who is brave enough to break you in must also know that you will chain him down and want to procreate because, girl, you have rose-colored glasses on when it comes to men, and I have to be the one to say it, but there is no Mr. Right."

"You bet," Sara agrees with enthusiasm.

"Or Mrs. Right," he adds. "We're nearly finished with college. This is the time we should live our best life."

"Absolutely!" Sara agrees.

"See, Sara and I are all over it. In fact..." Ethan turns his attention toward Sara when he adds, "Maybe we should have fun together, Sara? You screw around. I screw around..."

I let out a gasp of surprise at the sincerity in his tone. Sara pivots on her spot and stares at him like she's unsure what to say. A sliver of tension cuts through the silence. This is the first time I've heard Ethan speak to Sara that way. "As if!" he blurts out, ruining the moment.

Something unreadable flashes across Sara's face before she turns away and says, "Good, 'cause I'd rather poke holes in my eyes with toothpicks dipped in hot sauce." I can't help but wonder what just passed between them, the mystery of it all leaving me with more questions than answers.

He rolls his eyes and whispers so only I can hear him, "Someone's had a visit from Aunt Flo."

I sigh, rolling my eyes in frustration. "Why, 'cause a woman can't reject you?"

Monday rolls around, and I'm one subway stop away from Midtown.

Before Gabe's debt became a huge problem, I applied for a six-week internship program at the best venture capitalist company in New York, Slater Corp. Out of over one thousand applicants, they accepted me, and today is the final meeting with the CEO, Julius Slater.

I've already met the Human Resources Director and the Interns Manager, Debra. Despite her unruly hair that seems to have a life of its own, there was no mistaking the intelligence that shone in her weathered eyes.

But I'm feeling really nervous today. Even though I

know I'm accepted into the intern program at one of the top ten Forbes companies on the rich list, I can't shake the feeling that something could go wrong.

I stand and move toward the exit doors as the subway slows. Staring at myself in the glass-door reflection, a whisper from Mom carries its way into my heart. And a hand steadies me on my shoulder.

You've got this, Rosie. Now go get 'em.

I close my eyes, and when I open them, I see my reflection again. This time, my jaw is set, and my eyes burn with an intensity to succeed and optimism only my mother could whisper to me from the grave.

"Fifth Ave Stop."

I straighten my white blouse and run my hand down my fitted-to-the-knee black skirt. My brown hair is neatly pulled into a top bun, a stark contrast to the bleached blonde wig I wear at the Vanilla Club.

I applied a slash of liquid eyeliner and a light layer of mascara to elongate my lashes for a natural look. A mushroom-colored blusher highlights my cheekbones, and a touch of lip gloss adds some shine and color to my lips.

The doors pull open, and I tug my crossbody bag so it settles on my hip before stepping out onto the sidewalk.

A five-minute walk later and an introduction to security, I'm on my way up the elevator to the fortieth floor.

The top floor.

I've been to the Slater Corp headquarters before, but every time I enter the building, its sheer scale and architecture put me on edge. Today, however, I'm headed to the top floor for the first time.

As I step into the marble foyer, I'm struck by the realization that someone had a dream and created all of this. The enormous slabs of marble, worth millions of dollars, cover every surface. The floors, countertops, and walls not covered in panes of glass are veined with streaks of black-and-white marble that exude cold and assertive energy. It's clear that Slater Corp is a powerful entity, a leading venture capitalist valued at forty billion dollars, according to the financial review.

Soft elevator music lulls me into a false sense of relaxation, but as the doors ping open and I step out on the cold, black marble tiles, my relaxation dwindles. Walking toward the reception desk, I feel a comforting hand on my shoulder, and I smile, knowing it's my mom looking out for me.

A woman in her late twenties dresses me down with her eyes and asks, "Can I help you?'"

"I'm Rosie. I'm here for the internship."

"Of course you are," she quips, with the word sounding like a foul taste on her lips.

What the fuck is her deal?

"Thank you." I smile sweetly, even though I want to shake her out of her rude coma.

The receptionist motions toward the boardroom, where people are scattered around the large, oversized space. I immediately recognize Debra, the woman I have been having my pre-meetings with.

"Rosie, welcome. Come inside, please," Debra greets me as I enter.

The glass pane at the back of the boardroom overlooks Manhattan below. Four interns around the same age as me sit around the table, eagerly waiting to hear from Debra and the owner, Julius, who has yet to join us.

Apparently, Julius always spends time with his interns, believing they are the key to the future. I am beyond excited to meet the man I've read about and admired.

I sit next to a girl with kind blue eyes and a huge smile.

For the next half-hour, we will listen to Debra about our induction and what to expect during the six weeks we are here.

Starting next week, we will work on a transaction specifically picked for us by management. We will conduct the due diligence and assist with the work needed to buy the company. Of course, we have to sign a nondisclosure agreement, and between the five of us, we can't get paper to pen quickly enough when the agreement hits our desks.

A knock at the door interrupts our conversation, and a man I recognize from the newspapers walks in, wearing a sharp navy suit that matches his deep blue eyes. A warm smile spreads across his face as he greets the group, and although there's a sense of familiarity about him, I can't quite place it. With his striking looks and chiseled features, he could easily pass for a model if he weren't already a successful CEO.

As he speaks, the women around me are swooning over his every word. "Hi, everyone. I'm Julius Slater. Welcome to Slater Corp and the internship program." Debra stands immediately to shake his hand, and he nods, gesturing for her to sit back down.

Julius walks around and introduces himself to each of us, and when he comes to me, I introduce myself and smile. "Looking forward to working here, Mr.—"

"Call me Julius, please," he says, looking down at my name tag that Debra made us pin to our outfits.

"Rosie..." He turns back to Debra.

"Rosie West, sir," she confirms, and I'm curious what discussions have taken place without me being present, especially when a flash of recognition crosses his face. "Top of your class and granted into Trinity University on an academic scholarship."

"Yes, sir," I verify, surprised he's across that level of detail in his position.

"I make it my business to know the students who excel," he says, looking down at his watch as he sits back in his seat.

The door opens, and in walks another man. "Right on time," Julius says as I follow his gaze to the door.

My mouth falls open. It's *him*.

Holy shit. My heart thuds in my ribcage, and a wave of lightheadedness washes over me. Vin sits down in the empty seat beside Julius.

"You are in for a treat, ladies and gentlemen, because I'd like you to meet my brother and CEO of the London office, Vincent Slater."

"Hello," Vincent says in that dark, gloomy voice I immediately recognize.

I shrink a little in my seat, hoping to be invisible as discomfort cloaks me.

No, he won't recognize me.

I was in a wig, wearing heavy makeup.

It was dark.

So dark.

"Vincent is my brother. He is your mentor and instructor for the next six weeks."

Oh, fuck me.

His eyes move slowly around the boardroom, and my pulse quickens as I wait for him to reach me. When his gaze finally lands on me, it's like time stands still. I can feel his intense stare, and my heart sinks like a pit in my stomach.

Fuck, he recognizes me.

I want the ground to swallow me up whole.

He stares at me for a beat longer than necessary, sending sparks of electricity shooting up my spine and around my shoulders. Then immediately disarming me, he moves to the next person.

I let out a breath I didn't realize I was holding.

Okay, maybe he didn't recognize me.

Who am I kidding?

The guy was an A-class jerk hole. Okay, so he's richer than the rest of the population. That would explain his membership in the Vanilla Club and his sheer and utter arrogance.

But fuck, I'd have to endure him for my entire internship?

I completely miss most of what Julius says after that. My mind is a tornado of thoughts as panic chills my skin. Yet, he appears calm and composed as ever.

My heart is pounding, and I struggle to keep my breathing steady. I try to keep my focus on Julius, who is speaking about the company and the internship, but I can't help stealing glances at the man sitting next to him. I can't help but be distracted by his presence in the room.

How the fuck am I going to go with him, mentoring us for the entire program?

As it's time to go, I'm relieved to be the first to get up. Walking toward the door, a sense of heaviness lifts from my shoulders. The tension in the room is suffocating, and I'm glad to be leaving it behind.

I walk out across the marble floor toward the elevators.

"Hey, Rosie, wait up."

Turning around, I'm relieved to see the girl I was sitting next to approach me. Despite her small stature, she commands attention with her bold glasses and wide blue eyes, a striking contrast to her delicate frame.

"I'm Angela," she says, pointing to her name tag. "Ugh, I hate these things."

"Rosie." I smile back at her, realizing she already called

me by my name. "You obviously already know that." I shake my head with a nod of laughter, and she smiles back.

"Sounds so exciting, don't you think? I can't wait to start next week."

"So exciting," I say, trying to hide my frayed nerves.

I hit the elevator call button, and more students have approached by this time. I stare down at their name tags, trying to memorize who each person is.

Max has black-slicked hair and an angular face. A sense of familiarity between him and Fae makes me think they may know each other.

"We have landed the jackpot. Do you know how rare it is for a CEO to mentor his class of interns?" Max inquires.

"The Slater brothers don't seem as ruthless as their reputation," Dane adds to the conversation. He's tall and slender, and his quirky tie hints at a sense of playfulness and creativity.

Angela leans in and whispers so no one outside the group can hear what she's about to say. "Vincent is the ruthless one. I heard he just fired his entire legal team."

"Why?" I swallow down the lump in my throat.

"Probably looked at him the wrong way," Dane adds.

Well, that wouldn't surprise me. The man is a living jerk-hole.

"I mean, he's cute, though," Fae says, flashing a smile that reflects the cool light. She's a tall, slender woman with teeth that appear ghostly white. "They both are!" she gushes. Beautiful and dressed in designer threads, she is obviously from one of the most expensive colleges in Jersey—my guess, a Princeton undergrad.

Angela laughs, and Dane and Max roll their eyes in unison.

The elevator doors open, and I shake my head. I just

want to leave this building and go back home. I don't want to think about his burning eyes and how they confuse me.

"Trust you to say, Fae." Max folds his arms across his chest, crumpling his expensive suit.

They do know each other. I guess that isn't uncommon, especially if they are from the same university.

"Where are you all from? Princeton?" Angela asks, wriggling her nose, and I stifle a giggle.

"How'd you know?" Fae replies without looking at her.

"Was it the suit?" Max adds with a gleeful smile.

"Or my Prada?" Fae pops her shoulder as she clutches her prized possession worth over three months' rent.

"Just a guess," Angela retorts, and immediately, I know I will be friends with this girl.

Slater Corp only recruits from the two major universities, Princeton and Yale. Lucky for me, this year, they opened up to small universities in the Jersey district, and Trinity University was open to apply—a small business university fast getting a reputation for becoming one of the best business universities on the East Coast.

"I'm from Jersey Tech," Angela says.

"Where you from, Rosie?" I step into the elevator and turn to find Dane staring at me.

"Trinity University."

Fae sniggers, but I'm too wound up over my new asshole mentor to say anything.

The rest of them clamor inside, and I drift to the back. A voice calls my name, and I look between Max and Fae. Debra is running toward the elevator, and as it closes, Max extends his arm, blocking the doors from shutting.

"Rosie, I'm glad I caught you. Do you have a minute?" she asks, slightly breathless.

Oh fuck.

All eyes shift to me.

"Of course." I smile and inch forward. Fae doesn't move to let me pass. Instead, Max beside her turns, and I brush past him and into the foyer.

"Come with me, please," she says, turning, and a lump forms in my throat as the ding of the elevator chimes, shutting behind me.

Debra is walking back to the boardroom where we just left.

Where Vincent is.

Double shit.

4

VINCENT

My brother looks at me, eyes wide with disbelief. "She did what?" His pretty boy face shows shock and awe.

He's the one who talked me into returning to head up the Internship program with his naïve optimism. But he doesn't need to know why I really came back from London.

Vengeance is mine.

I repeat myself, which I don't like to do.

"She threw a drink on me at the Vanilla Club, ruining my Brioni shirt." He laughs, the sound bouncing off the walls of the empty boardroom. "It's not funny, Julius. She accused me of touching her."

Unusually, I feel a bead of sweat forming on my forehead as I wipe it with the back of my hand. I'm normally so calm.

"You're telling me you don't want Rosie in the internship program because she tipped a drink on you?" he inquires with a curious tone.

To be honest, I don't want Rosie in the program because

she rubs me the wrong way. "Yes," I snap. "And she's not a good fit."

He raises a thick eyebrow at me, then returns his attention to the paperwork on the table. "Actually, Vin, I beg to differ. Rosie is here on a scholarship from one of the smaller business universities we partner with, and she's top of her class. In fact, she's perfect for the program."

What the fuck?

"Give me that," I say, snatching the folder from in front of him and scanning Rosie's file from top to bottom. It's a transcript of her academic achievements, and I quickly realize she has a list of high marks and impressive accomplishments.

Dammit, he was right.

She scored in the highest percentiles for every class.

I let out a throaty groan.

Not only does she have brains, but she also has a killer figure hidden under a tight black skirt today. I have to admit, she's even more gorgeous without all the makeup on her face.

"It doesn't matter." I exhale loudly, pushing away the folder and sliding it back to Julius. "I just asked Debra to call her back in here to let her go."

"You can't do that!" Julius shakes his head.

"I can do whatever the fuck I want." I hiss as my hands steeple across the cold boardroom table.

He stares at me directly, a hint of frustration in his voice. "You've made that point many times before." He sighs. "I'm constantly dealing with the fallout from your office rampages and trying to put out staffing fires."

I scowl at my brother, wondering if he'll ever let this go. "I get results. I don't tolerate incompetence, and I'll never apologize for that."

"Yes, but there are ways to fire people, Vin," he reminds me. "Lambasting the entire legal team over the company loudspeaker for all to hear is not one of them."

"They had it coming," I retort. "No one loses twenty million on my watch."

Julius runs a hand through his tousled brown hair, eyeing me up and down. It's shorter than mine and neatly frames his face. He has softer features than I do, but we share the same sharp jawline. His eyes are kinder than mine, which are dark and heavy with the burdens I carry.

Growing up, we always had girls chasing us, but I pushed them away because they were more trouble than they were worth. They always wanted more than I could give. Instead, I had a specific taste in women and let an exclusive madame handle my needs at home and abroad—no fuss, no strings attached, and certainly no relationship headaches.

My brother smiles and twists his lips. "Are you saying you can't handle her, brother?"

"Oh, I can handle her." A vision of her long legs spread eagle over my table comes into view as I imagine slamming my flat palm against her fleshy ass while driving my cock into her.

"How about this, then?" Julius' voice cut through the X-rated Rosie carousel looping in my mind.

"I challenge you to see out your time here, and if by then, you don't think she's a good fit in the workplace, then get rid of her. Either way, you will be gone back to dismal fucking London, and she won't be your problem ever again."

I dust off a speck of lint from my pinstriped Tom Ford suit and contemplate his offer. The fucker knows he has me.

Rosie was in her final semester before graduating,

according to her dossier. She is twenty-two years old and has a nearly perfect GPA. On top of that, she cut a seductive figure in lingerie and student attire but has a noteworthy aversion to me.

Now, I have to teach her for the next six weeks, and the prospect is already causing me frustration.

I run my tongue over the top of my teeth and say, "Fine." I see him grin before I add, "Not because I'm giving in, but because I like a challenge."

A rumble of a chuckle left his chest. "You give in? Hell would freeze over before Vincent Slater ever gives in."

"We wouldn't be where we were today if we were soft like you."

He erupts into raucous laughter, and damn, it feels good to be back. I've missed my brother. London is cold, dark, and just the way I like it, but I hadn't realized how much I miss this place until now.

I hear a faint tap at the door. "Enter," I announce with a newfound sense of determination.

The animosity between us is stifling, but that simply means I have the power to make Rosie's time here a living hell. I won't let my dear brother in on the details, of course. After today, he won't even step foot in the offices of the internship program, which is one level below our executive floor.

My plan is to make Rosie's life here miserable, pushing her to her limits and seeing what she's truly made of. Then, I will watch as she crumbles under the pressure and leaves on her own accord. Everyone has crumbled under me, and she will be no exception. I give her two weeks, a rueful smile tugging at my cheeks.

Debra pokes her head inside the door, her wispy hair untamed as though she's had an argument with the weather and lost. I can't help but wonder why she doesn't take better care of herself and her appearance. I make a mental note to bring up her shabby appearance with Julius. Maybe we ought to pay her more or perhaps we ought to offer our staff some more free amenities such as onsite beauty services.

"I have Rosie here for you."

I nod curtly. "Thank you, leave us." The rushed click of her heels sounds against the polished black floor.

"Take a seat, please, Rosie," Julius says in an even tone.

She sits beside me, and I can't help but let my gaze wander down to where she's crossed her long legs in their noir pantyhose.

Stop fucking looking, Vin.

Her foot hangs in the air, tapping erratically as if nerves are wracking her body.

"So it appears you and Vincent are already acquainted," Julius says, jumping right in.

I lift my gaze and meet her anxious hazel eyes with a steely glare. She swallows and straightens her back, sitting up tall and rigid. Her confidence is something to admire, especially since most of my adversaries do much worse under the Slater brothers' interrogation.

Clearing her throat, she tries to compose herself. "Yes, sir, I wasn't sure if he recognized me at the meeting."

Seriously? I could effortlessly summon the exact color and shape of the eyes of the fierce lingerie waitress so deeply etched into my memory.

"I could spot you a mile away." I keep my eyes fixed on her as those same eyes that I had memorized now glare back at me with disdain. Call me sadistic, but it is rare to have the company of a woman who dislikes me as much as she does.

As I wait for her response, a tense silence envelops us, and her unprofessional behavior dawns on her. Abruptly, she shakes off her previous glare of disdain and replaces it with a neutral expression.

She clears her throat and looks between Julius and me. "I was groped, and I threw a drink on Vincent."

"You can address me as Mr. Slater," I interject, though a part of me wouldn't mind if she called me 'Sir' again. I watch her flinch at my assertive tone as I continue, "And you just assumed it was me who did that to you?"

She peels back into her chair, rolling her shoulders inward and feeling uncomfortable.

"I just assumed..." she says, her voice trailing off. But even though I feel like I have already given her a hard time, I can't let her off the hook that easily.

"Well, you assumed wrong," I assert. "There is no way I would ever touch you."

She swallows audibly, and I find myself inexplicably drawn to the motion of her throat as she does so. "Well, that's fine because it works both ways, sir," she retorts with a professional smile.

But the way she elongates the word 'Sir' makes me want to pry her legs open and slam into her tight little cunt as punishment, exactly the opposite of my former words. It's a strange feeling to be frustrated and attracted to her at the same time.

Julius' gaze shifts to me, and I can feel the weight of it on my face. I can't deny that there's something about Rosie that intrigues me, but it's nothing more than a mild attraction.

"Glad that's sorted," Julius says, breaking the tension in the room. "Now, Rosie, given your choice of employment, I'd suggest it's best to keep that private. Not many interns work as lingerie waitresses at the most exclusive club on the East Coast."

"Well, with all due respect, I'm not most applicants," Rosie responds, her confidence oozing out of every pore.

Julius and I exchange a look. While we appreciate confidence, we have no tolerance for ego in this building. It's only big enough for Julius and my egos.

Rosie lets out a sigh and rubs her temples, appearing distressed. "Look, I'm sorry. I'm not normally like this," she says before looking between us. "The truth is, I need the money for my sick father."

I'm caught off guard by her words, and suddenly, I find myself looking at her with a sense of empathy I hadn't felt before. Perhaps, there's more to her than meets the eye.

"I'm sorry to hear that. We both are," Julius says in an even tone, then turns to look over at me to agree. I shift in my seat, trying to remain inconspicuous and nod in agreement.

"Studying and trying to pay for his medical bills isn't easy, and my job as a librarian wouldn't cut it... so..." she explains, trailing off.

"So you turned to lingerie waitressing at Dante's club," I interject, my mind wandering to how she would look in a tiny tartan librarian's outfit.

Dammit, Vin, get a grip, I scold myself silently.

She lifts her head and defiantly sticks out her chin. "Yes. You do what you can for the ones you love. I won't apologize for that."

I feel a stirring inside of me. Fuck, I know that. That is exactly why I'm here. Maybe we have something in common, after all.

When Julius pleaded for me to come and head up the intern program, I saw it as the perfect opportunity. It provided the ideal cover for my true purpose, seeking truth and revenge. My eldest brother's death would not be just another faded memory, a mere shrine to visit. No, that fucker would pay for his sins, whoever he was. And I knew with certainty that it wasn't Montero, the man currently serving time in jail for Edgar's murder.

She lowers her head to the table. "That's if I still have a job there. I haven't heard from them since your call to Dante."

Dante, an old friend and loyal to a fault, would do anything for me, and I would do the same for him. So when I placed the call to Dante, I did so to scare her. Not for any other reason. I hate Charles, the cocksucker I was with and understood Rosie was the actual victim in all of this. Not the dickhead associate I was with who, after too many drinks, touched something that didn't belong to him, something that belonged to...

I don't know who Rosie belongs to, and I shouldn't spend any more time thinking about it.

"You have your job," I reply curtly, not wanting to discuss the matter any further.

I made sure Charles paid dearly for his actions. I didn't disclose to her the lengths I went to, to ruin him. Not only did I have him blacklisted from every exclusive club in the country, but I also made sure every person he met would know what he had done. I contacted his business associates and made it clear they could no longer work with him if they wanted to maintain their reputation. I even went as far as to have a private investigator dig up dirt on him, which I used to blackmail him into giving me everything he had. His pregnant wife is in the midst of leaving him after receiving a barrage of lewd photos of him and underage girls. She'd be taken care of. I'd make sure of that. Considering the nature of the man she was married to, I would do whatever it took to make sure he suffered for what he did.

I hear her take a sharp breath as she looks up at me. "Thank you," she bites out through a tight jaw. I can't help but smile, knowing that I made her nervous.

She takes her fingers to the lapel of her blouse and loosens it from around her long, swanlike neck. For a moment, I can't take my eyes off her, and I find myself momentarily distracted by the outline of her bra through the thin fabric of her blouse.

My mind wanders back to the bustier she wore at the Vanilla Club. Her breasts pushed up to perfection. A scatter of pins shoots up my spine, heating my shoulders.

"Right, well, it's settled then." My brother stands, cutting the tension in the room, and walks over to Rosie, shaking her hand. "We look forward to having you in our intern program, Rosie. If there's anything you need, feel free to approach Vincent or me while you're here."

I observe as she shakes his hand with a firm and rigid grip. A person's handshake can reveal a lot about them, and this twenty-two-year-old from Jersey had rocks in her fists and steel arms.

"Thank you, I can't wait," she says.

Julius turns to me, giving me a warning stare, before marching out of the boardroom. But his warning means nothing to me.

She extends her hand to me, and I stand. "Thank you, Mr. Slater."

"For what?" I ask.

"For letting me keep my job and place here in the intern program."

I let out a laugh. "I wanted you gone the second I saw

you here, and as for your lingerie job, well, if you want to put yourself in those situations, you deserve to be there.”

Her jaw goes slack as shock rings across her rigid body in a visible jolt.

She squeezes my hand tightly, and the warmth of her touch is something I want to hold on to.

I hold on for a little longer than necessary.

“Sir, I’m sure you’ve never had to put yourself in those situations before, but we weren’t all born into privilege.”

She slides her hand out before I can say anything and quickly flees out the door. Irritation flickers up my arm where her touch lingers and burns its way like a stick of dynamite wanting to explode.

I watch her hips sway with each step as she walks away from the boardroom, and something unexpected happens.

A grin lifts my lips, as next week can’t come soon enough.

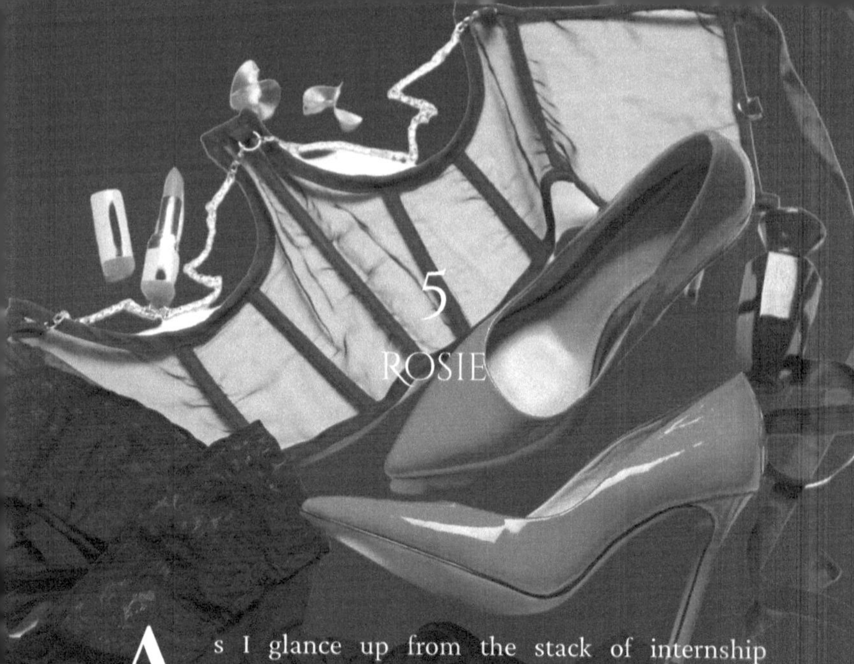

5

ROSIE

As I glance up from the stack of internship documents, I realize I've read them so many times this week that I now know everything I need to know about Slater Corp. My mind drifts to his haunting dark green eyes and broad muscles as an errant shiver rolls down my arms.

The unwelcome voice interrupts my thoughts.

"I wanted you gone the second I saw you here."

I force a tight smile, knowing I worked hard to earn my spot, and I'm determined to do whatever it takes to not only keep it but to excel in the program, making them hire me after graduation in May.

Needing a break, I make myself something to eat, then when I'm done, I clean up the house. The sun has dipped below the horizon, and Ethan and Sara have come home. When they see me, their faces drop.

"What the fuck are you doing in your pajamas?" Ethan asks.

"My shift got canceled, so it's Netflix for me."

"Not a chance." Sara sets her backpack down and pulls

me up from the arm of the couch. I let out a deep rumble and groan, giving in hesitantly.

"Get her ready, Sara, and I'm not taking no for an answer." Ethan throws his keys on the countertop, the cookie jar stopping them from completely sliding off. He goes straight to his room, the opposite side of our bedrooms.

"Ethan, what are you talking about? Get me ready for what?" I whine.

"We are going out. And I have just the place," Ethan says, his voice dwindling down the hall from his room.

"Oh, he does!" Sara shrieks, pulling me toward my bedroom.

"I just want to stay here tonight, Sar."

"What, why?"

"Aah, well, for a start, the semester starts up on Monday, and so does my internship."

"Pfft," she rounds out a sound. "Even more the reason to get out and let loose on the town."

Reluctantly, she drags me into my room. I flop on my quilt as she opens my closet, and the screeching sound of metal against metal as she slides the hangers makes me pull my pillow over my head.

When the god-awful sound stops, I fling the pillow away and sit up to see her holding my red satin dress.

"Ooh, this is spicy," she exclaims.

"Can you tell me where we're going?" I stand and pick up the dress.

It's a halter neck and falls to the knee. I've only worn it once before, and that was at the Vanilla Club.

"This is for the Vanilla Club," I say, jamming it back onto the hanger.

"I thought that was only lingerie," Sara says, raising an eyebrow.

"This was a dress-up night. They sometimes have masquerade-themed nights too."

"Ooh la la," she singsongs. "I wonder if I could get a gig there."

I let out a laugh. "Yeah, like the esteemed Dr. and Dr. Walters would let you work in an establishment like that."

She rolls her eyes. "True, but I bet you earn more than a graduate at med school."

"I would if I worked full-time with tips."

I flick through my clothes. They're so different from my persona at the Vanilla Club.

I reach for a button-up shirt and skirt. "Here."

"Oh God." She rolls her eyes and grumbles.

"What?" I look down at my selection and twist my lips.

"Come on, what else do you have so we're not too slutty, or that screams 'stay away, I'm a virgin.' "

Laughter escapes my lips. "Shit, it's not that bad, is it?"

An hour later, the three of us are riding the subway to Manhattan, already feeling the effects of the lethal cocktail that Ethan prepared before we left. The drink was made up of half a bottle of Cointreau and a mixer, and we're all feeling a little buzzed. We're only a few stops short of Central Park, which is the only information Ethan had offered up as to our destination.

As we ride, my mind can't help but wander back to Monday's inquisition, replaying the questions and doubts in my head.

I twist my lips into a rueful smile, still finding it hard to believe that my mentor is the same man I accused of assaulting me and I threw a drink on. "Vincent Slater," I say, the name escaping my lips before I can stop it.

"What about him?" Ethan turns to stare at me curiously.

"Who?" Sara asks.

Shit, I said his name aloud. Well, fuck it. I may as well tell them.

I take a deep breath and continue, "Vincent Slater is the arrogant son of a bitch I threw a drink on at Vanilla Club." My hands clench into fists involuntarily, the memory of that night still fresh in my mind.

Sara's eyes widen in disbelief. "Wait, what?"

I nod, my expression grim.

Sara splits into laughter. "The person you threw a drink on was *the* Vincent Slater?" *How does everyone know who he is and I don't?* Then it dawns on her. "And your internship is at Slater Corp?" Her hands fly to her mouth in disbelief. I guess it is kind of hard to believe.

Ethan lets out a drunken chuckle. "I'm surprised you didn't get fired. Vincent is…" His voice trails off as he shakes his head.

"Me too," I reply. "I think he feels sorry for me."

"What was his reaction when he saw you at the interview? Did he recognize you?" Sara asks.

"Immediately." I nod.

"Wait, why did he feel sorry for you?" Ethan interjects before I can answer Sara's question.

They are fumbling over the details, so I have to at least tell them something. "Okay, so it went like this. I walked in and first met his brother."

"Julius Slater," Sara adds because we spoke of him before when I first got the internship. He is the well-known brother of the two. Hell, I didn't even know he had another.

"He seems nice," I respond.

Sara waves her hands for me to continue, sitting on the edge of her seat, waiting in anticipation.

"Then in walks Mr. Slater. He's here from London, heading up the program. He immediately recognized me. I know it because I saw it in his eyes, but he didn't say anything. It was only after the meeting that both brothers called me back in. It's then they hammered me with questions."

"God, like what?" Sara asks.

"Like the flipping obvious! Why are you a lingerie waitress?" Ethan lets out a laugh, and Sara silences him with a look so I can continue.

"Especially with an IQ as high as yours," Sara adds.

"But I have to lie, right? Because I'm petrified he'll kick me out of the program after I threw a drink on him and basically accused him of assault."

We pull up to another stop as Sara leans in curiously. "So what did you say?"

"I lied, obviously. I said I worked at the Vanilla Club to afford the medication for my sick father."

"Oh my God. You didn't," Sara exclaims, pulling her hand to her head as if she's in distress.

"I didn't want to divulge my brother's money troubles. You try and think of something in that situation," I snap back at Sara, feeling defensive.

She holds her hands up in defeat. "Okay!"

"Well, I can see why," remarks Ethan.

They know about my dead-beat drunk dad and that I have nothing to do with him. He washed his hands of being a parent when I was a kid.

"It's like swapping out your dad for your brother… the apple doesn't fall too far from the tree," Ethan adds with a knowing look.

I shoot him a scowl. "Okay, that's the story," I say quickly.

Sara looks back and forth between Ethan and me. "Is he good-looking?" she asks, causing me to pause and Ethan to turn toward her.

"If he's anything like Julius Slater, he must be hot," she adds before continuing, "Imagine if he was your first!" She lets out a giggle, and I roll my eyes.

"Where did that come from?" Ethan looks at me with a shocked expression.

"He's a real jerk," I say. I refrain from mentioning how his intense gaze had me feeling like I was on fire.

"He's just as ruthless in business as he is with women," Ethan adds. "That's what I've heard, at least." I'm tempted to ask for more information, but I know that would raise suspicions.

Ruthless is an understatement.

"I couldn't care less. I'm in the program, and I'll prove to him what I'm capable of. That way, he'll have no choice but to favor me among the other four interns for a position after graduation," I say determinedly.

"Damn right, Rosie!" Sara high-fives me.

"We're almost there," Ethan announces.

"I hope this party is worth it," I mutter, secretly wishing I could be at home in my cozy pajamas, watching a romantic comedy.

Ethan walks ahead, wearing jeans and a white T-shirt, looking like a model from the GAP, and as he turns, a wicked smile spreads across his cheeks. "Oh, it will be."

Sara shrugs beside me. "You know he gets all the best invites. How *do* you get them again?"

He grins his boyish grin, and we sigh.

Sara holds up her hands. "I don't want to know," she admits.

During the ride on the subway, he brags to anyone who will listen about hooking up with a girl whose family owns half of Manhattan. A few people glance over, but for the most part, it's just another day in the city. "She's booked the entire Sky Deck for a private party," he says with a sense of pride.

Sara shakes her head and punches him in the arm. "Seriously?"

He raises his eyebrows. "Yeah, she wasn't the best, but a fuck is a fuck."

"Oh my God, Ethan!" I give Ethan a sharp kick in the shins with my pointy heels, causing him to let out a yelp of pain and clutch his leg.

"Good! It's guys like you that put me off sex," I whisper, intending only for him and Sara to hear me. However, as people turn to stare at me, I realize that I'm clearly drunk and need to muzzle myself before I say anything else embarrassing.

He laughs. "Did I mention the drinks are on the house?"

Like, Ethan and Sara need to worry about that. Ethan's family runs a successful business in textiles, while Sara's parents are both cardiothoracic surgeons. Not that you'd know it. They are so down-to-earth.

Sara and I exchange knowing glances. "Okay, so maybe I like you a little more right now," I admit.

It's late. I'm not sure how late because I am drunk, dancing like I don't have a care in the world with Sara beside me.

Sky Deck is full of twenty-somethings, lithe bodies, and fancy faces. A famous singer, Kit Jones, is here as well as other notable celebrities whose faces I know but whose names have slipped my inebriated mind.

Ethan isn't wrong. He is connected in ways I didn't know and has landed the party of all parties to end the vacation.

The music changes and Sara exclaims, "I love this song!" She runs her hands down her tight black dress and closes her eyes, getting lost in the beat. I'm about to warn her that guys are swarming around her, but someone's hands are on her waist before I can.

She smiles, going with it, and I relax, returning the smile. The guy is tall, blond, and good-looking, and he spins her around into his body.

As I sway my hips to the music, a voice chimes in beside me, "Having a good time at the party?" I turn to look at the guy standing next to me. He's handsome with tousled brown hair and a mischievous grin, and I figure he must be a friend of Sara's guy.

He moves well on the dance floor, and I notice his dazzling white smile as he draws closer to me.

"You bet!" I slur in my drunken state.

"What's your name?" he asks, his words slightly slurred as he steps closer, invading my personal space with his face. I catch a whiff of sweet rum on his breath, which fills my nostrils.

"Rosie," I yell back, completely absorbed in the amazing song over the speakers. It's only when he tilts down and his mouth is beside my ear that I jerk. "Pretty name," he growls out. "Darian," he adds. "Nice to meet you, Rosie. How about a dance?"

Before I can respond, his hand circles my waist, and I let out a reluctant sigh. *Well, what's one dance?* I'm alone anyway, with Sara sucking face somewhere in the crowd.

"Looks like you answered for me," I reply, widening my eyes.

"You look gorgeous." He breathes out, his hot breath landing on my shoulder.

A small chuckle escapes my mouth, and I roll my eyes.

"What?" He looks at me with surprise.

"I'm wearing jeans and a tank top," I point out.

"So?" he yells back, and the aroma of alcohol pours from his breath. Not that I'm one to talk. I've downed too many champagnes and practically French by now.

When he pulls me close, I let him, but I really should stop leading this poor sucker on. It's going nowhere. Instead, I close my eyes, willing him to disappear. Vincent Slater's full lips and sharp jaw instantly come into view, and I inhale sharply. A hand lowers from my waist to my bottom, and a thickness presses against my stomach. Immediately, my eyes snap open, and I pull back. "Thanks for the dance," I say, wanting to get away.

"Hey, wait," he says, his grip firming around my wrist and pulling me tightly into his grasp.

"Let go of me!" I shout, struggling against his tight grip on my wrist. I scan the dance floor for any sign of Sara, but all I see are unfamiliar faces. I'm alone.

Finally, his grip loosens, and he releases me. I breathe a sigh of relief and take a step back. But then I notice a shadow behind him, and familiar features stare back at me as I look up.

Vincent Slater.

"Oh fuck."

Shit. Did I just say that aloud?

My sudden outburst takes him by surprise, and he shifts his gaze to Darian, muttering something under his breath that I can't make out. I'm lost in a drunken haze of confusion and fear. Darian's eyes widen in terror before he swiftly steps away and disappears into the crowd.

What the hell did he just say to him? I wonder, my mind racing with unanswered questions.

As I look up and meet Mr. Slater's intense gaze, a sense of excitement courses through my veins, mingling with fear and uncertainty. His eyes bore into mine with fierce intensity, and a thrill of anticipation for what's to come washes over me.

6
VINCENT

Harry practically begged me to come to a party at Sky Deck when I told him I was back in Manhattan. Despite my reluctance to attend a party filled with people under the age of twenty-five, I agreed to come. However, I would have preferred a quiet drink at a pub where we could catch up without all the noise.

Harry and I are close friends who attended boarding school together with Julius and Caleb. I kept in touch with Harry and Caleb regularly over the years, but it didn't replace the weekly in-person catchups the four of us used to have, and I miss that.

A beautiful blonde woman and her friend had cornered Harry and me, but I had no intention of taking her home, even though she suggested otherwise. Fortunately, Harry had taken both women who were hitting on us to the bar with him, leaving me in peace.

The woman—*what was her name? Donna, Diana?* Fuck knows. She couldn't handle my needs, so I wasn't even going to bother with her. No point leading her on from the outset.

Harry can take care of them both.

My gaze is pulled to the dance floor, and that's when I spot Rosie. She moves her curves to the beat like she doesn't have a care in the world.

I find myself entranced by her, unsure of what it is about her that captivates me. She's dressed in skin-tight jeans accentuating her shapely curves and a lilac tank top revealing her midriff. She is dressed for a hot chocolate at a café, not an invite-only party at Sky Deck. There is something liberating about her disregard for how she dressed, and I'm inexplicably drawn to her because she doesn't give a fuck.

I don't even realize my attention is still on her after the song ends and the next one starts playing. I lean against the wall, curiously watching her.

It's pretty obvious she has had a bit too much to drink from her unsteady movements, and I'm not happy about it. To make things worse, some sleazy guy is moving in on her, trying to take advantage of her drunkenness, and she has no fucking clue what she is getting herself into.

As soon as the guy's hands dip below her waistline, a surge of anger flows to the surface, and I know I can't just stand by and watch. Despite knowing that I shouldn't get involved, I quickly push my way through the crowd toward her, determined to put a stop to what's happening.

And fuck.

Here I am.

The thin and low-quality material of his T-shirt slides between my fingers as I pull him away from her, my height towering over him. Shock registers on his face as I lean in close and whisper in a menacing tone in his ear. "Touch her again, and I'll fucking kill you."

It only takes one look, and he's gone.

My gaze shifts to Rosie, and I catch her staring at me. Despite the chaos around us, my focus drifts down to her exposed waist, then back up to her startled face as her chest rises and falls quickly.

"What are *you* doing here?" she asks, her voice laced with anger. She straightens and pulls her hair behind her ears, looking at me expectantly.

"It seems you've got yourself in a bit of a hands-on issue again, Rosie."

A tinge of embarrassment spreads across her cheekbones, but she narrows her eyes and bellows, "I had it covered."

"Don't just stare at her..." a woman suddenly appears from nowhere and exclaims, "... by all accounts, dance, dance, dance!" She then grabs my arm and forces it onto her friend, Rosie.

My hand curls around the soft skin of her waist, just below the hem of her tank top. The warmth of her skin as my fingertips press gently into her bare skin sends a rush of heat through me, igniting a new kind of desire.

She gives her friend a look, then gazes up at me in shock, "Oh no, you don't have to..." Her words trail off, and I'm slightly offended that she doesn't want to dance, but she'll dance with the dickhead who tried to get into her pants.

I place my other hand around her waist, holding her close, pushing the thought away.

"Maybe I want to," I say, and she looks at me curiously as her hips slowly move to the music. "Who was that gregarious woman?" I ask.

"Gregarious?" She rolls her eyes at my comment, and my lips flatten in response. Then, sighing, she relaxes her arms. "Sara. She's my roommate. I'm here with her and Ethan."

"Your boyfriend?" I ask.

"Hell no," she scoffs, and I'm oddly relieved to hear that. I pull her even closer so that she's touching me, and I take in her scent of vanilla and orchids. It's sweet and forbidden, yet I can't help but be drawn to it.

She's your fucking intern.

Let her go.

Walk away.

Okay. Just one dance. Then I'll let her go and walk the fuck away.

An intern and a lingerie waitress. A deadly combination.

She fumbles her hands around my neck, her nails grazing the back of my neck.

"What are you doing here?" she asks, looking up at me through her thick lashes. "Aren't you a bit too old for this kind of party?" She's teasing me.

"Exactly how old do you think I am, Rosie?"

She shrugs. "Thirty?"

"Thirty-two. And that's old?" I mutter, my piercing eyes holding hers.

"I guess not," she says, swiping her bottom lip with her tongue. My eyes momentarily drift downward, imagining her thick, full lips leaving a ring of lipstick around the base of my cock. I snap my eyes back up to hers.

What the fuck, Vin?

"You're twenty-two. Isn't that too young to be drunk and a lingerie model?" I ask, my tone coming out colder and more formal than intended.

Her brown eyes widen like saucers, and her hand balls into a fist around my neck.

"Do you want to throw another drink on me, Rosie?" I ask, pulling her closer until she's pressed against my shirt. She gazes up at me as something flares behind her eyes.

"More than you know," she whispers.

As our gazes lock, the air between us becomes charged with an electric intensity. Frustration wells up inside me, and I have an inexplicable urge to lean in and kiss her.

I quickly push that feeling deep down low and abolish it from my mind.

"Get in line," I respond.

Her hands unravel from the nape of my neck. "Thank you for the dance." Her voice wavers.

"The pleasure is mine, Rosie. Now go home. And stay out of trouble."

I hold onto her hips a moment longer than I should, her piercing eyes glued to mine.

"Maybe I just enjoy a little bit of trouble," she whispers, her eyes daring me as she juts out her chin in defiance.

Fuck me.

A wave of irritation washes over me, and I have a strong urge to punish her for her disobedience with a bruising hickey.

I press my thumbs into her hip bones and pull her close until her body is pinned against my firm chest. Gazing into her hazel eyes up close, I can't help but notice the way they seem to shift in color, appearing more green than brown with hints of gold around the pupils. Their depth and richness pull me in as if I could get lost in the stories they hold.

I drag my mouth down to the side of her face and around to the curve of her cheek before saying, "I won't repeat myself. *Go home.*" I emphasize the last part with a low growl.

I feel the pounding of her temple as my free hand rests

against her skin. She nudges her head, but I pull away before putting myself in a situation I'm not sure I can get out of. Even though a part of me may want to teach her a lesson in talking back, I know it's not the right thing to do.

I observe her wild eyes and tousled hair with a smirk. "If you don't go home now, you can forget about coming in on Monday," I say, suddenly needing her to leave.

She gasps audibly, taken aback by my words, and I watch her demeanor shift. Instead of instilling fear, she steps closer to me, closing the gap between us. Though she seems confident, I sense her uncertainty. Her hands snake around my waistband and palm my butt, dragging me close to her. Then I notice something in her eyes that has me hard almost instantly.

"Are you sure you want me to go home?" she asks with an innocent look that has me suddenly confused.

I let out a low growl, wondering how this little thing has me dumbfounded. Unable to help it, I lower my lips to her neck, tugging on her soft skin with my teeth and sucking hard, eliciting a gasp and a moan from her. As she presses herself into me, I warn her with a husky voice, "I'd break you, little one."

I turn to leave but not before catching a glimpse of the same desire in her eyes as in mine.

"You're back!" Harry says as he sees me approach.

When I turn, she's gone.

Good.

More women surround me, but I'm not interested. They can't give me what I need, which is hard—no-strings-attached fucking.

I slide my phone from my back jeans pocket and make a call. A moment later, and it's done. A regular girl, Heidi, is on her way to my penthouse. All I have to do is slide away from Harry and his harem of girls. He won't even know I'm gone.

"Nice to catch up, man," I say, throwing back the rest of my whisky and relishing the fresh burn as it slides down the back of my throat.

"So good to see you, Vin."

"Maybe next time we can actually get a conversation in before you get distracted," I say, raising an eyebrow as I watch the girls next to him.

"Sure. I know just the place," he says, smiling into his beer.

"I bet you do." I shake his hand and take my leave, the woman beside him licking her lips as her gaze hovers down the open neck of my shirt to my tan skin.

"Sure you don't want to join us?" she asks in a whispered shout.

I laugh. And so does Harry. "He has a certain type, sweetheart. Don't you worry. I'll keep you company."

I give him a knowing nod, then turn around, heading for the exit.

Hours later and I'm cock deep inside Heidi's ass, punishing her and letting out my frustrations on her.

I'm staring at the back of Heidi, her short black hair doing nothing to distract me from visions of Rosie and the defiance in her hazel eyes. A frisson of anger floods my veins, and I slam into Heidi even harder. She lets out a moan akin to a wild animal, but she hasn't used her safe word.

She can handle me.

My grip around her neck tightens as her moans grow more savage and airy.

"Come *now*," I command, then almost instantly, she comes in a fit of an explosion. I close my eyes, absorbing it all, then hazel eyes and perfect tits invade my view. The shape and size belong to Rosie. I sheathe my teeth, my body contorting and convulsing, irritation coursing through me, and with one last thrust, I slam into her and come in a rush, Rosie's sweet, tight pussy clenching around me.

Heidi is panting when she says, "Sir, that was..."

Her voice brings me back to the present, and I gasp, coming to grips with my own insatiable orgasm and the image of Rosie now invading my sex life.

Opening my eyes, I let out a long, drawn-out exhalation and swipe the beads of sweat with the back of my hand. Then, I lean back and slide out of Heidi, crawling off the bed, no less frustrated or irritated. "What? I always make you come multiple times, Heidi," I bark, my voice harsher than I intend.

She rolls on her back and twists her lips into a smile as she's thinking. "You certainly do, Sir. But that was something else," she says, oblivious to my turmoil.

My gaze falls upon her, and I scoff in disbelief before I turn abruptly and march toward my oversized en suite bathroom with firm, deliberate steps. I discard the used condom and step into the black marble shower.

"Until next time, Sir." I hear Heidi's voice reverberate through the bathroom door. She knows the drill—they all do. A business transaction based on an exchange or orgasms and, of course, a nondisclosure agreement.

I reply with a curt goodbye and flick the faucet. The searing heat lands on my sensitive skin, and I welcome the distraction, although brief.

What the fuck was I doing thinking about Rosie when everything about her frustrates me?

My body contorts with irritation.

I had hoped that sleeping with Heidi would scrub Rosie West from my mind, but I can feel the rage building up inside me as she once again takes over my thoughts.

I lather my body with fragrant and sweet soap. The scent reminds me of her, and I let out a moan as my hand rubs up and down my dick. It lengthens on its own accord, and damn, the next thing I know, I'm fisting myself hard and fast. Water sprays off my hair onto the wall as I pump harder from base to tip. With a groan, my body instantly flushes with heat, the intensity of the sensation radiating from my shoulders and fanning outward.

My teeth graze so hard against my bottom lip I taste the metallic tang of blood on my tongue. I stroke my cock harder than ever before as milky fluid spills onto the black marble wall.

Okay, so she's intriguing.

No one ever intrigues me.

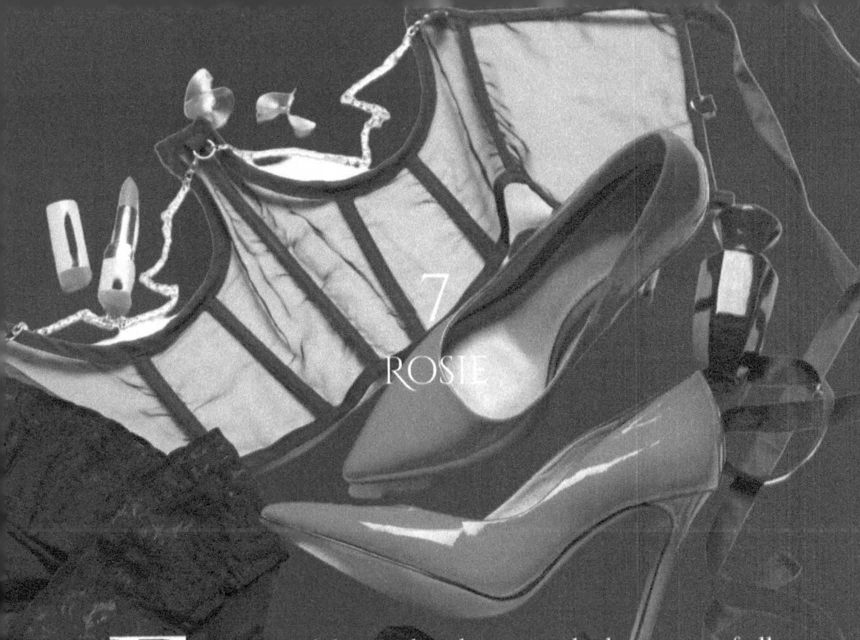

7

ROSIE

For most of the weekend, I nurse the hangover of all hangovers and have barely recovered when Monday morning rolls around.

Late Sunday, Ethan finally returned home after what started as Friday night partying and turned into a wild party weekend. Sara spent Saturday at her parents and Sunday waking up with a random guy. After she got rid of him, we spent the afternoon lazing about in our pajamas and eating way too many chocolate chip cookies.

I diverted the conversation when she asked if her matchmaking skills with the 'hot tall guy' she pushed my way worked out. I couldn't bring myself to tell her that the guy she basically forced upon me was Vincent Slater. And worse, I couldn't admit that some part of me liked it.

~

As I push through security and swipe my card in the elevator to the fortieth floor, my heart beats louder and louder as I ascend into the lion's den.

I may have been drunk enough to flirt and touch his brick-like ass, but I wasn't drunk enough to forget Vincent's searing lips biting the soft skin of my neck. Whenever I'm around him, I can't decide whether to kill or bait him with my flirtatious advances.

But then I don't know if he loathes or wants me.

The way his haunting eyes held mine shot slivers of need up and down my spine that I had never experienced. Then when he told me to go home? Well, fuck, he doused out my flames. But that didn't stop me from thinking about his possessive touch and damning words for the rest of the weekend. That, and the parting words he said to me in that velvety voice of his. *"I'd break you, little one."*

What did that mean, and why am I so curious to find out?

Exiting the elevator, I try to push away thoughts of Vincent, but my heart is still racing at an alarming pace.

I meet the other interns at the boardroom table, where chatter fills the space as we wait for Vincent to arrive. Debra bursts through the door first, her hair still frazzled from last week and her wide smile contagious and warm. "Right. I, for one, can't wait to get started." She beams. "Let's get up, grab your things, and I'll show you where your desks are."

We all bounce out of our chairs like eager little bees on the first day of school, but we know what an opportunity this is. We beat out over a thousand other applicants to be here, and the five of us know that an internship at Slater Corp will put us in good stead for future employment after graduation.

"Hey, Rosie, how was your weekend?" Angela asks over her bold glasses. She falls into step beside me as we follow Debra out of the boardroom and down the large marble foyer toward the elevators.

"Went too quickly. Yours?" I reply, welcoming the distraction of wondering where Vincent is.

"Same," she says, glancing down at my outfit and side-stepping as she does so. Then she adds, "Love the dress."

Automatically, I run a hand down the side of my pinstriped black and white dress, which falls to the knee and pulls in at the waist with a black patent belt. The thick straps cut down to a square neckline, revealing my crisp white blouse underneath. My hair is pinned up in a high chignon, with loose tendrils of hair falling around my face, and a light dusting of makeup powders my cheeks.

A far cry from the sheets of makeup I wore at the lingerie club, which, fortunately, I still had my job after a slap on the wrist.

"Thanks." I smile back. "So, Jersey Tech, that's not too far from Manhattan is it?" I ask.

"No, it's not too bad, but my parents have secured me an apartment in the city while I undertake the intern program. Saves me commuting each day," Angela says before adding, "How about you... from the city? I didn't get to ask you the other day."

"No. I wish. I'm commuting from Saddle Hills, so it takes me about forty-five minutes on the L train," I reply, feeling a twinge of envy for her easy access to the city. "But it's worth it for this opportunity."

"Oh, I can imagine! Saddle Hills is a bit far out, but I've heard it's a lovely area. And you're right, the opportunity to work in the city is definitely worth the commute," she says, nodding in understanding. "I've had friends who've commuted even longer than that for their dream job. Plus, you can always use the time on the train to catch up on reading."

"So true. And I am a bookworm so I really don't mind.

I'm currently rereading *Wuthering Heights* for the like the fifty-seventh time."

Angela laughs out loud, her eyes twinkling with amusement. "That's a feat. Obsessed much?"

I chuckle as Debra chimes in, "It's great to have a mix of city and suburban interns. We'll learn a lot from each other's perspectives."

As we reach the elevator, my nerves start to kick in again. I take a deep breath, reminding myself I've earned this internship and can succeed.

The tall blond man presses against me, his shoulder nudging me as we cram into the elevator. He's wearing another weird tie today, with pink flamingos on a blue background. It's kind of throwing me off.

What was his name again? David? No, I think it's Dane.

"Hey!" He pops an eyebrow and tosses Angela and me a flirty all-American smile. Debra is behind us, talking with the other interns about the program, which I'm trying to overhear, but he isn't letting me have a word of it.

"Rosie, right?" he questions, looking hyped as he gazes at me.

He has way too much cologne on and is either hiding smoking dope or trying to impress a girl.

I turn my head to the side, trying to catch a break. "That's me. Dane?" I query, and he smiles, happy I've remembered who he is.

"Hey, I'm Angela," Angela says, shuffling closer and running a hand through her short bob.

"Hi," he purrs with a flirty smile.

I have to bite my cheek from laughing. Really, is it that easy? Do we all just settle for whoever shows us an ounce of attention? And since when is the word 'hey' a come-on?

As soon as the elevator doors ping open, I burst through them, relieved to be out of the cologne-smelling elevator.

After taking a deep breath, I stand wide-eyed, taking in the opulent surroundings. Even the non-executive floors are impressive, with walls covered in expensive veined marble and large windows on either side that let in fingers of light throughout the space.

Soft chatter from the others bounces around, and Debra walks toward the front reception desk, where a young girl greets her with a friendly smile.

"Clarissa, good morning. I have five eager interns ready to be shown where they will work for the next six weeks."

"Of course. Everything is ready, Debra. The induction material is on their desks."

"You're an angel. Thank you," Debra says with a smile.

"Mr. Slater is scheduled to come down at lunchtime," she adds, and nerves dance in the pit of my stomach. *Lunch?* I thought he would be here first thing with us.

What will we be doing until then?

Debra turns to face us. "Right…" she claps her hands together, "… the morning will be spent going through safety and induction, policies, and procedures."

A groan filters out from behind me, and Debra raises an eyebrow.

"I'll have you know, being here in this building, we have a strict code of conduct that all employees must adhere to, and that includes you, Mr. Jones," she states while giving Dane a pointed look.

Angela smirks beside him, eager to get his attention, and he returns it with a wink.

"Come on then." Debra gestures with over-the-top enthusiasm.

We're led into a vast space with a U-shaped arrangement of desks facing a single table and whiteboard, presumably where our boss and mentor, Mr. Slater, will sit. Beyond that, there's a breakout area where additional desks with partitions are located. The room is bathed in natural light pouring in from the oversized floor-to-ceiling windows that offer an unobstructed view of the bustling streets of Manhattan below.

We settle into our seats, and I gaze at the mammoth document in front of me. I read the front page of the bound document, '*Slater Corp Code of Conduct,*' and inwardly groan. I want to start the internship, not read a bunch of nonsense.

I've never worked for a large corporation and market leader, but I think their code of conduct is over the top. The code is thicker than some of my textbooks, and we are spending the morning going through it line by line. My eyes are nearly bleeding from boredom.

I gaze up, thrilled that I'm finally finished with the most boring document on the planet. Dane lets out a sigh of relief as he flicks through the last of the pages. Sitting between us is Angela, who lets out a puff of air and slams the heavy book on the table with a thud, indicating she's also finished. Debra has been gone for the last half hour, leaving us all to read the remainder of the code of ethics before we break for lunch.

To my left, Max and Fae diligently rush through the final pages. Fae finishes first and runs her hand down her blonde bob, curling both ends so they fall perfectly underneath her jawline.

I watch as she pulls out a compact of makeup and applies lip gloss, giving a final blot before snapping her compact closed. As she looks up and catches my eye, I get the feeling she doesn't like me. She offers me a meek smile before turning back to Max.

Max stares beside her unabashedly. He seems to be mesmerized by her, whereas I'm fond of her expensive-looking outfit—a navy jacket over a designer dress with delicate fibers. I couldn't help but compare it to my sale item from Gap.

I only shop during sales or promotions, waiting for Black Friday or seasonal sales to get the best deals. These clothes will have to do for a while longer, especially since the extra money I was earning from tips goes toward paying off Gabriel's debts.

"Are they real?" My eyes snap up to see Max's eyes fixed on Fae's breasts. Her blouse is unbuttoned and quite revealing, but what the fuck? *Did he seriously just ask that?*

She turns to him, a scowl spreading onto her face. "Of course they're real," she snaps back, throwing her compact in her purse for effect and dropping it on the marble floor with a thud.

Angela, who is next to me, lets out a low chuckle. "Real as Dolly Parton's tits they are," she mumbles, and I laugh loudly, filling the silent space.

That's when he walks in.

Of course.

I cover my mouth with my hand as his green eyes immediately fix upon mine. Strong, broad shoulders, poised and dressed in a midnight blue suit that was made for him, his piercing eyes make me shrink into the back of my chair.

"What's so funny, Ms. West?" he asks, his voice deep and authoritative.

I roll my lips in on themselves as I try to think of a reply that isn't so childish. "Nothing, sir," I say, forcing myself to meet his piercing gaze.

His eyes linger on mine for a moment, then he snaps them to the square table we all surround. "Good, because a code of ethics is not funny. Nor has it ever been. It is a serious standard we adhere to here at Slater Corp, and anyone who steps out of line is out the door."

Shit.

"Of course, Mr. Slater," Fae says.

Asslicker.

Angela nudges me, jolting me out of my thoughts and making me realize she's just as annoyed with Fae as I am. I shoot her a knowing look, silently acknowledging our shared frustration. It's clear that we have six long weeks ahead of us, and I know I will need Angela's support to make it through.

As Mr. Slater continues to speak, I find myself studying his every move. From the sharp lines of his jaw to the ruthless demeanor he displays during the discussion on the takeover, it's clear he is a businessman in every sense of the word. Despite the lack of emotion on his face, I can't help but feel a sense of admiration for his focus and determination.

He's run through the entire acquisition on the whiteboard when Dane interrupts, "So you're still going for the kill even though they're that vulnerable?"

Mr. Slater turns around, precisely replacing the lid of his whiteboard marker. "Of course. It's when they're most vulnerable that you have the greatest advantage," he replies, his tone confident and unwavering.

When he finishes speaking, a sense of unease develops, and I decide to voice my concerns. "But don't you feel for the owners of the other company?" I ask.

He lets out a loud chuckle that makes the hairs on my neck stand on end. "They shouldn't have gotten themselves into that situation to begin with," he replies with a smug smile, his words dripping with contempt for anyone who would allow themselves to be vulnerable in such a way.

"Absolutely," Fae agrees, tipping her chin and beaming in agreement with Mr. Slater.

My nostrils flare.

"There are only winners and losers in a takeover."

I twist my lips. Something doesn't sit right with me during the entire explanation of his takeover.

"Do you think there's room for shades of gray?" I ask, hoping to gain some insight into his thought process.

His eyes flicker to mine, and I think I sense disappointment there, but I can't be sure. "Absolutely not." He deadpans.

Still, I need to speak up. I have thoughts, and they're warranted. I should speak up. That's what this internship is all about. Learning, right?

"What is it, Ms. West?" He studies my face, his impatience apparent.

"Well, I just wonder if your approach could have been different."

He scoffs. "Go ahead. This should be interesting." He folds his arms and stares at me intently, the smug look on his face making me roll my eyes around the room. Fae smirks, and I wish I could wipe it off with barbed wire. Dane watches me, waiting for me to continue. I look over at Angela, and she stares up at me expectantly, giving me the courage to speak up.

"Maybe if you hadn't let go of the mid-level management and affected all the families with that single decision, the company could have been rebuilt and sustained itself. Instead, you came in and stripped it down to the bare minimum to purely increase profits."

He holds my gaze, and I feel the heat rising from my chest to the tops of my ears. *Shit, did I say the wrong thing? "Speak up,"* I tell myself.

"That's an interesting suggestion," he says in a low voice. "But there's no room for emotions in this business when it's all about the bottom line. If you can't lose them, I suggest you work at the local pet shelter." Max and Fae let out a laugh as anger roars in my ears like rainbows of hell. He turns his back on me, effectively dismissing me from countering him.

Mr. Slater was an absolute asshole from arrival to when I left, not only to me but to the others as well. But I did get the feeling he was being extra tough on me.

And that's pretty much how the first week goes, starting the semester at college and working part-time at my internship for two days.

One of the only things I have from Mom's belongings is my antique watch. She didn't have many possessions, but one I cherish, and as I stare at it, noting the time, I just want this Friday to be over.

Mr. Slater comes to stand over me, invading my personal space. My desk is situated along the glass windows, with a long partition separating me from Angela's desk opposite. The scent of his cologne assaults my senses, and I can feel his six-foot-three-inch presence beside me.

"Are we boring you, Ms. West?" he asks with a hint of sarcasm.

I gaze up at him and force a sweet smile, clenching my jaw tightly.

His gaze holds mine for a minute, and the air swirls and crackles around us. I drag my teeth across my bottom lip, waiting for him to leave. *What is he doing?* He bends forward so his face is level with mine. *Shit, what the hell?*

His dark green eyes search my face, dominant in his gaze, and I wither under his stare. His gaze drags down to my lips, and my heart is a thunderstorm in my chest. Then, as if I imagined it, he quickly snaps them back up.

"Well?" He tsks impatiently.

"Well?" I croak out.

"Your work, Ms. West," he states, raising his eyebrows impatiently. I'm sure there's a slight grin tipping at his lips when I realize I'm still staring at him.

I quickly shift my focus back to the paper in front of me and snatch it up. I turn, not looking at what I'm doing, and my cheek collides with his dick.

His. Fucking. Dick.

Oh my God.

Kill me now.

"I'm so sorry," I say, completely mortified from head to toe. Thank God none of the other interns can see me. I can't even look up at him. That's how embarrassed I am. Damn him.

When I finally manage to meet his gaze, I see that his jaw is clenched tightly, and he's speaking through gritted teeth. "I should think so."

As he takes the paper from my outstretched hand, I mutter under my breath, "Don't stand so close next time." I can hear him inhale sharply as his hand brushes mine, sending a spark through my body.

He walks over to the next desk, his shiny, expensive shoes mocking me from below the table as he talks to Angela. Irritation floods my veins, erasing the optimism I had felt when I finished my paper. I want to grab a tin of red paint and splatter it all over his expensive suit and pants, creating my own version of abstract art and ruining his handsome features.

I am so relieved to leave that I basically tumble into the elevator first, with the others piling in and pushing me toward the back. It descends with a soft tug, and Dane lets out a laugh. "Well, I don't know about you guys, but I'm loving this already," he says.

Agreement rings out in the elevator, but am I the only one infuriated by Mr. Slater's arrogance and genuine lack of emotion?

"Sure, the content is great if we weren't being taught by such an arrogant asshole," I snap, noticing that it comes out more forcefully than I intended. All eyes turn to meet mine.

"You're just too soft," Fae shrugs.

"You need to get some backbone if you want to be in this business," Dane agrees, taking her side.

I understand the ruthless nature of takeovers, but surely there is a way where all parties involved can be happy with the outcome. "I'm certainly not soft," I retort.

"No, you're not. But you have to agree, it's his kill-or-be-killed attitude that has made him a multimillionaire," Angela offers and shrugs.

"Well, I can't argue with that," I say.

"Ah, don't you mean billionaire?" Dane half-laughs, swiping his blond hair from his eyes.

"I know." Fae purrs as she stares into space, imagining her life with him.

"Honey, forget it. A, you're too young, and B, Vincent Slater doesn't date, "Dane adds.

"How do you know that?" I ask, my interest piqued.

"A friend of a friend who moves in those circles says he doesn't date."

"Why would he when he has girls literally falling at his feet with that much money?" Max adds.

"Hmm… interesting," Fae says as she gets lost daydreaming about Mr. Slater.

"Honey, you're hot, but I'm telling you, give the fuck up on Vincent Slater," Dane warns.

She smirks at him, and he shakes his head dismissively. "He's never been pictured with a woman. Some people think he might even be gay."

A laugh rolls off my lips, and all eyes turn to me, except for Fae.

"If he's gay, I'm Mother Teresa," Fae says with a chuckle.

"If you're Mother Teresa, then I'm the next Pope," Dane adds in agreement.

Laughter rolls around inside the four walls of the elevator as we all laugh at the absurdity of Fae ever being saintly.

The doors open, and they all file out, debating on whether or not Vincent Slater was, in fact, a lover of men.

The memory of his scorching touch on my exposed skin and the way his gaze stayed fixed on my eyes it was impossible for me to believe that Vincent Slater was gay.

Ruthless, yes. Gay, absolutely not.

My natural hair is pinned tightly underneath a long blonde wig cascading down my shoulders. I gaze at my reflection in the mirror, wearing a delicate lace one-piece. The one-piece barely contains my breasts, held together by a thin velvet belt fastened with a gold clip at my navel. I'm grateful for the hefty discounts we receive at the best lingerie store in town. Otherwise, I would be walking around in who knows what.

At the Vanilla Club, every girl can pick lingerie from Shop X, and Dante's agreement means we get designer pieces at wholesale prices.

The beautiful garment makes me feel like a goddess. It's Saturday night when my manager at the Vanilla Club calls me, informing me that one of the girls has fallen ill and they need me to take her place tonight.

I'm relieved I wasn't fired and even more grateful for the opportunity to work three more shifts next week. I just have to juggle them with school and not fall asleep at my internship.

There is no way I could turn down the extra shifts at the Vanilla Club, especially with the looming pressure of paying off my brother's debt. I have no other choice.

Grabbing a tissue from the box, I blot my Venetian red lips before laughing at my transformation from a studious intern to a scantily-clad waitress.

No more time to fuss.

Tips wait for no one.

8
VINCENT

It's past eleven, and I'm sitting with my two friends, Harry and Caleb, and my brother, Julius, at Sojos—a bar we often visited when I lived in Manhattan.

Harry, a successful investment company owner, is known for his charm and is quite the ladies' man, with a new romantic interest each week. Meanwhile, Caleb runs his own thriving tech startup, constantly coming up with innovative ideas and solutions that keep him on the cutting edge of the industry.

"I can't tell you how good it is to see you back here where you belong," Harry says, holding his beer out. Harry always makes me laugh. He and Julius were the popular guys at school, whereas Caleb and I were more reserved.

I clink my tumbler of Blue Label scotch with my brother's beer. "London has been my home for the past five years," I say as I take a sip. The burn catches in the back of my throat, and I relish it as the drink slides down.

"Nonsense! Manhattan is also your home," Julius admonishes.

I set down my drink. "It is nice to be back," I admit.

"It's great to see you in person, man. It's been too long," Caleb says enthusiastically, grasping my biceps and giving them a friendly squeeze. "But seriously, what are they putting in the water over there? Your muscles are huge!"

"I channel my frustration into working out," I share, prompting laughter from them all.

"I thought you fuck your way out of frustration?" Harry asks.

"I do," I reply, but it hasn't been enough. I've always been high-strung, but hitting the gym alleviates some of the burdens I bear.

"Well, I'm glad you're here," Caleb says, nodding firmly.

I respond with a nod and a friendly slap on his back.

"I think this intern program will be the perfect distraction for you, Vin. Get your head out of your ass and out of that icy climate," Julius expresses with a sly grin.

I shoot him a glare over the rim of my drink.

"And absolutely no more staff firings, agreed?" Julius follows up, giving me a pointed look.

Ah, so that's what's been bothering him.

"That was a ballsy move, Slater," Harry says. "Did you really fire all thirty-three people over the company loud-speaker?"

"They had it coming," I retort, unfazed by the consequences of letting go of incompetent employees. "And for the record, it's freezing here too."

Julius scowls in response, "What's really cold is the chaos you left for me and the VP of legal to handle after your outburst. Let's hope you treat your interns with more compassion." He raises an eyebrow at me, driving his point home.

"What's that?" I urge, and Julius rolls his eyes at me.

The conversation moves forward without me, and my

mind wanders back to earlier today when I stood behind her desk. Her scent invaded my nostrils, and I was already getting thick when I stole a glance down her shirt. But then she had to go and snap her head into my dick as she turned.

My cock pulses at the memory like it did today when she felt it.

"Slater, where are you?" Harry's voice breaks through the noise in the bar, packed with suits and late-night meetings.

Suddenly, I realize I'm being watched and find three pairs of eyes focused on me.

"I bet he's thinking about that certain intern," Julius teases, a playful grin spreading across his face.

"What are you talking about?" I ask, trying to keep my voice calm but feeling a knot form in my stomach at the mere mention of Rosie.

"You know exactly who I mean. That intern with the dark hair and the captivating smile. The one who's been drawing your attention all week." Julius playfully jabs me.

"I have no idea what you're talking about," I reply, striving for a casual tone.

"Oh, come on. I noticed how you looked at her on Monday. Plus, whenever I've asked you about the interns this week, you always seem to bring up Rosie," Julius observes.

I pause, slightly surprised by Julius' observation. I've never shown interest in a woman outside of the women I hire at the agency.

Even if I did, had I been that obvious that Julius noticed?

What the fuck?

"Who's Rosie?" Caleb asks, taking another sip of his beer and gesturing to the waiter for another round. I let out a groan, not wanting to talk about Rosie and wishing I could push her from my thoughts.

"Rosie is one of our brightest interns. Who also happens to work over at the Vanilla Club," Julius announces with a sly smile.

Little fucker.

"I mention her because she's the one who irritates me the most," I respond, attempting to justify my actions.

Julius laughs. "I'm sure that's it," he replies sarcastically.

"Wait, an intern at Slater Corp works at the Vanilla Club?" Caleb asks.

"She must be fucking gorgeous," Harry adds. "Only beauties work at the VC."

"She's fine," I respond, hesitating to confess her beauty to this crowd of clowns.

"Here's a story for you," Julius continues, ignoring me.

"*Don't,*" I say through gritted teeth, feeling my brother rile me up for no good reason.

"Oh no, we have to hear this," Caleb says, grinning from ear to ear.

"Vin entertained clients last weekend at the Vanilla Club, and dearest brother here spotted Rosie. Although unbeknownst to Vincent, Rosie was going to be one of his interns."

"Did you sleep with her, Slater?" Harry asks, a mischievous gleam in his eye.

"Of course not," I reply, rolling my lips in and draining the rest of my scotch. The image of her in lace lingerie has etched its place in my mind.

Harry frowns.

"Unlike you, I don't fuck everything I see," I add, trying to defend myself.

The waiter comes and goes, leaving a round of drinks on the wooden table. So much for a quick drink after work. Instead, we are really getting into it, knocking back one drink after another.

"Well, what happened then?" Harry asks, his eyes wide.

"She was groped," Julius says.

"Not by me," I snap, feeling a sudden surge of anger flooding my veins.

"You fucking can't touch them there. At least not on the ground floor. The rules are strict as fuck," Harry says.

"I bet you'd know too, Harry," Julius says with a knowing expression.

Not wanting my brother to finish the story, I quickly pipe up, "She turned and threw a drink in my face."

Caleb and Harry burst out laughing at my comment.

"Seriously? She actually did that?" Harry asks, his eyes wide with amusement.

"Oh, she fucking did," Julius confirms, sporting a grin reminiscent of a Cheshire cat that just devoured a canary.

"Yes, it was hilarious," I say, staring at Caleb and Harry with a deadpan expression, which only makes them laugh even harder.

"The great Vincent Slater, taken down by his scotch and a lingerie waitress," Harry remarks between chuckles.

"And *intern*," I grit out, feeling my anger flare up again.

"Fuck, she must be hot," Caleb says. "They only have hot girls over there. We must go back."

"No, that's not happening," I say firmly, not wanting to be reminded of the situation again.

"She's quite the looker," Julius agrees, and I can feel my irritation growing. "Absolutely stunning, to be honest," he adds, seemingly enjoying my discomfort.

"Back off Julius," I tell my brother, my voice low and edged with possessiveness, betraying my jealousy.

He casually raises his hands in surrender, taking note of the seriousness in my expression.

You haven't seen her in lingerie.

Caleb looks at me sideways. "So what happened next?" he asks eagerly.

"I threatened her job and left that evening," I reply curtly. "Then she turned up in my fucking boardroom on Monday morning," I add with a scowl, remembering the entire awkward encounter.

"You should have seen the expression on his face!" Julius interjects, chuckling heartily. I shift my focus to him and regard him with narrowed eyes.

"You know the Vanilla Club is just around the corner from here," Harry adds with a sly wink.

"Not. Happening," I grit out. Although my dick seems to have other ideas as it swells between my legs at the thought of her full breasts spilling as she stands over me in sexy lingerie.

As I shake my head, a bunch of women saunters into the bar, their tipsy laughter and loud voices filling the room, adding to the lively atmosphere.

"I'm guessing you're not with Andrea anymore after our night out last time?" I ask Caleb, wanting to change the subject.

"No, she was too much work. Needy as fuck. Great around my cock, though. She gave the best head. That's why it took me so long to give her the flick," he replies, his crassness making me shake my head.

"Honestly, I don't know why you bother with relationships when you only last five minutes with them," I remark, looking between Harry and my brother.

"You can talk, Slater," Harry replies.

"I don't date. I'm clear from the outset," I add, knowing they know everything about my lack of dating life. I haven't dated anyone since I lost my virginity to a high-class hooker my dad insisted on when I was fifteen.

"Exactly, so don't go giving out advice when you clearly don't know what you're talking about."

"I know you shouldn't lead a woman on," I say, and Harry laughs aloud while my brother looks a bit shocked that I'm calling him out for his player tendencies.

"Out of all of you, I'm the one who's been in a relationship the longest," Julius adds as I struggle to remember his ex-girlfriend's name.

"Veronica, wasn't it?" I ask tentatively.

"Veronica? What the fuck, Vincent? You haven't been away that long. It was Vanessa," he corrects me.

"Right, Vanessa," I say, draining the rest of my glass.

"She was nice," I admit, remembering how happy my brother was with her.

"Yeah, well, I fucked that up," he says, staring out into the bar with a look of regret on his face.

What the fuck was I doing?

I find myself walking through the large, black arched doors of the Vanilla Club. I have no idea what time it is, but Julius already went home with a woman he met at the bar, and here I am, being led to a table by a clearly drunk Harry and Caleb.

"This is a bad idea," I mutter to myself, but a part of me is intrigued to find out if she is working tonight. An even bigger part of me wants to bank an image of her in her skimpy lingerie to memory.

"Here you are, gentlemen. Your waitress will be with you momentarily," the hostess says with a warm smile as she escorts us to our table.

"Thank you," we reply in unison.

The club is dark and crowded, but it's always busy no matter the day of the week. This is a place where we often take clients and suppliers and sometimes even seal business deals.

I look around, my gaze flicking to the bar at the back and the ladies clad in lingerie, but none of them are her.

"She's not here," I say aloud, feeling a strange sense of disappointment at the realization.

"Fuck it. Who cares. Just look at these angels. My dick is getting hard. I fucking love what Dante's done here," Harry exclaims, his eyes wide and soaring like a fucking horny prepubescent kid.

A waitress appears and smiles down at us with a slow, sexy smile, but it's not Rosie, and I'm not aroused.

"Good evening, gentlemen, and welcome to the Vanilla Club. I'm Kara. What can I get you?" she asks.

"I'll have a top-shelf scotch," I reply, trying to ignore Harry's inappropriate comments.

"Mm," Caleb murmurs, his eyes wandering blatantly over the waitress' breasts. It's almost uncouth.

The waitress smiles back at him.

"She wants a good tip, Caleb. Keep your dick in your pants," I say under my breath.

Harry and Caleb order beers, purposely ignoring my advice.

"Of course. Hold tight. I'll be back in a moment," Kara says before disappearing.

"She's delicious," Harry says, licking his lips.

"Keep your dick in your pants," I repeat, but Harry just laughs aloud.

I look around, feeling restless and uncomfortable.

"Maybe she's working upstairs," Caleb offers, knowing me too well.

"Upstairs, they can fuck," I say, my mind suddenly going to the possibility that she might be a sex worker. The drinks from earlier swirl in my stomach, threatening to come up. "She wouldn't," I hiss out, feeling defensive.

"Why not?" Caleb asks, his curiosity getting the best of him.

"Because..." My voice trails off as I try to come up with a reason.

"They're not supposed to fuck upstairs anyway," Caleb adds.

"Have you ever heard of it happening?" I ask, unable to resist the urge to know if Rosie gave sexual favors in exchange for money and tips.

"What difference would it make if she did?" Caleb continues to pepper me with questions I'm in no mood to answer. "It would be perfect for you. No commitment, just an exchange. You're still sleeping with hookers, right?"

"Keep your fucking voice down," I whisper-shout, and he just laughs. "They're escorts and only from the Carnegie Agency in London. Here, I have a few girls I keep. They know the deal," I explain, trying to defend myself.

Caleb rolls his eyes. "So cold, Mr. Slater."

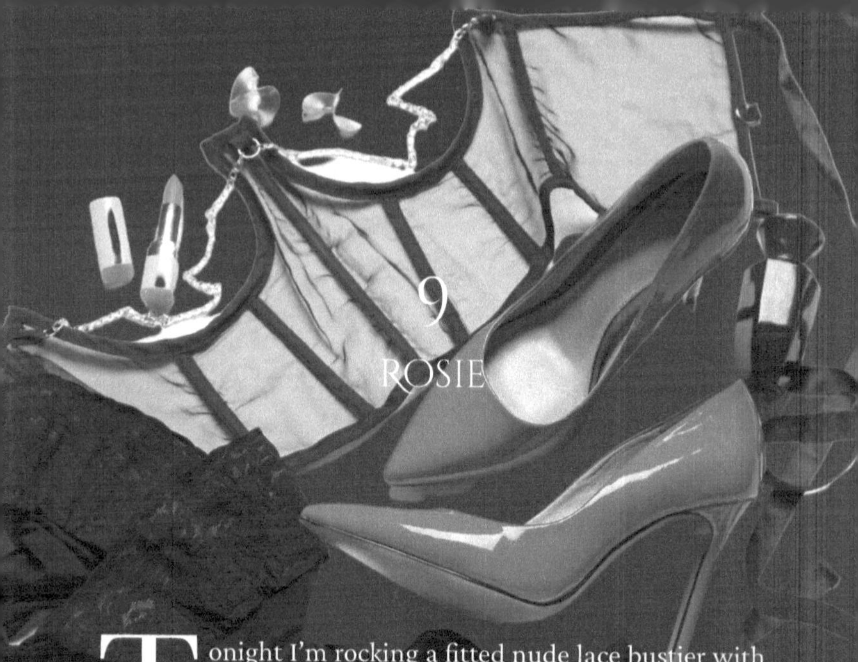

onight I'm rocking a fitted nude lace bustier with a sweetheart cup. The lace is so soft and pretty, straining against my natural curves, making me feel confident and sexy. I love the delicate fabric—it adds a touch of allure to my look, and I'm hoping the tips will be large tonight.

As I strut past my tables, I keep in mind that making my customers happy is the key to getting good tips. But it's not always easy—they always want to touch—and I have to politely yet seductively stroke their egos. These men are powerful and wealthy, and their egos are more fragile than glass.

I smile at the gentleman who stares directly at my chest, offering him another beverage before my shift ends. He nods, not even bothering to meet my gaze. According to him, my face is in the middle of my chest.

Okay, I know I'm a lingerie waitress, but with men like this, it's no wonder women are obsessed with romance novels. It's a way to escape from the not-so-great reality out here.

I saunter back to the bar and place my order with Jesse. He's as flirtatious as ever, flashing his stunning smile and winking at all the girls around. I know he's harmless, so I let it fly.

"Order up, Rosie," he says, purposefully grazing my arm and letting his hand linger on top of it after he places the drink on the silver tray.

"Thanks." I smile in reply.

The place is bustling tonight. The cool, velvety melodies from the high-quality sound system fill the air. Aromatic wafts of cigar tobacco swirl around the room, and men are laughing and boosting each other's confidence as they relax in plush wingback chairs and luxurious leather sofas.

Even more than usual, I feel exhausted and eager to head home. My shift ends at two, but tomorrow—now today—I have a considerable amount of homework to catch up on from the first week.

Suck it up, princess.

I remind myself that I need this job.

Exhaling a puff of air, I smile at the men seated at the table. Then, with a smile, I slide my hand from Jesse and automatically return to my table. "Here we are," I announce as I lean down and place the drinks in front of each man who ordered. "I'll leave you in Kara's capable hands now," I say, offering a sweet smile and hoping they'll generously tip me before the night is over.

However, one of the men, Elliot, grabs my hand. I politely extricate myself from his grasp, feeling uneasy with the attention. He's wealthy, influential, and just like the other guys in the bar. Elliot is a big name in the tech world, and all the girls working here are well aware of who these men are.

Earlier in my shift, a few of them had pulled me aside to

fill me in on the scoop about Elliot. He can be rather aggressive but can leave a fat tip if you play your cards right.

"Sorry, sir. I'm sure you'll find Kara more than hospitable." I smile and wave, turning on my heel and disappearing past the row of main tables and down the other side of the building where the staff dressing rooms are located.

My stilettos click against the wooden floor as the music slowly fades into the background. Then, unexpectedly, I feel a firm tug on my arm and quickly spin around.

"I *said* wait," Elliot states, looking down at me.

I immediately step back, feeling uneasy. "Excuse me," I say as I pull my hand from his tight grip, but he steps closer. His eyes roam over my body, and I recoil, feeling uncomfortable with his gaze.

A shiver of fear rolls down my spine and settles in my stomach as I realize we are alone. I can't believe he got past security. "Move away from her," a familiar commanding voice from behind him states, and my breath instantly hitches in my throat.

I glance over his shoulder to spot the silhouette of a tall man with broad shoulders and piercing green eyes staring intently at the man confronting me. Relief surges through me as I recognize him, and then it hits me.

What on earth is Mr. Slater doing here?

A mix of relief and curiosity washes over me at Vincent's presence.

Elliot pivots. "Mr. Slater," he exclaims, instantly releasing my hand. Vincent fixes him with a stare intense enough to wake the dead. I can feel the tension between the two men, and it's evident that Elliot knows Vincent and is intimidated by him.

"I suggest you leave the lady alone, Ellio*t*." He enunciates the T with such force, sending a shiver down my spine to the tips of my toes.

I'm beginning to realize the power Vincent has over people, and somewhere deep inside, it excites me. As Elliot steps out of my personal space and backs away, I can't help but feel drawn to Vincent and the way he commands respect from those around him.

"Right then. Sorry," he says to me, then hastily walks back down the dark corridor.

Great!

And just like that, I can kiss my tip goodbye.

Fuck!

How would I explain this to my brother?

Vincent steps closer, and I catch the familiar scent of his excessive cologne, which deliciously sweeps between us. He's wearing dark pants and a crisp white shirt with the sleeves rolled up, and his golden forearms are exposed, veins laddering both arms. His light brown hair is tousled and soft—the kind of hair you could get lost in for days. It's that damn clean and silky.

"Are you all right?" he snaps the question, running a hand through the hair I was just swooning over.

I gaze up at him, his eyes narrowing and his jaw tense as his hands knead together in front of him. *Why is he always angry with me?* I didn't ask him to step in.

"I'm perfectly fine," I reply with equal tenacity. "You shouldn't have done that."

"Is that so?" he asks before crossing his arms over his chest. His gaze runs down my body slowly, painstakingly slowly. Suddenly, the hallway becomes a blast furnace as something swirls between us.

I snap out of it quickly, swallowing the sand in my throat. "Because I had it," I say in a rush.

He steps closer, and the music fades in the background as blood pools in my ears at his proximity. "This is a dangerous job, Ms. West."

I pin my back against the wall, feeling the coldness against the heat that has engulfed my skin, and I let out a small gasp. His eyes darken at the sound, and my entire body is now alight as his gaze dips from my eyes down to my lips.

"I can handle it," I say, lifting my chin, but my voice is breathy and hot.

A smirk pulls from his beautiful mouth. "Oh, I have no doubt you can, little one."

Little one.

Why does it thrill me when he calls me that?

As he comes closer, his dark features become more distinct. His easy-going demeanor suggests he's had a few drinks tonight. I take this as a cue to speak my mind, even though I know I probably shouldn't.

"Listen, for what it's worth, I'm sorry I headbutted your dick today."

Oh my God, did I just say that?

As he stares at me intensely, his voice lowers to a low, seductive tone, and his hand firmly presses against the wall beside my head. "I do not want to talk about work while I'm here, and neither should you."

Oh.

My lips part before I can stop them, and the words tumble out, "You're a regular here, huh?" I cringe at how childish I sound and quickly move past the awkwardness, focusing on his striking almond-shaped eyes instead. They seem to have a mesmerizing effect on me.

Then, with a slow, seductive grin, he replies, "I am now."

He's flirting with me?

I can't tell if this is a good or bad thing. On the one hand, he's sexier than sin, and I can just imagine his chiseled six-pack beneath those perfectly tailored suits. But, on the other hand, he's my boss and has been a complete asshole to me since we first met.

I can't help but feel lost and inexperienced. I mean, let's be real. I'm a damn virgin. But he probably thinks I'm some kind of sex goddess. They all do. I put up a convincing façade, but I'm a bundle of nerves deep down.

Ugh, why is he staring at me like that?

I feel like I'm about to implode.

His hand glides down my shoulder, and I feel a sudden surge of electricity as his fingers brush against my bare skin. My eyes flutter closed as I instinctively run my tongue across my bottom lip. He inhales sharply, and the next thing I know, his fingers are brushing against my bottom lip. A shiver runs down my spine as my nipples harden against the fabric of my lingerie.

My mind is racing as I try to process what's happening. I'm acutely aware of every sensation—the warmth of his hand on my skin, the softness of his touch on my lip, and how my body responds to him. I feel the warmth of his body and sense he's close, but then, just as I think he may kiss me, I feel nothing. It's over. His hand falls from my face, and I find myself struggling to catch my breath. My eyes open, and his eyes hold a dark intensity that leaves me feeling exposed and vulnerable.

It's all so confusing. On the one hand, I'm attracted to him, his good looks, confidence, and power. But on the other, he's my grumpy boss, and I'm his intern. I can't help but wonder what he sees in me or if he even sees me.

Holy fuck.

It takes me a moment to peel myself away from the wall, my body feeling hot, sweaty, and flushed, with a growing dampness between my thighs. He continues to stare at me, and the thudding in my ears is so loud it feels like a kick drum. He looks me in the eye and says, "Good-bye, Rosie."

Walking away, I sway my hips just a little bit more, leaving him with something to remember. I glance back over my shoulder, catching him watching me with a hint of frustration in his eyes, and I say, "Goodbye, Vincent," because he is no longer Mr. Slater to me.

My heart is pounding so hard that it feels like I'm at a death metal concert. It's nine on a Monday morning, and I'm sitting around a table with fellow interns, clutching my piping hot coffee in a flimsy to-go cup. I almost spill it down my outfit, but I quickly grab a napkin and twist it around the cup to make a makeshift coffee cup sleeve.

Angela is seated next to me, and I can't help but like her. I'm even thinking about inviting her out with Sara and me.

Fae triple-checks her makeup in the compact mirror while Max is glued to his phone beside her, and Dane sits close to Angela, making it clear they have feelings for each other. I tap my foot uncontrollably under the table, barely having slept for two hours after my shift at the Vanilla Club. I'm still frustrated and confused about my encounter with Mr. Slater.

What was I even thinking?

And I called him Vincent.

And why can't I get his searing touch or the way I

sensed he might kiss me in that dark hallway out of my mind?

And I'm pretty sure I was not imagining how his eyes were raking up and down my body like a predator.

"You look tired, softy," Fae says, raising a perfectly sculpted eyebrow. I inwardly cringe at the pet name.

Yeah, no. She's not calling me that.

My eyes meet hers, and I see her perfectly coiffed blonde hair and flawless makeup. She snaps her compact shut with a click and looks me over. "Hot date?" she adds, sounding almost amused.

Oh, if you only knew.

"Yes, with your boyfriend," I say with a tsk, smiling sweetly.

"You wish," Fae retorts.

"Oh, wait. You don't have one because your head's too far up your ass." Laughter fills the room as she gasps in shock, then quickly composes herself.

"Oh snap, Rosie!" Dane chimes in, still chuckling. Fae rolls her eyes at me and says, "Who needs one when you can have plenty?"

Max perks up at this, saying, "Room for one more?" and nudges Fae with his shoulder.

She stiffens and responds with a scoff. "Ugh, you wish. I only date older men." She then gives him the cold shoulder.

Rolling my eyes, I chuckle. "Of course you do."

Vincent strides into the room, and the chatter immediately stops. Perfect hair, smelling like pure dirty sunshine. He's dressed in a sharp suit and cleanly shaven. You wouldn't know he was at a lingerie club and slightly intoxicated just a few hours ago. "Fuck me," she whispers under her breath, and a hint of a smile plays on his lips, if only for a millisecond. His eyes meet mine, and I quickly look away, pretending to focus on something in front of me.

"Good morning. How did everyone sleep?" Mr. Slater asks, taking his seat at the front of the table. *The sarcastic snake.*

Everyone responds, practically cackling in unison.

Fae: "Perfect."

Max: "Good."

Dane: "Great."

Angela: "Like a baby."

I keep my head down, pretending to read the agenda in front of me. "And how about you, Ms. West?" he asks in a cool tone, and I lift my face to meet his stare. It's penetrating, cold, and detached, a complete shift from his heated gaze at the Vanilla Club.

"Like a rock," I quickly reply, trying to sound casual. It's a lie, of course. I look like crap, and he knows it.

He steeples his hands in front of him and refocuses his attention on the group. "Good. We won't tolerate people nodding off in class. This internship is a once-in-a-lifetime experience," he warns, and nods of agreement ripple through the room. "Time-wasters can leave," he adds, his gaze flickering over to me. I swallow the wet sand in my throat, feeling exposed.

What the hell?

I might be exhausted, but I refuse to show it. There's no way I'll give him the satisfaction. If Vincent wants me out the door and out of this hard-won internship, he's going to have to try a lot harder than this. I grip the underside of my seat with white-knuckled force, barely containing my anger. Well, if I was tired before, I'm fucking livid now.

I'm wide awake and more determined than ever to ace whatever he throws my way.

Bring it on.

It's late afternoon, and I'm caught between feeling amped up on too much caffeine and exhausted. At one point, my hand starts shaking, and I have to stop it. I guess my body can't handle double shots, but I know that now. Between the shaky hand and heart palpitations, it's like I'm riding a wave. *Is this what drugs would feel like? Why would anyone do that?*

My brother was the one in our family who partied hard and hung out with dangerous people in the opposite side of town in Silverton. I stayed away from all that stuff, not wanting to fry my brain.

My best asset was my brain, not my D cups. Sure, maybe I was lying to myself when I said that, but it was the truth. I got accepted into Trinity University based on a near-perfect SAT score, not my looks.

"Ms. West. Are we boring you?" Mr. Slater's voice snaps me back to reality, and I realize I've been staring out the window on the thirty-ninth floor. *Dammit.* How did I let that happen? I've been so careful today not to appear tired. "Of course not," I retort, holding his gaze. I wonder if anyone else notices the tension between us.

Blowing out a steady breath, I flick my gaze down to the work in front of me. Today, we're assessing a company's financial position, and I enjoy working with numbers, so the analytics are interesting. In truth, I've already finished the assignment, which is why I started daydreaming in the first place. Still, I can't afford to be cavalier, especially since he's looking for any excuse to throw me out.

Gah.

I notice Fae lingering behind as we all file out for the day. She sidles up to Vincent, saying something flirty with a smile. I glance sideways and feel a weird sensation inside me bordering on jealousy and hatred, but I can't be sure. *Why would I be jealous?* It's pretty obvious Mr. Slater likes the company of girls fawning over him, and Fae is gorgeous, smart, and obviously his type.

Vincent politely entertains her and smiles, and Fae is in heaven. It's written all over her face. The way she bats her pretty lashes at him makes me sick.

As I pile my books into my satchel, I turn to Angela and whisper, "Is it me, or does he pick on me?" I nod toward Vincent, making sure he can't hear. "I definitely saw Max on his phone today, and he said nothing!"

Angela laughs. "I think he picks on everyone, but maybe you more." I scowl and flare my nostrils. "Forget about it," she says, tapping me on the shoulder. "Remember, he didn't get to where he is by being nice."

I blow out a breath. "Nice? I don't think he's ever heard of the word."

Angela laughs, and my tense shoulders relax as my arms fall to my side. Dane steps between us. "What are we bitching about, girls?" he asks, already packed up for the day.

Angela and I exchange a knowing glance, not wanting to discuss Mr. Slater in front of Dane, especially with Vincent still in the room. "Nothing," she offers, placing her hand on his forearm. His eyes shift to hers, and I know the subject is closed.

"We're getting a drink at Sojos. Wanna come?" Angela offers.

"Not tonight," I reply, completely down from my amped-up caffeine hit earlier.

"I'll let you off tonight, but next time you're coming." She widens her eyes and lowers her chin, giving me a pointed look.

"Okay, deal." I smile. "Come on, let's get out of here," I say, not wanting to stay a minute longer than I have to. I need sleep more than I need food right now, and every minute counts.

As I exit, he calls out my name, causing me to glance back. "Ms. West, I'd like to speak with you for a moment," he says, and I stop, frustrated.

"Shit," I mutter under my breath, knowing that Angela can hear me.

"Go. I'll see you tomorrow," she offers before leaving with Dane. "Be nice. He obviously likes nice girls," she adds, eyeing Fae.

I turn around to face him, putting on a fake smile, while Fae remains in front of him as he leans against the desk. His charcoal suit, crisp white shirt, and navy blue tie accentuate his biceps, causing me to inhale sharply.

"I'll see you tomorrow, Fae," he says with a lopsided smile, but his tone is final, and she doesn't look pleased. She presses her lips together, watching me walk over to him.

Her Hollywood face turns to his, and she smiles widely. "Look forward to it, Mr. Slater," she says in a flirtatious tone that makes me roll my eyes.

His eyes dart to mine, and they narrow. *Shit, did he just catch me rolling my eyes?* I curse myself for not being more careful.

I can't even look at him as she walks away. I'm leaning against the desk with my satchel slung over my shoulder, and he's on the other side, holding onto the desk for support. He's so close that I can smell his fancy cologne, but I try to play it cool and not let it affect me too much.

"You wanted to see me, Mr. Slater," I say, trying to shake

off the weird feeling I get around a man who should be too old to be anything else but my intern teacher.

He looks down at me, and I instinctively want to step back from his intense gaze, but I force myself to stand tall and meet his eyes.

"I won't tolerate tiredness and daydreaming at my internship, Ms. West," he says sternly.

Shit.

I remain silent, knowing that staying quiet is best when you don't have an ace up your sleeve.

"Did you hear me?" His voice booms, filling the empty office, and I roll my lips inward. I can't lose this job.

"Yes, sir," I speak like a marine, steadfast and determined.

His eyes flicker when he hears the word 'sir,' and there is a heat behind them I can't ignore.

Does he like it when I call him that?

His gaze roams over my lips.

Wait, what?

Honestly, I don't know where that came from. We aren't in the Vanilla Club. That's what we use there. It's the only address we can use unless the men ask us to call them by another name. He knows this. I know he knows this by the way his eyes hold mine.

Fuck.

I adjust my posture, feeling a blush creeping up my cheeks and reaching the tips of my ears.

"Mr. Slater, I mean," I correct myself, and he blinks. A veneer of professionalism takes over him, replacing the heat I secretly crave in his eyes.

"Good," he says with a sharp edge. I watch his hands grip the table, fingers curling around the edge with force, and it seems like he is just as angry as I am.

"You can leave now."

Our eyes lock, and at that moment, I feel something there like I felt at the Vanilla Club. But then, why is he so cold today?

Ugh, why do I have to stare like a complete idiot?

I break the gaze and quickly gather my things, moving to leave. As I stand, I realize the gap between us is small now, and my heart races. He's so tall, even sitting down, and the scent of his expensive cologne fills my senses. I step to the side, trying to create more space between us and rush out the door, feeling the heat of his gaze on my back.

Once I'm clear of him, I take a deep breath, unaware I had been holding it in the whole time.

IO

VINCENT

My corner office, situated next to Julius' office, offers a stunning view of the Manhattan skyline. It's late, and everyone has left for the day, but I'm still thinking about Rosie with her bow-shaped red lips and fiery attitude. I'm stewing over her, especially when I know I went too hard on her earlier and can't figure out why.

While I had been drinking her in throughout the day, I couldn't help but feel frustrated with myself. All I could think about was the image of her pinned against the wall, and my hand between her legs. In my mind, she had been wearing the pretty lace bustier she had on at the Vanilla Club that accentuated her full breasts and a tiny belt that emphasized her waist. The thought of running my hand between the clasps, unhooking them, and ripping off her lingerie had crossed my mind several times.

Jesus Christ. My dick is getting hard just sitting at my desk thinking about her.

I shake away her memory and the dichotomy of Rosie's

that exists—the intern and the lingerie waitress—both so different but fiery as fuck.

My phone illuminates the mahogany desk, distracting me from work and the stirring in my pants. The name of my ex-CIA man flashes on the screen.

Justin has been working for me exclusively for the past year and has recently managed to place a mole in the same jail cell as Montero, the man convicted of Edgar's murder. But Montero is just a small fish. I want the shark, and I'm willing to use blood as bait if that's what it takes. Eagerly, I click to answer the call.

"Justin," I say into the receiver.

"Boss, I have something..." he pauses, and my heart begins to race.

"Well, go on," I snap.

"Not over the phone. Meet me at the Vanilla Club Thursday at ten?"

My mind wanders to her, the swell of her breasts, her golden skin, and the orchid scent of her body wash.

"Boss?" The voice on the phone brings me back.

"I can't wait that long," I say.

"I'm outta town. That's the earliest I can come back."

"Fine," I say and hang up, tossing my phone across my desk.

It's unlikely Rosie would work during the week, although I try to convince myself that it doesn't matter, even if she did. But who am I kidding? It's a fine line I'm skirting, and as my dick strains against my pants' zipper, I am not so sure I can stop myself from crossing it.

The truth is, I need to hear what intel Justin has, and I will meet him at any time necessary. There is nothing more pressing than to find the real killer.

The brother my family never speaks of.

Because it's too painful.

Edgar.

He's the oldest, followed by me, Julius, and my sister, Victoria. I know for damn sure Montero, who is in jail for his murder, isn't the person responsible.

The air is cold, and I'm sad because summer is fading into fall. Edgar has me on his shoulders as he darts in and out of the manicured gardens at our Connecticut home. He's eighteen, and I'm seven. I love him so much because he plays with me when Daddy is too busy.

Daddy is working in the office inside, and Mommy is with my sister, Victoria, and my brother. The four of us just went for a swim, and I'm hassling Edgar to stay out with me when I should be getting ready for dinner. But I love summer, and I adore my older brother.

"Again!" I say, gripping onto my brother. My legs squeeze around his neck, and my hands ruffle his soft brown hair.

"Vin!" he scolds. "Not again!" I hear his moaning, but I can tell he's smiling. Secretly, he loves doing this. I'm his favorite, and he isn't shy about it.

"Oh, please," I whine, putting it on especially so I know he feels bad.

He grips my legs. "Okay, just one more time around," he says with a sigh as he bounces on his feet.

"Can we go all the way 'round this time?"

"You want to do the entire lap of the property?" He tilts his head, and I peer over, nearly toppling him forward.

"Ah!" he shrieks, holding my legs tight before he regains his balance.

"Oh, please, Eddie! Please, please, please!" I ruffle his hair and bob up and down on his shoulders.

"*Oh, all right!*" *he replies and, without warning, launches forward. I let out a wail as he glides with ease, taking my skinny weight on his shoulders. I bob up and down uncontrollably as he runs like lightning.*

Edgar speeds past the pool and patio and rounds the corner. Then he runs toward the steel arched front gates. "Booster time!" he yells, and I squeal uncontrollably.

I tug the tips of his ears, the sign for a boost of speed, like I've done so many times before, and he immediately picks up the pace. That's his secret go-to button for extra speed.

I laugh uncontrollably as I bounce around like a plastic bag in the breeze, bobbing up and down, holding onto the crown of his head for dear life.

We reach the steel front gate, and he turns and arrows back to the sandstone house. In the distance, I hear a car and what sounds like arguing. I don't think Edgar does, as he's making motor sounds with his voice.

He grips my shins harder, and I forget about it and enjoy the ride back to the house. He launches toward the final corner, where I can see Daddy working from the window.

Daddy is focused and doesn't take his eyes off his screen. I notice a phone in his hand, and he is yelling at the person on the other end. I don't think I've ever seen him so mad. It's scary. I think my brother sees it too because he slows down when we reach his office and taps my shins, a silent warning to be quiet.

A crack sounds like it's in the distance, and the next thing I know, I'm flung off Edgar's shoulders and hit the hard travertine tiles. Searing pain shoots through me, and when I open my eyes, Edgar is on the ground too. But why are his eyes closed? I shuffle over to wake him, thinking this is another one of his games. Then I notice a red streak on his shirt. Blood seeps from underneath his body and starts to pool around my knees.

I scream.

. . .

I decide to take a detour and stop on the thirty-ninth floor before making my way down to the busy streets of Manhattan. As I step out of the elevator, an eerie silence greets me, signaling that everyone has gone home for the day. However, as I approach my teaching office, I can't help but feel a strange sense of unease. I enter, and my gaze fixes on Rosie's empty desk.

What the fuck, Slater?

Shaking my head, I pivot and head toward the elevator when a noise catches my attention. My instincts kick in as I approach the source of the sound—the restroom.

Despite the late hour, I quicken my pace, knowing something isn't right.

As I reach the restroom door, it swings open, and a familiar figure emerges. "Rosie?" I call out, recognizing her despite the dim lighting.

"Vincent?" Her response sends chills down my spine. Something is wrong.

Without warning, Rosie suddenly collapses, her body swaying uncontrollably as she falls toward the floor. I react instinctively, lunging forward and catching her just before her head hits the ground.

"Rosie!" I cry out, hoping for some kind of response, but she remains unconscious in my arms.

A cold sweat breaks out on my brow as I hold her face. Despite my efforts to stay calm, a knot of anxiety tightens in my chest. Checking her vitals, I continue calling out her name until finally, she regains consciousness.

Relief floods through me as her eyes flutter open, revealing huge hazel irises. "What happened?" She gasps, her soft breath brushing against my cheek. "I'm sorry," she says, closing her eyes and leaning into my touch as my hand absentmindedly strokes her cheek.

"You fainted," I say, and Rosie abruptly straightens up as my hands release her. "Jesus, Rosie, what are you doing?" I ask, watching her sway slightly on her feet.

"I'm okay," she insists, attempting to squirm away from me.

I hold her close, and she inhales sharply. "You are far from okay."

"I'm just a bit dizzy, that's all. Must be my blood pressure acting up," she says.

Her face comes close to mine, and I'm tempted to claim her, but I push aside my desires, knowing she's vulnerable and needs care. "Come on, let's get you home," I tell her. "Where to?" I ask.

"Saddle Hill, Jersey," she says, dusting back the tendrils of hair that fall across her cheeks. I'm drawn to her before the reality of what she said hits me.

"Jersey? What the hell?" I snap out of my lustful thoughts as I realize the length of her commute, not only to the Vanilla Club but to the office too.

She straightens, her eyes suddenly wide as if taken aback by my reaction. But seriously, am I the only one concerned about her well-being? *Is there no one else?*

"Do you really take the subway to the city for the intern program?" I ask in disbelief, and then it dawns on me that she works at the Vanilla Club at night. "And you commute back from there after midnight?"

Her expression transitions from confusion to irritation as she scowls at me. "My private jet is currently on loan," she snaps back sarcastically.

A sudden rush of heat courses through my body as I gaze into her intense hazel eyes. The urge to silence her smart mouth and take her in my arms becomes almost overwhelming.

"I know exactly how to silence that mouth," I say with a hint of desire in my voice, watching as she takes in a sharp breath. Her full lips part slightly, and I can't help but wonder how they would feel against mine.

"We need to get you home," I say, pushing those thoughts aside and reminding myself that she is vulnerable and in need of care. I take a step back, giving her space to regain her composure, but I feel a mix of emotions stirring within me.

After I'd gotten home, I realized I'd left my workbooks at Slater Corp. I was in a rush to get out of there after Mr. Slater warned me, and I'd forgotten them on my desk. With school tomorrow, I had no choice but to take the subway back to the city and retrieve them. But as I walked down the subway steps and entered Slater Corp, I suddenly felt dizzy and unsteady on my feet.

The next thing I knew, I was collecting my books and walking out of the bathroom when I saw Mr. Slater, concerned, staring back at me. Then, I opened my eyes to his voice. I had never heard him sound that way like he was in distress when he called my name. I opened my eyes and felt his warm hands on my cheeks. I leaned into his soothing touch, feeling safe and protected.

But now, his grip on the steering wheel of his luxurious car is so tight that it seems like he regrets offering me a ride home. I'm dying to understand why he's behaving flirta-tiously one moment, then suddenly annoyed with me the next, but I'm too afraid to confront him.

"Thank you for driving me home," I say, attempting to ease the tension.

"When was the last time you ate, Rosie?" he asks, his jaw clenched.

"Um…" I think for a moment. I skipped breakfast and grabbed a quick apple during lunch while I studied. Surely, that's not all I've eaten. I wrack my brain for more.

"So I thought," he says, taking the next exit and slowing down as he spots the neon lights of a diner.

Is he taking me to dinner?

A wave of uncertainty washes over me as he opens the door and leads me to a booth, muttering, "This will have to do."

I'm unsure of what to make of this situation.

The diner is dimly lit, with a handful of customers inside, their quiet chatter filling the air. The scent of greasy food and stale coffee hangs heavy in the atmosphere, and he guides me to a booth in the back, away from inquisitive gazes, and grabs a menu as we go.

As we get comfortable in the booth, a waitress approaches, plucking the pencil from above her ear. "What can I get you, folks?" she asks warmly.

Mr. Slater glances over the menu and orders two chicken salads. The waitress takes the menu and heads off, leaving us in silence.

"What if I don't want a chicken salad?" I ask with a chuckle, trying to lighten the mood after the tense car ride. I tuck a strand of hair behind my ear and look at him.

He smirks and shakes his head. "Sorry, Rosie, but you'll eat what I order," he says teasingly. "Can't have you studying all day and forgetting to eat. It's not healthy."

I roll my eyes playfully at his concern. While I appreciate the sentiment, I'm not sure how to feel about his bossy attitude toward my food choices.

I shift uncomfortably in my seat, feeling frustrated and embarrassed. Deep down, I know he's right about taking better care of myself, but I can't stand being told what to do. The fact that it's him giving me orders only makes it worse.

A part of me wonders why he even cares. It's not like he has any real concern for me, right? I try to push the thought away, not wanting to dwell on it any longer.

Mr. Slater leans back in the booth, his finger loosening his tie as he stretches his arms across the back of the seat. The movement causes his white shirt to hug his muscles tightly, and I feel a sudden heat rise in my body. It's like we're creating our own microclimate in the air-conditioned diner.

"You need someone to look after you," he says, breaking the silence between us. His words make me uncomfortable, and I shift in my seat.

"I can take care of myself," I retort, trying to sound confident despite the lump in my throat.

"Clearly," he replies, his face twisting into a scowl.

The tension between us is palpable, and the awkwardness is weighing heavily on me.

After a moment of hesitation, I give in. "Fine, I forgot to eat today. With school and work, it's been a little chaotic lately," I confess, feeling a pang of guilt for neglecting my health. I leave out the part where I feel crazy pressure from Gabriel to take as many shifts as possible to pay back his debt.

"Then stop working," he states firmly, his intense green eyes locking onto mine.

I let out a laugh at his suggestion. "That's not possible,

Mr. Slater," I reply, feeling a strange flutter in my stomach at the sound of his name on my lips. I recall the hours I spent googling him over the weekend, reminding myself of the ten-year age difference between us.

"We've established that you can call me Vincent outside the office," he reminds me, his voice taking on a darker note.

I run my tongue over my bottom lip and watch Mr. Slater-Vincent glance down at my mouth, inhaling sharply. Damn, he's handsome.

The sudden awareness of his attractiveness catches me off guard, and I quickly look away, feeling a flush scale my neck.

"I don't like you working there. It's not safe," Vincent continues, his concern evident in his voice.

I roll my shoulders in a nonchalant shrug. "It's okay," I reply, not wanting to cause any more discomfort. However, I'm taken aback when I see a look of genuine concern on his face.

My stomach rumbles in appreciation when the waitress arrives with our chicken salads.

"Thank you," I say, feeling grateful for the distraction. I take a bite of the juicy chicken and savor the flavors, enjoying the break from the intense conversation.

"I'd like you to visit my physician," he says, his eyes fixed on me but not touching his food.

I quickly swallow the chicken in my mouth, feeling slightly uncomfortable with the suggestion. "That's not necessary," I say, shaking my head.

"It's not a request, Rosie," he says firmly, and I feel a bit taken aback by his sudden shift in tone. I take a few more bites of my chicken salad, mulling over his request. It's been a while since I've been to the doctor, and I have been feeling more fatigued and dizzy lately.

After a moment, I nod. "Fine, but on one condition."

His lips twist into a satisfactory smile, and he leans back in his seat. "Already negotiating, Ms. West?" he teases.

I straighten my posture and dab my mouth with a napkin before responding. "I believe I am," I reply, feeling a bit more confident now that we're back to a more professional tone. "But first, I have a question for you."

He leans in closer, giving me his full attention, and I can't help but feel a surge of electricity pass between us. I remind myself not to get swayed by his appearance, with his strong jaw, full lips, and skin the gods would envy. Taking a deep breath, I steel myself and ask the question that's been bothering me all day, "Why were you so cold to me earlier?"

He holds my gaze, and it's as though we are trying to read each other's thoughts.

"Perhaps I was a bit rough on you. I guess I thought you'd quit by now."

"I'm certainly not quitting," I exclaim. "And yes, you are harder on me than the other interns."

"You tipped a drink on me and accused me of assault, Rosie."

I tilt my head and swallow the lump in my throat.

"You said some not-so-nice things to me that day we met as well," I offer up, and he tilts his head curiously. "You're not my type... and something tells me you're not easily satisfied," I say, rattling off the exact words spoken to me that have stuck with me.

He looks surprised by my admission.

"I was with a bunch of guys who like that kind of nonsense. It was just banter."

"So you didn't mean it? Is that what you're saying?"

Vincent takes a sip of water and sets his glass down, his intense gaze locking onto mine. "I'm sure whoever gets to satisfy you is one lucky man," he says, his voice low and seductive.

Oh God. *You*. I want *you* to satisfy me.

I take a sip of my water and clear my throat. "So when you said I'm not your type…" I let the question hang in the air, and my heart hammers in my chest, waiting for his response.

He leans forward, his eyes locked on mine as he speaks. "You are every man's wet dream, Rosie West," he says, his voice low and husky.

His words send a chill down my spine, and I can feel my cheeks flush with heat. I take a moment to compose myself before deciding to take a risk and push back.

"So what kind of man are you, Vincent?" I ask, arching an eyebrow and trying to hide my nerves.

"I'm a man of my word, Rosie. And I always get what I want." There's a hint of a challenge in his tone, and I can't help but feel a thrill of excitement mixed with apprehension.

"And what is it you want?" My voice comes out soft and flaky.

He pauses, letting the question linger in the air before continuing. "I don't date, Rosie."

Before I can say anything else, the waitress comes by to refill our water glasses, breaking the tension between us. I take a deep breath and try to collect myself, hoping to make it through the rest of the meal without making a fool of myself.

We finish the meal quickly, and Vincent pays the bill, leaving a generous tip for the waitress. Then we walk back to his car, and he enters the address on the satellite naviga-tion. As we drive, I can't shake off the need to know more about why Vincent doesn't date.

The silence is suffocating, and my curiosity is getting the better of me.

He breaks the silence first. "So, it's settled. My secretary will call and arrange a visit from my physician," he says firmly.

"I guess so," I say absentmindedly as I notice the familiar houses in my suburb come into view.

"You seem lost in thought," he observes.

"I was just thinking," I reply, avoiding his intense gaze.

"About what?" he presses, and when my eyes flicker to him, his stare is direct and unnerving.

"Nothing important," I say with a shrug, trying to seem nonchalant. But my heart is pounding in my chest, and my mind is filled with thoughts of him.

Disappointment flickers across his powerful features as he brings his gaze back to my street. He looks down at his map and slows down the car, and I see the light on in the house, realizing that Sara and Ethan must be home.

I quickly clear my throat to speak up. "This is fine." I tell him to stop the car a few yards away from my house, and he reluctantly complies, his disappointment evident in his eyes. He quickly kills the engine, and I gather my things.

He exits the car and strides over to my side, opening the door and offering me his hand. I take it, savoring the way his skin feels against mine. Despite feeling stable on my feet, I'm not quite ready to part ways with him. I lean against the car and watch him close the door.

He stands in silence with a pensive expression etched across his face.

"Thank you," I whisper softly.

"You're welcome," he responds, and there's a moment of silence between us that's thick with tension. I feel a fluttering sensation in my stomach.

"Is there something else you want to ask me, Rosie?" His voice is dark and low, stirring something between my thighs.

"Why don't you date?" I ask, my voice low and husky. *"Because you're every woman's wet dream,"* I add, echoing his words earlier. My chest rises with my rampant breath, and his eyes flare with heat.

He steps closer so his body is pressed against mine, his heat seeping into me, and I can feel his breath on my neck. I can't move, can't breathe, and can barely think. His eyes lock onto mine, and I see something raw and primal there that sends tendrils of heat down my spine. I know I should be scared, but all I feel is an intense desire to be taken by him.

"I take what I want from women."

What does that mean?

As his hand firmly grasps my chin, his breath hot and heavy against my lips, a jolt of electricity surges through me. His eyes lock onto mine, and I'm completely drawn in, powerless to resist. He leans in slowly, his lips tantalizingly grazing mine before he plunges into the kiss with a fierceness that takes my breath away.

I gasp as his tongue invades my mouth, and my body responds to him in ways I never thought possible.

His hand tightens around my hair, pulling me closer to him as his tongue continues to explore my mouth. My fingers grip his shirt tightly, pulling him closer as his body presses against mine. His hard length is evident through his pants, and the desire coursing through me is almost too much to bear.

This is so wrong, but I can't bring myself to care. All I want at this moment is for Vincent to take me, to possess me completely.

But as suddenly as it started, he pulls away, leaving me breathless and wanting more. He leans his forehead against mine, his breath hot on my skin.

"Go inside, Rosie," he commands, his voice thick with desire.

I nod, feeling a hot flush spread across my body. Then, not trusting myself to speak, I peel off the car door and stumble toward my house.

As I make my way to the front door, I can feel his eyes on me, burning into my skin. *What was I thinking?* This is Vincent Slater, my boss, and he just kissed me like he owns me.

My mind is racing with questions, but one thing is clear.

Vincent Slater has awakened a hunger in me I never knew existed.

Stepping into my house, I close the door and can't shake off the feeling that everything has changed.

12

VINCENT

I t's Thursday, and all I can think about is Rosie and that kiss. Honestly, I hardly fucking recognize myself. I haven't seen her since Monday night when I drove her home, and I slammed my lips on hers. Soft velvet lips left their searing mark on mine, and it took everything for me to pull away and not bend her over the hood and fuck her senseless.

I'm driving absentmindedly to the Vanilla Club in my Porsche when my phone rings, pulling me out of my Rosie-filled haze. It's my sister, and I answer it immediately with a smile. "Victoria."

Her excitement is contagious as she asks, "How's my brother?"

I chuckle. "More like, how's my celebrity sister?" I can't help but feel proud of all the hard work she's put into her singing career.

Despite our five-year age difference, Victoria and I are incredibly close. As I talk to her, I feel guilty for not returning her calls since I landed in Manhattan.

"Oh, please!" She laughs, her warm and homey tone

bringing back memories. "Obviously not famous enough for my oldest brother to call me back!" she scolds, and I wince.

"Sorry," I say, not wanting to let her down.

"That's okay. Listen, I'm back in Manhattan next week. The record label has me performing in Times Square for a promo launch of the new album. I'd really love it if you and Julius could be there."

"Of course, we'll be there," I say without hesitation. "Are you seriously performing in Times Square?"

A shrill rings down the phone, and the sound of her excitement make me smile. "Can you believe it? It's finally happening Vin!"

"I'm proud of you, sis," I say as I pull into the valet parking of the Vanilla Club.

"Thanks, Vin. Enough about me, What have you been up to? We should try to organize a family dinner. Mom mentioned she's upset that you haven't been to the house yet."

I feel terrible about not visiting her in person since arriving in town, but I've been avoiding my father.

"I'll pass on dinner," I say. "But I will call Mom."

"Forget it. You're coming. You can tolerate Dad for a few hours. If I can, you can."

"How do you do it?" I ask, letting out an exaggerated sigh. "You always manage to persuade me when I wouldn't budge an inch for anyone else."

She chuckles before adding, "I'll text you the details."

The club is dimly lit, with thick cigar smoke filling the air. A stunning lingerie-clad waitress leads me to my table, but my eyes can't resist roaming the floor in search of Rosie.

I shake my head, wondering why this woman has such a strong hold on my thoughts, and then I spot Justin at the corner table, puffing on a cigar. He stands up as soon as he notices me.

"Mr. Slater," he says, stubbing out his cigar in the marble ashtray and shaking my hand. Honestly, I don't know why he is so formal, especially with all the under-handed shit he has done for me. Must be all that CIA training still in him.

I grip Justin's hand firmly. "Justin," I say before we take a seat at the table.

The waitress approaches us and asks, "What can I get you, gentlemen?" I look her up and down, hoping she'll stir something in me like Rosie does. But there's nothing, no spark of desire.

"What would you like, sir?" she asks me.

"Whisky neat." I sniff. "Blue Label."

"Of course, sir," she replies with a seductive smile, but I don't react. Even the way she addresses me as 'sir' doesn't do anything for me like Rosie does in her lingerie. It's like she could be any ordinary store attendant.

Ugh. What the fuck?

I need to get laid.

The waitress turns to Justin and asks, "And for you, sir?"

"The same," he replies.

Justin is built like a tank, with tattoos covering his arms, but his friendly face belies his deadly skills. Justin, also known as the 'Smiling Assassin,' is an ex-CIA agent trained in combat, MMA, and intelligence tracking. He's led his team to capture and kill some of the world's top terrorists. Now, he works for me along with his three-man team.

I got rid of my old team, the ones my father recommended, who had made slow progress over the years, always hitting dead ends or insurmountable roadblocks. Now, with Justin on my side, we're making steady progress.

The waitress departs, leaving us to our conversation. I loosen my tie and undo the top button of my shirt, getting comfortable. "So, what couldn't you tell me on the phone?" I ask, leaning forward in my seat.

He leans in, pulling his chair closer to the round table. "I have some news on the man working on the inside," he says. I stare at him, hope rising in my chest. "He's gaining Montero's trust every day. He's even sharing the same cell with him."

Montero, the thug charged with my brother's murder, was sentenced to thirty years without parole at Great Meadows State Prison. When the guilty verdict was announced, my family breathed a sigh of relief. It was the end of a chapter in their eyes. I remember that day vividly, even though I was only seven at the time. Dad looked down, finally at ease with the decision, while Mom, Julius, and Victoria cried tears of relief. I was numb, in disbelief. I couldn't understand why they were so relieved. Montero's sentence didn't bring my brother back.

I didn't know it then, but that day planted something inside me. Something I knew I would have to see through to the end. They called it a hit gone wrong. I overheard my parents talking about it during the trial. They shielded me from most of it and even convinced the prosecutors not to put me on the stand because I was a minor. But on that last day in the courtroom, I was there to hear the sentencing. And even then, I knew something wasn't right.

A hit gone wrong.

It took a level of skill to shoot from over two hundred

yards away on the quiet country streets of Connecticut. It didn't make sense. Things weren't right, and Montero's sentencing was only the beginning of my quest to find the truth behind my brother's murder.

Not that my parents were eager to discuss it. Time passed, I finished my schooling, started my own business with my brother, and indulged in various sexual escapades, realizing I was dominant in the bedroom, much like my approach to the boardroom.

But something was missing. In my early twenties, my brother's death began to call out to me. I begged my parents to share any court documents and memories they had of the case. My mother couldn't bear to speak of it, and my father avoided me as usual. When I finally cornered him, he would snap at me for dredging up the past and give me the basics. I understood why he was upset, but I just couldn't let it go.

And that brings us to the present.

The waitress arrives with our drinks and sets them on the table before quickly retreating.

"How is he sharing the same cell with him?" I ask, eager for any new information.

"He's Montero's cellmate. His previous cellmate had an unfortunate accident and was transferred to a lower security prison while he recovers," Justin explains with a wry smile. I can't help but laugh at the irony.

"My guy says Montero likes him."

"What have you got for me?" I ask anxiously.

"We've finally got the confirmation we've been looking for," Justin says, a serious look on his face.

My heart races with anticipation. "Is it about the Family?" I ask, my jaw tense.

"Yes. Montero just admitted that he was working for

the Gambino Family at the time of your brother's murder," Justin reveals.

I slam my hand down on the table in relief, causing our drinks to rattle.

"Tell me everything," I demand.

For the next hour, Justin tells me about all the conversations that have taken place between his mole, 'Gino,' and Montero. Although nothing else stands out as much as that admission, it's all about trust. Gino is gaining Montero's trust more and more every day. Now I know exactly which family this gun-for-hire was working for at the time of Edgar's murder.

The next step is to find out who ordered the hit and why. I know for a fact he wasn't alone because he had an accomplice. I heard it in the voices when Edgar ran along the fence line of our property. I heard it, and I know for certain it wasn't just my imagination.

I don't know what time it is, but Justin left a while ago, and I'm on the top floor of the Vanilla Club, trying to get my head back into the game and my dick aroused by the gorgeous women up here. But mainly, I am trying to forget about Rosie West and her pillowy lips. I drain the contents of my drink and hand a hefty tip to the women dancing seductively in front of me.

It's no use.

In a sea of half-naked women, all I see is Rosie.

13

ROSIE

My phone rings when I'm already snuggled up in bed, rocking my cozy floral PJs, and ready to crash after a couple of crazy days at school. Seeing the Vanilla Club's number, I figure they might be hooking me up with extra shifts for the end of the week. But instead, my boss is practically begging me to come down to the club since one of his top girls, Carlotta, got hit by a car.

At first, I straight-up say no. I mean, virgins don't work the top floor. Obviously, my boss doesn't know that. Heck, only my roomies Ethan and Sara are in on the secret. I never broadcast it, and there definitely isn't a neon sign on my forehead shouting, *"V-Card up for grabs."* But when he mentions I'll just be waiting tables on the top floor and raking in double the cash, I quickly change my tune and say yes right away.

I know I'll be kicking myself in the morning when I have to force my eyes open just to stay awake at Slater Corp, but there is no way I can pass up that kind of cash. Gabe is seriously in need of the money.

As I stare at my reflection in the mirror, I can't help but think back to the incident when I threw a drink in Mr. Slater's face. His anger was palpable, his face fierce. I crack a smile at the memory.

Wearing a midnight blue lace bustier and black leather shorts, I adjust my long blonde wig and admire myself in the mirror. My thoughts drift back to the first night we met and the explosive kiss we shared on Monday night. Mr. Slater might be cold, distant, and grumpy, but Vincent is warm, kind, and insanely sexy.

I leave the staff quarters and find myself looking around the ground floor in search of him, my gaze lingering on the table where we first met.

No matter how hard I try, I can't forget that kiss on Monday night. The way he took control and claimed me with such intensity should make me want to flee, but it isn't his dominant touch, I fear. The memory of his hard and fast style and lingering taste had me craving more. It was so arousingly hot, but I knew deep down I couldn't give him what he needed from a woman. I'm too inexperienced and clueless about the things he desires. But as I stand here in my sexy lingerie, feeling the heat rise in my cheeks, I contemplate what it would be like to surrender to his demands.

I shake my head and climb the spiral staircase, pressing my hand against the curved metal rail for support while my black heels click against the floor. The booming music from downstairs reverberates through the room. Reaching the top step, I pause and survey the area. I've been here before on random errands, but I don't often spend time up here. Maybe if I did, I'd be better equipped to give him what he needs.

The top floor is cozier and more intimate than the level below, featuring ten massage suites along the sides, each marked by a red leather door. We're all aware that more than just massages are happening behind those red doors.

I shiver at the thought that my life could take that turn if I sacrificed my values for money. What if Gabe and I run out of time to find the money? *What if?*

"No," I mumble to myself, determined not to let that happen. I have to find a way to help him. With that in mind, I head to the bar for my instructions.

Leather sofas are arranged for maximum privacy, with a stripping pole in front of each lounge area. The lighting is dim, and the corners are intentionally shadowy. Women I recognize dance, strip, and flirt around tables, hardly maintaining modesty.

Dante enforces a rule that no one can be fully naked, but I don't see the point since our outfits already reveal so much, particularly up here.

I suppose that's what the private suites are for. As I pass by them on my way to the bar, my hand brushes across the luxurious red leather. I admit I'm curious. Sometimes I wish I had lost my virginity a long time ago like everyone else, but now it's become a big deal.

I catch sight of my friend, Simone, dancing provocatively with a man in a suit. She shoots me a surprised wink when she notices me. I smile back and proceed to the bar, leaning against the cool gold surface encasing it.

Everything up here is even more upscale than downstairs if that's possible. Gold finishes extend from the bar to the ceiling, where oversized chandeliers hang. The black leather armchairs and loveseats are accented with gold trims. The ambience is sophisticated and laid-back without being ostentatious.

"Rosie!" Freddie shouts when he sees me coming his way. Freddie is awesome, and I really enjoy hanging out with him. I wish he was downstairs more since I've had enough of Jesse's constant flirting. But, as it turns out, I'm not the only one with a few girls starting to get fed up.

"Hey, Freddie," I say, meeting him halfway for a quick cheek kiss.

"He's so desperate he called you, huh?"

"Wow, thanks!" I pretend to be mad, crossing my arms.

"Nah, you know what I mean. You're almost too sweet and innocent for this place," Freddie whispers.

"Ugh, whatever!" I grumble, but my heart's racing like crazy.

"It's hard not to get caught up in it, right?" He looks into my eyes, and I can't help but grin.

I have to admit, I'm a bit fascinated by all the skin on display. Gorgeous women everywhere, and men who just can't get enough of them. There's something about a woman calling the shots that's really attractive.

"Maybe." I shrug, a grin spreading on my face.

"You're a dirty bird." He chuckles, and I join in the laughter.

"So what's in store for me tonight? Did Tony tell you what I'm meant to be doing?"

Freddie grabs a rag from his waist and starts wiping up the spill on the counter. His tall frame, brown eyes, and chocolate hair frame his face.

Freddie's always had my back here. From dealing with catty coworkers to handsy patrons, he's been there for me, and I'm genuinely grateful.

I don't know too much about Freddie beyond our break-time chats. I know he's a gay man who kept it a secret from his posh Manhattan family and that he feels secure and appreciated working here. He can be his true self at the club. It's kind of sad, really, but we have something in common. I told him my only family is my brother and a dad I barely know out there in the world.

When he inquired about my mom, I shared that she had passed away. He thought that made me fiercely strong-willed, but I figured he was just being nice. Although deep down, I knew he was right. Fending for yourself during those vulnerable teen years can make a girl tough.

"You'll be roaming tonight. Savannah, Josie, and Simone are working the room, so just float between tables and handle any extra requests," Freddie tells me.

I tense up, a shiver running down my spine. "Requests?" I ask nervously.

"Not that kind of request!" he clarifies, and I let out a sigh of relief.

He chuckles. "Would it really be so terrible if a good-looking guy asked you for a BJ?"

"Freddie!" I snap back.

He looks past me to the dimly lit area where men are checking out the women. "I'd do it in a heartbeat. I'd be balls deep, gagging. Some of these guys are seriously fucking hot!"

I roll my eyes. "You slut," I tease, and he chuckles.

He studies me closely. "Are you sure you're okay being up here?" he asks, and I know what he's getting at.

He knows I haven't had many boyfriends before, and although I've never explicitly said I'm a virgin, I think he suspects.

I press my lips together and stand tall. "I'm perfectly fine," I reply.

"That's the spirit," he exclaims, tucking his rag into his

belt and gesturing toward the corner table. "Why not start there and work your way around? I'll see you in a bit."

"Great," I respond, smiling wide, and turn to the table he's pointing at.

As soon as I brace myself against the cool metal of the bar, my smile vanishes. I'm rooted to the spot by the sight of familiar green eyes gazing back at me.

14

VINCENT

My attention is yanked away from the lap dance by the sight of familiar brown eyes gazing back at me. My hands clench into fists at my sides, irritation bubbling beneath the surface.

What is she doing up here?

Dante had assured me she only worked on the ground floor when I checked in with him this week. I guess I was being a bit nosy, but it was only to ensure my intern wasn't involved in any sexual activities. At least, that's what I kept telling myself.

A half-naked woman is curling around me, but I can't focus on her. My mind is consumed by the sight of Rosie at the bar in the littlest black leather shorts. *Why is she here after fainting on Monday?*

The thought of her blatant disregard for her health and welfare drains the blood from my face, but it goes straight to my dick. Even from across the room, she makes me hard.

As she peels herself off the bar and pushes away her blonde wig, her surprise is replaced by a steely determination. My dick hums in my pants as she strides toward me, breasts shimmering and bouncing with each step. She comes to a halt at the edge of the leather sofa, her thigh tantalizingly close to mine. I can sense the warmth radiating from her body, and I'm tempted to reach out and touch her, but my anger holds me back.

What is it about this woman that captivates me so much?

"What can I get you, sir?" She purrs, and I swear if she calls me 'sir' one more time, I'll punish her with a firm smack on her enticing backside.

I run my tongue over my lips, enjoying the anonymity game she's playing while another woman grinds on my thigh.

Rosie's eyes lock on mine.

Her golden skin illuminates in the dim lighting, and her lips are painted with a popping cherry red. I prefer her natural hair color to the blonde wig, and as I imagine her leaving a red ring around my dick, a low groan escapes my lips, though she can't hear me over the loud music.

"Whisky neat," I order, admiring her natural curves amidst the sea of silicone. Her eyes linger on my open white shirt, and I know she's drawn to me too. I felt it in our kiss Monday night. She didn't pull away from my bruising force.

I did.

I contemplate bending my brother's rigid moral code and claiming Rosie for myself. After all, I'm only here for a brief period, and what he doesn't know can't harm him. She pivots and walks away, and I knowingly follow her every move.

Her hips sway in sync with the slow, sensual rhythm, and I find myself hypnotized by her movement. When she pauses at another table and flashes a seductive smile, I experience a surprising twinge in my chest that I swiftly dismiss.

As I watch the man's gaze linger on Rosie, a powerful wave of jealousy washes over me. I cringe as the man with a pointed nose and poorly fitted suit touches Rosie's arm. I can feel my blood boiling as I imagine him touching her again. I clench my fists, trying to contain my rage.

I catch Rosie's eye, and for a moment, we share a silent understanding. She politely removes herself after taking their order and heads to the bar. The man looks up at me, his gaze hard and challenging. But I'm not afraid. I stand my ground, my eyes locked on his. The anger pulses through me, and I can't understand it.

"Are you okay, honey?" Brie asks as she grinds down on my leg.

"Fine," I reply. I flare my nostrils at the intrusion but force myself to settle back into the leather and let her do what she does best. I try and focus on Brie, but unavoidably my focus drifts to little miss not-so-innocent Rosie. At twenty-two years old, she is in dangerous territory and doesn't even fucking realize it.

A strange possessive sensation rises within me.

Brie straddles me like a rodeo rider, bucking and encouraging me to let loose.

I take a deep breath, trying to relax and enjoy the sensation of Brie's body pressing against mine. But my eyes keep darting back to Rosie, who's sitting at the bar, her gaze locked on mine. Even with Brie's grinding, all I can think about is the electricity between Rosie and me.

I imagine it's her on top of me, and a surge of desire courses through me.

"That's it," Brie says, smiling as she can feel my length and girth between her legs.

Honey, that's because of Rosie.

The bartender interrupts our moment, saying something to Rosie. She turns abruptly, taking away any moment we just had. Then she grabs the drinks he gives her and heads back toward the jerks who touched her before.

Brie tosses her hair as she moves her head up and down on top of me. She thinks I'm enjoying this, but I'm not. I ignore her and fixate on Rosie as she moves through the crowd.

She places the drinks on the table where two men sit. One is loud and boisterous, while the other pays no attention to the woman grinding on him. The loud one gets up and approaches Rosie, and my blood spins like a centrifuge.

He's saying something, and I lean past Brie to get a better view. Rosie's smile turns into a forced one as the man's hand lingers on her waist. I grip Brie tightly on my lap, feeling a surge of protectiveness. Suddenly, the man pulls Rosie closer, and she jerks away from him, her expression shifting to one of alarm. My fists clench as I see the fear in her eyes, and I know I have to do something.

What the fuck?

Physical contact is allowed up here, but that is too rough. Anger rises within me, and I stand up abruptly, catching Brie before she falls off my lap. With determined strides, I approach their table, and the scent of Rosie's perfume infiltrates my senses. I push it away. I don't need the distraction now.

"I'm waiting for my drink," I snap with barely-there control.

Her eyes find mine, and she steps away from the man, bending to lift the tray on the table.

"Fucking impatient, Slater?"

What the... who the fuck is this clown?

"Do I know you?" I sneer, my tone sharp and cold.

"No, but I know you," he replies, his voice laced with hostility as he stands up and confronts me. His dark features and brown eyes are menacing. He turns, a smirk playing on his lips, then he reaches for Rosie again and swats her on the ass.

A surge of energy courses through me. I'm like a wild dog, the heat soaring as I grab his shirt and land a punch on the man's face. The force of my blow sends him reeling backward, crashing to the ground with a thud. I'm breathing heavily, my chest heaving with a mix of anger and adrenaline.

"No!" Rosie screams, and suddenly a group of people swarms around us. He gets up again, and I manage to land another punch before being dragged away. Blood is on his nose and mouth and on my shirt as we are pulled apart.

Rosie is shaking, and her eyes are wide with fear as she runs over to me.

"What are you doing here, Vincent?" she asks, her voice tinged with panic.

I move toward her, and her body shudders as I wrap her in a protective embrace.

"Trying to forget about you," I whisper into her ear, the irritation at my inability to forget her evident in my voice.

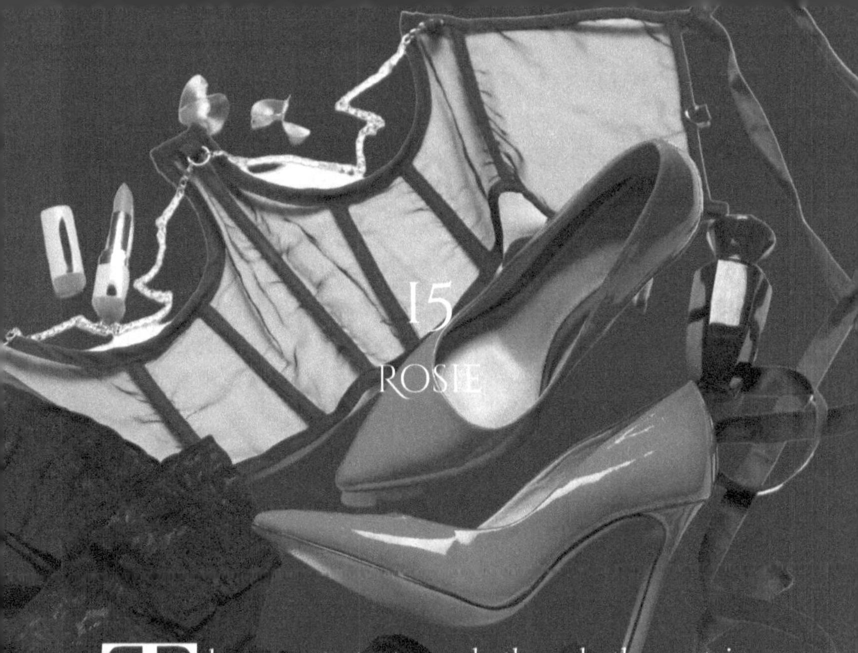

15

ROSIE

The sun starts to peek through the curtains, casting a soft mix of amber and tangerine light in the room.

Lying in bed, I'm still buzzing with adrenaline. I haven't slept at all. Instead, I've been going over the whole night in my head from when I saw Vincent at the Vanilla Club getting a lap dance to when he punched the guy who touched me without a second thought. And then his last words before he left without saying anything else, *"Trying to forget about you."*

The memory of Vincent's appearance sends a tingle of arousal through me. He was clean-cut and well-shaven, wearing a dark tailored suit. But that night, his crisp white shirt was open, revealing a glimpse of dark chest hair and a sun-kissed tan. His sleeves were rolled up, displaying his strong biceps as he casually rested his arm along the back of the sofa. His broad fingers were tantalizingly close to my legs, and it was a struggle to keep my composure.

The more I thought about Vincent and his possessive attitude, the more I craved him. I longed for his touch, his

141

body, his everything. It was like a magnetic force attracting me to him, despite my best efforts to resist.

His confession lingered with the possibility of something more, and even though I ached for his lips on mine, he hadn't touched me. When my shift ended, I checked my phone and saw a message from an unknown number lighting up the screen.

Unknown: *My driver Jason is out front and ready to take you home.*

When I walked out, a black car and a middle-aged man greeted me with a tip of his cap. I climbed in immediately, grateful for the ride, and saved his number in my phone, then typed out a reply.

Me: *Unnecessary, but thank you.*

I toss and turn in my bed, my mind consumed with thoughts of Vincent. *What the hell am I doing playing this dangerous role?* He sees me as something I'm clearly not, and if he finds out I am a virgin, he might run or, worse, laugh. But despite the confusion swirling in my head, I can't deny the pull he has over me.

I spring out of bed and slide into my slippers, determined to start the day. In a few hours, I'll come face to face with Mr. Slater, the CEO mogul. But I wouldn't forget Vincent, the sexy man who makes me ache between my thighs with equal parts frustration and desire.

It's Vincent in my dreams.

It's Mr. Slater when I wake.

Assessing myself in the mirror, I notice smudged black eyeliner mixed with purple bags under my eyes. There is also a smear of red lipstick that I couldn't completely remove with makeup remover. My brown hair is knotty and disheveled from tossing and turning all night.

I look like a raccoon.

Shit.

An hour later, I'm feeling more like myself. I've chugged my morning coffee and am about to leave to catch the subway into the city when Ethan opens the door and walks out. I do a double-take as confusion sweeps over me. He's leaving Sara's bedroom, not his own. He's shirtless and in boxer briefs, his morning wood clearly evident. I race to keep my eyes anywhere but down there.

"What the fuck, Ethan?" I protest at his morning glory and the fact that he's leaving Sara's room.

He brings a finger up to his lips to silence me. "Shh," he whispers as he closes the door behind him with a click.

A smile peels onto his face, his shaggy blond hair tousled. "Sprung," he says with a chuckle.

I set my coffee on the counter and fold my arms across my body. "How long has this been going on?" I huff out, feeling slightly betrayed by my two roommates and close friends. "And for heaven's sake, will you do something about that!" My eyes dart down to his impressive appendage, then quickly back up.

He lets out a low chuckle and adjusts himself. I'm curious, but I don't dare stare. I wonder how big Vincent is. I imagine him hiding a glorious washboard of muscles underneath his broad chest, muscular arms, and a huge dick.

He'd know exactly how to take my innocence.

I snap back to reality as I hear the splashing of coffee, and I look up to find Ethan pouring himself a cup.

Was I just seriously thinking about my first time with Vincent?

"Are you okay?" Ethan asks, staring at me. A warmth spreads across my cheeks to the tips of my ears. "I'm fine. Back to you," I reply, trying to brush off my fantasy.

"It's a recent thing," he says, shrugging like it's not a big deal. I realize Sara will think it's everything, and I don't want her to get hurt. I straighten in my seat. "Don't hurt her, Ethan," I threaten.

"Jesus Christ. Morning to you too," he mumbles, scratching the crown of his floppy blond hair.

"I'm serious," I counter. "She likes you. I know she does."

A slow smile crosses his face. "I like her too," he admits, and it takes me aback because Ethan doesn't like anyone. He uses women and enjoys it. That's what college boys do.

I bring the remnants of coffee to my lips and swallow it. "Good."

"Good," he repeats, and I feel a sense of unease wash over me.

I let out a low groan, uncertain of how this is going to end. What if something goes wrong? Something always goes wrong. Then one of us will have to move out.

"You look like shit," he remarks, his eyes assessing me as he quirks a brow.

"I haven't slept. I'm working overtime at the Vanilla Club," I explain.

"How can you work, do your internship, and school?" he asks incredulously.

"I don't know," I admit, feeling overwhelmed by the mounting pressure. "I'm not sure how long I can keep this up."

"Do you really need to work this much? Can't your brother sort something out himself?" he suggests.

In my inebriated state, I let it slip to Ethan and Sara about my brother's financial problems, and now they know why I work so damn hard. If it weren't for my dear brother, I could ease up and maybe even look for a job with better career prospects.

Lingerie waitressing is a means to an end.

Shit, that reminds me, I haven't replied to his messages about my latest tips. I'm falling behind on my communication with my brother.

"I do," I respond to Ethan's first question with a sigh.

"It's such a shitty thing to do, you know. Put you in this situation when he's the one who fucked up," Ethan comments, shaking his head.

"What am I supposed to do? I'm all he has, Ethan. I'm sure you'd do the same for Desiree," I explain.

He laughs. "Fuck that. My sister can fend for herself. It's the only way she'd learn not to fuck up again," he says, staring down at me with his elbows resting on the countertop and his face opposite mine.

"Cold," I respond.

"Real," he counters. "Don't fuck up your future on your wayward brother, Rosie."

I shrug it off, trying to make light of his comments and really not wanting to think about it with a heavy head and no sleep. The truth is, I will have to confront this situation sooner or later because I'm burning out fast.

He pushes off the counter, the muscles in his back rippling as he moves toward the sink, and again my mind transfers over to Mr. Slater.

"Let's be honest. My parents would bail our asses out anyway." He laughs.

"Oh, to having wealthy parents." I chuckle alongside him.

"It has its cons, too, you know." His face falls as he turns toward me.

"Only a rich person says that." I laugh, and he shoots me a scowl. "Please, like what?"

"Like, I have to go to this charity ball this weekend because they are out of town, and it's going to bore me to death. Like, literally suck-my-eyeballs-out boredom. There's a real chance I could turn to dust just sitting there."

I laugh, and something flickers across his eyes, like an idea yet to be birthed, and before he says it, I'm already shrinking back into my seat.

"Come with me," he says with wide eyes.

"No," I reply, standing and walking over to the sink.

"Please!" he pleads.

"Take Sara!" I say, washing up my coffee cup and setting it on the dish rack.

"She's having dinner at her parents. Come on, it will be fun," he begs.

I laugh. "You just said it's boring, and you'll turn to dust."

"I did," he says, following me as I gather my things and prepare to leave.

"But it's boring because old wealthy people are there."

He grabs my arm and spins me around to face him. "Might be good for you. All the biggest businesses will be there, CEOs, important people," he says, and dammit, I hate when he's right. Networking would be a good opportunity in such a competitive field of graduates. "Network with these guys and actually do something for yourself for once, Rosie."

I shake off his grip and walk out of the kitchen, letting out a groan.

"Have I ever told you how manipulative you are?" But something inside me tweaks when he tells me to be selfish. It can't hurt, not that I'll have anything to wear.

"You could even wear something from Sara's wardrobe," he calls to my back, almost reading my mind. He's talking quicker now, knowing he has me teetering on the edge of committing.

Over the years I've known Sara, she's attended many balls with her family of surgeons. Surely, she would have something, but still. I snatch my house keys and throw my crossbody bag over my shoulder, aware that Ethan hasn't moved from his spot in the kitchen.

"I'm probably working," I say, knowing I couldn't turn down a shift, not when my brother needs me.

"Think about it, please? You'll be doing me a solid. I won't die from boredom with you there, and I can introduce you to some heavy hitters in the business world."

I turn and see a wide smile on his face. No wonder he is so good at getting women to bend at his every word. He is smart, funny, and says exactly what I need to hear to get me over the line.

"I'll think about it," I say and meet his pleas with a smile, then close the door in a rush.

"You're coming, Rosie West," he yells from the kitchen, and the sound travels through the crack in the door, making me chuckle.

~

Because I had fallen asleep on an older woman's arm without even realizing it, I almost missed my stop on the subway. If she hadn't gotten up on the previous stop, I would have missed it and potentially lost my internship. The woman smiled and apologized for waking me before leaving her seat, showing her kindness. *What a sweetheart.*

As I enter the office building and make my way through security, I realize that my mind is a haze of thoughts. I don't even remember getting off the subway. But one thing that keeps looping in my mind is Mr. Slater—Vincent—was at the Vanilla Club trying to forget about *me*.

I smile at the receptionist, but she stares at me longer than necessary, causing me to run a hasty hand through my windswept hair. I'm acutely aware that I look like I haven't slept in days in a workplace filled with immaculately dressed people, but what's with her attitude?

My chestnut hair is pulled back in a high bun, but a loose strand has fallen from the wind and brushes against my cheek. Dressed in a fitted black skirt and blouse, my heels are high and the same ones from last night—shiny black pumps.

I didn't have the energy to search for another pair when I kicked them off.

A wave of nerves washes over me as I catch my reflection in the thirty-ninth-floor windows.

I spot Angela in the tea room, and she rushes over to me with an excited smile. "Good morning," she exclaims.

"You seem extra cheery," I reply, intrigued.

"Yes!" she whispers, leaning in close to my ear. "Dane and I slept together... and oh God, I really like him."

My eyes widen in shock. "What?" I question loudly,

causing everyone in the room to turn and look at us. Dane smiles sheepishly while Fae and Max stare at me like I've lost my marbles. *Whatever.*

Angela chuckles nervously and tugs on my arm, leading me to the kitchen area.

"Let's grab some coffee," she suggests, her eyes avoiding mine. As she busies herself with the coffee maker, she fills me in on her latest romance. Apparently, it started with a kiss at Sojos last week and has quickly escalated into something more serious.

Despite the twinge of envy I feel at Angela's newfound happiness, I'm happy for her. Her face is glowing with excitement, like a beacon of light in the dimly lit kitchen. But as I sip my coffee, I wonder if it's really that easy for some people to find romance and, potentially, love.

Why can't that be me? Or maybe the real question is, why don't I like anyone except *him*?

We return to our desks, the hum of small talk enveloping me as I fidget in my chair, trying to find a comfortable position. My colleagues' conversations weave through the air, the buzz of their chatter familiar and distracting.

As Mr. Slater enters, the atmosphere in the room shifts, and I feel a change within myself. My heart rate quickens and butterflies flutter in my stomach. His mere presence radiates power, commanding everyone's attention. We all fall silent, preparing ourselves for the day ahead.

Today, he's wearing a charcoal suit, black shirt, and tan loafers, and I can't help but admire how he's the epitome of a handsome man in a suit. His aftershave lingers in the air, and I sit up straighter to catch more of it. His attractiveness is distracting, but he doesn't even glance my way.

Throughout the morning, Mr. Slater pays me no attention, leaving me feeling annoyed and disappointed. I'm not sure what I expected, considering the past two weeks have felt like a surreal dream I don't want to wake up from. But now, I'm beginning to understand how absurd the entire situation is.

Despite my exhaustion, I push through and manage to impress myself with the work I've accomplished. I can only hope Mr. Slater will be impressed too. I wonder if my motivation to succeed comes from trying to impress him or the fear of being kicked out of the program because of my supposed wayward devotion.

After lunch, I'm at my desk analyzing the data when I sense his presence before I see him. That damn cologne and the memory of his kiss will be the death of me. I look up to find him standing beside me. He stares at my work, and I swallow as his scrutinizing eyes wander over my scribbles and conclusions.

"Very good," he comments, glancing briefly at me, but his voice lacks any warmth. "However..." He leans in closer to me, his eyes fixed on my work. Instinctively, I follow his gaze, pulling my eyes away from his chiseled jawline. "However..." I whisper, noticing the vein in his neck tense up. He inhales sharply before regaining his composure, a flicker of something passing over his face. "However, you're missing the entire point," he states in a detached and icy tone, sending a chill down my spine.

My focus immediately sharpens, snapping me out of my lovesick daze. I look down at my work, which I'm sure is correct. "I don't understand," I reply, acutely aware of the nearby interns listening in. Although they can't see us, I'm certain they can hear us.

"You misinterpreted the data," he states firmly,

pointing to a specific section of my work. "This here is a loan, which is a clear liability."

I quickly glance over the line his finger indicates and cross-check it against the company's actual figures. I curse under my breath as I realize my mistake.

His gaze returns to mine, his face just inches away, and I find myself torn between wanting to kiss him or strangle him. At this point, I'm not entirely sure which one I want to do.

In a matter-of-fact tone, he delivers the crushing news, "That's a fail," causing my shoulders to sag with disappointment. A hint of tenderness replaces his cold, steely expression for a brief moment, but it quickly vanishes, leaving me uncertain if it is real.

"You should know better, Rosie," he says, his eyes narrowing. Then he stands and walks away, not giving me another glance. I let out a frustrated sigh as I watch him leave, walking out the door without giving me a second glance. I should have known better than to push his buttons, but I want him to see me as a valuable asset, to recognize that hiring me was not a mistake, and I have what it takes to be here, just like all the other interns.

Angela's face appears from around the corner, and she sighs while blowing a puff of air through her cheeks.

Feeling defeated, I let my head fall into my hands. "He's harsh," she consoles me. "But don't be too hard on yourself. The only reason the rest of us got it right was because he helped us."

He helped them?

I sit there with my head in my hands and feel my emotions starting to rise. *Why am I letting him affect me like this?* I'm angry with myself for making a mistake. Yet, I can't shake the feeling that he wants me to fail.

He could have easily stepped in and guided me, just like he did with the others earlier. Instead, he let me struggle on my own, waiting until I finished. It's almost as if he wants to trip me up and watch me fail. But I won't let that happen.

Without thinking, I launch out of my chair and follow him out.

16

VINCENT

Rosie barges into my office, with my secretary, Julie, red-faced, behind her. I had just finished a quick call with an update from Justin on my burner phone.

"I'm so sorry, sir. I... I couldn't stop her," Julie stammers.

"Thank you. I'll take it from here," I say, slightly intrigued by this ballsy interruption.

Julie closes the door, but it's not the scared look in her eyes that grabs my attention. It's the wildness in Rosie's. She's mad, ferociously mad, and it's a turn-on.

"Come in," I say calmly, fascinated to have this woman all to myself. "Although, I can see you already are."

"Mr. Slater," she snaps, her breath short and rampant, her chest rising and falling.

I sit down to hide the twitch in my pants.

"Sit down," I bark, motioning for her to take a seat in the leather seat opposite mine.

She stares at the seat, then her gaze lifts back to mine. "I'd rather stand, thank you," she hisses, and fuck, it's hard to stay straight-laced when all I want to do is bend her over and fuck her hard on my mahogany desk.

It's been so hard not to touch her, and having her here, all alone, I wonder how long I can keep my needs in check. Julius' strict code of conduct can fuck off for all I care.

I'm staring at her, my eyebrows raised expectantly, and she lets out an audible exhalation. "Fine." She flops on the chair in front of me, then crosses her long legs.

My eyes lower to her legs, then snap back up to her eyes. "What can I do for you, Rosie?"

"I think you're being unfair," she accuses, her ankle swinging back and forth with clear irritation.

I raise my eyebrows in question. "And how do you think I'm being unfair?" I ask.

She looks flustered and out of place as she marvels around my office, the huge expansive windows behind my desk masked by the backdrop of Central Park. "You're clearly singling me out for some reason."

I wet my bottom lip with my tongue as I consider what she's said. A blush fills her smooth cheeks to the tips of her ears. That's the second time I've seen her blush, and I sure as hell didn't pick her to be shy. Not with that fire inside her.

She fills the silence, but I'm not entirely listening as I'm drawn to her lips, her floral scent, and her breathy voice that's sounding more and more alluring by the minute.

I affect her.

I know I do.

"Mr. Slater," she says, and I snap to attention.

"I just want to help you improve, Rosie," I say, my tone sincere even if my actions were intent on driving her away for fear of getting too close.

We stare at each other for a moment, neither of us

knowing what to say. Admittedly, I'm drawn to the beautiful woman in front of me, and I'm compelled to say something.

I round my desk and stand opposite her, leaning back on it. She stares up at me as the gap between us closes, and I lean down to her. I lift her chin in my hands, her soft skin like butter between my fingers.

"I said to you, I'm Mr. Slater here, your mentor, and as your mentor, I need to be firm if I want you to succeed. And you, more than anyone here, Rosie, have that ability."

"I see," she registers.

I stroke her chin and draw her closer, battling against my own desires. "But, little one, I'm Vincent everywhere else."

"Can we talk about what happened last night?" Her voice is gentle, and it stirs something warm inside me.

My tone is possessive and intense as I declare, "I don't like other people touching you."

"Oh," she whispers.

My voice drops to a low growl, and I notice her swallow. I let my eyes linger on her lips, feeling drawn to them.

"Because..." she prompts, her voice soft and hesitant, then she runs her tongue over her bottom lip, making me lose control.

I press my hands firmly against her cheeks, pulling her toward me as I kiss her passionately. As we kiss, my hands roam down her back, drawing her closer to me. She moans softly and wraps her arms around my neck, intensifying the kiss. The heat between us builds, and I know I want her—*right here and now.*

When we finally break apart, her face is flushed with desire. "I don't know what's going on, Vincent," she says, her voice filled with uncertainty.

I pull her close, and she nestles between my thighs. Then I lean in to capture her lips again, but she hesitantly pulls away, reminding me I haven't answered her question. I've been sending her mixed signals, and it's because my head is a clusterfuck of emotions whenever she's around.

One minute, I'm distant and aloof, and the next, I'm painfully hard for her.

"You're all I can think about, Rosie," I confess, my voice rough with emotion. "I don't understand why you're the first and last thing on my mind every day."

A look of disbelief crosses her face, quickly replaced by a smile. "I can't get you out of my head either," she confesses, and I feel a warmth spread through me.

"I need to see you tonight," I insist.

"I'm working," she says with a frown.

"Then I'll be there. I can't stay away from you any longer," I reply determinedly.

As soon as I step into my penthouse, my mind is consumed by thoughts of Rosie. I quickly take a hot shower to refresh myself before meeting up with Caleb and Harry for drinks.

I relish the feeling of the searing hot water against my skin, but I switch the handle to cold to jolt my senses. It's like a mini challenge that prepares me for the unexpected.

My thoughts drift to Rosie once again. She's so talented, confident, and determined, but I can't help but feel like there's a vulnerability she is hiding from me. It's when she blushes, and I don't understand if it is me or something else. Despite my expertise in reading people, I find myself unable to fully decipher her. But maybe that's what draws me to her—the challenge of unraveling her complexities.

Then thoughts of Rosie in my office replay, and my lathered-up hand connects with my already erect cock. A shiver rolls across my shoulder blades as I begin to stroke it. From base to tip, I grow harder, with the brutally icy water, a dichotomy of Rosie in her lingerie and student Rosie in my office. I lick my wet lips, imagining running them across her breasts and taking her erect nipples between my fingers. But it's her eyes that have my body on edge—big, beautiful, and feathered by the longest lashes. The way she stares at me has the air drawing from my lungs. I stroke faster, my grip firm with each demanding pull until my balls contract and hot jets of liquid ribbon accent the marble tiles.

The sound of glasses clinking and music thumping fills the air at a busy bar downtown where I meet Caleb and Harry.

"Slater, you're looking sharp." Caleb slaps me between the shoulder blades as I sit down.

"Thanks," I say, taking a sip of my beer waiting for me. "I need a break from the office."

Harry nods in agreement. "You've been working nonstop lately. It's not that foxy intern keeping you busy, is it?"

I pause for a moment, my mind wandering to Rosie. "She is so frustrating."

Caleb's eyes widen in surprise. "Frustratingly hot?"

I nod, taking another sip of my beer and putting it down with a thud. "Fucking hot."

Caleb scoffs. "Don't dip your pen in the company ink,

Slater. Julius will have a conniption. He's already pissed at you for your firing rampage."

I shake my head. "It's not like that. She's just different."

"Different, how?" Caleb asks, raising an eyebrow.

"I don't know," I admit with a sigh. "I can't explain it."

Harry grins. "Can't stop thinking about her, can you?"

I roll my eyes, but there's a small smile tugging at the corner of my lips. "Maybe."

Caleb's expression is a mix of confusion and disbelief. "Since when do you like anyone, Slater?"

Fuck knows.

I don't date. So why am I even considering it now, and with an intern, no less? I take a gulp of my drink, trying to sort out my thoughts.

"I don't. You know that."

Caleb leans forward, his eyes glinting mischievously. "Well, then, why don't you explore it? You never know where it could lead."

The memory of her soft lips on mine, the way she fits perfectly in my arms, it's all too tempting. I can't let myself get too attached to an intern, but at the same time, I can't seem to resist her. It's like a constant battle in my head, and I don't know how much longer I can keep pushing her away.

"That's what I'm afraid of," I admit.

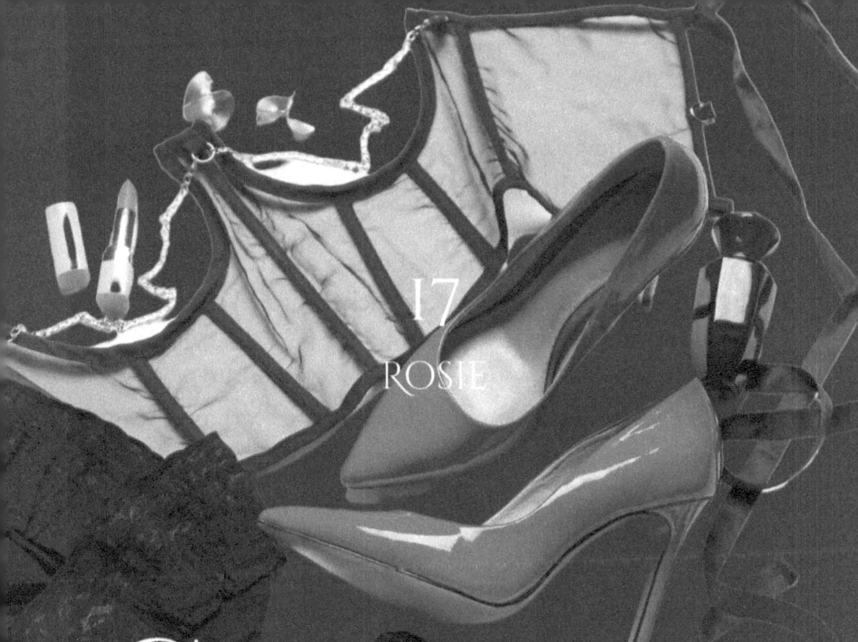

Carlotta, the girl who was hit by a car, is still recovering in the hospital, and they are short-staffed, so I'm up top again tonight.

I shake my head as I wait for the drinks from Freddie.

"Don't look now, but hunky-as-fuck Mr. Slater just appeared," Freddie says as he hands me the drinks.

I swallow the lump forming in my throat and mutter, "Oh my."

"Someone a stalker?" Freddie jokes. My eyes are still on him as the weight of Vincent's stare is heavy on my bare back.

Heat shoots up my spine. Tonight's outfit is a bikini-style top and short shorts.

"He's coming," Freddie says. "Straight toward you. Fuck's sake, why can't he like dick?"

My eyes widen in alarm and anticipation. I don't know what to expect. Even worse, I don't know how I feel.

"Rosie," Vincent says as he approaches me.

I turn, and our eyes connect. A warm, unexpectant smile blossoms on my lips. "Vincent."

His eyes hover across mine and lower slowly. My chest rises and falls as the silence eats between us, and the chemistry swirls.

"I don't like you working up here," he says.

"I'm surprised they let you back in after yesterday," I tease, ignoring his statement but happy he's here with me.

"I think you're forgetting the power I have, little one." I roll my eyes because I know it riles him up. "Perhaps I want to keep an eye on the things dearest to me," he adds, leaning in.

My heart thuds in my chest, and his gaze hovers over my lips. He's so close, and I can smell his expensive aftershave, and a need overcomes me. But then I realize I'm at work.

"I have to deliver these," I say, but I'm so out of my league and flustered it comes out in a rush.

He steps back, a frown forming on his face. "Don't let me hold you up then," he grunts out, and my insides liquefy. He hasn't even touched me, and I'm imploding. My tongue sweeps across my bottom lip, and I pick up the tray with a grip-like force.

He clears the way for me but just stands, watching me walk past him. I'm so tempted to look around but fear I'll fall flat on my face. I feel his stare all the way to the table, where I set down the drinks.

It's Friday night, well, actually early Saturday morning, but you wouldn't know it. The place is abuzz with exclusive clientele. The curved sofas are full, as beautiful women dance provocatively in front of guests. I smile as I lift my gaze toward the bar, noting his eyes aren't on any other waitress but me.

He leans back effortlessly. His shoulders are strong and broad as he takes a drink to his lips.

I'm suddenly nervous but excited. He is here just for me, and the idea has me happy dancing on the inside. I don't care he is ten years older, nor the fact he is my mentor. I sashay back to the bar and brush past him, purposely touching the expensive fabric of his shirt.

"Don't tease me, little one," he says as I pull up beside him.

"Freddie, table three will have the same again, please," I say, smiling.

Freddie flicks his gaze between us, then gets straight back to work. He knows Vincent is here for me too, and my chest pounds with excitement like a hammer striking steel. Intentionally, I lean over him to grab something from the bar.

He inhales sharply before pulling me toward him, his voice dark and urgent. "Come here." My hands land on his chest, and my arousal throbs between my legs. His hand wraps around my bare waist, pulling me closer, and my heart is deafening in my ear.

He lowers his face to mine and whispers, "I've booked a suite tonight." His fingers stroke my bare skin, sending shivers down my spine. Suddenly, my jealousy flares up, and I wonder who he's booked it with. He must see the look on my face because he quickly adds, "I was hoping it was you that would be joining me."

He's asking me? *Oh.*

"I don't..." I falter. "That's not part of my job description," I admit. But suddenly, with him, I wish it was.

"Well, I will get thirsty in there, so book me in for three cognacs. Each ten minutes apart from the other."

"Drinks are up." I turn to find Freddie. His grin shoots from ear to ear. He must know something is up by that Cheshire grin.

I remove my hands from Vincent's chest and snatch the drinks with enough force that things nearly topple over. He shoots me one last look, then disappears to help another waitress with her order.

Vincent pulls the key with a red ribbon attached to it from his pocket without waiting for a reply. "I'll see you in there, little one," he says, his voice low and seductive.

I'm left speechless as he turns and walks toward the end suite, suite seven—my lucky number.

As I watch him enter the suite, my heart races with anticipation. His gaze collides with mine, sending tingles throughout my body. He's just looking at me, but it feels like so much more. Slowly, he closes the door behind him, leaving me standing there, wondering what the hell to do next.

Ten minutes drag on and on, and finally, it's time to bring him his requested beverage.

"Hennessy," Freddie's voice slices through my thoughts.

"Thanks," I say quickly, eager to bring Vincent his drink on time.

"Where's that going?" Freddie asks with curiosity. The asshole knows exactly where it is going. He's in charge of the keys to the suites, for fuck's sake!

"Suite seven," I mumble, and it's barely audible.

"Vincent Slater," he says.

I nod, then rush off, so he can't get another word in.

My heart is racing, and my palms are sweaty with anticipation. I take a deep breath and walk toward the door. As I approach, my hand trembles slightly as I reach out to press the doorbell. I hesitate for just a moment, then take a deep breath and push the button.

When he opens the door and sees me, his face breaks

into a smile that has me forgetting our surroundings and the reality of our situation. "Hello, beautiful."

The room is not at all what I expected. Soft rose paneling lines the walls, and the heated marble floors radiate warmth through the worn soles of my heels. Candles flicker in every corner, casting shadows that dance across the walls. The lighting is dark but still ambient, and a four-poster bed dominates the center of the room, with a dancer's pole in front of it.

Vincent gestures toward a leather sofa and table beside the bed, where he wants me to put his drink. As he closes the door behind me, I swear my heart is so loud he can hear it.

The soft music playing in the background creates a romantic vibe, and I'm taken aback by the beauty of the space. It's nothing like what I expected. I'm not sure if I was anticipating whips and chains, but this is just beautiful. I set his drink down on the table and stand there, taking it all in.

Vincent saunters toward me, stopping when he's only a few inches from me. The scent of him is intoxicating, and I have to fight the urge to reach out and touch him. He pushes a strand of hair back from my face, and once again, I see that soft, delicate side of him that's not at all like the ruthless man he displays to the world.

I close my eyes at the feel of his hands on my face, and his thumb slides down my cheek, running over my bottom lip. I want him so badly, with his lips on mine again. When I open my eyes, we're staring at each other, and I know he wants this just as much as I do.

I can't stop thinking about our kiss earlier, and before I can stop myself, I launch at him like a bull out of a cage, my lips landing on his.

He pulls me close, his large hand circling my bare back as his strong fingers pull me roughly into him. I open for him as his tongue sweeps inside my mouth, and I moan with pleasure. His erection presses against my stomach, and it feels so good. I wonder what it would be like for him to be my first. His hand drops to my behind, and he pushes me into his thick erection.

My panties are getting wetter by the second.

He pulls back for a moment and says, "I'll see you in ten minutes." His eyes are wild with lust as he drinks me in.

"What?" I'm a chaotic jumble of emotions and thoughts. All I know is I need more of him.

"Delayed gratification, little one." He smirks, and I'm more aroused and excited.

"Ten minutes, Sir," I whisper, and his eyes flicker with even more fire. I turn to leave, excitement blooming in my chest and pulsing between my thighs.

Opening the door, I take a moment to adjust to the bright lights and loud music outside the suite. My lips tingle from Vincent's kiss, and I run a hand through my hair, feeling a bit disheveled.

Screw the other tables now.

All I want to do is serve Vincent Slater.

I walk around, absentmindedly collecting a few empty glasses and taking more orders, but my head is in the clouds as I count down the minutes and seconds until I see him again.

"Order for table fourteen," Freddie says, and I step forward to take it.

Two other girls are waiting for drinks, so I hover around them, waiting for my turn without letting Freddie chew my ear off with questions.

"And this is Hennessy for Vincent," he adds

"Thank you," I respond, unable to contain my smile.

He narrows his eyes at me. "Go have fun."

"I don't know what you're talking about," I reply, feigning innocence.

He raises an eyebrow. "Honey, I can tell if you've sucked the man's dick by the smudge of your lipstick."

I widen my eyes. "I have not!" I say quickly, though the thought of taking Vincent Slater in my mouth has me wild with desire.

"Not yet," he says. "But it's wearing thin."

Shit. Note to self, *Must carry lipstick somewhere in this scrap of clothing I'm wearing.*

I let out a chuckle. This is the most fun I've ever had at work.

I deliver the drinks to table fourteen and set them in front of the four men. As I turn to leave, one of them grabs my wrist.

"Do you work the pole?" he asks, staring me up and down.

"No, sir. I'm just your waitress," I reply with a warning smile.

"Shame," he says. "Those titties and that ass should be where they belong."

I swallow hard. I've never had anyone speak to me that way, and I cringe, suddenly feeling cheap.

Walking away from him, I steady myself and knock on the door to suite seven. He opens it in a rush, and his face falls. "What's wrong?" he asks, his hand cradling my back as he gently guides me inside. He's so tall, this close, and strong, and all I want is the feel of his hands on my body.

I set his glass of Hennessy down, and he keeps his distance, leaning against the back of the red-leather door.

He's a picture of beauty, but he won't come near me. He thinks it's him. I need to reassure him it's not.

I walk toward him and stop just in front of him, gazing up into his green eyes as he looks down at me. "Everything's fine," I say softly. "Will you kiss me now, Vincent?" I practically plead because I don't want to waste another minute without his lips on mine.

He smiles, pleased at my request, before lowering and brushing his lips across mine. His tongue brushes across my lower lip, and that familiar ache between my legs grows at the connection.

His hands spread across my backside, curling underneath my cheeks, pushing me into his body. He's strong and firm everywhere. My hands make their way to his hair as I struggle to hold him as the kiss deepens. His thickness grows, and a deep growl in his throat reverberates in our mouths.

I know I should tell him, but he'll leave me when he finds out I'm a virgin. Men like him don't do virgins. Men like him have experienced women knowing exactly what to do.

His lips leave mine and ladder down my jaw and neck. His breath is wet and rampant as he trails my soft skin with nips and bites.

"God, you smell amazing," he says, his voice thick with desire. "I need you, Rosie." He groans, trailing his tongue up my neck to my jaw.

My heart is pounding, and I can barely catch my breath, but I don't care. I want him too badly to stop now. I pull him back to me, and our kiss becomes fast and heady. He holds back just enough to keep me wanting more.

Wrapping my arms around his neck, he digs his fingers into my flesh and lifts me, my legs wrapping around him.

He leans on the wall, and his erection presses against my wet folds, the leather the only thing separating us.

"Grind up on me," he whispers, and I'm so aroused I don't care about being embarrassed. I rub myself against him as he supports my weight effortlessly. Every part of me tingles with need.

"Harder," he commands, and I do so eagerly, lost in my need for him. I'm aware of how it must look, but I can't bring myself to care. The sensation builds inside me, pushing me higher and higher toward my climax. He takes my mouth in a searing kiss, and the sound of his groans only serves to heighten my pleasure. Suddenly, I explode, my body convulsing around him as I reach my peak.

When I come down from the high, I struggle to catch my breath, my heart racing. I can feel his heart pounding against me as we catch our breaths. Finally, I slide down his body and look up at him, still in a daze from the intensity of our encounter.

"See you in ten minutes, little one," he says with a smirk, and I'm left reeling, barely able to stand as I try to collect myself.

18

VINCENT

The second hand slowly makes its way around the oyster-faced Patek Philippe watch, making me impatient. My strained erection barely goes down, wanting only Rosie. It's simple—it wants what it wants.

The women dancing on the poles barely register, Rosie is my wrecking ball, and I don't need to understand why. She's just a distraction from the real reason I'm back in Manhattan.

The soft chimes of the doorbell sound, and I know it's her.

I steamroll toward the door, swinging it open to reveal her in a leather bra and short shorts, every man's wet dream. But I care about the size of her intellect.

"Your drink, sir," she says, a naughty smile on her lips.

I take a sharp intake of breath. This little minx has me so wound up upon her entrance. *What is she doing to me?* "Please enter," I say, her submissive address arousing me even more.

I slam the door shut and snatch the drink from her

hands before she can put it down. My lips are on hers, and she smiles against mine. I set the drink down while pushing her onto the sofa. I'm on top of her now, trying to calm myself down because I don't want her to run.

She pulls me to her and kisses me, tasting of berries and vodka. Did she have a shot of something? I sense she's nervous, but why? She works *here* and has balls of steel.

I kiss her back with force, my body on hers with suffocating need. I run my hand up her thigh slowly, my thumb skimming across the hem of her shorts.

"Vincent," she says, and I'm kissing her neck now, unable to take my lips away from her buttery skin. I want to make her mine, have her here and now, and...

"Vincent," she says louder this time, and I stop nipping her neck and stare down at her. Her eyes are wild, and she's breathing rapidly. She's fucking beautiful. "I'm a virgin," she says, her eyes wide.

I chuckle at her claim of virginity, but the intensity of her gaze makes me pause. I sit up and create some distance between us. Is all of this a façade? Is she masking her own vulnerability with bravado? The minute she caught my eye, she looked out of place working here, but could she be?

"No, you're not," I say, hopeful, trying to dispel the tension in the room.

She sits up, pushing me away from her, and studies me with confusion.

"I understand if you don't want to..." She trails off, hesitating.

Her defenses are up, and I can feel her slipping away from me. I can't let that happen. I don't care if she's a virgin or not.

"Come home with me," I blurt out, desperation creeping into my voice.

Her eyes widen in surprise.

"What?" she asks incredulously, looking at me like I've lost my mind. "I'm at work!"

"Fuck it. Say you have a headache or something. I'll pick you up in five."

I stand, gazing down at her. She's beautiful, intelligent, and a *virgin*. She looks at me skeptically, and I can sense her resistance, but I don't want to let her go yet.

"How are you..." I shake my head in disbelief but not wanting to get into this with her now. "Rosie, don't make me wait," I say in a low, commanding voice before turning and walking out of the room, leaving her behind.

As she emerges from the back exit, I'm relieved and quickly open the car door for her. She slides in, wearing an over-sized coat over her leather outfit, and I struggle to resist the urge to touch her during the short drive to my penthouse.

I'm not sure what I'm doing, bringing her back to my place like this. But my desire for her is too overpowering to ignore.

"How are you still a virgin?" I ask, breaking the silence in the car.

She shrugs and stares out the window. "I just haven't found anyone I like enough, I guess."

"You're twenty-two, Rosie."

"I've kissed a few guys," she admits, and the thought of her lips on someone else makes me feel possessive. But then it hits me.

She's never been with another man.

She's never had her pussy eaten out or been devoured like a queen should be.

I let out a slow breath, shaking my head. "You're looking too hard," I say as I pull into my garage.

"Maybe," she responds, watching me as I park the car.

After killing the engine, I step out and walk over to her door. She looks nervous, biting her lower lip. I extend my hand, and she takes it without hesitation.

We walk to the elevator, and I pull out my card to swipe it across the reader. The penthouse is called, and the elevator begins its ascent. "So, you're telling me no one has ever…"

She swallows hard and nods.

"I want to be your first," I cut in before she can say anything.

"Why?" she asks, trying to understand my motives.

"I don't know, little one. There's just something about you," I reply honestly.

We stare at each other in silence as the elevator's soft music plays.

She dips her chin and admits, "There's something about you too, Vincent. I want my first time to be you."

The door pings open, and I lift her into my arms, kissing her roughly. I soon realize my own strength and pull back, trying to be gentler. She's a virgin, and I need to calm the fuck down.

Her legs wrap around my midsection, and I feel the warmth of her body against mine. I walk slowly, taking in the feel of her in my arms and the scent of her hair surrounding me.

As soon as we enter the living room of my penthouse, the lighting automatically switches on, and she detaches herself from me to look around.

"Wow, this is beautiful," she remarks.

So are you, little one.

Guiding her to the kitchen, I grab two glasses, placing them on the counter. When I open the refrigerator, I'm relieved to find it stocked with my favorite foods, courtesy of my thoughtful housekeeper, Shirley.

Every time I fly back to the States, she's always there with my preferred snacks and drinks.

My eyes scan the selection of chilled wines before settling on a vintage that catches my attention. I grab the bottle of vintage red and open it.

While I pour the wine, I watch her admire the artwork on the walls and the plush textures on the floor. Something about having her here in my penthouse feels different, but I push the thought aside. I'm not one for attachments, especially with interns who are ten years my junior.

Her eyes flicker across the art on the walls to the furniture carefully selected. I hired the best interior decorators to decorate my apartment, and it shows. No expense is spared, from the leather sofa to the expensive chandeliers and multimillion-dollar artwork I collect from my travels.

The house is minimal, the way I like it—clean and sparse. The elevators open into the main foyer and living area, and the kitchen is along the floor-to-ceiling windows. From up here, Central Park looks like a square green patch. It's quiet, the way I like it. A world away from the busy streets below, where taxis and people flood the sidewalk.

Up here, it's my sanctuary. I keep it bare so my mind stays clear and focused. The only color is in the artwork and salt and pepper rugs that furnish the heated marble floors.

I walk over to her. I don't want to rush her into anything, but I'm so impatient with need it hurts. I'm fighting a battle with myself to be gentler.

"You've done very well for yourself," she says

"You sound like it's a bad thing." She picks up the glass, and I clink it with her.

"Only if your wealth has been to the determinant of others."

"There are always winners and losers, little one," I say as my eyes meet hers.

"They call you ruthless for a reason," she states.

"*They* can call me whatever the fuck they want. I don't give a damn about their opinions," I say with a cold tone, downing the drink.

"Of course, you don't," she replies, and there's that sass again.

No one ever speaks to me like she does, and the boldness stirs a primal desire within me.

She takes a large gulp of her merlot and sets the glass down, her hands shaking slightly. I sense her nervousness, and it makes me wonder what she's thinking.

Is she regretting being here with me? Is she scared of what might happen next?

I move closer to her, my hand gently resting on her waist. "Is this what you want to be discussing, little one?" I ask, unable to hide my need.

"No," she says in a scratchy, low voice. "Show me your room."

19

ROSIE

His warm hand envelops mine, causing my heart to race as we walk down the hallway. My palms are sweaty, but he doesn't seem to mind. As we pass by two guest bedrooms, I catch a glimpse of his slightly open office door. The mahogany desk with ornate carvings catches my eye. Everything in the apartment is sparsely furnished and minimally decorated, with no objects out of place.

Clearly, he's a bit of a control freak.

My heart races with anticipation as we approach a set of double doors adorned with gold knobs. Vincent reaches out and turns them, pushing open the doors.

The room is stunning, with an oversized bed dressed in navy satin sheets taking center stage. The walls are paneled in white and adorned with minimalist artwork, except for one striking piece. A large cream rug covers the marble floors, and I can't resist kicking off my heels to feel the plush fibers under my feet.

As I step forward, I notice him watching me with a

strange expression on his handsome face. It's as if he's never seen anyone enjoy life's simple pleasures.

"Join me, I say, extending my hand.

"What for?" he asks, looking bewildered. "You look like you're doing some kind of rain dance on my expensive rug."

"Don't knock it until you've tried it, Sir," I say, twisting my mouth. His eyes flicker, and I know he likes it when I call him that. *Does he have a dominant streak?* It's starting to fit the picture with the way he likes me calling him Sir and making me wait to orgasm.

The thought stirs something inside me.

He slowly and meticulously steps out of his tanned leather pointy loafers and sets them to the side.

"Today," I tease, laughing at him.

He rolls his eyes and takes my hand as he steps on his rug, probably for the thousandth time.

"What's so special about this?" he asks, confused.

I laugh as he presses his foot up and down. He looks adorable, and I'm struck once again by the unique blend of power and gentleness that this man embodies.

"Just relax and feel the sensation of the rug on the bottoms of your feet," I say.

He steps a little lighter this time, and it's then I can see his expression changing. He's no longer in his head anymore but in his body.

"See?" I say.

Suddenly, he hoists me up, and I instinctively wrap my legs around him. I can't help but let out a small yelp, but the excitement coursing through me is undeniable. As he sets me down on the bed, I land with a few playful bounces.

"I'm a pretty patient guy, Rosie, but I don't know how much longer I can resist you," he says in a low, serious tone, his earlier playful demeanor gone.

I clench at his authoritative tone and straighten up on the plush backboard, setting myself upright. He unbuttons his shirt and pulls it off, and I gasp at the sight of his chest. *How embarrassing.* He must have heard me because a smile spreads across his lips.

He's all curves and muscles, not an inch of fat on him. He's cut like a diamond, and I'm drooling over him as he unbuttons his pants and lowers the zipper.

Vincent drops his pants and briefs all at once, and his huge engorged dick juts away from his stomach. My gaze keeps drifting back to his impressive length, and a surge of desire courses through me. I can't stop fidgeting with my fingers now damp with sweat. But with him, he makes me feel safe. Trying to calm myself, I stretch my hand out on the smooth and luxurious sheets, enjoying their softness and silkiness.

"Get over here," he beckons, motioning for me to come closer.

I playfully roll my eyes, trying to hide the nervousness in my belly. "If you wanted me closer, why throw me on the bed?" I quip, hoping to ease the tension.

He lowers his chin and stares at me intensely, causing heat to pool between my legs. "That mouth, Rosie... I know exactly how to shut it up." His voice is rough and suggestive, and I feel a shiver run down my spine and nestle between my legs.

Oh.

I shuffle toward him, feeling awkward and bouncy as I move closer to the edge of the bed. Heat spreads through my chest as I kneel in front of him. Grasping my chin tightly, he runs his thumb along my cheek and lifts my face to look at him. "Don't ever be embarrassed in front of me. This space is for you to explore your own needs. Do you hear me?" His voice carries a hint of annoyance and assertiveness.

I nod in agreement, feeling a bit uncertain about my own needs. But I know that anything with him involved is something I want to experience.

His hand glides down to my jacket, pulling it off my shoulders. The cool air on my skin sends shivers down my body. Kneeling in black leather shorts and a bralette, I can feel his possessive eyes scanning me up and down as if I'm completely naked.

He unzips the front of my top between my breasts and tosses the flimsy piece of leather aside. My breasts spill out, and his eyes widen at the sight.

My heart is racing as his hands slide over the fabric of my shorts, tracing the curve of my hip bone with his thumbs. He steps forward, his naked body a striking contrast to my own. Without thinking, I reach out and run my hand over his chiseled abdominal muscles, eliciting a sharp intake of breath from him.

Does he like it when I touch him there?

As I look up at him, he begins to pull my shorts and thong down until I'm completely naked before him. I try to stifle my shyness, but it's overwhelming.

"Stop thinking," he commands as if he knows what's going on in my head. "You're fucking exquisite, Rosie," he continues, trailing his finger over my collarbone and down my body, caressing one breast and then the other.

His touch elicits an uncontrollable gasp from me.

I can barely control myself, and he's only touching me. I suck in a breath, the pads of his fingers in deep exploration as they swipe the breath from my lungs. His eyes watch my every reaction, like he's deep in fascination.

His finger ladders down my front, rolling onto the

indent of my stomach. He travels lower until he plays with the neat strip of hair above my folds.

"I need to stretch this delicious cunt." He breathes heavily, his fingers delving inside my folds. His crass words should make me pull back, but I find myself leaning into him.

He hisses as his fingers find my wet spot, and I groan. "Fuck me," he says, slipping a finger inside me and inching back and forth. His lips trace mine, and I shut my eyes, trying to absorb the sensory overload feeling.

"Your soaking, Rosie." He licks my bottom lip, and I know he's barely holding on. As his jaw clenches, he surges forward, pressing his lips against mine with an almost overwhelming intensity. Expertly, his fingers glide up my folds to my clit, and he finds just the spot that has me teetering. Reaching up, I grip his shoulders for support, then he swallows my gasps with kisses.

"I need to taste you." He removes his fingers, and my legs are heavy from the orgasm that's building and just about to rip through me. Dragging his fingers up to his mouth, he licks them and groans. "Delicious," he says as I watch on, panting.

"Open those lips," he commands, and I do as I'm told. "Suck, little one."

His fingers enter my mouth, and I lick my juices off his finger. I suck his finger from base to tip and watch him suck in a sharp needy breath. It's sweet and slightly tangy. I don't care. I'm so hot right now I'd do anything Vincent asked of me.

I lower my hand to his dick and touch him. I don't really know what I'm doing, but I pull it down. He's heavy, thick, and smooth all over.

I take him in my hands, stroking him back and forth

slowly. He closes his eyes momentarily, then opens them abruptly. "Lie down." His hands remove mine, and I'm left wondering if I was doing it right.

I do as he says, my mind swirling with need and apprehension. I'm scared. I'm thinking about the pain. *Will it hurt?* Everyone says the first time isn't enjoyable. I want this time to be enjoyable for him *and* me.

He walks over to his side drawer and pushes a button. It glides open, and he pulls out a condom and rolls it on himself quickly. His biceps pop as he holds himself firmly.

Well, fuck if that isn't the hottest thing I've ever seen.

"This may hurt for a second," he says as he comes to lie on top of me. He balances his weight carefully, but the weight of his dick rests against my thigh. It's hot and heavy, and I swallow the cement in my throat.

I want him.

I've never wanted anyone as much as I want him.

"But I've got you, Rosie." His sincere look pulls me out of my whirling mind, and when his mouth drops to mine, I'm completely his. A slow, passionate kiss ensues that reaches the tips of my toes. He shifts on top of me, and his thickness nestles between my folds.

I'm wet and aching all over, so ready, and my heart is pounding in my ears.

My hands skirt around the smoothness of his waist. His kiss turns urgent, and his dick nudges against my opening as I shift my hips to accommodate him.

"Open for me," he murmurs against my lips, his kiss becoming stronger and wetter, making me ache all over for him.

He enters me quickly, and I wince at the size of him stretching my tight walls, making it more than uncomfortable. He stops for a brief moment before pushing deeper. I groan and suck in a needy breath as he fills me completely.

"Baby, I'm only halfway." He groans. "I need more," he says on a hiss, and I know he's close to losing it. His kisses are now landing on my neck, more ferocious in their assault. "So... fucking... tight." He growls, his eyes blazing with desire and assertion.

Heat slashes through my chest as he nudges even deeper, and I know he's all the way in when he moans at the connection before moving out again. With every movement, I feel the muscles in his back contort.

He rolls his hips in again, pushing further and harder, and this time it's not as painful. He's stretching me with each thrust, and the pain gives way to a delicious fullness. The throbbing sensation returns, and he's moving quicker now.

The power radiating through him as he roughly enters me sends an overwhelming pleasure through me.

Oh God.

Feels. So. Good.

My body quakes and pulses until an orgasm rips through me, and I let out a moan. "Rosie, you're squeezing me so tight. I can't... fuck!" Vincent hisses out as he rolls into me harder and faster, losing control as he comes in a rush.

As I pant, lightheaded and dizzy, he rolls off me and disappears toward his bathroom. I look around and see a few specks of blood on the sheets. *Oh God.* When I look up, he's watching me. Naked, his dick still hard, he walks over to see what I'm looking at. A ghost of anguish flickers across his beautiful face.

"Are you okay?" I ask, suddenly feeling self-conscious.

Does he regret taking my virginity?

Shit.

His expression shifts, a smile spreading across his face as he sits beside me. His lips capture mine in a forceful kiss, his tongue dancing with mine and setting my body on fire.

I can't believe how much I crave his touch.

"Shouldn't I be asking you that?" he finally responds to my earlier question.

I brush it off and focus on the present. "That was nice," I say, running my tongue over my lips.

"Nice? I'm not sure I'd describe myself as 'nice,' little one," he replies, raising an eyebrow in amusement.

I sense a warning in his tone, but I ignore it.

"So, what happens now?" I ask, hoping for some clarity about our relationship when we return to the real world Monday morning.

He looks down at me, a mischievous glint in his eye. "Now, I'm going to give you a bath before I fuck you again."

Oh boy.

20
VINCENT

Rosie's hair cascades loosely around her shoulders, and I can't help but feel in awe of her beauty.

I guide her into my sunken marble tub, admiring her naked body as the light reflects on her silky skin. She steps into the tub and lowers herself into the water, smiling as she does so.

"This is beautiful," she says, her voice genuine and hitting me in the chest where I thought I was void of feeling. I watch as she glides her hand across the smooth surface of the water, then I settle into the seat beside her, feeling the hot water glide up my legs to my waist.

"I had it craned in through the window. It's one piece crafted from a rare Turkish marble," I explain. Rosie gazes up at me in disbelief, and I'm unsure if she's disappointed or amazed. "It's one of a kind," I say, my voice low as I stare directly at her.

I know she knows I'm no longer talking about the bath. Her eyes dip low as her tongue traces across her bottom lip, causing my dick to swell.

"You're dirty, Rosie. Let me wash you," I say, maneuvering her so she sits between my legs with her back pressed into my chest. The scent of orchids and vanilla takes a deep dive into my nose, and I lean in for more. It drives me wild like a caged animal, and I let out a groan.

"What are you doing?" She giggles and presses into me, making the water ripple and slosh around us.

"Your scent..." I trail off, unable to finish my sentence.

She twists to face me and smiles sweetly, and a foreign feeling envelopes me, settling in my stomach. Suddenly, London, my home, is the furthest place I want to be.

I push away the thought and remind myself why I'm here. I'm here to find my brother's killer, nothing else.

"I'm under no illusion what this is, Vincent," she says with her back against me, catching me off guard. I run the sponge down the curves of her shoulders, pausing to construct my response. It doesn't take long.

"Good," I respond. Because I'm not capable of anything else but fucking.

"Doesn't mean we can't have fun, though," she says playfully, and I observe a smile tugging at the edges of her mouth as her chin draws down to the slope of her shoulder.

"Fun is for amateurs. When I'm done with you, you won't be able to walk for a week," I say, matter-of-factly, unable to keep the smile from my face as I bury it in her silky hair.

She giggles before adding, "Then you might have to explain my absence from the intern program."

I glide the sponge down her front, between her breasts, and she moans.

"Tell me about your family," she says, stroking my leg.

"Do I have to?" I ask.

She turns to face me with wide eyes. "I want to know more about the man who just took my virginity."

I chuckle. "Well, then... there's Julius, me, and my sister. My relationship with my father is strained, but I'm close with my mom."

"Why is it strained?" she asks.

"That's a topic for another day," I say, closing the door on the conversation. "My sister's in town, actually, so we're all catching up for dinner next week."

She absentmindedly strokes my thigh, and I enjoy the sensation of her touch. "What's her name, your sister?"

"Victoria, but she goes by Viki Slate."

Suddenly, she turns around to face me, causing water to splash over the edge. "The singer? Your sister is Viki Slate?"

"Sure is. Guess she's become a bit of a hit in the last year." I feel protective of her but guilty at the same time because I know I should be there for her more. Dad certainly wasn't.

"I love her music. It's got a bit of a jazz kick, like Amy Winehouse."

I laugh at her enthusiasm, and she punches me in the arm.

"If you say so." I shrug. "I don't really listen to music."

"What?" she says in disbelief as her eyes connect with mine. I run the sponge across her collarbone with one hand and cradle the nape of her neck with the other, pulling her toward me. I slide the sponge down the column of her neck and feel her swallow beneath my hand.

"Music isn't my thing," I whisper in a low voice as I slide the sponge down her chest, between her breasts. I trace the curve of her breasts and take the roughness of the sponge across her sensitive nipple. A fresh wave of arousal fills her cheeks, and she sucks in a breath at the sensation.

Her rosy pink pebbles harden and lengthen as I wipe the course sponge across them. I'm transfixed by her response, and my dick swells.

"Music isn't a thing, Vincent... it's a feeling," she says, breathy and hot. Her voice makes me want every inch of her. I trail the sponge across her right breast, slowly circling her skin and nipple.

"Pleasure is my thing," I say, my voice low and greedy, as I feel my hard dick taking up space in the searing water.

I lose the sponge and spread her legs, pulling her toward me so she is straddling me. "Hard pleasure, little one."

A fire dances behind her pretty brown eyes, and I warn her with my tone, but she doesn't seem to hear it with the needy look she's giving me. She wants this as much as I do. I greedily thrust two fingers inside her, and she closes her eyes and gasps.

"I want to break you, little one," I say as I'm rough with my fingers, hard and fast. But I don't care. I can't control myself around her. "Do you want more?" I ask, her eyes squeezed shut, and she's lost in the feeling of my fingers deep inside her.

She nods, unable to utter the words. I add a third finger, and she exhales with a moan that has my dick almost parting the water. I rake my tongue across her nipples, branding them with my stubble. Her soft skin is a greedy invitation for my mouth only. She squirms, and her orgasm builds as she clamps down on my fingers. I imagine her doing that with me inside her, and a groan pulls from my throat.

"Come, little one." I breathe across her nipple then I clamp down on it hard.

"Oh God," she yells out as an orgasm tears from her. I

leave my fingers inside her, letting her ride it out as I watch her unfold on top of me.

Eventually, she opens her eyes, and I slide my fingers from her. "I'm not done yet."

My hands circle her hips as I drag her out of the water. Her thighs squeeze around my hips as my lead boner weighs a goddamn ton.

I take her in, wet hair, flushed cheeks, and bruising redness across her tits and chest where my mouth ravaged her skin. "Against the wall," I command. I open a drawer, grab a condom, and wrap myself quickly. My dick is heavy and needs draining.

She's still panting from her orgasm but does as I ask and is a foot from the wall when I close the gap between us, kissing her hard. The force of my kiss drives her back against the wall, and she squeals at the cool connection of the marble slab on her hot back.

Her body is hot and smooth, and her large breasts are against my chest.

With one quick motion, I grip her hip and pull her legs up and around my waist. "Let me know if I'm too much," I say. "Your safe word is blue. Say it, and I'll stop immediately." She nods, and without another warning, I maneuver myself toward her entrance and slide into her delicious wet folds. We groan at the impact. "So fucking tight," I bite out.

Her hands grip the backs of my shoulders as I pump her harder. She grabs around me each time I slide in and out of her.

With each pounding thrust, I stretch her more and more. I'm hard and fast and can't control it much longer. I feel my orgasm building—my legs are heavy, and blinding heat shoots up my spine.

She's moaning loudly, and the sound is enough to drive

me over the fucking cliff with ecstasy. My hips rock hard and fast as she slams against the wall, the sound of our skin slapping echoing throughout the bathroom.

"Vincent," she breathes out as her hands dig into my shoulder blades, her fingernails digging into my firm skin.

I pull back suddenly, realizing the savage force I'm delivering into her vanilla pussy. "No, keep going," she says on a shaky breath. "Please." It's in her breath and voice that she's pleading with me, and I continue with hard, quick thrusts. I'm losing control and sense of time and space, giving it to her hard and relentlessly. I press my lips to hers, and it's wet, firm, and sensual.

"I can't hold it any longer. Give it to me," I command. Rosie moans out a breathy moan and clamps down on me as an orgasm shatters from her.

A moment later, an orgasm rips through me, and I grit my teeth, absorbing the explosion.

I rest my head against the cool wall as beads of sweat slide down my spine. Our chests are heaving against each other as we try to claim a morsel of the thick oxygen swirling between us.

Fuck, I was rough. Carnal and lost in the moment. *Did I hurt her?*

A flicker of worry shoots through me, and I peel myself off the wall to assess her. "Look at me, Rosie," I demand, and she opens her heavy eyes. "Are you okay?" I ask, and before I realize what I'm doing, I set her down and explore her body for any marks or bruising.

"I'm fine." She breathes out on a scanty breath, but I'm certain I pushed her too far. It's the last thing I want when I've just claimed her as mine.

"I'm fine," she repeats as though sensing my disbelief.

Seeing the reassurance in her eyes, I scan her from head

to toe because I'm all but done with her. "Let's get cleaned up."

~

We're heading back to her place, and it's already past four. No way in hell was she riding the subway at this hour. Was she insane? Did she really think I'd let her go from my penthouse to her place on the subway?

My mind drifts, wondering who she has in her life to protect her from making such poor decisions.

As we smoothly ride along the freeway, she begins to ask me more questions about Slater Corp.

It's my turn now, and I want to know her reasons for working at the Vanilla Club. Now that she's mine, I don't want her working there anymore. *What's wrong with her father that she has to work at the Vanilla Club to pay for his medical bills?*

"What's wrong with your father?" I notice her tense up in her seat, but I push on, "You said your father was unwell, and that's why you work at the Vanilla Club to earn enough money for his treatment," I remind her.

"Oh, right," she says, and when I glance over at her, she has a strange expression on her face, one of turmoil and conflict.

I immediately back off. "You don't have to tell me," I say, surprised at my own admission. I usually push further when someone seems uncomfortable, but with Rosie, I retreat. *What the hell is wrong with me?*

"I... um... kind of lied," she admits.

I grip the steering wheel tightly, my knuckles turning white. "You lied about your father being ill?" I ask, feeling betrayed.

"Yes," she replies quietly.

"Why?" I demand harshly.

She sighs and admits, "I started working at the Vanilla Club a few months ago to help my brother, Gabriel. He put my name down on a loan with a loan shark without my knowledge, so now they can come after me. Not that I have much money, but it's my mother's jewelry and keepsakes that are most precious."

I reach out and place my hand on her thigh, waiting for her to continue.

"My mother died three years ago. She was hit by a car walking home from my graduation ceremony. The driver was drunk. Completely mowed her down in the crosswalk and continued driving after he hit her."

"I'm sorry, Rosie." She reciprocates by rubbing her hand on mine. "No wonder you are so strong and independently fierce," I add, and she looks my way, her eyes softening.

"Thank you," she says, and my heart aches for her because I know how hard it is to lose someone you love. But I don't dare tell her about my brother—that feels too personal.

"Why didn't you just tell me the truth in the interview?" I ask.

"Because it's embarrassing. Working as a lingerie waitress to pay back my brother's debt? Come on." She shakes her head. "I thought you hated me, Vincent."

"I know I have a reputation, but I could never hate you, Rosie," I reply, and she smiles slightly, but it doesn't reach her eyes.

"Did you think I'd remove you from the intern program?" I ask.

She nods but remains quiet.

Maybe she's right.

"And your father?" I continue, wanting to know more about her.

"Alive and well, unfortunately. Last time I heard, he was upstate, mixing with the wrong crowd. I don't have anything to do with him. My parents divorced when Gabriel and I were kids."

This poor beautiful woman, all she needs is someone to take care of her for a change. But I can't dwell on that feeling. I'll be back in London once my business is finished here, and this thing we have will be a beautiful memory.

But for now, she is all I need.

The roads are empty as we cut through the I-95 in New Jersey back to her place.

"So now you know about me. But what I don't know is something about you," she says, her cheeks blooming with heat.

"Go on," I reply, curious about what she wants to know.

"You like it hard, have you always?" she asks, surprising me with her directness.

"Yes, little one," I reply, not wanting to give away too much.

"Why?" she presses.

"I just do." I shrug, not wanting to delve too deeply into my preferences.

I notice her wriggling in her seat, trying to get comfortable. "Are you sore?" I ask, feeling guilty about how rough I was with her in the bathroom.

"A little," she admits, waving her hand dismissively.

"Are you like that with all your girlfriends?" she continues, staring at me with wide eyes.

"I don't have girlfriends," I reply curtly, flicking my eyes back to the road as I take the exit for Saddle Hills. "But why do I think you already know that?" I add, smirking.

She huffs out a laugh. "I may have asked around about you," she admits with lighthearted innocence.

I glide my Porsche around her neighborhood, committing it to memory. "Well, don't believe everything you hear," I caution.

"Is that so?" she challenges.

My gaze flickers to hers as we stop at a set of lights. "Yes. Ask me if you want to know anything about me, and I'll give it to you straight, Rosie," I say firmly.

She swallows and blinks at my words. "So if you don't have girlfriends, do you have regular girls for sex?"

I roll my lips inward. "Yes, I use an escort agency that takes care of my needs. Or did, before you."

We ride in silence the rest of the way to her house, and I pull up out front, killing the lights and engine. "Thank you for driving me home," she says softly. "And tonight," she adds, her eyes drifting down to her lap. "I don't expect anything from you, and understand if this is a one-time thing." Her voice is low, not quite a whisper.

"What?" I ask, wondering if she's misread this entire evening.

"You know, do the innocent virgin a favor and all..." She trails off, her voice uncertain.

I unclip her seat belt and pull her by the chin so she's closer to me. Her eyes widen as they fix on mine.

"I may have taken your virginity, little one, but I'm nowhere near done with you yet," I assure her.

"Oh." She breathes out, and the warmth of her breath tickles my lips.

I lean in and kiss her hard on the mouth before releasing her quickly. I wait a beat for her to open her eyes. "I will give you everything your body craves, so you will be ruined for anyone after me," I promise her.

Her teeth rake across her bottom lip as she bites down. "And what will you get out of it?" she asks.

"You," I reply flatly. Rosie's eyes widen, and I can see that she's surprised by my answer. For some unexplainable reason, I'm in awe of this beautiful woman, and after tonight's admission, I feel a pull toward protecting her, even when I know she doesn't want or need it. I want to be there for her.

"Just me? And no one else?" She's asking if I'll be fucking on the side, but the thought of fucking anyone but Rosie is the furthest thing from my mind.

"I want you all to myself, Rosie, and you can have me all to yourself. Tonight was just a prelude."

"I don't want to wait till next week to see you," she says, her voice soft.

"I cannot wait that long. I'll be in touch," I whisper before we kiss again, and the heat between us ignites immediately. I pull back and say, "I have work to do, Rosie. Leave now before I change my mind and fuck you on my leather seats."

She giggles and steps out of the car. Her hand lingers on the door as she leans in to whisper, "You wouldn't want to ruin those leather seats, Vincent."

My lips quirk into a smirk as I watch her straighten and saunter to her front door. She glances back at me, her eyes alight with a playful glint before disappearing inside.

I remain in the car for a moment, savoring the scent of her on my skin and the taste of her on my lips. But soon, the reality of my work and the real reason why I'm back in town creeps back in, and I force myself to shift my focus.

Driving back to my penthouse, my mind races with the night's events. I know I shouldn't get involved with Rosie, especially with my plans to leave New York soon, but I can't help the magnetic pull I feel toward her.

When I arrive, I park the car in the garage and head inside, ready to dive into Justin's transcripts and forget about everything else. But even as I pour over the conversations with convicted Montero and Justin's planted mole in jail, my mind keeps wandering back to the brunette beauty who has somehow captured my attention and stirred something inside me.

I know I should stay away, but I also know I won't be able to resist her for long.

I can't shake the feeling that she's meant to be mine.

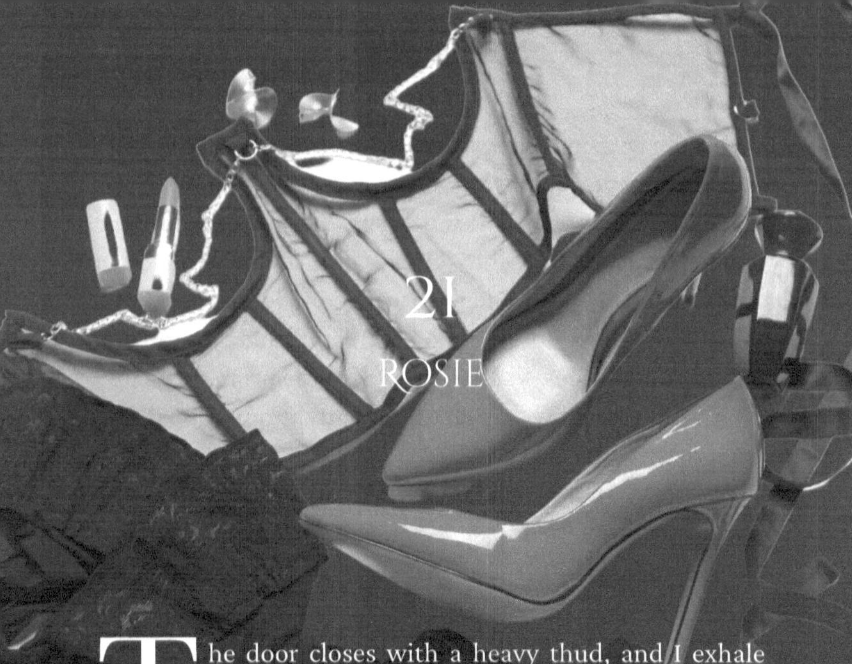

21

ROSIE

The door closes with a heavy thud, and I exhale deeply, my heart pounding in my chest, drowning out the silence of the empty house. It doesn't matter that everyone else is either asleep or out, and I can't shake the rush of heat that spreads across my skin.

I can't believe it. *I'm not a virgin anymore,* is my last thought before my eyes close, and I fall into a dreamless sleep.

When I wake, my body is sore and pulsing with remembered pleasure. It wasn't a dream. Vincent Slater took my virginity, and it was a mind-blowing experience.

I giggle into the sheets, still feeling the tingling sensation in my body. Forget the idea of waiting for the perfect man and falling in love. Desire won in the end, and I'm happy to have lost my V-card to a man like Vincent Slater.

The romantic part of me, nurtured by reading Shakespeare, Darcy, and Brontë, was slowly dying as I watched my roommates engage in meaningless hookups and was approached by men who held no interest for me. Vincent Slater was different.

For starters, Vincent didn't run when I confessed to being a virgin. He was powerful and dirty, and he knew how to fuck. That was enough to turn me on and push aside any notions of traditional romance.

I can't help but wonder what's in store for us.

Would he stay true to his word?

Would I be able to handle the intensity of our connection?

All I know is that, for now, I'm completely and utterly under his spell. And as I close my eyes and let out a contented sigh, I know I want more.

So much more.

"I will give you everything your body craves, so you will be ruined for anyone after me."

I already knew he was right. Vincent Slater already knew my body inside out. It's as if he has a roadmap to every inch of me, then it hits me.

He is going to be returning to London.

Between school, my internship, and extra shifts at the Vanilla Club, It's been a while since I've caught up with Sara.

I'm in the kitchen when I hear movement from Ethan's room, which means he has company. I hope it's Sara. *God, what if it's not?* I don't want to catch him with someone else. Suddenly, the door flies open and out walks Sara with a bright blush on her cheeks.

I'm relieved to see her face.

"You naughty little minx!" I laugh at the sight of her, knowing exactly what she's been up to.

Sara smiles and sits on the stool beside me. "I know."

She giggles, and I hug her. "Ethan said you caught him sneaking out of my room the other day."

"You betcha. God, you even smell like Ethan." I pull away, not wanting to smell him on her.

"Oh my God, the sex, Rosie!" She giggles louder, and I can't help but feel happy for her, yet something is stopping me from telling her about my night with Vincent. I think it's because it doesn't feel real.

"I like him so much," she confesses, and I stare at her with concern.

"You do?" I ask because even though Ethan admitted he likes Sara, I'm unsure of Ethan's true intentions, and I want Sara to guard her heart.

She twists her hair as she nods. I pull her in for another hug and confess, "I'm happy for you." Because the truth is, I really am.

They are the biggest players I know— check that. Vincent Slater tops that now that I know he has a call agency he uses for sex. I let out a slow exhalation as a pang of jealousy swirls in my chest.

It's just sex, I remind myself.

Delicious, toe-curling sex.

The scent of dirty sex and sweat brings me back to the present, and I pull back from Sara in a rush, saying, "Okay, you need to scrub him off you, girl. Stat!"

She apologizes and pulls her hair back from her shoulders. "Oh God. Sorry!"

"Please just promise me one thing?" I ask as I take my coffee to my lips.

"Shoot," she says.

"I don't want to sit on any... you know..." I widen my eyes, trying to drive home my request. "This is communal furniture." I gesture to the small room with a couch, two armchairs, and a rug.

"Too late!" She throws her head back in a nervous laugh but doesn't say anything.

"Sara!" I scold her, aghast.

"Okay, so we may have done it on the couch last night," she confesses with sincere eyes, but it means nothing because I'm mortified.

My eyes dart to the couch we all sit on, and my hands palm my cheeks as I wrinkle my face in disgust.

"I swear it's clean, don't worry." She rolls her lips inward to try and stifle her giggle.

"Oh my God, seriously?"

She holds her hands up. "Okay, okay, I promise from here on out, no fucking in the communal area."

"Jesus Christ." I breathe out. "Good."

It's then that Ethan strolls out. "Morning!" He groans through a yawn.

"Morning," we reply in unison.

Something passes between them, and I feel compelled to let them have that and look away. I clasp my coffee mug and draw it to my lips.

He pulls her into his heady chest, and she wraps her arm around him.

"How did my girl sleep?" he asks lazily, and I can't help but swoon. I've never heard Ethan refer to any girl as his girl before.

"Perfectly," Sara replies sweetly, and suddenly, I feel like the third wheel.

Draining the rest of my coffee, I walk over to the machine and hit the flashing button. I need another.

"Tonight is the charity ball," Ethan says to no one in particular.

"I wish I could go with you." Sara lets out a low grumble over the purr of the coffee machine. "You know how persistent my parents can be."

I turn and rest against the counter, taking my steaming cup of coffee to my lips. The steam billows over the edge, and it's the nearest thing to a facial I've had in years. "Don't mess with her parents," I say, aiming my bullet stare directly at Ethan. There's a not-so-subtle nod I give him.

He narrows his eyes. "It's a good thing you're coming with me then, so Sara doesn't need to disappoint her parents." He smirks devilishly.

I had thought about the ball in my limited head space, and I couldn't come up with a good enough reason to turn him down.

"Yes! I have just the gown for you too." Sara's eyes widen as she imagines this outfit in her head.

"Ugh. You know I have to work."

"What time?"

"Ten," I reply on a white lie as I turn around.

"What time?" Sara repeats in a stern voice.

Fuck, she knows I'm lying.

I slam my hand on the counter and turn around. "You should be in the CIA... you're a human lie detector sometimes."

"You know it, now spill," she counters.

"Fine. I start at midnight."

"Perfect," Ethan says triumphantly.

"Dress her well, Sara. This is fancy as fuck," he says, and I roll my eyes at his back as he walks out of the kitchen and back to his room.

"Come back to bed, Sara," he says, his voice disappearing down the hallway.

Okay, third wheel here. I frown. I was hoping to spend today with Sara.

She smiles widely. "He is so good in bed," she whispers from across the counter.

"Ugh," I say.

"Honestly, you don't know what you're missing out on," she says, and I look at her surprised. "No, not with him. Okay, yes, with him." She shakes her head. "I mean sex. You being a virgin and all." She shrugs.

"Well," I say. "I had sex last night," I blurt out. And I wonder if it's because I secretly want what she has—to be part of the sex club.

"Oohh my God!" Her eyes widen in fascination. "Tell me who!" she demands, intrigued, her face lighting up.

"Just a guy from my internship," I quickly say with a steady delivery. Well, I'm not lying, *exactly*.

"Sara!" Ethan's voice yells from the bedroom. "I have wood I need taken care of."

"Oh my God!" I yell back. "Seriously?" I look at Sara, and she's in hysterics laughing.

She launches off the stool. "I want to hear all about him. Just a little later, okay?"

"Sure." I drink the remainder of my coffee, but I'm already scouting the keys, ready to leave the house.

I cannot be here knowing they are fucking in the room next door.

As I stare at my reflection, I'm taken aback by the sight before me. The navy blue sequined dress hugs my curves so tightly that breathing feels like a luxury. But it's worth it, as the sweetheart neckline accentuates just the right amount of cleavage. Loose waves cascade down my shoulders, adding a touch of glamour to the look. I strut in my strappy heels, which are so high that they'd make a lesser woman tremble, but I'm a pro at walking in them, thanks to my experience at the Vanilla Club. And my makeup? It's a subtle kind of pretty—pale pink eyeshadow highlighting the green of my eyes, with a catlike eyeliner completing the look.

When Sara and Ethan walk in, their jaws drop in unison as they take me in.

"Holy shit," Ethan whisper-shouts. "You scrub up well, Rosie."

He's wearing a navy suit, his short blond hair coiffed neatly atop his head.

Sara had insisted on color-matching us for tonight's ball, and at such short notice, she pulled it off.

"So do you." I widen my eyes at the view. He is a handsome guy, and there's no wonder women fall at his feet.

"Don't get any ideas," Sara says, whipsawing between us. "Oh, hang on... wait..."

I shake my head, begging her not to say anything. I play along, hoping she remains silent about spilling that I'm not a virgin anymore. In the brief moment we had this evening to chat, I admitted it was nothing but a fling and quickly moved on from the topic.

"Please." I roll my eyes because as much of a nice guy Ethan is, there's no way I'd ever go there. He's more like a brother than my own brother sometimes.

"Virgins are like kryptonite!" he preaches while swiping his finger side to side.

I let out a groan. "I don't have to go to this thing with you," I say.

"You know you want to. All the big CEOs will be there. And I know how much you want to mingle."

"I'm not in the mood to mingle," I say as my eyes drift back to my reflection.

"Don't worry. They will come to you," Sara scoffs, and I can't help but smirk.

She thrusts a golden clutch into my hand. "Take this," she says, and as I take it in my hands, I instantly recognize it.

It's her Louis Vuitton purse, and as much as I should say no, I can't. "Oh my God, thank you!" I squeal and give her a hug.

She squeezes the bag, then lets me go abruptly. "Oh, I almost forgot." She disappears, and I hear her rustling around.

"Hurry up, Sara, we have to go," Ethan says, slipping his phone from his suit jacket and beginning to scroll.

I hear her walking back from her bedroom, holding up tear-drop earrings. "These will go perfectly."

"When did you get these?" I say, threading them through my fingers. There are five drop diamonds with a sapphire in between.

"Don't worry, they are fake," she muses out loud. "But no one will know."

A smile crosses my lips. "I don't care if they are. They are stunning," I say, taking them to my ear and sliding one inside the hole, then the other. I clip the backs and pull my hair over my ear, admiring them. "They are beautiful," I mutter.

"Whoa." Sara is watching me in my reflection. "Now you're ready," she says with a satisfactory nod.

"Thank you," I say, pulling her in for a hug. My movement is restricted as the dress claws around my waist, sucking every inch of space between my skin and fabric.

"Oh God, I don't think I can eat a thing in this." She releases me and laughs. Ethan raises an eyebrow.

"That was always so tight on me," she says wistfully.

"And you're tinier than me," I say in jest.

"Yup!" We laugh, and it hurts.

"Oh God, don't make me laugh. I have no room for that in here."

We walk into the large ballroom, and my mouth drops open in awe. I've never seen anything like this, and I'm clearly living under a rock with the peasants.

Crystal chandeliers hang from the ceilings over each of the round tables draped in crisp linens. Lilac and cloud-white orchids spill from tall vase centerpieces as a live orchestra plays classical music, welcoming the mingling guests.

There is serious money here, and suddenly I feel self-conscious and out of place. As if reading my mind, Ethan takes my hand in his. I look down at him in surprise. "Stop fidgeting," he says with a brooding smile.

I smile back, thankful for his friendly gesture. "Come on, let's do a lap," he says, squeezing my hand in his.

"Okay," I mumble hesitantly.

"Relax, princess. I'll have you home before midnight."

"My carriage will take me to the Vanilla Club." I laugh.

"Who knew Cinderella moonlit as a lingerie waitress." Ethan laughs, and I smile, suddenly feeling more relaxed.

"That's Connor and Lourde Diamond," he says, and I

follow his gaze to where he is tilting his head and nodding hello at a gorgeous brunette.

"She's stunning," I admit, as her genuine smile flickers from Ethan to me.

"They are brother and sister and heirs to the Diamond Media fortune. Their parents host this event every year, and it's the ticket on everyone's social calendar."

I turn to him. "I thought this was a business ball."

"Philanthropy and big business go hand in hand, just like wet sheets to a teenage boy."

"Ew, gross," I scoff as he chuckles beside me.

I squeeze his arm, thankful for the invite, as he introduces me to one important person after the next. He's right. Everyone who is anyone is here. I've just met three CEOs of Fortune 500 companies and their wives.

We coast through the large expanse of arched flowers, and it just dawns on me to ask Ethan an important question. "So, how did you get this invite?"

"I didn't. I'm here in place of my parents, who are in Rome."

"And how did they get a ticket?" I ask, realizing all I know about Ethan is that his parents own their own business, but that is the extent of it.

He takes two glasses of champagne from the waiter, who walks past and passes one to me. I sip the champagne, and damn, it tastes delicious, unlike the stuff I drink.

"Well, because they are worth two hundred million," he says casually, and I choke on the next mouthful of champagne. I suck it down without spitting it out and take a lungful of needed air.

I jerk on his arm, and he turns abruptly. "What the hell? I knew you were rich, but that's..." I shake my head. That amount of wealth is mind-blowing. There are too many zeroes, I can't even imagine that amount of wealth.

"I don't tell many people because of that very reaction." His features morph into a scowl.

"Does Sara know?" I ask in a whisper because I am in serious shock.

Why does he rent with us in our modest house, eat noodles, and drink the cheap wine I buy?

"No, not yet. I try to live my own life."

My eyebrows pinch together in confusion, and as if reading my mind, he continues, "I like her. I don't want this getting in the way. She knows my parents own a large company, but that's about it."

I smile into my drink. He really does care for Sara, and I melt a little.

He continues to point out noteworthy people of importance, and we stop to say hello to a few more people before he dips his head toward a group of men ahead. "And there are the Slater brothers." My heart stops as I stare in their direction.

Vincent's brother, Julius, is staring directly at me while I see the shape and cut of Vincent's back. He is engrossed in conversation with an older man and hasn't seen me.

Julius offers a wave, and I falter. Then he leans in, whispering something to Vincent, and smiles. Vincent turns, and his dark eyes feverishly find mine in less than a second. His stare is fierce and ignites something within me that spreads like wildfire across my skin, sending every single nerve-ending alight.

Then his eyes flicker to Ethan's, and I realize I'm still holding his hand. *Dammit.* Last night, Vincent gave me multiple orgasms, and tonight it looks like I'm with another man. *What must he think?*

"Why is Vincent Slater staring at you?" Ethan turns to me, his grip tightening. "Do you know him?"

My skin gives rise to thousands of goose bumps, and the heart in my chest feels like it's going to explode out of this goddamn dress I'm wearing. Suddenly, I get the urge to flee. I give a feeble wave to not seem impolite, then tug the crook of his elbow and head for the opposite side of the ballroom.

"Shit!" I mutter under my breath. "Don't you listen to anything I say?" My voice is angry, but I'm not frustrated with Ethan. I'm furious with myself for getting myself in another situation that would piss Vincent off.

He stops me when we are out from underneath Vincent's excruciating glare. Ethan turns to me. "What the fuck is going on, Rosie? Do you know Vincent?"

"Yes." I breathe out, slightly dizzy from holding my breath. "My internship is with Slater Corp." My eyes raise in a question. I did tell him this.

His lips curl to the side as he chews the inside of his cheek. "Now that rings a bell."

"No shit, that rings a bell," I blurt out, my head in a flurry of emotions.

I practically accost the waiter walking past me and swipe another champagne from the tray. I lug it down, draining the contents in one go.

"Okay, slow down, Cinderella. Do you want to tell me what's going on and why Vincent was glaring at me like he was going to take me out back and bury me with bullet holes?"

"Not really," I say with a scowl. I really don't want to discuss anything about Vincent Slater when I feel his eyes all over me. Also, Ethan is my friend, but he's not the kind of friend you can curl up with a cup of tea and air your dirty laundry to.

"Fine," he says coolly, looking over my shoulder. "I spot Mr. and Mrs. Devigne, and they are calling me over."

"Oh God, take me with you," I beg, not wanting Vincent to tear strips off me.

"Of course. Mingle. That's what we're here for and forget about the Slaters. He won't miss you in this sea of pussy."

"Jesus Christ," I mutter, my eyes widening to the size of saucers at his admission. "I thought you liked Sara."

"Oh, I do. But a guy can look," he says mischievously. "Just like Vincent Slater was eye-fucking you too. Don't think it's just you. Vincent has a reputation."

Oh God, not you too.

"Those boys put the *P* in playboy." He leans closer and whispers, "If he knew you were a little virgin..." He laughs, letting the sentence hang in the air.

A chuckle escapes me as I struggle to compose myself. Ethan shoots me a sideways glance and scowls before leading me through the bustling crowd toward an elderly lady bedazzled in diamonds, beckoning us over.

As we chat with the lady and her husband, my mind can't help but wander back to Vincent and his intense gaze. I can still feel the heat of his eyes on me, and it sends a shiver down my spine.

I take a deep breath and force myself to focus on the conversation at hand. After a while, Ethan and I excuse ourselves and continue to mingle, meeting more important people and making small talk.

But no matter how hard I try, I can't shake off the feeling that Vincent is watching me from somewhere. It's like his gaze is imprinted on me, and I can't escape it.

We've finished dinner, and while Ethan indulged in a sumptuous three-course meal of silky, buttery pastry, white fish, and truffles prepared by a world-renowned chef, I'm so famished I could eat a horse and its offspring. Still, I won't risk busting a seam open, no matter how delicious the parfait looks.

Vincent's intense gaze on me only adds to my jealousy. I can't tell if he's angry with me or if he's imagining what it would be like to have me at his mercy. I secretly hope it's the latter.

Seeing how easily the Slater brothers attract gorgeous women like moths to a flame is maddening. They bask in the attention shamelessly, and it's no wonder I feel like I'm on the outside looking in.

All night I've been a bundle of nerves, watching Vincent and Julius with their harem of women, desperately wishing I was the one by Vincent's side. But he hasn't even bothered to come over and speak to me, and I refuse to be just another one of his conquests.

At least Vincent doesn't look pleased about it. Julius, on the other hand, is loving it.

I've had the opportunity to meet and network with numerous influential individuals tonight, gaining valuable insights into the corporate world. A few CEOs even expressed interest in potential employment opportunities for me after I complete my final semester of studies.

Of course, there was also some touching and grabbing, but I like to think they were simply being friendly. After all, their wives were likely nearby, probably mingling around the Slater brothers. Despite all this, I choose to remain naïve and resist accepting that all men are deceitful creatures.

Guzzling down the remnants of my champagne, I'm

pleasantly tipsy, but the fact I didn't eat anything for dinner is starting to hit me. I need to sober up before my shift at the Vanilla Club. I can't afford to lose my job there.

A towering presence looms behind me, and the scent of his expensive cologne wafts through the air. A smile creeps onto my face, unable to resist the comforting familiarity of his aroma.

Vincent always manages to make my heart skip a beat. I had been hoping to avoid him all night, but now that he's here, nerves flutter in the pit of my stomach.

I turn to face him, and he slides into the empty seat beside me where Ethan had been sitting earlier. "Well, aren't you something," he says, his eyes roaming down my body teasingly. The heat rises to my cheeks as I try to play it cool.

"It's the dress," I say with a half-laugh.

But damn, he is the one that's fire. His tuxedo fits him like a glove, accentuating every curve of his body. His broad shoulders are practically bursting out of the jacket, and his dark hair is styled to perfection. As his intense green eyes lock onto mine, I can't help but feel a little weak in the knees.

He leans in close to me, his voice commanding. "I don't know who that man is on your arm, Rosie, but I forbid it."

22

Vincent

The words leave my mouth quickly, and even quicker is her reaction.

"You forbid it?" Her beautiful eyes widen as she mocks in a question.

"I don't know what games you're playing, Rosie."

"I'm not playing any games. I assure you," she defends with a knowing nod. Her hands fall into her lap, and her thumbs fidget. I watch her as she does this and snap them apart.

I make her nervous. It's not my intention to, but she just drives me mad.

I've never let myself care for a woman before Rosie, then she goes and does this?

When my brother told me to turn around, she was the last person I expected to see.

She looks absolutely beautiful. Her soft hair cascades down her shoulders, and her natural makeup shows off her smooth skin and full lips.

I did a double-take when I saw her. And that something inside of me that I pushed to the furthest points of my ribcage twinges. Then I saw him. A young good-looking blond man holding her hand, and my mind swirls with a million different scenarios. None of which are good.

She was in my bed last night, and now she's holding hands with him. If we weren't at such a noble charity ball, I wouldn't be holding myself back from launching at him and finding out who he is.

My brother sensed it, too, distracting me with beautiful women all night. Leaving was futile between him, Caleb, and the women vying for our attention.

Except here I am, and I won't let her go anywhere until I find out who the hell this man is.

"Last night, I took your virginity, and tonight you're holding onto another man. You have a date." I sneer, barely able to control my rage.

"Calm down," she says, taking stock of the vein protruding from my neck. "He's not a date... he's my roommate."

What the fuck? Her roommate?

"He's a friend," she bites back in reply, and I should be more at ease with her words than I am. *But they fucking live together?*

I'm agitated and fucking pent up with rage. What is it about this woman that gets my balls in a knot and sends my mind into overdrive?

"You're one to talk," she says and seems looser than normal with her speech. *Is she tipsy?* My gaze flickers to the empty glass of champagne in front of her.

I shake my head. Now she's drinking too? "I didn't come here with a date, Rosie," I state.

She throws her hands up in the air, obviously not caring that we are in a public space with prying eyes and open ears. "I told you he's my roommate," she says louder this time.

Restlessly swiping a stray hair from her face, she looks around for someone, probably the guy she arrived with. "Where's your *roommate* now?" I tease. This conversation is not going as I planned. I want to take her to bed and fuck her senseless.

"You don't own me, Vincent," she says. "You'll be back in London in a few weeks, back to your call girls."

The thought puts me on edge more than it should. "It doesn't mean I don't care about you." Her hazel eyes soften. "I'm sorry. I just saw you with him and didn't know what to think." I shake my head, trying to get a grip on these feelings I have.

"We're just friends," she whispers reassuringly, and the way she's looking at me has me believing anything that comes out of her mouth.

"Let me make it up to you," I lean forward and reply in a dark whisper.

"Mr. Slater, I'd love you to, except I'm working tonight."

I quickly force a smile and swallow down my jealousy. "Is there anything I can do to stop you from working at the Vanilla Club?" I ask.

She shakes her head. "You know I don't have a choice," she reminds me.

"I can pay back your brother's debt."

She lets out a laugh, but I'm not. "You're serious?"

"Deadly. I don't like you working there."

"I don't have a choice," she rounds out on a huff before adding, "Gabriel got me in this mess, and I'm determined to get myself out of it."

I quickly lift the scowl, settling on my features. Rosie is fiercely determined. It's what attracted me to her in the first place. But if she doesn't want my help, I can't help her. Nor can I stop her from working there and getting eye-fucked by strangers.

I need to take control of my emotions and create some space between us, even if it is just for tonight.

"Monday night. My place," I say, and her hazel eyes soften just as a booming voice interrupts over the sound system, and a light shines on the podium on the stage.

"Ladies and Gentlemen, please take your seats. Our last auction item is about to begin, and we save the best for last."

I curse under my breath, wanting to spend more time with her.

"Excuse me, Mr. Slater, you're in my seat." Her roommate stares down at me, and Rosie straightens, putting space between us.

Ignoring him, I keep my eyes locked on her. "This conversation isn't over, little one," I tease, leaning forward to capture her attention. Her guard momentarily slips, and I am flooded with warmth.

Reluctantly, I stand to face the interruption in front of me. "And you are?" I inquire.

"Ethan Sanderson."

I recognize the name instantly, and it takes only a moment to realize who he is. The Sandersons, owners of a textile business. "Son of Darla and Duke?" I ask.

"That's me," he replies, staring back at me confidently.

I smile, familiar with his family's business as our company has had dealings with one of their competitors. A small family business turned wealthy.

"We're not for sale," he retorts as he takes his seat.

I grin, impressed by his confidence, reminding me of myself at his age. "Everyone has a price," I say with a smirk.

He scowls, but I turn away and head back to my table without another glance.

The gentlemen around us raise their paddle sticks with their auctioneer numbers on them, getting excited. They believe they have it in the bag, competing against each other at lightning speed. A smile traces my lips, enjoying the game of cat and mouse.

Sipping on my Hennessy, I watch as the bidding for a weekend in St. Barts rapidly increases in price. My brother turns to look at me, nodding with his eyes wide.

I shake my head, and Caleb on my right chuckles quietly, just loud enough for us to hear.

The man with the paddle raises his hand again, offering another thousand dollars to round out the bidding to one hundred thousand dollars.

His weak offer is more than his competitor's, but it sends the weakest message of all. He's tapped out, even with his winning bid. Connor Diamond holds the auctioneer hammer in his hand. He raises it, and my brother shoots me a what-the-fuck-are-you-waiting-for glare. I drain the rest of my Hennessy and set it down.

"Going once, twice, and three times..." Connor pauses, and I wait. He scans the room, and I watch the highest bidder act like he's won the damn prize already. Then, I raise my paddle. "Two hundred thousand," my voice booms around the room, drawing gasps thick and fast.

My brother chuckles, and Caleb remarks, "Vincent strikes again, ruthless as ever."

The bald man turns to face me, and his expression drains of color as he recognizes me.

"Well, well, well, Mr. Slater, what a bid," exclaims the auctioneer.

I shoot a glare at the underbidder, daring him to make a move.

Connor Diamond continues with the auction, "I have two hundred thousand dollars, going once. Going twice…"

He raises his hammer and looks toward the weak bidder. With a shake of his head, he accepts defeat.

"Sold to Vincent Slater of Slater Corp!" announces Connor as he slams down the hammer, and cheers erupt throughout the ballroom.

As I glance over at Rosie, I notice an expression on her face that I can't quite decipher. Her arms are folded across her chest. *Is she angry with me?*

The thought of taking her away to St. Barts, pampering her with every luxury, and making her unable to walk straight for a week flashes through my mind.

Maybe that's exactly what I'll do.

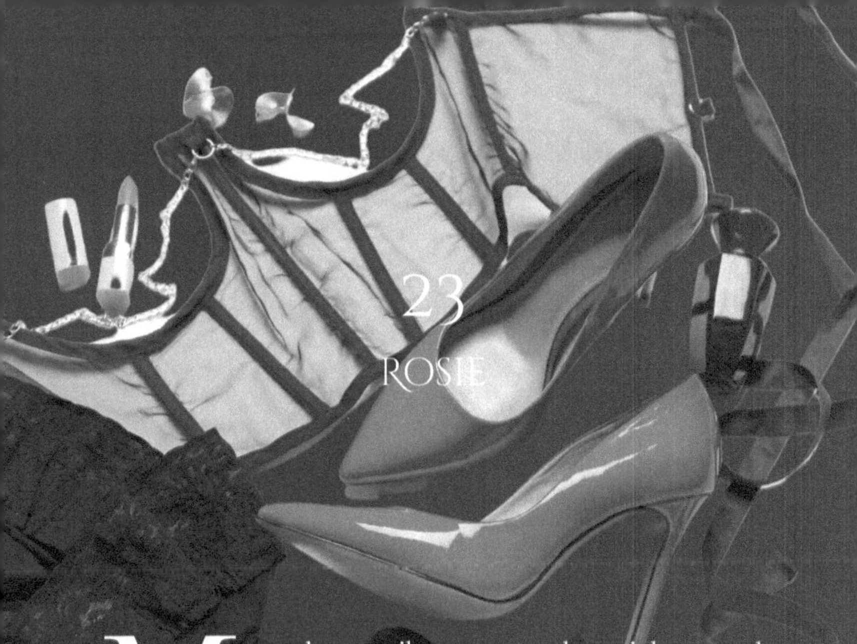

23

ROSIE

My phone vibrates on the night stand, interrupting my thoughts, and I reluctantly answer it, wanting to hold onto the memories a little longer.

"Hello?" I say into the receiver.

"It's me, sis." My brother's voice comes through.

"Oh, hey, Gabe," I respond, rubbing my eyes. *What time is it?*

The amount of light flooding my room suggests it's late, but since my shift finished at four in the morning, it should be expected. If it weren't for Vincent's driver waiting for me after work to take me home, I would have been even later.

"Where are you?" His tone is clipped, and suddenly, I sit upright. It's Sunday, and we had plans to meet for coffee.

Shit.

My brother lives in Silverton, which is on the west side of Jersey and considered the wrong side of the tracks. He said he would be in Saddle Hills on Sunday, so we had made plans to meet up during the week.

"Shit! Sorry, I overslept," I mutter sheepishly.

215

"Fuck's sake!" he shouts, and I jerk the phone away from my ear in surprise. Before I can reply, he continues. "Look, sorry, that's fine. I'll just come to you. I'll be there in fifteen."

The phone goes dead, and I'm left staring at it for a moment in disbelief.

Since when does he get angry like that?

I quickly slip out of the sheets and take a sip of water from the bottle on my nightstand. The memory of Vincent in his tuxedo last night and the way his possessiveness softened when he admitted that he cared for me has me smiling. I know I shouldn't feel like there's something more between us, but I can't help it. He's leaving soon, and I'll probably never see him again.

I change into denim shorts and a ribbed T-shirt, then moisturize my bare face and brush my long hair, smoothing it to the side.

As I step out of my room, there is a sudden knock on the front door. I glance around, but I don't think anyone's home. It's ten o'clock, so I assume Sara and Ethan have gone to the Sunday markets. Although, it's strange that their door is closed.

Walking to the front door, I open it to see a shadow of my brother standing in the door frame, but his usually handsome face appears crestfallen and weighed down. Purple bags hang heavily under his blue eyes, giving him a gaunt appearance.

He greets me with a groan as he walks past me into the house, kissing me on the cheek. "Hey, sis."

I respond with equal coolness. To be honest, I'm not in the mood for my brother. I want to bask in the memories of last night, holding onto them for just a bit longer. In other words, I want to be selfish and not deal with *his* bullshit.

I shut the door and make my way to the kitchen to pour us each a glass of water.

"You got anything stronger?" he asks with a laugh.

I check the clock. "It's only ten in the morning."

"It's five o'clock somewhere, right?" he jokes, and I thrust the glass of water in front of him.

"Dad used to say that," I recall with disappointment.

"Yup," he says, slamming down the water like it's the last glass before diving into the desert.

"Dad's a drunk, brother," I say, assessing him. Neither of us has spoken to Dad in over ten years. He isn't part of our lives, and that's just fine by me.

"What the fuck is going on? You look like shit." I'm straightforward and abrupt, but I don't care. My brother looks terrible, and I'm all he's got. If I can't tell him the truth, who will?

"I'm fine." He shrugs off my question but is lost in thought.

"Clearly, you're not," I snap back. I'm hungry and impatient, so I open the cookie jar, dig my hand in to fetch a chocolate chip delight, then pass the jar over to him.

I pick off the chocolate buds and eat them first.

He takes a bite. "These are not as good as Mom's were," he says, and a flicker of sadness passes over his pale skin.

I let out a sigh. "Mom sure knew how to bake," I reply solemnly. I reach out my hand across the counter to his. "What's going on?" I ask gently.

"I've just got some people breathing down my neck, sis."

"Who, the loan shark or someone else?"

Gabriel isn't a stranger to trouble. He has gotten involved with the wrong crowd after Mom's death, but I thought it was just him rebelling and mourning her.

"You know I don't want to involve you in my mess," he says, casting his eyes low to avoid me.

"Fuck that! You involved me the minute you asked me for financial help," I say, raising my voice in irritation. We're past that point.

"Rosie, you don't want to know," he says, snapping his hand away and coming to stand. There's a silence that descends over us, and I don't like it. I don't like this space between us.

We were always so close. Since a young age, we were only there for each other. If he's in trouble, I can help.

"Wait there," I say.

I stride toward my bedroom with a clear purpose in mind. I reach into my closet, past my favorite romance novels, and grab my tin box. On my bed, I open it and take out as much cash as I can, leaving myself enough for rent and essentials before closing it back up.

Returning to the kitchen with wads of cash in my hand, I hold them up and say, "Here, take it."

He stares at the money in my hands, and there's a flicker of relief in his eyes, though it quickly fades. "I can't take this," he says, crestfallen. His once-handsome features, with blue eyes, sandy blond hair, and a strong jaw, have morphed into those of a broken man. I force the money into his hands, and he reluctantly takes it from me. "Rosie," he says in a low voice.

"I'm working more shifts next week at the Vanilla Club, so I'll send more as soon as I get it, okay?" He's taller than me but seems so slight today. "Thanks, Rosie," he says in defeat.

"How much more?" I ask almost begrudgingly because I need to know what level of shitstorm he is in.

"A lot," he says, but his eyes don't meet mine.

"What the hell?" I raise my hands above my head. "I thought you were paying off your loan with the loan shark. What the fuck have you done now?" My voice is raised, but that's only because I'm scared of losing the only other family member I have.

"*Rosie.* It doesn't concern you."

"Damn right, it does," I snap. I've always been the bossier of us, even though he is older, and I'm not going to stop now.

"You're not going to let this up, are you?"

I raise my eyebrows, my hands landing on my hips as I wait for his response with a scowl.

"I'm in deep with the wrong crowd, sis."

"Are they from Silvertown?"

He nods, and I cringe. "Mafia trouble?" The Angelinos are the mafia family that runs that side of town. Everyone knows it but chooses to ignore it until it affects them. He doesn't have to say it. It's apparent in his eyes.

"Fuck, what have you done!" I say in exasperation. "Just move here," I offer, knowing that's not going to solve anything, but if he's closer to me, then maybe I can keep an eye on him more.

He laughs at my naive request. "Not that simple, sis." He shakes his head and tucks the cash into his back pocket.

I stare at him. His worn jeans are old, and his shirt is crumpled. He smells of cigarettes, and he's skinny. Too skinny.

"Hey, it was nice to see you, sis," he says. "You look really well," he adds with a smile.

"Thanks," I reply, but I am distracted, unsure how I can alleviate his problems.

"How's that internship going you were telling me

about?" he asks, grabbing one last cookie before heading toward the front door.

"Huh?"

"The internship?"

"Oh, it's great. I really like it, but you know me, I love everything to do with the world of big business."

"You were always the clever one," he says with a wink. "Got that from Mom's side," he adds as his smile slips.

He's nearly out the door now, and I'm following him. "Hey, why don't you stay a little longer?" I ask because I'm trying to seriously problem-solve a way out of his issues, but I need more time. "I can make us some sandwiches."

"People to see, places to go," he says and leans in to kiss my cheek.

"See you soon?" I say, but it comes out as more of a question because I really don't want my brother to go.

"Sure," he replies, but he's pulling away. Sadness sweeps over me as he descends the stairs two at a time and disappears out of sight.

I'm still in my head when I hear a rustling inside. Someone's here. *Shit.* I close the door quietly and turn around to find Ethan and Sara staring at me.

I know that look. They don't like my brother. They've met him numerous times before and aren't afraid to come forward with their mutual dislike for him.

"Don't look at me like that," I say and peel myself off the back of the door.

Now I need a coffee.

I walk past them, lift the black plastic handle of the percolator, and pour a steaming cup of coffee into my favorite polka-dot mug.

With my back turned, they sit at the counter, the sliding of stools echoing in the small space.

"You work your ass off, and you just give him your money?" Sara observes with a sigh. "I don't get it. You're so smart, Rosie, but with him..." She lets her voice trail off into the silence.

I turn and rest against the counter. Sara and Ethan look like they've been having sex all night. Her hair is matted and wild, and if I'm not mistaken, there's a hickey on her neck she tried to cover up with her top, but it's peeking out.

Ethan at least has a shirt on, but his hair is wild, and he appears completely relaxed except for the scowl he plastered on his face.

"Look, he's in trouble," I say.

"He's always in trouble," Ethan states, taking a hand to his tousled hair.

"He's older than you! Let him sort his own shit out," Sara says.

"I'm all he's got," I defend with more force than I mean to.

"I know," she says quietly. She turns to Ethan and puts her hand in the crook of his elbow. "We just worry about you, that's all."

I let out a deep sigh. "I'm fine," I say. "Thank you, but I'm fine," I repeat. "I think he's in serious trouble," I share, worry setting in. "Anyway, let's talk about something else."

"Uh-huh. Yes, let's," Sara says.

I shake my head subtly and whisper, "Not in front of Ethan."

She looks at me cryptically before pulling Ethan close to her. "Ethan, sweet pea, you promised me you'd get me that almond chai and a croissant for breakfast?" She looks at him with come-fuck-me eyes, and I giggle.

He scowls momentarily before pulling her in for a passionate kiss. "Be right back."

She waits for the door to click shut, then says, "'Okay, spill, what's the dirt on your sex god?"

I let out a laugh. Keeping Vincent a secret from Sara is hard, but I feel it's necessary. Just because if I tell her who the man is that I lost my virginity to, it feels real. And that scares me. It scares me because I've never had anyone before, and Vincent, he makes me feel a spectrum of emotions that have me questioning what we really are to one another. I don't think I can handle Sara's questions too.

Sara raises an eyebrow at me. "Amazing? What does that mean?"

I take a sip of my coffee to stall for time, trying to come up with a non-committal response. "Just that he's a really interesting person."

She fakes a yawn. "Oh, boring! Come on, at least tell me something saucy."

I roll my lips inward and blush.

"Oh, hello!" she yells out. "What is it?"

"He is very possessive, and I think I like that."

"What, in the bedroom?" she asks wide-eyed.

"Yes, it's such a turn-on. I kinda want more of it."

"Rosie has a kink! Good. About time you explored your own sexuality."

"I guess," I say, biting my lip.

"Is he older?"

I nod. "Yes."

She narrows her eyes. "So he has experience then?"

"A ton of experience," I admit with a giggle.

Well, you get pounded by him for as long as you can," she says with a dirty grin. " 'Cause let me tell you, there are serious duds out there."

"I bet," I say, thinking about Vincent's long, thick dick and how much I miss it.

"So when am I going to meet the man who's making you blow like Krakatoa?"

We chuckle. "Soon," I say, clearly lying. Because the truth is, this perfect specimen of a man will be flying back to London in a matter of weeks, and all this will be a distant memory.

A sense of melancholy washes over me just as the door clicks.

Ethan enters carrying a bag of fresh pastries and a tray of coffees. "What did I miss?" he inquires as Sara releases a hearty laugh.

"Nothing. Absolutely nothing."

24
VINCENT

All day I've been thinking about sinking myself deep inside her. It's amazing how much this unassuming wallflower has been on my mind since the charity ball.

Today, Rosie looks stunning with her light brown hair styled in a sleek top bun, hazel eyes accentuated with layers of mascara, and bare lips that appear temptingly pouty. Her attire comprises a black high-neck blouse, tight black skirt, and black stockings.

She and four other interns are intensely focused on the task I assigned them.

Despite my awareness of the need to be cautious, I have found myself repeatedly glancing at her when nobody is looking. It's a complicated situation since I'll be returning to London soon, and any man would be fortunate to be involved with a strong and intelligent woman like Rosie. And the fact she works at the Vanilla Club has become clearer to me. She's not just beautiful and smart but also fiercely protective of her brother and willing to jeopardize her safety to help him. I'm in awe of her independence but also frustrated since I could easily alleviate her concerns if she would accept my financial assistance. Nonetheless, she's not like the other women I've encountered, and I'm considering this when a blonde enters my peripheral vision.

Fae is in my face again, and I'm irritated that it's not Rosie chasing me instead. "I've been calling you, Mr. Slater," she says, batting her fake eyelashes at me. "Didn't you hear me?"

"What do you want, Fae?" I ask coolly, my patience waning.

She's your typical private school girl from a well-off middle-class family—some intelligence but money-hungry and a social climber. Definitely not my type.

My dick practically goes into hiding whenever she approaches

"Can you tell me if this is how you would do it?" she asks, motioning to her desk. I follow her to her desk and find the problem I've given them to work on.

As I read it, I'm not surprised. She gives the Princeton response—the carbon copy of answers. It's not wrong. It's just not good enough.

"You can do better." My response is curt. She stares at me with that daft look she has given me before. "You need to think outside the box."

"Excuse me, Mr. Slater," I hear her voice and immediately flicker to her desk. "In a minute, Rosie," I reply and notice her expression change as she looks between blondie and me.

A brief smile flickers across blondie's face, and I immediately feel remorse.

Slutty socialite. She has nothing on Rosie. Absolutely nothing.

"We don't take carbon copy elitists here. We need free thinkers, and I don't think you have it," I say, staring at her flatly.

Her twisted smile freefalls as I deliver the ruthless blow. I'm not lying. If she can't take it, she's in the wrong business. There is no room for weak emotions in the cutthroat world of mergers and acquisitions.

My gaze rises to Rosie, and I catch a hint of a smirk on her face.

Her desk is a mess as usual, with pens and pencils strewn in every direction, papers haphazardly stacked, and a coffee mug leaving a stain on the desk.

"What can I do for you, Rosie?" I ask quietly, moving closer to her and away from prying eyes.

Her eyes flicker with arousal, and she combs my body with her gaze before sucking in a sharp breath. "I'm finished," she says.

"Are you?" I say in a low voice as our eyes collide, my eyebrow arching with double meaning.

Reluctantly, I remove my focus from her and to her work, finding myself speed-reading just to return my attention to her. But I'm engrossed in her work. It's very good, and my girl deserves a reward.

I move closer to her, and my hand slides underneath her dress and up high on her thigh. She freezes momentarily but then relaxes as her lips part and her pupils dilate. The scent of orchid body wash drives me fucking crazy.

"Good work," I whisper in a low, heady voice.

Screw it.

My fingers graze her sex, and she looks at me with longing. "Eyes on the screen," I command, slipping a finger beneath her panties and plunging inside. She's so wet.

Fuck me.

I have to keep up appearances, so I point to her laptop and say loudly, "This part needs a bit more work." She moans in agreement, and I add another thick finger, watching her cheeks flush a crimson red.

"Other than that, Rosie, you've done a good job. Well done," I say, whispering, "Delayed gratification, little one."

I remove my finger and take one to my lips. Her delicious nectar fills my mouth as she looks up at me with desire-laced hazels. I remove my finger and bring it to her face.

"Suck," I command. Without waiting for a reply, I quickly nudge her mouth with another finger. She opens, and I push inside as she circles my finger with heady need. My dick throbs, and I'm barely holding it together when I imagine fucking her on the desk in front of everyone to see. I need to remove myself from temptation and get back to the class. "I have work to attend to. See you at the end of the day with your reports."

One of the boys asks, "And if we finish before then?"

"Go through it again," I snap. "And again."

I smile to myself as the elevator takes me to the executive floor. Who knew leaving London could be so much fun?

As soon as I flop into my straight-backed leather chair, I slide out my phone to message her.

Vincent: *My place, 6 o'clock. I'll send my driver to Sojos to collect you.*

That way, she can't get spotted getting picked up from the office. My brother would shoot me if he knew, but screw it. Him and his rules can take a hike.

It only takes a few minutes for a reply to bounce back.

Rosie: *I was hoping you'd say that.*

I inhale sharply, staring at the words on my screen before thumbing out a reply.

Vincent: *I need to taste you.*

I know I'm crossing the line, but I honestly can't control it. Staring at her all day has my balls blue and swollen with need.

Rosie: *Yes, Sir x*

My dick twinges against the seam of my pants as I read and reread her words. Even they make me hard. I find myself hesitant to pull my eyes away from the screen, but I reluctantly break my stare and carefully slide my phone aside.

I'm knee-deep in addressing a problem with the London office when my email pings from Justin. At the same time, my brother walks in. Ignoring him, I open the email from Justin.

"Where have you been?" he questions, sliding onto the chair opposite.

"Interning, brother," I say absentmindedly and click open the email.

I quickly read it. It's short and to the point.

From: Justin Moore
     To: Vincent Slater

I'm meeting my guy tomorrow. He has news. I will keep you updated.

J

Adrenaline courses through me. *Fuck yes.* I'm getting closer.

Soon my brother's death will not be in vain.

Soon, I will find out who was really behind the killing and why.

The scapegoat in the penitentiary was just the fall guy, and I am determined to see this through. I will have my vengeance.

"Haven't seen that look for a while," he says, and I realize I am with company.

Julius stares at me, and I know that look he's giving me. I've seen it many times before when I tried to convince Father and him to reopen the case and look harder for the actual person behind his hitman-style death.

Each time I was shut down, I was met with a steely gaze and guilt for not letting it go. How could I when deep down in my soul, I knew the person responsible had gotten away?

"What are you doing here?"

He steeples his hands in his lap and scowls. Then he lets

out a dismissive sigh. "Tell me. Fuck, brother, tell me it's not to dig up the past again."

I have two choices, lie or tell him the truth.

I smile darkly. "That fucker is going to pay."

He rakes a hand through his hair. "Fuck, Vin. Not again," he spits out. "Let our brother rest in peace. You weren't the only one affected by his death. You digging up the past affects all of us."

"So it should. You were his brother, too, even though you don't remember him. He adored you."

His lips flatten into a thin line. "I knew it was too easy to get you here. I should have questioned you. What on earth was I thinking? You would drop everything in London to intern here?" He shakes his head, but he is being tough on himself.

"I'm a terrific liar," I say with a smirk. "And turns out interning isn't a bad job," I admit, leaving out the part where I have the most fun I've had in years, and that's all to do with a specific lingerie waitress with an IQ of 122.

"Is it?" he says, raising an eyebrow in question.

I smile but say nothing.

"Don't fuck her here," he says, reading my thoughts. He is my brother, after all. "You know how strict I am on business and relationships. It fucks it all up. And we have worked so very hard not to fuck it all up," he says in a stern voice.

"Relax, brother," I say darkly. Perhaps eating her out splayed across my office desk shouldn't occupy my mind as much as it does. He pins me with a stare.

"I would appreciate it if we kept this between us," I say.

"So you don't want Father to know this time?"

"No," I say. "I don't need his bullshit guilt clouding my decisions. I will find the fucker responsible, and then I will seek retribution." My hands grip the pen in my hand, and it cracks beneath my grip.

"Seek retribution?" His eyes are wide now, full of concern. "What does that mean?"

"I'll do whatever it takes," I say, determined to destroy the person or people responsible for my brother's murder.

"Fine. I'll keep it from Father because I don't want to worry him. He's not getting any younger, you know."

I shrug. I should probably visit the old man. I called him when I arrived but haven't swung by this week to see them.

"I also know there is no stopping you, Vincent." He stands, and I join him. "You are one determined motherfucker." He smiles wistfully, then turns and heads toward the door before adding, "Just be careful."

"It's not me I'm worried about," I add with a knowing smile.

He stops, looks back at me, and shakes his head. "Promise me once this is done, even if you uncover nothing, you will move on with your life."

I stare at him in confusion. My life hasn't stopped. It's fucking flourishing—businesses, money, a thriving empire. What the hell was he talking about?

"Sure." I nod, wanting to get him out the door so I can get into the business of crucifying this motherfucker who took my brother away from me.

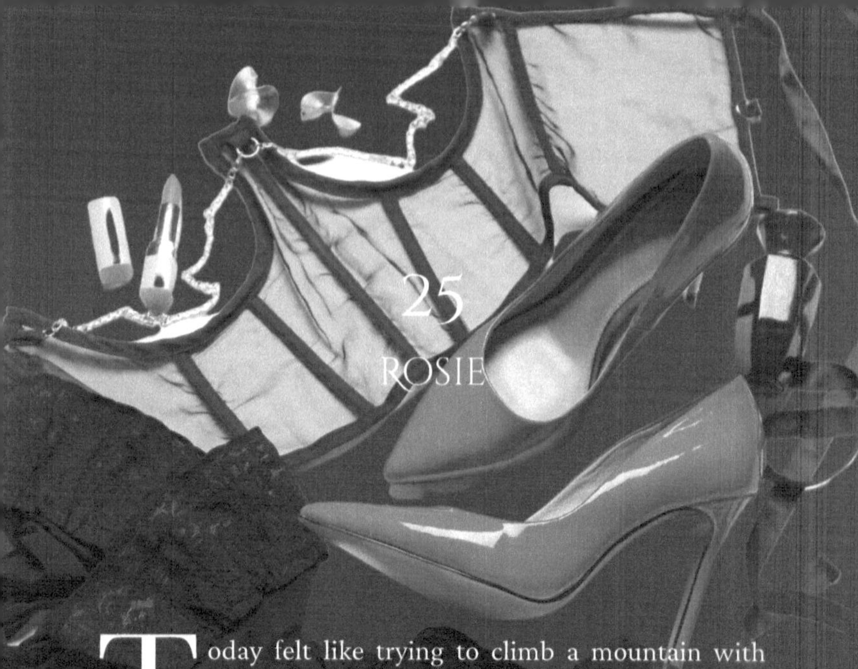

Today felt like trying to climb a mountain with weights tied to my ankles. I tried with a steely determination to focus on my internship program because that is exactly why I'm here. I need to ace the class, get offered a job after graduation, stop working at the Vanilla Club, and get on with my life. I haven't actually thought through what that looks like now we are together, but Vincent will return to London soon, and I'll be back to my own life.

Still, Vincent's sharp jaw, high cheekbones, and beautiful big green eyes have distracted me way too many times to count today. I even had to check myself a few times when bitchface, Fae, stole his attention as waves of jealousy rolled over me.

As promised, his driver collects me from the Sojos and drives me to his place, where his concierge addresses me by name. The entire drive to his penthouse, it's like he left me hanging after I tasted my arousal. The way he pushed the boundaries today was such a goddamn turn-on, and I'm so hot right now I could combust with need. He's all I can think about.

As I ascend the private elevator to Vincent's penthouse, my heart beats like a kick drum. My thumbs are clammy and moist as I clasp them together in an iron grip.

The elevator doors open, and I walk inside, my heels clicking across the floor. A moment later, he floats into view like a mirage in the Sahara.

He's lost his jacket and tie and has unbuttoned his shirt a few buttons, revealing his sun-kissed tan chest. I smile, and his eyes turn dark, hurtling my lady parts into aching overdrive.

"Come here," he growls out, beckoning me with a single finger. His voice is rough and commanding, sending shivers down my spine.

I close the distance between us, my heart pounding in my chest. His strong hand grabs the back of my head, tilting my face up to his, and he devours my mouth in a fierce, hungry kiss. It's as if he's been waiting for this all day, and I eagerly respond to his urgent need.

When he breaks away, I'm left gasping for air, my body trembling with desire. With one hand around my waist, he pulls me flush against him, and I can feel his hard, muscular frame pressing against my own.

"Hello," he murmurs, his dark eyes smoldering with lust.

"Hi," I whisper back, barely able to speak.

We stand together staring at each other, and I'm in absolute and utter awe of the man looking down at me.

"Tonight, Rosie, I'm going to show you how a real man eats," he says, his voice low and suggestive.

I quickly reply, "I've already eaten." But my words are barely audible. In truth, I don't want food. I want him to take me, teach me, and use my body in ways I never knew possible.

A devilish smile spreads across his face as he stares at me in wonder. *Oh fuck, that's not what he means.* Embarrassment swarms me, and I blush from my toes to my crown.

"I have waited all day to feast on this," he says, his hand pinching my folds over my skirt. I let out a yelp, followed by a giggle.

Oh, dear God.

Is it possible to faint from his dirty words? I feel like an idiot.

He pulls on my hand, and the next thing I know, he's dragging me down the hall and into his bedroom. He leads me over to the edge of the bed, and with one quick motion, he finds the zipper at the back of my skirt and lowers it. The black skirt slides down over my heated thighs, and he kneels before me, helping me step out of it.

My hands roam into his thick mane of dark brown hair as I stare down at him. He dives between my scrap of underwear, licking me through the lace of my thong. The fabric rubs against my clit, causing delicious friction, and I gasp at the connection.

The sensation is overwhelming, pulling another gasp followed by a moan. "Holy fuck," I whisper, unable to contain my pleasure.

He darts inside again, and I'm so aroused I think I might combust.

I'm unsteady in my heels and falter with my balance. I try to shuffle out of them, but his hand steadies my movement.

"Leave them on," he barks, and his hand circles the

backs of my thighs, holding me in place. His tongue runs down the inside of my thigh, and I quiver with anticipation. "Enough foreplay. I need you on my tongue, little one."

His hands come up to my thighs, and he pulls hard on my thong. I hear the fabric tear and sharply inhale as I look down to find a hole where my lace was once sewn together.

I'm too startled to say anything, and I watch the beautiful man take what he wants. Without warning, his strong tongue slides into my wetness, and my hands fall into his hair for support.

Feels. So. Good.

"Fuck," he mumbles against me as he drags his tongue up my folds, expertly circling my clit with just the right amount of force. I suck in a lungful of air, my hands circling the roots of his hair.

He continues his relentless assault, and my knees grow weak. My body aches and heats all over. "Vincent," I whimper, breathless.

At the sound of his name, he only intensifies his ministrations until I can't hold it any longer, and I groan as a tidal wave of an orgasm crashes over me. "Oh my God," I moan out between strangled breaths.

When I open my eyes, he's already lost his shirt and pants, standing before me with a thick and long erection. "Fuck, I could die a thousand deaths in that tight little pussy," he growls.

I moisten my lips with a quick flick of my tongue, feeling a surge of desire coursing through me. But just as quickly, a thought dawns on me.

Shit, am I supposed to...

"I need your lips around my cock," he says darkly, and my body responds with an ache that leaves me trembling with desire. "I will teach you," he adds, sensing the fear that flickers across my face.

He slips his boxers down, and his voice is coated with desire as he commands, "On your knees, little one." I do as he says, and he steps out of his briefs.

Grabbing his thick dick between my fingers, I pull it down to my lips, hoping my limited experience won't make me a complete novice.

He hisses as I sheathe my teeth and take him in all the way. As his hands take hold of my head, his fingers tangle in my hair, guiding me with firm but gentle pressure. "Take it like you own it." His commanding voice leaves me with an overwhelming need to comply. I suck harder, and he moans out in pleasure. The sound has me dripping in arousal. I adjust to the rhythm he sets, his grip tightening on my head. "Rosie," he hisses through rampant breaths. "You're a good little student, aren't you?"

I clench at his words, trying to please him even more as I continue licking and sucking his shaft. "Jesus Christ," he bites out before pulling himself out of my mouth and dragging me up to him.

Fuck, did I do something wrong?

I'm left uncertain as dark green eyes stare back at me. I watch his broad chest rise and fall like he's just run a marathon. "I don't want to come in your mouth... yet."

A flash of disappointment flickers through me.

He smirks darkly. "My girl wants to taste me?"

I nod. The thought of swallowing his release makes me drip with arousal.

"I will tell you when. Now, I want you on the bed, on your knees." He slaps me hard on the ass, and the sting reverberates between my thighs, leaving me aching with desire.

The tear of a condom packet and the slap of a condom cut through the silence, and my nerves are on edge with anticipation as I spread out on the bed, fully exposed for his viewing pleasure. He stands watching at the foot of the bed, and although I'm slightly nervous, I'm also incredibly aroused.

"Face forward." I comply, then feel the bed dip as he climbs on and behind me, his hand sliding down my spine and hovering over my ass. His mouth places hot, wet kisses down my spine as I wrestle with containing the inevitable orgasm building inside me.

Vincent gets into position, then, with one deep thrust, he's inside me. "Shit!" I squeak out from the sudden fullness of him. He's fucking me hard with no warm-up or slow intimacy like the first time.

The force has me jolting forward, and his hand quickly circles my hip bones, holding me firmly in place. His grip is bruising, but I don't care.

A strangled moan escapes at the overwhelming feeling of being owned by Vincent Slater.

He slams into me, and I'm buckling with every thrust.

"Take my cock like a good girl," he growls out.

The headboard hits the wall with furious thuds, and his hands slide up to my breasts, cradling them firmly in the palm of his hands. His grip is no less punishing, pulling me back as he pounds into me.

Sensation overload builds quickly inside me, and I can feel the heat eclipsing my body. "Holy fuck. So... good," I pant out. I'm on the edge when the pads of his fingers twist the buds of my breasts. "Oh my God! Yes, like that." I moan out in pleasure and pain as a wave of sensation takes over my body.

"Vincent!" I yell out as I come in a rush. He thrusts a few

more times, hard and fast, and as I clench around him, his cock jerks, and I know he's going to come.

"Fuck," he groans with a deep, guttural sound, slapping my ass hard as he ejaculates.

"Aah," I squeal from the sharp impact.

He lowers his head on my back while he's still inside me and kisses my spine. "I want to live inside you, even if I don't understand it," he says between intakes of air, and his possessiveness is contagious. I want him so much, even for this short time.

The bed shifts, and I turn to see him disappear into his en suite to clean up. I roll over on my back and nestle onto the soft bed linen, closing my eyes.

As I hear his footsteps, I open my eyes to find him watching me, naked and undoubtedly looking like I've just been thoroughly fucked. I can't help but wonder how I ever survived without Vincent's touch.

"I want you every night, Rosie," he says as he cleans me with a moist towel. There's a hunger in his eyes that makes my heart skip a beat.

"What?" I ask, completely caught off guard by his statement.

"Stay with me here," he clarifies, his voice deep and seductive.

I shuffle up the headboard, trying to make sense of his sudden invitation. "I can't," I say firmly. "I need to work at the Vanilla Club."

"You don't need to. I can pay your brother's debt, whatever the cost," he offers, and I can feel the weight of his words and the depth of his concern for me.

I shake my head, refusing to get him involved in my brother's shady schemes. "No, I won't allow that," I say, my voice filled with fierce determination.

He frowns, but his expression softens as he reaches out to cup my cheek. "Fine, work, but come back here afterward. I can't be away from you that long. And there's the fact that it's not safe for you to ride the subway in the middle of the night," he insists.

I let out an exaggerated sigh but a small smile tugs at the corners of my lips. It feels good to have someone care about me once in a while.

I turn to look at him, and our eyes meet. At this moment, I feel a connection to him that I can't explain. It's as if we're speaking a language that only the two of us understand.

"Okay," I say softly. "I'll stay."

We indulge in the buttery steak from Palmero's restaurant, and the conversation flows as if we've known each other for years rather than just a few weeks. We discuss his business, his sister's career, and current events. When he brings up my brother, I steer him away from the topic, and the insurmountable pressure slowly eats away at me, shift by shift. I do everything in my power to avoid the discussion altogether, and thankfully, he doesn't continue to press.

On the drive back to my place, he reaches over and rests his hand on my thigh. It feels comfortable like it belongs there. When we're together, he's not the ruthless CEO, and he makes me feel like it's just him and me in the world. "I'll ask my chauffeur to collect your things," he says as the car roars around the street.

"That's not necessary," I say. "I can just bring a bag to work."

He stares at me. "And what will that look like?"

I'm aware of my mistake. "It's pointless to send your chauffeur all the way to Jersey on my account. I can just say I'm visiting a friend in the city if anyone from the intern program asks."

"I can have him here in the morning to pick you up," he says, placing his hand on my thigh.

"Not necessary," I reply. "I'll take the subway like I do every morning and come back to yours after work."

I wonder what I'll tell Sara and Ethan. I decide to say I'm staying with a friend from the program who lives in the city. It's only temporary, anyway. As we near my house, I realize I don't want to leave him yet.

"I've never met anyone like you, Rosie," he says, and I turn to face him.

"Ditto, Mr. Slater." I purr, and he turns to me, his eyes darkening. Arousal crosses my face, and he reads me all too well.

We pull into my driveway, and he kills the engine. I know Ethan has football training on Monday nights and comes home late, and Sara is visiting her parents for dinner. It's still early, and the house is dark, so I know she isn't home yet. "Do you want to come in?" I ask, all breathy. His fingers run along the inside of my thigh, making me hot and needy.

"You know I do," he says darkly.

26

VINCENT

Her room is bright, full of books and colors bursting from every corner. It's a goddamn migraine upon entry.

I gaze at the mismatched linen, plants, and odd objects scattered on her bookshelf. Everything is clashing and chaotic.

It's so colorful it hurts my eyes.

"Fuck!" I trip over something, and she laughs, the sound sweet and hitting me somewhere between my heart and ribcage. I rub my shin, dulling the shooting pain up my leg, and the pain subsides quickly.

I watch her bend over, and my dick thickens as I imagine taking her hard and fast from behind. She scoops the fallen soil back into the potted plant before placing it back on the stand.

Who has a goddamn prickly cactus in their bedroom? She straightens, and I'm still watching her like some weirdo, unable to stop staring.

"This is me," she utters, completely comfortable in her own space and obviously clueless about her effect on me.

"It's a train wreck," I say.

She shrugs and laughs it off as she comes to sit on her floral quilt. I move toward the bookshelf, and my face falls. She's a fucking romantic. Darcy, Shakespeare, and Brontë all stare back at me. Although they've been dead for a long time, I have this gut feeling that Darcy, Shakespeare, and Brontë are all laughing at me, and I can't shake the feeling.

Dear God... Is that the Twilight *series?*

Fuck.

I swallow the lump in my throat and turn around to face her. "You believe in happy ever afters?" I ask because I'm shocked into honesty.

Her eyes widen as she crafts her answer carefully. "I do, Vincent. I... er... I did until I met you."

"Thanks," I mutter, taken aback by her words.

"No, that's not what I mean." She shakes her head, looking nervous. "You're returning to London. You don't date. There are a million red flags."

I'm reassured, but then the reassurance quickly vanishes, leaving a sting in its wake. Suddenly, there's something inside me that wants to know if we can be more.

"And if I wasn't returning to London?" I ask. Because I wonder if she's feeling this insatiable attraction that may just be more than desire. And although it's ridiculous to think I could ever be anyone's boyfriend, I need to know.

"Well, I guess if you wanted..." She pauses. "We could give it a shot?"

"A shot?" I kneel in front of her and spread her legs apart abruptly.

She stares down at me, her eyes flaring, "Uh-huh, a shot."

"If I wanted to be boyfriend material," I say with my hands in speech bubbles. "I could. Maybe I could with you, little one," I say, and I'm more surprised at her than the words that slipped out of my mouth. But this woman makes me feel more alive than ever before.

I glide my fingers up her thighs and push across her thin thong. Then, thrusting two inside of her, I watch her inhale sharply.

"And why would you want me as your girlfriend when you could have anyone in this world?" she whispers on a smatter of disjointed breaths, brown eyes heady with lust and untamed desire.

"I like you a lot, little one," I growl out, watching her writhe at the force of my fingers stretching her.

"I like you too."

I remove my fingers and bring them to her lips. Her tongue darts across and sucks in her arousal, and I groan.

I push her back and watch her slide down her panties. Then I quickly unzip my pants to wrap myself.

Laying on top of her, I glide into her. She's tight and wet. Oh, she's so fucking wet.

We both moan out as I stretch her with my girth.

"Who makes you this wet, Rosie?" I ask, needing her to understand that only I can bring her this kind of pleasure.

"You." Her breath catches as I push in impossibly deeper.

"Christ," I bite out as heat slashes across my chest and down my thighs. "You're mine, Rosie," I say firmly. "And everyone needs to know that you're taken. No one else can have you."

I grab her by the waist and pull her to me, crushing her lips to mine. She moans into my mouth, her body melting against mine with my claim. This is what she wants and needs—to be controlled and dominated.

And I'm more than happy to be the one to do it.

I push inside her harder as our rhythm takes over. We're kissing and fucking, and I'm lost in another world. I'm lost in *her* world, and it's a world I want to stay in.

Her little moans flow into my ear as her hands roll across my arms, wrapping around my muscles. She's close.

I grab her legs and lift them over my shoulders, needing to give it to her deeper. She moans out as I hit her deep inside her back wall.

"Oh God, Vin." Her hands are in my hair, pulling at the roots. I inhale sharply, trying to fill my lungs with oxygen, but it's leaving me quicker than I can regain it.

She lets out a loud moan as she comes in a rush. My balls rise, and I'm there with her, in an orgasm that rips through me. I rest my hand on her neck and kiss her lips before rolling off to my side.

Our panting and sharp breathing fill the silence. She reaches over and rests a hand on my cheek. "Quite the teacher," she says, smiling.

"Quite the student," I respond with a wink.

I pull her close to me just as a sound from outside catches my attention.

"Shit," she says as she pulls away. "That was the front door."

I'm lying on her hideously uncomfortable bed, watching her freak out. Why is she so worried about what her roommates think?

"Rosie? Is that you?" a voice sounds from beyond her bedroom, seeping into the cracks.

"Quick," Rosie says in a panic. "She tosses me my pants." I can't help but chuckle.

"This isn't funny!" she says, jerking down her dress and fixing her hair.

"It actually is," I reply, still laughing.

"Oh my God. Vincent, if you don't get up now and put your pants on, so help me God…"

I laugh even louder now, unable to control it.

"Coming!" Rosie yells over my laughter.

"You're not, but you could be," I tease, unable to stop myself.

She rises and lifts a hand to her temple like she has a headache. I zip up my pants and move toward her, pulling her close to me.

"You have to learn not to give a fuck about what other people think, little one."

"What if they think… I'm sleeping my way to the top." She stares up at me with a pained expression.

"Then they don't even know the Rosie I know. Because she is beautiful, intelligent, and certainly can make her way to the top in the corporate world."

Her expression softens at my words, and she gently runs her hand down my cheek. Her demeanor shifts suddenly as a flash of apprehension crosses her face. "But she's never met you or ever seen me with a boyfriend."

Boyfriend.

Alarm crosses her hazel eyes. "Sorry, no, that's not what I meant…" Her voice trails off before she quickly follows it up with, "Is that what we are now?" She's all flustered and red with embarrassment.

"Lead the way, *girlfriend,*" I reply, and she smiles before quickly leaning up and kissing me passionately. I squeeze her ass, and she moans in my mouth.

"Oh God," she shrieks, steadies herself, and opens the door.

Her roommate is in the kitchen with her back to us, fixing herself something to drink. She must hear our footsteps because she turns around. Her eyes widen when she takes me in, then they immediately fall back onto Rosie.

"Sara, this is Vincent," Rosie introduces me, then turns to me wide-eyed.

"Vincent, this is my roommate, Sara."

"No shit," is her reply.

Am I the only one who thinks this is amusing?

"I guess we have a lot of catching up to do," Sara says, flashing a smile as wide as the Brooklyn Bridge while Rosie's shoulders relax, and she laughs.

"Well, we better do it now since Rosie will be staying with me for a while."

Sara's jaw drops open, and Rosie turns to me with a scowl. "Well, Friday through to Monday, right?"

"Right. Thank you, Vincent," Rosie says with an acidic tone that only makes me smile wider.

"It's probably best to tell her now so you two can catch up on everything," I say with a wide grin.

Her eyes widen, and she shakes her head, a mischievous glint in her gaze.

"I'll see you tomorrow," I say, kissing her cheek. She holds me close for a moment before I pull away.

I turn to leave, but before I do, I take a moment to address Sara directly. "Nice to meet you, Sara," I say with a polite smile, noting her assessing gaze fixed on me.

She mutters a brief goodbye and offers a meek wave as I open the door and make my way out. From behind me, I can feel Rosie and Sara's eyes on my back as the door shuts.

I bound down the stairs, taking two at a time, and hop back into my Porsche parked in the driveway. Revving the engine, I relish the roar as I accelerate through the dark streets of Jersey, unable to wipe the grin from my face as I contemplate what Rosie and Sara might be discussing.

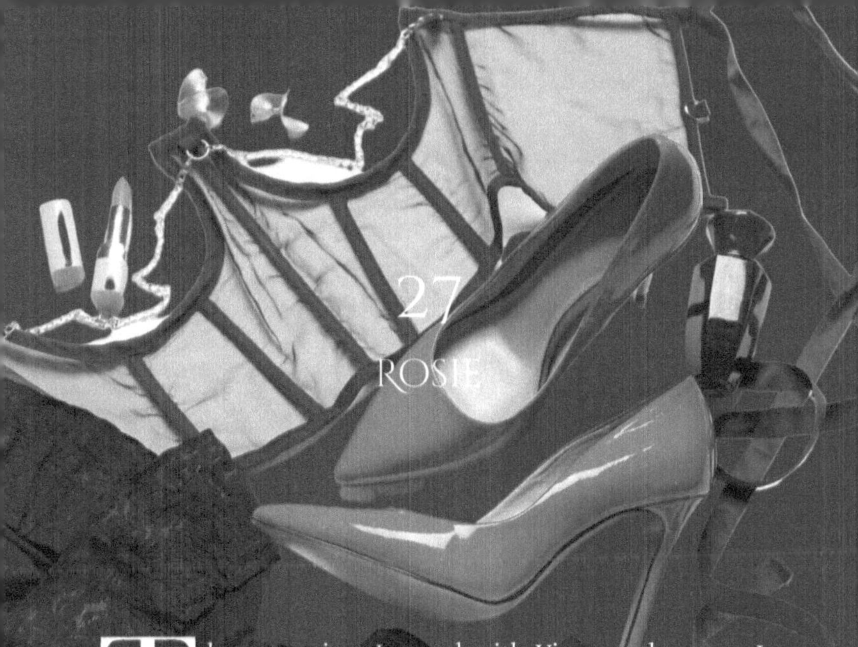

27

ROSIE

The more time I spend with Vincent, the more I realize this could be more than just a fling. I've only caught a glimpse of his deeper side these past few weeks, but I sense there is so much more to him.

I stare at the door, watching him shut it behind him. I'm beside myself, to be honest. Moving into Vincent's penthouse for the weekend while I'm in the city for my internship feels like a dream.

"Look at you," Sara says, glancing at me and breaking my thoughts. "What the actual fuck? When I said to let loose, I didn't think you'd lose your V-card to one of the most eligible bachelors in the world. Holy shit, Rosie!"

I let out a nervous laugh because I need to remind myself that before me, he had others. But when I'm with him, he makes me feel like I'm the only person in the world who matters.

"I'm serious. I don't want to see you get hurt. Did you ever think he was only interested because you were a virgin?" Sara's pointed stare makes me feel uneasy.

"I didn't think of that. He probably has never had a

challenge. Women fall at his feet, and I threw a drink on him!"

"He isn't the guy for you, Rosie. He lives in London, for a start, not to mention his cutthroat reputation and Casanova tendencies. What happened to waiting for the one, being in love?" Sara raises a valid point.

I shrug, knowing that we entered this with the notion that it was just a bit of fun, with no commitment and certainly no relationship. But it's not so black and white anymore.

"We're just having a bit of fun while he's here. We know it can't go beyond that. We've discussed it," I say, but as the words leave my mouth, I can't help feeling pained at the thought of a world without Vincent in it. I try to ignore the disappointment settling in my belly, but the truth is, I'm falling for him, and I know it's not going to end well.

It's ridiculous how much I miss Vincent, even during my business acquisition class. I'm practically counting down the seconds until Friday. Professor Turlot is droning on about balance sheets and financial statements, but all I can think about is the last time I saw Vincent and how I can't wait to see him again.

Then, my phone rings, interrupting my daydream. I quickly realize I forgot to silence it and see 'VS' flash across the screen. My heart does a little flutter.

Professor Turlot catches my eye and scowls. I mouth out a 'sorry' and quickly silence my phone before dragging it down to my lap and out of sight.

We spoke for an hour last night, just talking about

everything and nothing, and it felt like I'd known him for years.

But I also know I shouldn't get too excited. No one can take care of me like I've always taken care of myself, and I'm not sure I'm ready to give that up. Still, my heart seems to have its own ideas, and I can't help but feel drawn to Vincent.

I quickly type out a message to the man who has my heart captive.

Me: *Sorry, in class.*

VS: *I don't give a fuck. I need to see you.*

My stupid heart takes off like a jet plane, and smile broadly.

Me: *I need to see you too, but I have classes till Thursday.*

I look up, but my mind is still consumed by Vincent's message. The words echo in my head, drowning out the professor's lecture. I wait anxiously for the three dots to appear on my phone screen, indicating Vincent's response. Finally, they appear, and I feel a jolt of excitement. I quickly read his message, my heart racing as I respond.

VS: *Shame. Don't you want my tongue lapping up your tight cunt...*

. . .

Oh, dear God.

Me: Yes, Sir, I do.

 VS: Do you crave my thick cock in your mouth, little one?

Oh, holy fuck balls. I'm wet with arousal just from his messages.

Me: Oh God, yes.

I'm so wet with anticipation I struggle to thumb out my reply.

VS: Good girl. I'll be thinking of you deep-throating me while on my conference call x

Three long days and nights until I'm back between his silk sheets, doing all the dirty things I want to do with him. I blush, discreetly pack up my things, and creep out of class. Nothing, I repeat nothing, can make me focus after that distraction.

 As I'm walking off campus, Angela texts me to join her and Dane at a nearby bar. I oblige, but my disappointment is palpable when I see Fae and Max sitting with them, drinking at a table.

Angela spots me and waves me over. I wave back, weaving my way through the crowded bar filled with college students drinking and watching a sports game on the screen. I'm hungry, tired, and really don't want to be here, especially since Fae, who has disliked me from day one—probably because I didn't bow down to her like she's used to—is here.

"You made it!" Angela pulls me in for a hug, then drags a chair from the table next to us to make space for me.

"Hey, girl!" Dane greets me with a kiss on the cheek.

"Rosie!" Max smiles.

"Hey, guys," I reply.

Fae says, "Hey, softy."

"What the fuck, Fae?" Angela responds.

Fae looks alarmed at the questioning gaze as she shifts her eyes from Angela to me.

"I think we've established Rosie is certainly no softy, especially after she followed Mr. Slater out of the room the other day when he reprimanded her," Max says to Fae.

Oh shit, they noticed that.

"Yes, I saw that. You better not be trying to butter him up so you can get a job after this," Fae says with a sly smirk.

I let out a nervous laugh, remembering how he pulled me into him and slammed his lips on mine right inside the confines of his office.

I straighten up, addressing the table, "Mr. Slater had every right to tell me I got something wrong. I just wanted to clarify his reasoning."

"He does pick on you more than the rest of us," Max says.

"It's probably because she's the smartest one here, and he wants to push her even further," Angela adds.

"She is not!" Fae interrupts.

I take a sip of water, hoping to deflect any further questions.

Fae's smile betrays her thoughts. "Hmm, maybe I can also go to his office and clear up a few misunderstandings." Her comment elicits laughter from the table.

Fae's face contorts with disgust. "Why can't I do that too?"

Dane takes a swig of his beer before chiming in, "Because Rosie isn't trying to suck his cock."

I choke on my water as laughter erupts around the table. Fae shrugs her shoulders. "Well, take away the grumpy personality, and the guy's a fucking god," she crows.

I remain silent because truly I have no words, just a promise of what's to come when I see him. My phone buzzes in my purse, and I pull it out. The initials 'VS' light up the screen, and fuck, it doesn't take a rocket scientist to figure out who's calling if any of my friends saw it on screen. I quickly pull it closer, hiding the screen from view.

Angela looks over at me and furrows her brow. "Who's that?" she inquires.

"Oh, no one," I say, immediately regretting not making something up.

"Do you normally blush when no one calls?" Fae scoffs. "Oohhh, someone has a man," she continues.

"I do, as a matter of fact. Just a guy I met on campus," I say to get them off the scent quickly.

The bar erupts as a team scores on the big screen television. Max and Dane are distracted, and Fae corners Angela asking her about the latest Couture store opening in Soho.

I take the opportunity to reply to Vin.

Me: *Sorry, just having dinner at Stomp with the other interns discussing you, of course.*

Three dots appear immediately.

VS: *To be a fly on the wall there... if I gave a fuck.*

I let out a chuckle and promise to call him when I finish.

We fall into a discussion and eat dinner around the table. By the time the waitress clears the table, Fae has a harem of men around her while Max, Dane, and Angela are watching the game, which I have zero interest in. I go to stand when Angela reaches for my wrist. "You're not going yet, are you?" she asks.

" 'Fraid so, but I'll see you on Friday."

"Okay, let's grab lunch then."

I nod, feeling guilty for not telling Angela about Vincent.

But then again, the internship will be over in two weeks, and he will be back in London, so it's like none of this means anything anyway.

Liar.

28

VINCENT

It's been over an hour since she texted me, and honestly, I've never done this before. I wonder how I got here.

I'm across the street from Stomp, waiting for her. It's not like I can blame the whisky I had in the office earlier either because I'm sober as fuck, and I'm still here. Waiting for a woman. But she's not just any woman. It's Rosie.

While waiting, I even dialed up a call girl, hoping she'd pull me away from this person I've become. But I couldn't do it. The mere notion of sleeping with anyone else made the bile in my stomach lurch into my throat. I hung up before she even answered.

After a few more agonizing minutes, I finally see Rosie's silhouette emerge from the bar. She's dressed in black tights and a sweater, and my heart skips a beat at the sight of her. She's my pretty, stubborn, fiery intern, and I can't decide which part of her I'm drawn to the most.

She turns and starts walking down the street, heading south toward the subway. I hide in the shadows, watching her every move, even though she can't see me. As she fades into the distance, a feeling of longing and yearning takes hold deep within me.

I step out from the shadows and catch up to her. "Hello, Rosie," I say with a smile, and she turns.

"Vincent!" Her brown eyes light up, and a smile spreads across her face. I'm filled with a sudden surge of happiness.

Up close, I notice she's removed her makeup, and her bare face remains. Her skin is smooth, and her natural hair falls around her shoulders. The remnants of her eye makeup linger as smoky dark eyes stare back at me, and I can't help but be captivated by her natural beauty.

"What are you doing here?" she asks, still smiling.

"Time is a curse when I don't get to see you 'til Friday," I reply, my eyes fixed on hers.

Her eyes widen with excitement and nerves, and she bites her bottom lip, making me want her that much more. "Do you have any idea how hard it was for me to watch you in there?" I add.

"What... why?" she asks, a hint of confusion in her voice.

"Because you're my girl, Rosie. I don't want other eyes on you but mine."

Her eyes sparkle mischievously as she leans in closer, her lips curving into a playful smile. "So possessive, Mr. Slater," she whispers as we fall into step.

As soon as we turn the corner, I pull her toward me, my back hitting the wall, and her body crashes into mine. I whisper into her ear, "Call me, *Sir*. You belong to me and only me."

"Yes, *Sir*," she whispers, her eyes filling with desire and anticipation. I can feel her body pressing harder against mine, her breaths coming out in quick pants.

My girl wants to play, and the thought has me pulsing with need.

"I want to show you more." My question comes off as a statement because I know she can handle it.

She nods in agreement as her pupils darken with a need that matches mine.

"Kiss me, Sir," she says, and fuck, the ways she looks at me through her long lashes, a slashing heat rolls down my thighs and hits my dick.

I pull her chin toward me and feel her breath on my face. "No topping from the bottom, little one."

The cool air prickles against my skin, but the electricity between us is hotter than hell. I can tell she's not sure what I just said, but I'll show her exactly what I mean this weekend.

I lean in, our lips mere inches apart, and I see the hunger in her eyes.

My lips crush onto hers, and damn, they're soft, warm, and perfect for mine. Rosie moans loudly as I plunder her mouth with my tongue, the sound making my cock strain against my zipper.

I'm rough and bite her lower lip, but I don't care. I need all of her. My hand gropes her ass, pressing her into me as I suck on her neck, leaving red marks on her skin.

Her scent is intoxicating, fueling my desire to have her. I slide my hand up her sweater to her lace bra, fondling her breasts expertly, feeling her nipples harden under my touch. She moans louder, and it's pure ecstasy.

We break apart, panting, and stare at each other. Her eyes are wild, lips swollen.

"Car, *now,*" I command, breathless.

~

After I close her door, I climb into my seat.

"Slide your panties down now. I want to feel your wetness on the drive home," I order, and she moans in response. It's clear she craves my dominance and touch.

Starting the car, I watch as she slides her panties down and hands them to me. I bring them to my nose and inhale her scent deeply. "Fucking delicious." I let out a guttural growl as I pull the car onto the highway.

"Where are we going? I have school tomorrow?" She hesitates, looking around.

"Do you want to go?" I ask. The thought of not seeing her until Friday is unbearable.

I slide a thick finger inside her, giving her a taste of what's to come, and she moans loudly as her head tilts back against the headrest. She rakes her teeth against her lower lip and takes in a deep breath. "No."

"Good girl," I say, rewarding her with a second finger. "I should make you wait like you made me wait for you."

"I didn't know you were waiting," she responds, and I thrust a third finger inside her, causing her to squirm with pleasure.

I smirk and twist my fingers, watching her body arch and writhe with pleasure. I know I'm pushing her to the edge, but I can't help it. I need her to know how much she belongs to me, how much I own her body and soul.

Suddenly, I pull my fingers out, leaving her gasping and desperate for more. "Please, Vincent," she begs, her voice thick with need.

"Not yet, little one," I say, my eyes locked onto hers. "You have to earn it."

Her eyes widen with excitement, and I can see the

hunger in them. I know she's ready for whatever I have in store for her. I reach over and grab a silk tie the back seat and hand it to her. "Tie your hands together," I command. My gaze drifts between the road and her, watching her closely as she willingly complies.

With her hands tied, she looks up at me with an expression of pure submission and anticipation. "What are you going to do to me, Sir?" she asks, her voice barely above a whisper.

A smirk crosses my lips as I think of all the things I want to do to her. "You'll just have to wait and see," I say, my voice deep and commanding.

The tension builds between us, and I know it's going to be a long night filled with pleasure and pain, but I can't wait to see the look on her face when I finally give her what she wants.

It's past ten when we arrive back at my penthouse. Desperate to have my way with her, I lift her and throw her over my shoulder as soon as the private elevator doors open. Her hands are still bound together, which only increased her arousal on the drive home.

"Let me touch you, Sir," she pleads.

I reign in my control slightly and hold onto the thread of patience I have around this vixen. I set her down on the bed and untie her.

"In good time. Strip," I order in a dark, needy voice, and I see her swallow down her throat.

"Yes, Sir," she says, catching on quickly. Like the perfect student, she knows what I want.

"Do you remember your safe word?" I ask.

"Blue, Sir," she says, and she sucks in her lower lip as she pulls off her sweater and throws it to the floor.

She drops her panties, standing in front of me in nothing but a bra.

"You're fucking beautiful." I marvel at her—smooth skin, taught stomach, and long legs I need around me.

Patience.

"Put your clothes on the dresser," I command.

"Really?" she asks, perplexed by my request.

"Do you want to disobey me?" I ask.

"Maybe," she says, and I slap her ass cheek. She lets out a gasp, and my hand rubs against her cheek, taking away the sting.

She leans into my shirt, her skin hot and eyes closed. I snake a line of kisses down her neck, and she tips her head up and moans before I abruptly let her go. "Go," I say, and her eyes snap open.

She picks up her clothes and does as I ask. Then she stands in front of me as I tilt her chin up to me. "Do that again, and you'll be crawling on your knees."

Her chest rises and falls, and the thread of arousal swirls between us. Is it possible she's more aroused? My girl likes to be told what to do.

"Yes, Sir," she moans out.

I let her go, then step behind her and slide my fingers across the clasp of her bra, releasing it with one snap.

I place her bra in my suit pocket, then take my naked queen in.

My hands run down the hollow of her back to the curve of her bottom. I slide past her hole, and she gasps. "I will give you pleasure, Rosie, but you have to trust me."

I slip between her thighs, wet and hot, as I spread her legs wider with my hand. I sink a finger into her wet folds, and she lets out a moan. Then pulling the silk tie from the side table, I slip it over her eyes, fastening it at the back of her head.

"Do you trust me, Rosie?" I ask, tilting her head to the side as I enter her with another finger, dipping in and out of her faster.

She moans, and the sound has my dick swelling with need.

"*Rosie*," I command as I stop finger fucking her delicious cunt.

"Yes," she breathes out. "I-I trust you," she says, barely able to utter the words.

I add another two fingers so I'm four fingers deep, just to see if she can take it. Her legs begin to buckle as she groans louder. I pull my fingers out, and she whimpers in frustration.

I pull her over to the bed and guide her on her knees at the headboard.

I slide in between her legs, my head at her opening.

"Sit on my face, little one. I want to be coated in your juices."

She lets out a shallow breath as she hovers carefully above me, taking her hands to my hair and feeling her way around as her sense of sight is removed.

"Don't hover, *sit,* Rosie," I command as my hands grip her hip bones.

She moves lower, and I tease her with a flicker of my tongue. She lets out a groan, but she's still too far away. Without warning, I tug her down onto my face so her complete body weight is on me and run my tongue up and down her wet, slick folds.

She groans loudly, and I growl against her, knowing the vibrations will heighten her need. Her hands fist my hair as she begins to move quickly, riding my face.

Tastes so fucking good. I hum with pleasure.

"Come for me, baby," I growl out into her pussy, feeling her walls clench around my tongue as she comes undone.

I lap up every drop of her sweet nectar, savoring her taste.

She collapses onto the bed, panting heavily as I crawl up beside her, my face glistening with her juices.

"Good girl," I praise, keeping my fingers inside her and riding out another wave.

I drag my fingers, wet with her arousal, up to her ass and circle the entrance. She sucks in a breath, one she can't seem to catch as I deprive her of more oxygen.

I slip out of my trousers and briefs, then unbutton my shirt. She's removed the neck tie from her eyes and is now watching me. "That was—"

I cut her off with a consuming kiss, our teeth clashing with bruising force.

"Does my girl want to please me?" I ask, my throbbing dick reminding me of her answer's importance.

"Yes, Sir, very much," she says, but a flicker of trepidation mars her hazel eyes.

"Only honesty, little one."

She remains silent, and I bite her lip.

"For this to work, we have to be honest with each other," I say, tipping her chin up to mine. Her eyes lift to meet mine.

"I'm not sure If you liked it last time." A faint blush washes over her skin, and my hand lands on her bottom hard with a stinging slap.

She moans, but this time it's deep and lusty. *She likes it. My girl is getting it.*

"I told you, don't ever be embarrassed," I say, rubbing my hand in circles across the mark and soothing it.

"I love your lips around my cock, little one, but if you want to learn, I will mentor you."

She rolls her lips in and smirks at my choice of words.

"I'd like that, Sir," she breathes out on a heady breath.

Pride swells in my chest. She is beautiful.

"On your knees," I command in a deep voice, one I know she loves to hear.

"Wrap two hands around the base of my cock and start fisting me like this." I role play for her, taking my cock in my hands, and her eyes light up at the sight. Then, I remove my hands and guide hers to my pulsing dick. My dick is heavy as she takes it in her grasp.

I sweep her hair behind her shoulders as I marvel at the woman on her knees. She's hard and quick, and fuck me, I inhale sharply. I'm not sure how long I will last. I've thought about her in this position all week.

"Now wrap those lips around me and suck hard," I instruct.

She does as told, and the minute her mouth hits the sensitive head of my cock, a flash of warmth spreads across my thighs. It's good, but I know my girl can do better.

I clutch her by the head, my hands wrapped in her hair, and move her in the rhythm I need. "That's it, little one." She sucks harder and deeper as she takes all of me, opening her throat for the head of my cock.

"My girl's a quick learner," I hiss out on a forced breath. My orgasm is building by the second. Sinking into her delicious mouth, her tongue slides down the entire length to the base of my cock, and my balls draw up.

I groan, then she moans around my cock and returns to the rhythm I set, except this time, she's taking me deeper. Saliva spills from her mouth as she gags at my size, but it doesn't slow her down. My breath shudders, and my fingers tighten in her hair.

"Oh, fuck." I'm about to lose it, and without warning, warm jets of liquid shoot out of me and down her throat.

I'm about to apologize for losing control when I look down, but I'm startled. Rosie's wiping her mouth with a grin and a twinkle in her eyes.

Could she be any more beautiful?

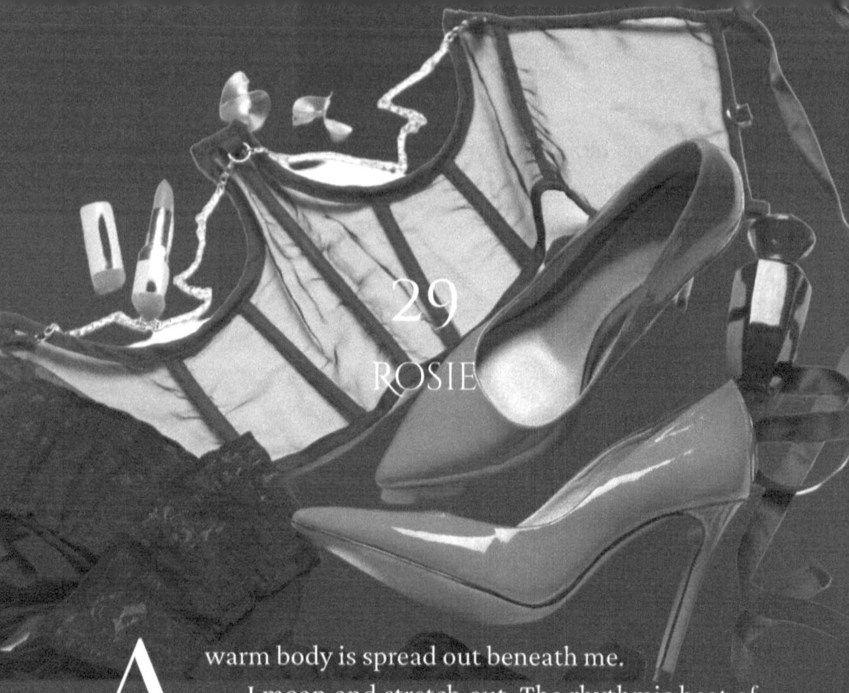

29

ROSIE

A warm body is spread out beneath me.

I moan and stretch out. The rhythmic beat of his heart is soothing and homey, and everything about last night comes flooding back in.

He couldn't wait to see me, so he came all this way to collect me.

The mere sound of his voice sends a thrilling wave of adrenaline through me, leaving me feeling electrified and alive. Something about his possessive nature draws me in, a quality that resonates with me on a deep and primal level.

I've never known the feeling of wanting to pleasure someone so much that it takes you over. The need for him to dominate me is nothing I've ever experienced and everything I want.

I crave it.

I need it.

I trust him explicitly.

I know he won't hurt me, even when he spanks me. The burn he takes away with tender strikes of his palm.

Gazing up at him from my submissive position on my

knees, I'm overcome with the need to bring him pleasure. The rush of exhilaration I felt as I fulfilled this desire empowered me, and I watched him lose control in response.

I let out a soft moan at the memory as I inhale sharply. Vincent's arms wrap around my body, and I look up to find him staring down at me.

Feeling happier than I have in a long time, I smile up at him.

"You're quite something to wake up to, Rosie," he says as he runs his fingers along the shell of my ear. I lean into his touch as his fingers trail down my jaw and brush across my bottom lip. Unable to resist, my lips part as his finger enters my warm mouth.

"What is it you want, little one?"

My sex clenches with desire as I suck and lick his finger, imagining I'm taking his entire length in my mouth. He lets out a deep guttural growl, and with his other hand, he grabs my hip and pulls my bare body onto his. I grind against him, and my nipples ache as they press against his chest. He removes his finger and kisses me deeply, his hands digging into my hips as I continue to grind.

As he pulls away, I'm left panting with insatiable need, and he stares at me.

"I'll be late for work, but only if you ask me." I realize he's just given me the power, and I take a moment to revel in it before answering.

My chest heaves with each breath, and my arousal is palpable. "I want you to fuck me, Sir," I pant out, and with that admission, his eyes darken, and he takes me in a punishing kiss.

. . .

"I need to fuck every inch of you," he says, and I'm a hot, heated mess. I don't even realize he's wrapped himself until he's standing in front of me.

"Remember your safe word."

"Blue," I say, marveling at the god in front of me—taught, rippling muscles carved into his abdominals like Mount Rushmore.

He tenderly brings his hand up to my cheek in a move that pulls a need inside my chest.

"On your knees, facing the headboard."

Oh God.

His words send shivers of excitement coursing through me. I do as he asks, feeling the weight of his stare as I kneel, naked and bare. Strangely, I'm not self-conscious. I sway my hips, moving seductively for my man, and I'm rewarded with a low growl of approval.

"Spread your legs wider," he says, and damn, I'm so wet, and we haven't even started.

"So beautiful," he whispers, and the bed dips as he climbs on. I'm panting with anticipation as his praise washes over me, sending all my senses into overdrive.

Without warning, his hand connects with my hip, and he thrusts inside me, slamming me forward. I let out a loud moan as he catches me from hurtling forward. A guttural sound escapes his lips, and I clench around him, trying to absorb every painfully pleasurable thrust.

He continues his relentless assault as my pleasure builds. My toes curl and dig into the sheets from the sheer force, but I can take it.

I want to take it.

I want to please him.

His hand circles around my neck, and I'm startled at the

connection. I arch, leaning into it, and it's the permission he needs to squeeze.

I'm panting, breathless and heady with need, and the pressure he's applying on my neck has every sense ignited tenfold.

"Cream on my dick, little one," he commands, and holy fucking shit. His dirty words are enough to tip me over, and an orgasm rips through me as I moan out his name. He sinks into me further, if that's even possible, and his dick jerks as his body shifts forward, and he spills into me. He releases my throat, and I glance back at him and watch as his eyes roll back into his head, beads of sweat sliding down his valley of muscles. He places kisses down my spine, and I try to catch my breath when he pulls out of me, and the bed shifts.

He has his hand out when he says, "Time to get cleaned up."

As I'm catching my breath, I can't help but feel a bit let down. I stare up at Vin and imagine what it would feel like to be held by him after sex and to wake up next to him every morning. But I push away the absurd thought and take his hand.

I know he's leaving soon and that he's not capable of anything beyond what we have.

After we've cleaned up and he's dressed, we're perched on black metal stools at his huge onyx kitchen counter, eating fresh fruit from a platter . Suddenly, it hits me like a ton of bricks. He's leaving for the day, and I'll be stuck here all alone in his massive penthouse.

He's scrolling through his emails when he notices me

frowning. "What's wrong?" he asks, a hint of concern in his voice.

"You're leaving me here all alone in this penthouse," I say, feeling a pang of sadness.

He thinks for a moment before suggesting, "Why don't you come to work with me?"

I stare at him incredulously. "Aah, for starters, your brother would know we're together."

He rolls his eyes. "When are you going to stop caring so much about what other people think?"

"I can't help it! Maybe you should start caring a little more," I say, feeling frustrated.

The back of his hand brushes my cheek and along my jaw, where he tilts my chin down. "I do care, little one."

As we sit there in silence, I can feel a sense of unspoken understanding fall between us. It's like there's a deeper connection between us that we're trying to ignore.

I look up at him, and he meets my gaze. We lock eyes for a moment, and I can feel my heart beating faster. I know that there's something more between us, something that goes beyond just physical attraction.

His hand lowers to my lips, and I feel the familiar pulse between my legs.

"I'm good here," I manage to say, my voice hoarse and breathless.

His tongue brushes the bottom of his lips, and I'm drawn to the glistening, full lip, feeling a wave of desire wash over me.

"Stop looking at me like that. I'm already running late," he whispers darkly.

"Sorry, Sir," I tease, and he inhales sharply.

"Are you disobeying me?" he asks, his jaw ticking with irritation.

I shrug, knowing I secretly want to be punished.

He quickly types out a text on his phone before grabbing my chin and pulling me closer to him. "I've canceled my housekeeper. You will be my housekeeper for the day."

"What?" I gasp in surprise.

"You'll clean every surface of my house in your bra and underwear," he says, his voice tinged with authority.

I realize this isn't the kind of punishment I had in mind.

"I have cameras everywhere, and I'll be watching you," he warns, his eyes gleaming with a hint of danger.

He kisses me deeply, then grabs his wallet off the counter. "I'll be watching," he says with a dark promise.

The thought of being his naughty maid for the day sends a surge of arousal through me. I vow to be the sluttiest little maid possible, eager to please Vincent in every way.

As I scrub the kitchen counters and wash the dishes, I revel in the feeling of the cool, smooth marble against my bare skin. I move on to the living room, and I can't help but sense Vin's eyes on me, knowing his desire grows with each passing moment.

I dust the bookshelves and run the feather duster along the edges of the furniture, my body twisting and bending in all sorts of provocative ways. I catch my reflection in the mirror and blush at the sight of my heaving breasts and flushed face.

As I make my way to the bedroom, I can't resist the temptation to run my fingers over the soft bed sheets. I giggle to myself, feeling a sense of anticipation building inside me.

I decide to up the ante and really show him what he's missing out on. I locate one of his cameras and angle myself in front of it. I accidentally drop something and bend over so I'm on all four with the camera on my behind. I widen my legs and slide my fingers underneath the lace of my panties, pushing them aside so he can see my wet and swollen folds. I let out a groan as I finger myself in front of him, thoroughly taking to my punishment.

30
VINCENT

Currently, I am watching my girl on my desk monitor. My mistake of leaving her evident as she's taking her punishment to another level. I watch her fingers slide into her tight cunt, and my fingers are itchy with greed.

She's now moving and grinding against my bedpost to the beat of the music echoing across the walls. While cleaning and wiping the surfaces, she wears sky-high heels that have me glued to the screen. Her motions send excruciating pain through my suit pants, and I can't take my eyes off her. I shouldn't be here today because I haven't achieved much since I arrived at work and switched on my monitor.

Wanting to praise her excellent work, I grab my phone and send a quick text.

Me: *Impressive work. I can't take my eyes off of you.*

. . .

Upon hearing the notification sound, she swiftly grabs her phone from the side table. As I zoom in, a smile lifts onto her lips, and I feel a strange warmth fill my chest. It's the same feeling I had this morning as I brushed her cheek. She types out a response, and my phone beeps.

Rosie: *Thank you, Sir. But I'd enjoy cleaning you more.*

Damn, her mouth. She's more dominant than submissive, and I'm surprised at how much it turns me on. Although all I want to do is dip my tongue in her sweet pussy, I have back-to-back meetings today, and I need to remind myself of that. Scowling, I quickly check the time and realize I have a ten-minute reprieve before my board meeting.

With my phone in hand, I punch out another text.

Me: *Lie on the bed and touch yourself but don't come.*

A grin lifts my mouth at the prospect of her reading that message. True to form, she picks it up and gasps. I find her eyes widen as her teeth dig into her bottom lip. That single expression has my dick pulling tighter against my pants zipper.

I'm aching for relief. My hand lifts off the mouse and down to the button of my pants. I'm about to relieve myself when I hear footsteps echo toward my door.

Fuck!

I quickly turn my monitor and mute the sound, but the

vision of her still remains on my screen. Right at that moment, Julius opens my door.

"What's this about dinner tonight?" he asks, clearly flustered.

"What dinner?" I ask because I have no idea what he's talking about.

"With our parents?"

Jesus Christ, I completely forgot. I shake my head. It wasn't like me to forget anything, but these last few weeks with Rosie have turned my world upside down.

"Fuck, that's tonight? Victoria's in town. She's performing in Times Square and booked Le Cirque afterward."

My eyes flicker to the screen momentarily, and I see her lie back on the bed, her knees hitched to the sky and slightly spread apart.

I swallow the thickness in my throat at the sight of her as I want my brother to fuck the hell off.

"Goddammit!" he rants, and I can't give a fuck about my brother's scheduling right now.

"If that's all, then..." I say, dismissing him.

His eyes dart to mine, and curiosity falls behind them.

Fuck. My girl is fucking her sweet pussy, and I'm not watching.

"I have important matters to attend to, Julius. Did you come here to vent about a scheduling conflict? Isn't that why Isabella is here to handle unexpected situations?" I respond, hinting at his loyal secretary.

I notice his jaw tick, then he utters through clenched teeth, "Yes, that's exactly why I have her."

What's that about?

It suddenly dawns on me that tonight will be more

bearable with Rosie by my side. I don't give a fuck what Julius has to say about it.

"I'm bringing Rosie," I declare.

He blinks and looks at me like I have two heads. I know it sinks in when his hands steeple at his hips and his face morphs into a scowl.

"I fucking knew it!" His voice is high and strained. And before I can answer, he's pacing my office from the wall to the glass window, back and forth like he has a million things on his mind.

"Fuck, Vin, I can't believe you're fucking your intern!" he spits out in a rant. The way he's carrying on has me wondering if his anger is less to do about Rosie and me and more about his own problems.

"I am," I say in a measured voice, but the mere confession of just fucking Rosie seems off. She's so much more, even if I can't admit it to her. "She's also living with me until I go back to London."

He stops and stares at me. "What? You've never lived with a woman! Now you choose to complicate things by fucking an intern and having her move in with you? What if she sues you? Sues us?"

I let out a laugh because I know Rosie, and she's definitely not after my money. She wouldn't even accept my offer to pay back her brother's debt.

"Oh, it's funny, is it? You've completely broken the strict code of company ethics and no intra-office relationships."

I rise because even though I don't give a fuck about the rules, I don't like seeing my brother in distress. "Since when have you known me to abide by rules?" He throws his hands in the air. "Listen, Rosie and I are just fucking. She's staying with me while she works at the Vanilla Club because she lives in Jersey, and it's easier to commute."

"Then what? What happens when you leave in two weeks to go back to the UK, and she is applying for a job here? Am I supposed to pick her because she was fucking you?"

"No, of course not. That's completely up to her and our rigorous interview process."

He seems relieved to hear that. "And she knows this?"

"It's not a discussion we need to have." He scoffs at my remark. "Not because we haven't gotten around to it, but because I know her. She's not like that. She's worked her ass off to get where she is on a scholarship after her mother was killed, and with no father in the picture, she takes care of herself and her older brother. She works at the Vanilla Club to pay back his debts."

He's surprised by my admission. "I thought it was because of her sick father."

"No, she was embarrassed to tell us the truth in case I fired her before even starting."

He narrows his eyes. "Sounds like you're getting attached, Vin."

I stare at my brother. He looks at me expectantly, and something pulls inside me. I do like her. She makes me feel something I buried a long time ago when my brother was murdered in cold blood.

"Do I need to remind you that I'm leaving in two weeks?"

A slow smile forms on his face. It's then I realize by not shutting him down, I've confessed to liking a girl to my brother. Something I've never fucking done. *Ever.*

"Get the fuck out," I say, and he lets out a deep chuckle before holding his hands up in surrender.

He's walking out the door when he turns and says, "You

realize Mom will think you're marrying her by bringing her tonight."

I widen my eyes. *Oh fuck.* He's right. Out of anyone, I care what my mother thinks, and I don't want to give her false hope.

"I'll make something up. Don't worry your little head," I tell him.

He lets out another laugh and shakes his head. "I hope you know what you're doing, brother." I watch Julius walk through the door and shut it behind him.

I dial my secretary, and she picks up after one ring. "Yes, Mr. Slater?"

"I don't want any interruptions Julie," I say.

"Of course."

I hang up and immediately turn up the volume and enlarge the screen. Soft, delicious moans come through my speakers. Her finger is inside her, and I sense she's close to coming.

Jesus fucking Christ.

My hand comes up to my chest as my naughty girl tugs at her hardened pebbles, kneading them between her fingers.

"Vincent," she moans out, and the thought that my girl aches for me has me hot with need. I unzip my pants and spit into my hand. I fist myself rough and hard with one hand, and with the other, I click on my mouse, activating the microphone on the camera in my bedroom.

"So fucking beautiful," I hear my voice through the speakers, and she lets out a groan at hearing my voice.

"Can I come, Sir?" She's rubbing her pussy faster now, alternating between her clit and her swollen folds. Tingles of heat slash my back, and I'm so fucking close to coming.

It's ridiculous what this girl does to me, and I need to tell her.

"I'm fucking myself to your sweet pussy."

She moans louder, and I want to reward my girl for pleasing me, but before I can reply, she is breathing out all hot and needy.

"Please, Sir," she pleads.

Her words are enough to tip me over, but I want to come with her, so I urge, "Come, now," as warm liquid drips down my cock and into my hand.

I watch her quiver and groan as she rubs her clit furiously and comes with an arched back off the bed.

She's mine.

My girl.

I don't know how I can ever let her go.

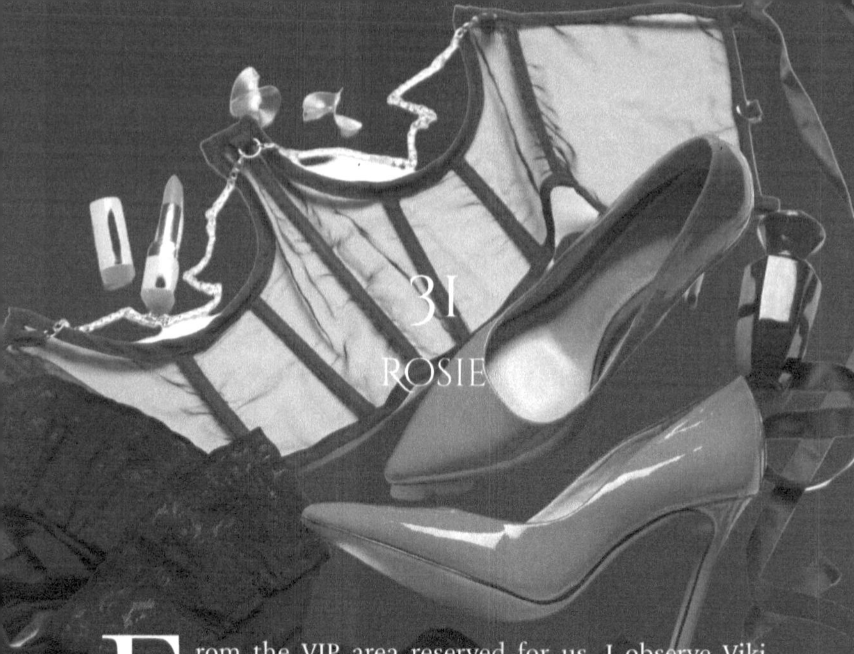

31

ROSIE

From the VIP area reserved for us, I observe Viki Slate slaying her final song. After my steamy encounter with Vincent earlier today, where I played the role of a submissive housekeeper, I didn't think anything could top it. However, Vincent surprises me by bursting home and inviting me to watch his sister's performance by his side.

To my surprise, he suggested that we 'accidentally' run into each other to avoid any questioning from his mother about our relationship. I understand the need for discretion, especially considering our age difference. So here we are, carrying out the plan flawlessly. Earlier, we bumped into each other, and Vincent introduced me to his parents, Tatiana and Edward, and brother without raising any suspicions.

Although he must have told his brother I was coming, Julius keeps up the act of not knowing me and maintains my cover.

As Vincent's sister mesmerizes the audience with her jazzy voice, I can't help but feel disappointed. Was I not good enough to be introduced to his parents? Am I not girl-friend material?

But I know the reality of the situation. Vincent is a billionaire business mogul, and I am just an intern struggling to make ends meet by working as a lingerie waitress. What could I possibly offer someone like him? Besides, I am ever aware that our secret relationship has an expiration date since he is leaving in just two weeks.

However, something inside me wants more from Vincent. There's something in his kisses and tender touch that make me believe there could be more to our relationship. But perhaps I'm just imagining it, and he's like this with all his submissives. I shake away these thoughts as the song ends, and the crowd cheers and applauds.

Vincent's touch on the back of my arm alerts me to his presence before I even see him. His cologne wafts into my nose, and I can't help but lean into his warmth, feeling at ease in his company. It's the first time he's been this close to me since arriving.

"I can't wait to get you home tonight," he murmurs in a gravelly voice, making me smile. Even though our time together is limited, this man means everything to me right now.

"Wasn't she something?" Tatianna turns to us, pride evident in her every word. Tall and slim with beautiful high cheekbones and a warm smile, she looks impeccable in her plum skirt and blouse with her dark hair swept up in a tight bun. It's clear that having her family together in one place brings her great joy.

Damn, moments like these make me wish my mother were still alive—someone to be proud of me, love me unconditionally, and always be there for me without fail.

Vincent's hand disappears, and the distance grows

between us. He steps away, and the warmth that once enveloped me turns cold.

"She is so talented," I say, trying to gauge Vincent's reaction to the space between us.

"Unbelievable," Vincent says, his expression stern. I exhale deeply, struck by how he can be so tender one moment and cold as ice the next. I glance up at him before feeling the weight of Tatiana's stare. She looks between us before smiling.

Did she see Vincent touch me earlier? I try to divert the tension by turning my attention to Edward, who is back on his phone, missing his daughter's incredible performance and standing ovation.

My exhale is drowned out by Julius' wolf whistling, and I look up at him with curious amusement. The Julius I know is a serious and professional CEO, so seeing him wolf whistle seems out of character.

Tatiana discreetly loops her arm through Edward's, trying to get him involved. It doesn't take a genius to figure out that Edward is more absent than present as a father, and the strain is evident between him and his sons and daughter. I wonder which is worse, having a drunk father who is absent or having a father who is present only in body but absent in every other way.

Tatianna enthusiastically asks her husband, "Don't you think she was amazing?"

He looks up to face the group. "Of course," he replies in a gruff voice, his face creased with lines. He has piercing blue eyes and a sharp jawline, traits that Vincent and Julius inherited. I wonder what else they have in common, especially since Vincent never talks about his father.

Vincent responds calmly, "I'm surprised you noticed."

Tatianna shifts uncomfortably as Edward locks eyes

with Vincent in a stand-off of sorts before turning his attention to me. "Tatiana tells me you're joining us for our family dinner, Rosie, is it?" he asks, his eyebrows raising in question.

I clear my throat and answer, "Yes, if—"

"She sure is," Vincent interrupts, causing me to swallow down the lump in my throat.

The awkwardness lingers in the private dining room at Le Cirque as we wait for Victoria to arrive. The world-renowned chef is known for catering to an exclusive upper-crust clientele with waitlists stretching for months. So, how did they manage to secure not only a table but the private dining suite on such short notice?

The private room is dimly lit, but a vintage chandelier delicately crafted and hanging from the ceiling illuminates the space with a soft glow. The table is draped in fine linens, and the air is infused with the mouth-watering scent of caramelized onions from the kitchen nearby.

I sit silently, listening to Julius and his mother exchange company updates when I decide to engage Edward in conversation.

"You have a very successful family, Edward. You must be proud of their achievements."

"Of course," he responds flatly.

Unperturbed, I persist, trying to get to know the family's patriarch better. "Did you help Julius and Vincent start Slater Corp?"

Tatianna gives me a friendly smile and a nod of approval.

I like her.

"No, that was all them," he says, a hint of disdain evident in his croaky voice. "I sold my company years ago."

"My father ran a successful business brokering

company where he managed the sale of numerous mid-to-large size businesses," Julius proudly interjects. "He did over a billion dollars' worth of transactions in his time," he explains as he sips his whisky.

"I see where your sons get their determination from," I remark, and Edward pauses, a trace of sadness crossing his eyes before he swallows down the amber liquid in one gulp.

The tension swirls around the table again, and I wonder if I said something wrong.

Finally, it's Tatianna who breaks the stillness with her words. "Rosie is such a pretty name. It was too loud to ask you anything at the concert, but tell me, how is it you know Vincent?" she asks, her tone curious but friendly, and I feel a sense of relief that the tension at the table is starting to dissipate. But then I suddenly forget what Vincent and I rehearsed earlier as a wave of panic crashes over me.

When I meet Vincent's gaze, a sense of calm washes over me. His eyes are cool, calm, and collected, and at this moment, I remember why I trust him completely. My initial panic disappears. "I met Vincent in London while traveling," I say.

God, that sounded so much more believable when it came out of Vincent's mouth.

"I see," Tatianna says with a tilt of her head, and I know she doesn't buy a word of it. I want to shrink into my seat.

"Hello, family!" Viki thrusts open the curtain to the private dining room and struts inside with huge yellow platform heels, and I couldn't be happier with the timing. She kisses her parents on the cheeks, and her mother brings her in for a large hug. She has to practically pry herself off her to give Julius and Vincent a warm embrace.

Vincent pulls her in for a hug. It's strong and inviting, and I can immediately sense their closeness.

"We are being rude!" she says as she pulls back from him and turns to me. Damn, this family and their gene pool. She is stunning.

Huge green eyes feathered by long lashes stare back at me. She's a lot shorter than her brothers, even with her platforms, but her presence is magnetic like it is with all the Slater siblings.

"Hey! I'm Viki," she says as she pulls me in for an embrace.

Julius lets out a chuckle while over her shoulder, I see Vincent watching on with a smirk playing on his lips.

"Victoria, meet a friend of mine, Rosie," Vincent says.

Everyone sits back down, and I pull back, suddenly aware of my intrusion into this family. Sensing my discomfort, Victoria reaches out and squeezes my arm as she whispers, "Vin doesn't have many friends, so you must be special. Thanks for being here." She squeezes me one last time before taking the empty seat beside Julius and me.

"Darling, you were extraordinary!" Tatianna claps her hands, and we all agree, giving her the adulation she deserves.

"Fuck, seriously, that was by far the biggest gig I've ever done. I'm still on cloud nine!"

"Language, Victoria!" Edward scolds her with a frown, and she lets out a giggle.

"Sorry, Dad."

I glance at her and grin. She's cool, and I like it. She's nothing like the professional, suave, and rugged bravado of her brothers. She's young and hip, and I'm getting her vibe completely.

The waiter comes around, and we order. By the time the entree is served, we've heard all about Victoria's latest album, new agent, and new security team. Julius is swept up in conversation with Victoria, Tatianna, and Edward when I feel Vincent's hand slide up against my thigh underneath the table. I want more of his touch, so I shift closer to him and revel under his possessive touch as I watch his family converse.

It feels so nice to be part of this.

Although I sense some fragments in Vincent's relationship with his father, seeing him surrounded by family is still heartwarming. I watch on as discussions fly around the room with ease, and a smile falls on my face.

"What do you think of the ceviche?" Vincent leans closer and asks quietly.

I take my napkin to my lips and pat them dry, his hand wandering higher up on my thigh. I inhale sharply as his fingers dust across the fabric of my panties.

I'm wearing a dress that he bought me for tonight—sky blue and knee-length, with a slit on one side, giving him perfect access.

"It's delicious," I respond, but it comes out breathy.

The rest of the meal is spent with Vincent, Julius, and his sister catching up. It's evident that Tatiana is very involved in her children's lives, and Edward is more absent than present. Vincent has practically avoided him all evening, while I sense that Julius and Tatiana are the peacekeepers in the family.

"I'm flying to Tokyo in two days," Victoria says after Vincent asks about her upcoming schedule.

"Tokyo?" Vincent repeats.

"Yes, it's a huge market over there. J-pop and all that."

"But isn't your music infused with jazz? I thought J-pop was another thing entirely. You're no BTS and BLACK-PINK..." I pause before adding, "That's a compliment, by the way."

"Who the hell is BTS and BLACKPINK?" I hear Vincent asking as laughter echoes around the table.

"Rosie knows." Victoria winks, then squeezes me on the shoulder. "You're right. That's K-pop, by the way. But K-Pop or J-pop, it's a huge market in Asia. My record hit number five on the Asian billboards just last week."

"I'm not sure I like you traipsing around the world, Victoria," Vincent says, and my eyes dart between them.

Victoria lets out an exaggerated sigh. "Please, Vin, don't be so overprotective. I have a bodyguard now."

"Yeah, Vin, don't be so overprotective," I tease, and Victoria giggles. Vincent looks between us, and a mischievous smirk creeps onto my face.

"See! Listen to Rosie. She seems like a fiercely independent woman. Not all of us need a man to protect us, Vin." Victoria tosses Vincent a pointed stare, but before Vincent can respond, Julius steers her attention with a question about her management.

Vincent runs his tongue across his lower lip, and his eyes seem to ignite like kerosene. It's a subtle movement, but it has me squeezing my thighs together under the table, trying to keep my composure. His phone lights up on the table and breaks the chemistry between us, and I release a breath I didn't realize I was holding as he flips it over, excusing himself from the table.

"I have to take this," he says, his voice cold and extinguished by the heat in his stare. I nod in understanding as I try and regain my composure.

"Let's see what this K-Pop, J-Pop nonsense is all about," Julius says as he scrolls on his phone. His eyebrows knit together in confusion as he stares at the screen. "It's like a rainbow-colored unicorn had an explosion of glitter," he announces.

Victoria and I burst into uncontrollable laughter, unable to contain our amusement.

Julius continues. "Seriously. though, when did music become so forced and overdone?"

Suddenly, I notice Vincent returning, but his appearance is strikingly different from before. He seems agitated, his chest heaving as if he's about to lose control. He slams his phone on the table with a swift motion, causing an immediate hush to fall over the dining room.

"Everything all right, son?" Tatianna asks, and he lifts his stare. He's practically radiating with anger, and I can feel the tension in the air around us. All I can think about is finding out what caused this outburst and getting him out of here so we can work through it together.

"It will be. I promise you that." His voice is deathly calm, although his demeanor is anything but measured. Julius stares back at him, and there is a silent discussion taking place between the two, which no one is privy to.

Julius shakes his head in a warning.

"What the hell is going on?" Edward interrupts, finally invested in his children.

"That phone call is the call I've been waiting for since I arrived in Manhattan. Finally, after all these years in the dark, I know the truth about Edgar," Vincent announces.

Julius shakes his head while Victoria lets out a gasp. Tatiana and Edward stare at their son, and I'm at a loss at what the heck is going on.

32
VINCENT

My heart is hammering in my chest when I hear the name of the person responsible for my brother's murder—Tony Gambino. Tony fucking Gambino, cousin to the Gambino Mafia family, was responsible for the hit on my brother and not Montero, the man rotting in the jail cell accused of his murder.

I'm barely holding it together when I return to the table, gripping my phone with white-knuckle force.

"Jesus Christ, Vin. Not here," I hear my brother say, but it doesn't register as I'm seething with rage.

Sharp pain shoots up my legs and back, but I push it away, spreading like an octopus to my arms and fingers. Pure vengeance leeches to every single crevice of my body. Rage floods every single cell of my body, and hatred seeps from my bones. I'm going to fucking end Tony Gambino. It's only a matter of time.

"You're talking about Edgar again? You can't be fucking serious!" My father pushes out his chair, the sound of the steel legs screeching across the floorboards. "I will not let you do this to our family again, Vincent," he hisses through a clenched jaw.

I feel Rosie's hand on my leg and push away the calming sensation it fills me. Now is not a time to be calm. Now is a time to find out why. I rise slowly and methodically walk over to my father as though in slow motion. With each step, I feel the rage build higher and higher.

"I think we ought to have a chat," I say, venom dripping from my words.

I see the fear in my father's eyes, and at that moment, I know he knows I know.

"I have no idea what you are talking about," he says.

I turn my back on him and face the table. "He has no idea what I'm talking about," I tease mockingly.

Faces stare back at me. Victoria and my mother have tears in their eyes, Rosie is willing me with her soft hazel eyes to calm the fuck down, and Julius is staring at me with curiosity.

A low rumble of laughter escapes my lips as I turn my focus on Father. I roll up to him, only a few inches away from him.

"Your firm brokered a deal for Gambino Construction, didn't they?"

His Adam's apple bobs up and down as he swallows. His eyes widen slightly before relaxing again.

"Don't even think about covering this shit up on me. I might have been seven, but I remember," I warn.

"What is he talking about, Edward?" Mom asks through glossy eyes.

"Edgar got in the way of that bullet," I snap in anger.

"Stop!" Viki yells through tears, but I continue the search for the truth, impenetrable in its pursuit.

"That bullet was meant for you!" I shout at him, and he quickly puts his hands up in surrender.

"No, son."

"Fuck you." I spit. All my venom and rage spill out as I lurch forward, grab my father by his shirt, and ball it between my fingers. I slam him back against the wall.

I hear yelling around me, but I'm blinded by my need for the truth, and I want his admission.

He lets out a moan at the impact, but he isn't fighting back. He knows he doesn't stand a chance.

A commotion erupts behind me, and hands claw around my bicep, pulling me back. I assume it's Julius, and I fight him off, throwing my father back against the wall.

"*Why?*" I yell, completely losing all sense of control.

My mother's perfume fills my nostrils as her nails dig into my arm. "Get off him, Vin, please. I beg you!" she shrieks, tears streaming down her face.

I immediately release my grip on my father. I can't bear seeing my mother like this. My eyes are wide, my chest heaving as if I've just sparred with a world champion. Julius is standing beside Mother, consoling her.

"Is it true?" My mother's question comes out quietly, and it's as though you can hear a pin drop as we await his response.

Of course, it was. My phone call with Justin confirmed it. The confession was extracted from Montero by our mole on the inside, who confirmed that he took the fall for the hit when it was Tony Gambino who had, in fact, pulled the trigger. But now it was their turn to hear it directly from my cowardly father.

His hand goes up to his chest, where I had him pinned moments before. My brother, Julius, steps closer and demands an answer from him. Father looks between us before focusing on Mother. She is staring back at him, fear and confusion sweeping across her face.

He takes his hand to his head when he admits, "It's true."

Mother lets out a loud shriek and collapses into a chair, sobbing uncontrollably. Viki cries hysterically, and Rosie pulls her in for an embrace as she tries to console her. Meanwhile, I am glued to the floor, watching my pathetic father finally admit what I had known all along.

I am suddenly alerted by a loud crunching sound and quickly turn my head toward the source of the noise. It's Julius, standing over our father, who is now lying on the ground after receiving a hard punch to the jaw.

Rosie is sitting across from me, looking up at me, and I can't help but wonder if she's terrified of me.

I have no memory of how I made it back home, but now I find myself in my cigar bar, sitting in my armchair with a neat whisky in hand. I don't even know why she's still with me. She deserves someone who can give her the happiness she deserves, and even though we work well together, I know our time is running out. I should end things with her and spare us the heartbreak.

But I'm selfish, and I can't let her go. I need her now more than ever.

"I'm sorry, I didn't know about your brother," she says, breaking the silence between us.

I down the whisky in one gulp and set the glass back on the table.

"You have nothing to apologize for," I say as the sting of the whisky lessens, having had a few since dinner.

"Come here, little one," I say, swallowing the thickness in my throat. I'm full of vengeance, and I need to calm the fuck down. My girl is the only one who can help me do that.

She slides across my lap and runs her hand down my cheek. I close my eyes and lean into the smooth touch of her fingers, relishing in the momentary peace it brings.

"Let me help you," she whispers, dusting her lips across mine.

My eyes fly open, and the calm is fleeting, replaced by the insatiable hunger I have for her. I pull her closer, kissing her more fiercely as my hands roam over her body, exploring every curve and inch. She moans into my mouth, and I feel myself growing harder with every passing moment. I need her now more than ever to help me forget the pain and anger consuming me.

I reach around her back, find the tiny zipper, and tug it down. The soft, cool metal is a stark contrast to the heat emanating from her body.

The weight of her dress shifts as it slides down and pools around her waist. Her hips tilt slightly, pressing against me, and my arousal grows with each passing moment. My eyes are locked on her as she stands up and lets the dress fall to the floor, revealing the curves of her body in a canary yellow bra that has my dick heavy like lead.

Her gaze lowers to the dress on the floor, then back up at me and a slow, sexy smirk tips into her cheeks.

She's left it there purposely.

For me.

I inhale sharply. "You were warned the first time you did that on my floor. Do you understand that you will be punished for your behavior?"

"Yes, Sir," she replies as she unclasps her bra and slides down her panties, letting them pool beside the dress.

I lean back in my chair and run my fingers across each other, admiring the beautiful disobedient woman standing in front of me. The light washes across her smooth skin as I slowly trail down the length of her stomach to her neat little strip of hair between her legs. Her confidence, standing there and letting me drink her in, is even more of a turn-on.

"So fucking beautiful," I say as I rise so we are standing together, only a whisper apart. I step behind her, my hand sliding down between her breasts and further to the indent of her stomach, feeling her tense at my touch. My lips trace the nape of her neck in bites and sucks.

I whisper in her ear, "You know what happens to naughty girls, don't you?"

She nods, her breaths coming in short gasps.

I take her hand and lead her down the hall toward my bedroom.

As I lead Rosie to the bed, I pick up the scarf I had left earlier. It's soft and delicate, perfect for what I have planned for her. She's watching me with a mix of anticipation and apprehension, and I know she wants this just as much as me.

Guiding her down on the bed, I slowly tie her wrists together with the silk scarf, feeling the softness of it against her skin. Opening my side drawer, I pull out a blindfold and some rope and slip it over her head. But before I do, I see a flicker of fear and excitement dancing in her hazel eyes.

Next, I move down to her legs, spreading them apart. Then, slowly yet meticulously, I tie the lengths of rope around each of her ankles, binding her to the bedpost and spreading her far apart.

Once I'm finished, I take a step back and admire my handiwork. She's spread out before me, completely at my mercy. Mine for the taking to do as I will.

I disappear into the kitchen and return with a glass of ice cubes. When I return, I watch as Rosie's chest heaves up and down with anticipation at the sound of my footsteps.

"By the time I'm finished with you, you'll be begging me to come," I whisper in her ear and kiss her bottom lip, biting down on it. She lets out a moan as I marvel at the goddess beneath me.

I slide an ice cube across her collarbone, watching as her body shudders in response. I repeat the motion, this time down the length of her chest, pausing to circle each nipple with the cold cube until they harden into peaks.

Rosie moans, arching her back as the ice trails down her stomach and into the V of her thighs. I move the ice back and forth between her legs, teasing her as she writhes and begs for release.

But I'm not ready to let her come just yet. I want to see her squirm and hear her beg for it.

I pull back what's left of the ice, watching as her body quivers in frustration. "Please," she whispers, twisting in her bindings.

"Please, what?" I ask, my voice low and husky.

"Please let me come," she begs, her hips lifting off the bed in a desperate attempt to find release.

I run an ice cube along the inside of her thigh, moving closer and closer to where she wants it most. "Not yet," I whisper, delighting in the way her body trembles in response.

I run it across her clit, and she writhes beneath me. Then I slide it down her folds to her puckered hole. She's shaking and thrusting, chasing her release.

Relishing how her body responds to my every touch, I continue, driving her to the brink of orgasm, then pulling back, over and over again, until she's a panting, begging mess beneath me. Finally, when I can't take it anymore, I slip the melting ice inside her, pushing it deep and giving her what she wants. "Come now," I command as I watch her fall apart beneath me, her body shaking with pleasure and crying out my name.

I'm consumed with need as I swiftly undress and slip on a condom. My cock feels like a heavy weight, dragging me down toward the bed. Then, climbing on top, I roughly devour Rosie's pussy, savoring the taste of her juices coating my mouth as she squirms and writhes beneath me. I'm a wild beast, taking what I want from her.

She cries out as I stroke and lick her from clit to back entrance. I savor the sight of her jerking against her restraints, her back arching off the bed as I pull another orgasm from her.

"You're cunt is fucking delicious, little one."

A soft moan slips from her lips at my words. My girl has a thing for dirty words, and it has a smirk pulling at my lips.

I undo her restraints and slip off her blindfold. Then I chase away her breathlessness with a chaste kiss, then pull back. "I'm not done with you yet. On all fours, facing the headboard." A flash of arousal sparks in her eyes, and she quickly complies.

I marvel at the sight of her, but my primal needs take over. Climbing behind her, I slap her ass, and she hisses out a moan. Then, instead of using my hand to rub out the sting, I lean down and kiss her red-marked cheek where the outline of my hand lingers.

Without warning, I slam into her, and she's propelled

forward, our movements rough and hard. I need her so much it consumes me.

"Oh God." She moans loudly into the pillow, and I feel a sudden pressure in my chest. I need to see her. Pulling out of her, I roll her over.

"Your sweet little cunt, I need it riding me," I growl in her ear while cupping her pussy. *My pussy.*

She moves, sliding herself over my cock, and lowers herself down. We move in unison, our eyes locked onto each other as the intense heat builds between us.

My hands circle her hips, slamming her down onto me harder as we find a sensual rhythm. This is intimate, too intimate, but I want and need her like this.

Her hands cradle around my neck as she deepens the kiss.

The orgasm builds between us, and something unspoken but potent swirls between us as our eyes connect.

"Vincent," she calls out between pants as her eyes flutter.

"Look at me, Rosie," I groan out so close, and she complies, steadying her gaze to mine.

Our bodies entwine, sweat slicking our skin as we climb together, both on the brink.

We come together, and I capture her breathlessness with a kiss. We stay like this, with her arms around my neck and mine around her waist, drawing her close.

It's at this moment that I am finally at peace.

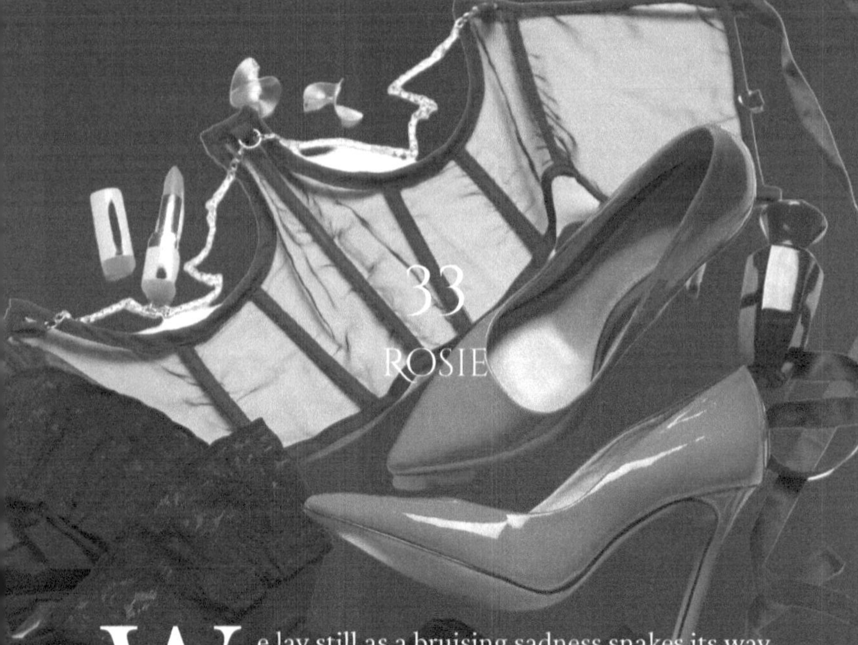

We lay still as a bruising sadness snakes its way into my bones. I don't want Vincent to leave, but I know he won't stay. He isn't capable of anything but what he's given me—no-strings-attached sex. I should be grateful for the time we've had and the brilliant man I've gotten to know. So, for now, I will press him close and cherish him.

Maybe even love him.

Eventually, we disentangle and get cleaned up.

Vincent walks back to the bed, then slides in beside me. His warm body heat radiates against mine. He drags my thigh on top of his muscular leg, and I melt into him, relishing the feeling of his strong embrace.

"I'm sorry you had to witness what happened with my family," Vincent says, disappointment evident in his tone. I hadn't even known he had a brother, let alone that he was murdered. But I hadn't had time to process anything with a grieving Victoria to console and an irate Vincent to deal with.

"What are you thinking about?" he asks, brushing his

thumb against my chin. "I've always said you can ask me anything," he adds when I don't answer immediately.

I feel a lump form in my throat as tears threaten to spill over. I swipe at them, willing them not to fall.

"Oh, baby, what is it?" Vincent asks, concern etched on his face.

I hesitate. I'm afraid of what Vin will think if I tell him the truth—that I'm falling in love with him, despite everything. But admitting to him that he is everything I've ever wanted will just make it that much harder when he leaves.

"I'm sorry about your brother," I say, choosing the safer option.

Vincent stares at me for a moment before speaking. "Don't weep over me, beautiful. I'm not worth the tears."

His reaction surprises me. I realize that he, too, is holding back for reasons I can't quite understand.

"That's not true," I say, meeting his gaze. The tension between us is palpable, unspoken words hanging in the air. But I push on, not willing to go there. "What will you do now, you know... with this information?" I ask.

Vincent's lips curl with venom as he speaks, and I can hardly recognize the cold switch that happens instantly. "My team is working on locating Tony Gambino as we speak. Once we get the word, he is a dead man."

I sit upright, feeling a sense of urgency. "Vin, no. You can't."

"Oh, I fucking can and will," he replies with a dangerous edge to his voice. "He will pay. He took the most important person away from me, Rosie. He will pay with his fucking life."

"But you'll go to jail for the rest of yours," I reason with him, my hands rising to his cheeks. It dawns on me that my man is blinded by pure and utter revenge. It has made him who he is, and it's his driving force. Suddenly, all I feel is pity that he has been robbed of any feeling.

"I have to do this," he insists. "And I shouldn't be telling you any of this, Rosie. But you... you bring out this other side in me that I buried a long time ago. You make me want to be a better man."

He turns away from me and rolls onto his back, staring up at the ceiling. "Maybe if we'd met under different circumstances..." His voice trails off.

Maybe he's right. Timing is everything, and the possibility of us being more under these circumstances is just too much. He's too blinded by anything else to see us for what we truly are to one another.

I'll be devastated when he leaves, but I don't think I could survive knowing he's rotting in a jail cell somewhere when I can stop it.

"Vincent, listen to me. If you do this, you will ruin your life. Everything you and Julius have built will crumble," I say, desperation lacing my voice.

"I don't give a fuck," he retorts coldly.

"Yes, you do," I exclaim, rolling onto him and punching him on the chest. "I won't let you do this."

He scoffs and pushes me off him. "You don't get a say," he growls out before storming out of the bedroom.

What the hell just happened?

When I wake, warm hands are wrapped around my stomach. I lean into Vincent's touch as he presses his chest against mine.

"We only have a week together, Rosie, and I don't want to spend it fighting,"

He turns me around, and piercing green eyes stare down at me.

"I don't want to fight either," I reply softly. Overwhelmed by emotion, I wrap my arms around him, unwilling to let him go.

His hand glides down the side of my naked body, and I shudder at the connection. He places soft, heated kisses at the base of my neck, moving up to my lips, which I willingly open for him.

He kisses me passionately, his tongue sensually massaging mine. It's as if he was born to kiss me.

He pulls back, his eyes intense as he gazes into mine. "I need you bare," he says, his voice low and urgent.

Oh God, yes.

This is what I need, to feel him inside me. All of him. No barriers.

I'm already wet with arousal and willingly part my legs as he positions himself between them. The head of his cock brushes across my sex, and I clench with a deep need as he quickly slides inside me.

Our groan of ecstasy echoes the room as he fills me completely.

"Fuck," he mutters, his eyes rolling back in his head. With each thrust, he stretches me, and I'm overwhelmed by the sensations coursing through my body, struggling to catch my breath.

I pull him down to me, craving the feel of his lips on mine. He groans into my mouth as our tongues tangle in a hot, breathless kiss.

It's sensation overload as he thrusts deeper, hitting that spot at my back wall, and I can't hold it anymore. Waves of pleasure wash over me, and I'm quivering around him.

He watches me with a look that wraps around my heart.

A few more thrusts and he's coming with me as I climax again, our bodies intertwined in a moment of bliss. He kisses me gently on the lips slides out of bed.

He returns from the bathroom, his naked body a symphony of muscles as I sit up and watch him. He seems so carefree and relaxed, a complete contrast from earlier at the restaurant.

I bite my lower lip at the sight of him.

"That lip will be the death of me," he says, coming to sit beside me and giving me a chaste kiss that pulls at my bottom lip. I giggle, but my mind is racing with thoughts about our relationship.

"Just so you know, I've only been on birth control since your doctor made a house call, but it's only been three weeks, so I'll grab the morning-after pill first thing," I say, trying to keep my voice light.

He gently guides my legs open and wipes me with a towel, his lips contorting into a smile. "Would it be the worst thing if I put a baby in you?" he asks, and I freeze at the question.

We haven't talked about the possibility of a future together because, until now, there hasn't been a real possibility. He lives in London, and I live in Jersey. He's thirty-two, and I'm twenty-two, barely paying my bills.

We're on different trajectories in life, aren't we?

Silence descends over the bedroom as he finishes cleaning between my legs, and he looks up to see my expression. "Why are you looking at me like that?" he asks, putting the washcloth down.

"You can't be serious?" I reply, feeling flustered. He stares at me blankly as I continue, "We haven't even discussed our relationship beyond next week, and now you're talking about a baby?"

He laughs nervously. "You're right. We haven't."

"Well, I just assumed you'd be going back home to London after the internship program," I say, feeling a knot forming in my stomach.

"And after I wrap up loose ends," he replies, his carefree face now replaced with a scowl.

I purse my lips, not wanting to argue with him and waste the little time we have left together. I can't stop him if he wants to seek revenge and throw away his life.

"Exactly. So, that's settled," I say, trying to sound confident, but my true feelings are anything but that.

"You could move to London after you graduate," he suggests, making it sound like a casual suggestion instead of a life-changing decision.

"What?" I'm taken aback, feeling confused yet exhilarated at the possibility of us not ending. "Is that what you want?" I ask, eager for an answer.

"I just know that you make me feel alive, Rosie, and I'm not ready to let go of that," he admits, his words impacting me deeply, but that's where they end.

His offer lacks the commitment and love I hadn't realized I needed until this moment.

When we met, I thought I could be the type of girl who loses their virginity without being attached and falling in love. But that's not me. I have fallen for him and need more.

He's incapable of more.

I couldn't possibly contemplate moving overseas with someone not willing to give me the love I deserve.

"I have my whole life here," I explain, and his face fills with sadness.

"Of course," he responds, sensing my hesitation. "It's late. Let's get some rest," he suggests, sliding into the sheets and leaving space between us.

My phone ringing jolts me awake, and I realize I am alone in bed. I quickly grab my phone and see my brother calling.

"Gabe. What time is it? Are you okay?" I ask, still half asleep.

"I'm coming over," he says.

"What? No, I'm in the city."

"Even better, so am I."

There are voices yelling in the background and muffled sounds. Gabe's heavy breathing travels down the line, and it's as though he's panting or running away from the noise as the voices become distant.

"What's going on?" I ask in a panic, now fully awake.

"I'm in trouble, sis. Now where the fuck are you?"

A loud bang sounds, and I pull the phone away from my ear.

"Text me the address."

Then the line goes dead.

My heart hammers in my chest. *Was that a gun?* No, he is in the city, and it's always loud and busy. It could have been anything.

I quickly text the address, throw on my dressing gown, and walk out to find Vincent in his cigar bar with a whisky in his hand. He's staring out the huge glass windows when he turns.

"Are you okay?" he asks.

"I should be asking you that, considering you're here and not in bed."

"Can't sleep."

"I see." There is a space between us that wasn't there when we made love earlier. It's as though he has put up a brick wall, and the feeling is fucking painful.

Instead of going to sit with him, I slide into the opposite armchair.

"My brother, Gabriel, is on his way over. He's in trouble. I'm sorry I didn't have a choice but to give him your address," I tell him, trying to focus on the here and now and not the future of what-ifs.

He set his glass down. "What kind of trouble?"

I avert my gaze from him, and my eyes wander outside. "I don't know what's going on, but I'm scared for him. Just like I am for you," I say as a solitary tear unexpectedly rolls down my cheek.

"Please, don't cry," he responds, his voice broken as he shifts his chair closer to me. With a gentle touch, he wipes away my tear using his thumb, and we're interrupted by his phone ringing.

He pulls my face toward him, and I feel like I'm about to break down. Suddenly, everything becomes too overwhelming. I've always been strong and independent, but the fear of Vincent risking his life and something happening to my brother is too much to bear.

"Wait here," he says, rising to answer the phone.

I watch him, feeling like he has enough to deal with without my brother coming in here with his problems.

I'm so done right now.

"Yes," Vincent says into the phone.

"Send him up," he states, passing a glance at me. "Yes, I'm sure," he barks into the phone before hanging up.

My heart pounds with anxiety and worry as I stand and walk toward him, determined to shield Vincent from my brother's problems.

"Vin, why don't you go back to bed? I'll be there as soon as I finish," I suggest.

The soft ding of the elevator signals its impending arrival at the penthouse, and Vincent grabs my hand.

Vincent tightens his grip and looks at me with a puzzled expression. "You don't want me to meet your brother, do you?" he asks.

I hesitate for a moment, unsure of how to answer. I know Vin feels a little hurt, but I'm only trying to protect him. Although I believe my brother is a good person at heart, he has a knack for doing underhanded shit, and the luxury penthouse we're in is already a giveaway, so introducing him to Vincent would be too risky.

"I will leave you alone once I know you're safe," he says through a strained jaw when I don't respond.

The elevator doors slide open, and I let out a soft "Okay," giving in to the fact that Vincent will stay by my side to confront my brother. Despite my fear and anxiety, I'm relieved I don't have to face my brother alone.

Sobs rise in my throat as I struggle to push them back upon seeing my brother. His shirt is torn, buttons are missing, hair is disheveled, and he's wet with perspiration. He also has a cut brow with droplets of blood streaming down the hollow beneath his eye. As he steps out of the elevator, his gaze flickers between Vincent and me.

"Gabe, what the hell is going on?" I shriek, unable to contain my shock.

Vincent steps forward to separate us. "Were you followed?" he demands.

"No, of course not," my brother replies as the two men face off.

"Good. I'm Vincent. If you ever put your sister in danger, I will fucking kill you," he warns, and I'm taken aback by his admission.

"Vin!" I yell, but he turns to me briefly and says, "I'll be in the office if you need me," before storming down the hallway, throwing my brother a corrosive stare.

My brother watches him leave, then turns his attention back to the penthouse, visibly impressed. "Is that your boyfriend?" he asks, touching the cut on his head.

"I believe we have bigger things to figure out than that, don't you think?" I respond, turning my back on him and walking into the kitchen. I fetch him a bottle of Evian, and he takes it absentmindedly, continuing to take in his surroundings.

"Look at this place," he says. "Rosie, ask your boyfriend for help. He clearly has it."

"I'm not asking Vincent," I respond firmly. "We got ourselves into this mess, and we can find a way out of it."

He continues to plead with me, and I feel a surge of anger. "So you'd risk my life over your pride?" he accuses, frustration creeping into his voice.

"My pride?" I retort, incredulous. "What do you mean?"

He takes a deep breath, looking like he's struggling to tell me something. "The loan sharks are run by the mob, sis. If I don't get them two-hundred grand by Thursday, I'm done."

"Two hundred grand?" I repeat, feeling the air dissolve in my chest as I sink down on the barstool. Desperate for answers, I plead with him, "What have you done?"

He paces nearby, and I feel my fury build when I stand and yell, "What have you done, Gabriel?"

He stops pacing, and I look into his eyes and see the fear and desperation there.

"It's Dad," he confesses, his voice low, and I take a step back at the mere mention of him.

"I'm sorry, okay? He came to me with a proposition to make money, and it seemed like a no-brainer at the time."

He looks at me, assessing my reaction as he waits for my answer. The room is silent except for the sound of my breathing and my heart is racing.

"I can't believe you did this," I say, my voice barely above a whisper. "You went behind my back and got involved with Dad, even after everything he did to us?"

"I know, I know," my brother says, desperation creeping into his voice. "But I didn't know what else to do. I'm in too deep now, and I need your help."

My heart sinks as I realize the trust we've built over the years has been shattered. I can't believe he went behind my back, betraying the bond we forged as siblings trying to make a life for ourselves without our mother.

Vincent charges into the kitchen, his face set like stone. My brother turns toward him, and I feel a sense of dread wash over me. "What the hell do you want?" Gabriel demands.

"I will pay your debt if you promise to stay the fuck away from Rosie," Vincent says, his voice cold and unyielding.

"N-no," I stammer. "Vin, No."

"I can do that!" my brother responds all too quickly, and I shrink back at the speed of his answer.

Does he never want to see me again, or does he want to keep me safe and out of harm's way?

I lean toward the former, considering how much he has tangled with my life in the last few months.

"No!" I repeat, but Vincent holds his hand up, silencing me with one swift motion. "Thought you'd say that." Vincent hands him his business card, then squares up to him. Now get the fuck out of my house," he says, his voice deadly stern, causing the hairs on the back of my neck to stand on end.

My brother looks at me one last time and says, "Sorry," before turning on his heel and disappearing into the elevator.

The soft ding of the elevator tells me he's gone, and I feel my heart shattering into a million pieces. I crumble into a flood of tears, my body shaking with sobs as I try to come to terms with the chaos engulfing my life.

34

VINCENT

Tomorrow marks the last day of the internship, and with it comes the end of the most magical weeks with Rosie staying with me. Waking up next to her, watching her sleep, and feeling her soft breath on my skin has been nothing short of incredible. But as much as I want it to continue, I know I have to let her go.

I shouldn't have let things go on for so long. I was selfish, taking what I needed from her without considering the consequences. Now, as Justin closes in on Tony Gambino's whereabouts, I know I have to act. I need to end this, even if it means taking a life. Once I have my vengeance, I'll have to leave the country and likely never return.

Justin may be an expert in covering up crimes, but there's always a risk. If I stay in the US, I'll be an easy target for the feds or the Mafia. And I can't be with Rosie if she's going to be a target. I could never forgive myself if anything happened to her because of me.

It wasn't such a good idea to open up to Rosie. In a moment of weakness, I asked her if having my baby was such a bad idea. *I don't know what the fuck came over me.*

That was last week, and we haven't discussed it since. Nor the fact that she basically refused to consider moving to London with me. That was a flimsy idea on my part, wafered in the heat of the moment. Still, although obvious, her refusal was a sucker punch to the gut, especially since I know the only thing keeping her here is her wayward brother.

It's late, and I have the interns downstairs finishing off some tasks when I decide to pay Julius a visit. Walking past his vacant reception desk, I notice his office door ajar and push it open. Inside I find his secretary Isabella sitting close beside him.

They look up, startled by my intrusion. "Hope I'm not interrupting," I say as I enter Julius' office.

"Of course not," Julius replies. His secretary then quickly exits the room. I can't help but wonder what that's about as I take a seat in front of him.

"Have you spoken to Mom?" I ask. "She hasn't called me back."

Since the fight at Le Cirque, Mom and Victoria haven't taken my calls, and I'm restless. I'd like to think it's because I'm waiting for a call at any moment from Justin telling me they've found the asshole who shot Edgar. But I know it's more than that.

I push away the tentacles of need, suffocating my heart in my chest.

"Vin?" Julius pulls my attention.

"What?" I look up and realize I completely missed what he just said.

"I said Mom is going through a lot right now," he repeats as he takes me in. I nod in understanding, hoping she will be okay.

Julius steeples his hands across the desk. "You were

right," he admits. "All along, you were right." He shakes his head.

I know it pains him to admit it, but all my searching and painfully dredging up the past has resulted in the truth. "Montero is in jail, but he isn't the one who killed our brother. I'm sorry I tried to stop you from finding out the truth," he admits.

"Thank you, Julius," I reply, accepting his apology and not wanting this to come between us.

He nods, grateful for my forgiveness.

We sit in silence for a few moments, each lost in our own thoughts. The weight of the truth settles heavily on my shoulders, and anger and frustration build inside me.

"Victoria hasn't called me back, either," I say wistfully. "But she's been in contact with Rosie."

Julius isn't surprised. "They seemed to hit it off at the restaurant before shit went sideways."

"Look..." he lets out a sigh, "... Victoria needs time too."

"What is it with everyone fucking needing time?" I question angrily.

He throws his hands in the air. "We've all been lied to, Vin. Dad has known the truth and kept it from all of us... Mom, Viki, even me. We need time to process this shit in our own way. You should know this. You've spent most of your adult life trying to find the truth, and now we know that Dad knew all along. It's just... we all need time."

I sniff and ask, "What about him?" I haven't spoken to him since that evening. That's not to say I haven't poured over the videos and transcripts from Justin and my team, who interviewed him about everything I need to know. I couldn't possibly sit opposite him and keep calm. No, that's why I paid Justin to do the interview, to dot the i's and cross the t's so we can have every shred of information we need.

"He's been cooperating with your team. You'd know that," Julius says.

"And he's kept the police out of it?" I ask.

"Yes, at your request."

Justin has extracted every last bit of information from Father about his dealings with the Mafia. It turns out, he brokered a deal between two companies, and unbeknownst to him, one was controlled by the Gambino Family. The deal went bad, and the Gambinos were after him because he brokered it. The deal lost them millions of dollars and sent their lead guy to jail.

"I can tell you not to throw your life away for vengeance. I can tell you to let the cops handle it. But I know it will fall on deaf ears." He leans in, steepling his hands together as he takes me in.

A smirk lifts onto my lips. "The less you know, the better," I admit, not wanting to implicate my brother in any of this.

He shakes his head and asks, "And how about Rosie? Have you thought about her?"

I feel a lump form in my throat at the mention of her name, but I push aside the sadness that threatens to consume me. I can't afford to be weak right now. There's no time for emotions. I need to remain strong to see this through to the end.

"I saw the two of you at dinner last week. I've seen the change in you over the last six weeks. That is her, brother. She brings out the side in you I miss. You used to be my brother who I could pass the time with jokes and laughs. But ever since Edgar, it's like your path was sent into another trajectory full of hate and vengeance."

I know he's right, but now, when I'm so close to finishing it, I can't back down. Not now.

"It's the man I had to become," I say.

He rises abruptly, pushing his chair back, and rolling toward the glass behind him. "That's bullshit. We all make choices in life. You've made yours, but that doesn't mean it's final. What you do next will steer your life. You're at a fork, brother. Rosie is your light. Don't push her away for all the vengeance in the world."

Sadness washes over me, but I push it down deep into the crevices of my stomach where the light doesn't shine. "I need to finish this," I press as I stand.

His piercing eyes fixate on mine, and he shakes his head. "Then get the fuck out of here. I have nothing more to say to you."

I stare at him one last time, seeing the fear in his eyes, the same fear mirrored in Rosie's hazel eyes. *Don't they understand that I need to do this for Edgar?* He deserves peace. He deserves the asshole who killed him to suffer and die. For people to miss the lowlife scum when I take his life like I miss Edgar every fucking day of my life.

I turn and walk out the door, slamming it behind me.

It's the end of the day when I return to the floor below and find my interns chatting. "So, we're all finished?" I ask bitterly. I'm angry, and it's evident in my tone.

They all turn, but Rosie's piercing look catches me off guard as she stares at me with disappointment.

Adding to her disappointment, I say, "There's always more you can all do." I stare at her before turning away and landing my gaze on each of them.

Yes, I'm being a dick. It's the day before the program finishes, and they have all completed their tasks pretty well, if I'm honest. But I don't give a fuck. One can always be pushing, but her gaze and disappointment feel like a stab to the chest. She's the last person I want to disappoint.

We're back at my place when she leans over the onyx countertop and asks, "What was that about before?"

"What?" I ask, even though I know exactly what she's referring to.

She tilts her head to the side. "You being an ass to us when we'd all finished the tasks you set, and we were just about to leave for the day."

I'm torn between answering to push her away or keeping her close because of my selfish needs. I know she's perfect, but I'm not, so I push her away.

"The day doesn't end because of the time, Rosie."

She lets out a sigh. "Don't do this," she pleads.

"Don't do what?" I yell, and she jerks back at my outburst.

Like ripping a band-aid off, I need to end this. I've been too selfish to see it before. But now, we're in too deep, and I won't bring her down with me.

"I'm going to take that shift tonight," she says, shaking her head.

Everything inside me ignites as a flurry of sparks runs down my spine. She hasn't taken any shift this week, and now...

I slam my hand down on the counter. "Why? I paid your brother's debt. You do that, and we're over," I spit out venomously.

She turns slowly. "We were over before we ever began, Vin."

I round the counter and reach for her.

"What?" she asks.

"That's not fair," I say.

"We never stood a chance, Vin. Not with all this hate in your heart. You don't have room for anything else. Not me, not your family, and certainly not yourself."

"I was only ever honest with you from the beginning, Rosie... when I said I didn't date."

She nods as tears prick the backs of her eyes. All I want to do is pull her in and take away her pain. But something stops me.

"I know," she says, and all of a sudden, it's like a door closes as she falls out of my grasp and disappears down the hall.

I'm in the cigar lounge when I hear her footsteps return. I hate she's leaving me to work at the VC, and I hate even more that I can't stop her.

I look up at her, and she's the most beautiful woman in the world.

"If it's okay with you, I'll move my things out tomorrow after the final class."

A lump swells in my throat, but I can't say anything for fear of jeopardizing everything I've wrecked my adult life for.

She looks at me expectantly, and all I can give her is a nod. Disappointment flashes across her beautiful hazels, then she turns and walks out.

A moment later, she's in the elevator on her way to the Vanilla Club, and I'm too much of a coward to stop her.

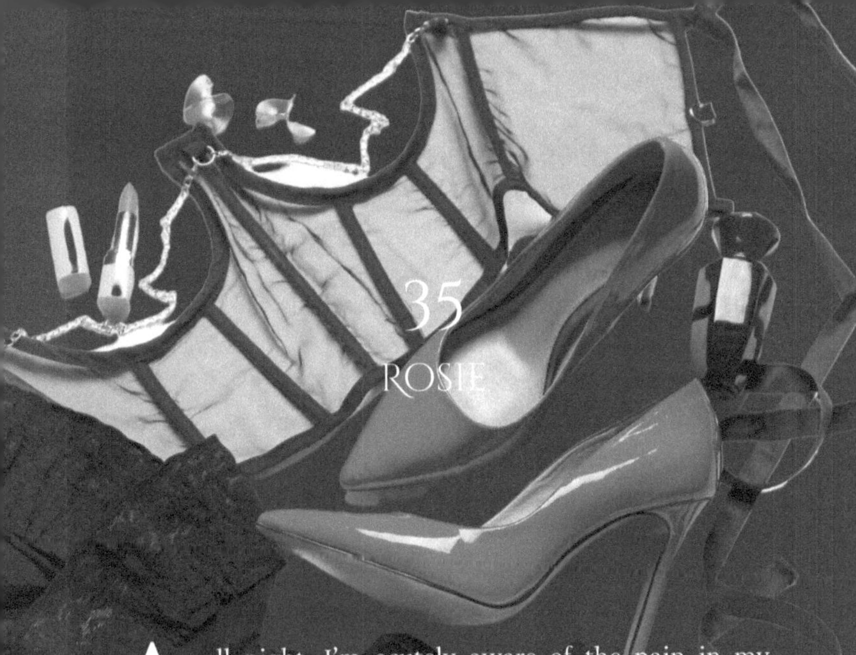

35

ROSIE

All night, I'm acutely aware of the pain in my chest. It's present with every touch and every flirtatious comment that's not from Vincent. I'm miserable, and I know it shows, but I can't do anything to hide the pain I feel. Maybe I shouldn't have taken the shift. I don't need to pay off my brother's debt anymore. He and Vincent sorted out the details during the week, and since my brother said he'd stay away from me, he's done just that by confirming everything with Vincent directly.

I'm downstairs at the bar, waiting for Jesse to prepare another round of drinks, when I see Freddie walk down the staircase. He offers me a weak smile. I swear that guy has a radar for emotions. He has this sixth sense about what people are feeling, even though my emotions are on full display tonight.

He knew about Vincent and me long before I even sensed that he liked me.

"Here you go, sugar," Jesse says with a wink as he slides the tray toward me. I grab the tray, but he stops me, his hand circling mine. "How's about a quickie tonight?" he asks. Flirtatiousness is one thing, but now this?

Uh, no, not happening. Ever. I need to make it clear. "What the fuck, Jesse?"

"I heard a rumor you've been upstairs in the suites."

"You heard wrong," I say, utterly taken aback.

He shrugs. "If you say so."

"I do say so, and for the record, there will *never* be anything like that between us. Your flirting is making me uncomfortable, so while we're at setting boundaries, you can stop that too," I say firmly.

He stares at me, poised to say something else, but then thinks better of it and rubs down the counter with the cloth that was tucked in his waistband.

Taking a momentary break, I step into the bathroom to reapply my lipstick. As I carefully touch up my makeup, the door suddenly swings open, startling me.

"Hell yes, sister from a different mister!" Kara stares me up and down, but I have no clue what she's talking about.

"What?" I ask, smoothing down my lace corset. Baby blue with a gold clasp and French knickers, it's a beautiful piece of lingerie, but tonight I don't feel special. My normal armor of confidence is wearing thin, and I'm questioning why I'm still working here, especially after fending off comments from the bartender.

"Laura heard what you said to Jesse when you were at the bar, and she told me."

I toss my head toward her. "Oh, that."

"Yes, that!" she says, exasperated. "Thank you! We're all pissed at how hard he's been flirting lately. Someone ought to shut him up."

I offer her a weak smile as I push away my golden Hollywood curls in the faux wig. "No problem," I reply, counting the minutes until my shift ends, and I can see Vincent again.

"You all right, hun?" she asks, tapping her hand on my shoulder as I pass by, causing me to turn. I'm about to crack like a dam and burst open.

I'm not okay, but I push on like I always have. "I'm fine." I smile at her reassuringly, even though my insides feel ripped apart.

It's been a bit of a rough crowd tonight, and I'm glad my shift is over. I unpin my hair and change into my boyfriend jeans and sweater, still wearing my black heels.

In my rush to leave Vincent's place, I forgot to pack sneakers. It's not like he lives too far from here, just a short cab ride away, but he hasn't texted me during my entire shift, and I know he's disappointed in me. But I'm disappointed in him too.

I even wonder if he'll wait up for me, but I shake my head, knowing it's just wishful thinking. Maybe I hoped he'd come to his senses and choose me over his black heart.

"What are you shaking your head at?" Freddie appears as I round out of the dressing room.

"Nothing," I say, surprised by the interruption.

"That's not what it looks like," Freddie replies, eyeing me with concern.

I sigh, feeling defeated.

"You've been moping around like a soggy noodle in a bowl of soup," he says. "You're lucky not to have any complaints from the men at your table tonight."

"I don't care anymore," I say because I think it's the

truth. I stayed here to help my brother out, but now that Vincent has stepped in, I don't have to be here anymore.

He raises his eyebrows. "Where's Mr. Slater tonight?" he asks, and I swallow.

"At home."

Shit. I haven't exactly told anyone that we're living together.

"Home?" His eyebrows knit into a question. "And you know that because you're with him?"

"I *was* with him, Freddie. He's going back to London, and I'm just..." I let the sentence hang in the air because I don't know what the hell I'm meant to do now. Forgetting about him is like forgetting how to breathe.

"Oh, Rosie. You don't fall in love with a man like Vincent Slater."

"Yeah, well, a bit late for that," I say, feeling tears prick at the backs of my eyes when he pulls me in for a hug. His arms wrap around my body, and I lean into his care.

"I'm so fucked," I whisper.

"All we need is a bottle of vodka, me, and your besties."

I nod into his shoulder. "Tomorrow," I say, wiping my tears from the back of my hand because tomorrow, the internship will end, I'll be moved out, and chances are I will never see Vincent again.

"I'll be there," he says, pulling me closer.

Freddie is called away, and we say our goodbyes. I text him my address and at the same time, fire off a text to Sara. It's two in the morning, but I know she's likely to be awake, especially since her last text to me was only an hour ago.

She's been out to dinner with Ethan, and she messaged me a blow-by-blow account of their evening. In the last text, she sent me a picture of the diamond earrings he just bought her.

. . .

Me: *They are beautiful.*

I reply before sending another text.

Me: *I'm back home tomorrow. You, me, Freddie, and a bottle of vodka. I need to forget.*

I place my phone in my backpack and walk out the staff entrance. Tonight is my last night with Vincent, and I don't want to argue. I want to be in his arms, immersed in his touch, and making love to the man who has stolen my heart for one last time.

I push open the door, and the cool spring air hits my face as a gust of wind spins a patch of leaves into a whirlwind. Suddenly, I hear a commotion behind me, and before I can turn, a blinding pain hits me across the back of the head.

The last thing I see is the gravel, then everything fades to black.

~

My eyes sting, and my head is pounding with pain. The metallic taste of blood is in my mouth, and I swallow the lump in my throat. I hear voices nearby that I don't recognize, and as I open my eyes, I realize I'm unable to move, bound with my hands behind my back. Alarm floods my body, heightening every sense as panic takes over. I jerk against the straps, but I'm unable to move.

I will myself to calm down and take in my surroundings—an old warehouse building, graffiti on the windows, and...

No, this can't be happening.

I attempt to move once more, but thrashing about only saps my energy without achieving a damn thing.

"She's awake," a dark voice from beyond the shadows says.

My heart rate hammers in my chest, fearing the worst. A lone tear falls down my cheek at the realization.

Vincent probably thinks I've gone home after my shift.

He won't be looking for me. No one will be looking for me.

I'm as good as dead.

36
VINCENT

It's after three, and Rosie should be home by now. I sit nervously, tapping my foot against the rug in my cigar bar. I have a sinking feeling she's left me. She couldn't even wait until tomorrow like she said before she left.

The truth is, I don't fucking blame her. For any of it.

I pushed her away.

Sadness settles in my heart like a heavy fog, suffocating any glimmer of light. It's a foreign emotion that seems to have melted away anger since Rosie arrived in my life. It's probably for the best, but I'm too pained to see it that way.

She deserves someone who can make her happy and give her his entire heart. Not someone tainted by the past. I pick up my phone and exhale a sigh before furiously typing out a message.

Me: *I wish you nothing but happiness, Rosie.*

. . .

I slam my phone down, pouring the remainder of the bottle of whisky into my glass and lugging it down.

A debilitating hangover jackhammers loudly in my head when my phone buzzes on my way into the office.

I slide it out of my suit pants and see Justin's name flash up on the screen.

"What's the update?" I ask eagerly.

"We have eyes on the target, and I'm getting the team together as we speak."

"Where is he?"

"In Silverton, Jersey," Justin responds.

My mind races. Silverton is the battle ground for the Mafia. Namely two families, the Gambino and Angelino Families who are often at war. It makes perfect sense for him to hide there.

"I'm on my way."

"Not so fast. Go to work, establish an alibi, and I'll call you as soon as we've assembled," Justin cautions.

I let out a frustrated growl, but I know he's right.

"Fine," I mutter, snapping off the phone in annoyance.

It's nine thirty, half an hour since the internship started, and still, there is no sign of Rosie. She hasn't missed a day of the internship since it started. Not when she worked back-to-back shifts at the Vanilla Club and not when she felt unwell.

Despite my best efforts to focus on the class, I can't shake the thought that something is wrong, and by nine forty-five, I can't focus on anything else but Rosie's whereabouts.

I check my phone. There's nothing from her. I look up to

find the interns busy finalizing a project when I discreetly call Angela over to my desk.

"Yes, Mr. Slater?" she asks.

"Angela, do you know where Rosie is today?" I ask, hoping she knows something.

She shakes her head. "I don't. Sorry."

I feel my apprehension increasing. And the feeling that something isn't right is suffocating me.

"It's strange that she's not here on the last day. We had plans to have lunch together," she says, a concerned expression spreading across her face.

"Thank you, Angela." I dismiss her with a nod, my mind racing with possibilities of what could have happened to Rosie.

I get up and walk over to the windows, staring down from thirty-nine stories high at a sea of people below.

Where are you, little one?

I decide to push aside my emotions and dial her number. The call goes straight to voicemail, and a shiver runs down my spine. Her phone never goes straight to voicemail.

I call her brother, having saved his number in my phone. I wait as each ring is left unanswered.

I storm out of the room, turning away from the windows.

Dane's voice fades behind me as he calls out, "Should we proceed without you?" But I don't look back.

My mind is racing with countless thoughts and worries, all revolving around Rosie's safety. I continue to walk, unable to stand still when my phone vibrates in my hand. I look down to see Justin's number instead of Rosie's or Gabriel's.

"Fuck!" I yell out in frustration, feeling helpless and

worried. I ignore the eyes shooting in my direction as I click on the call.

"What?" I yell into the receiver.

"We've got him. He's in an abandoned warehouse on the outskirts of Silverton," Justin says.

I'm compelled to find Rosie, but not when I am this close to getting vengeance on the man who murdered my brother.

"I'm on my way," I say firmly.

"Vincent, wait," Justin says urgently.

"What," I snap out impatiently.

"There's something else," he hesitates as he pauses.

"Spit it out," I demand, feeling a sense of foreboding wash over me.

"He's got Rosie, Sir."

I stop in my tracks, feeling as if the ground has disappeared beneath me. A cold hand grips my heart like an icy claw, squeezing it with a paralyzing fear.

"Is she alive?" I ask, barely able to breathe.

"Yes. I have a man with eyes on her. She's bloody and bruised, but she's alive. They must have been tracking you. I'm sorry. We'll get her," Justin assures me.

"You better," I croak out, my voice hoarse with emotion as I hang up the phone.

My girl is there because of me.

In an untraceable car, I arrive at the abandoned warehouse and veer into the back alleyway, away from the front entrance. I kill the engine and run toward the building, a good hundred yards in front of me. It's silent, and the smell of rubbish invades my nostrils, but a sense of calm hits me. I know that anything else would jeopardize her safety.

Justin spots me and motions for me to come over to where he and his partner are hiding out.

"Where is she?" I ask.

"At the right side. She's flanked by two men. Gambino's in the room beside her, and by the looks of the infrared sensor, he has another two men with him," he replies. "We're outnumbered," he adds.

"I know we're not," I say confidently. "Follow my lead," I say as I set off toward the entrance.

"Fuck, Slater," he hisses out, trying to keep up. "Stop. We will enter first to provide cover," he adds, pulling me back. But I push on.

"No one is getting her out but me," I insist.

"Fuck, at least take a piece," he says, shoving the cool heavy gun at my hip. I take it from him and tuck it into my waistband.

It's been a while since I've shot a gun, but I'm prepared to use it or my bare hands to kill the son of a bitch.

I proceed to the back entrance with Justin and his man flanking me on either side. I kick the door open, announcing myself to all who can hear me. It's the safest thing to do, given the circumstances. Creeping up on Gambino or any of his men could trigger something unexpected, and with my girl inside, I can't risk it.

The inside of the old abandoned warehouse is eerie and desolate. The air is thick with dust, and the silence is deafening, broken only by the sound of creaking metal and rustling debris. The walls are lined with peeling paint, and the concrete floors are cracked and littered with rubbish. The windows are boarded up, casting a dim light into the vast open space, and I'm growing impatient every second that ticks by without Rosie by my side.

"Where are you, you bastard?"

I take a deep breath and reach for my gun, feeling the weight of it in my hand. I grip it tightly, my fingers hovering over the safety switch. With a quick flick, I disengage the safety, the soft click barely audible over the sound of clapping. My attention diverts to the far corner of the warehouse, and I make my way toward it, determined to confront Tony Gambino.

As I approach, I see Gambino and his men spread out behind him, and I realize that we are seriously outnumbered.

"Well, well, finally, he works it out. After all these years, Vincent Slater is here to do what? Kill me?" Gambino's deep laugh echoes off the walls, and his henchmen join in, jeering and taunting me.

It's a trap. They knew I was coming after him, so they took Rosie as bait.

How did they know we were coming? There must be a mole in Justin's unit. That's the only explanation.

I take a step forward, the gun steady in my grip, my finger poised on the trigger.

"Let me see her," I demand, my voice firm and unyielding.

But Tony Gambino just shakes his head. "Not just yet," he replies with a sly grin, his eyes glinting with malicious intent.

The anger inside me is like a ferocious animal, clawing at my chest with its sharp talons, demanding to be released. It feels like a raging inferno that threatens to consume me whole, and I struggle to keep it in check.

"I didn't come here to play games, Tony. Where is she?"

Tony smiles, enjoying the power he holds over me. "You're not in control here, Vincent. You never have been," he taunts, his voice oozing with malice.

I take another step forward, my grip on the gun tightening. "I suggest you start giving me some answers."

Tony just laughs, his men laughing with him. "You're in no position to be making threats."

The tension rises, and the air is thick with hostility. I know I need to stay calm and focused, but all I can think about is getting Rosie out of here and making sure she's safe.

Tony, a short man with wispy gray hair, a balding head, and thin lips, runs his hand through his hair and wears a thick gold chain with a crucifix around his neck.

"I'm only going to say it one more time, Tony. Where is she?"

"She's fine," he says, waving me off. "Fiery bitch, that one. She roughed up Tommy Two-Shoes' nose here."

I look over and see his bloodied nose, and I'm fucking proud of my girl. But scared to think what drove her to do that. *Was he roughing her up? Was he... God...* not time to think about that.

"If you don't bring her to me now, I swear..."

"You swear what? You're clearly outnumbered," he says. "You're a few soldiers against an army." Laughter filters around the room, but he doesn't scare me one bit.

"Bring the bitch out," he says, waving to his henchmen in the back.

Immediately, the door swings open with a loud creak,

and one of Tony's men is holding her upright, her body limp in his grip. Her hands are bound, her face bloodied and streaked with tears, and a bloodied rag is tightly tied around her mouth, muffling her cries.

My heart races in my chest as I see the state she's in. Fury and panic course through my veins, mixing into an explosive cocktail. I feel my free hand ball into a tight fist, my knuckles turning white as my nails dig into my palms. My vision blurs with a red tint as I lock eyes with Rosie, silently willing her to hold on a little bit longer and follow my lead.

"You know, when I discovered you were after me, I couldn't help but take something dear to you yet again."

I feel a knot form in my stomach as I remember the sight of my brother's lifeless body, surrounded by a pool of blood. But I quickly push the thought away, focusing on the present moment and the need to save Rosie.

"For weeks now, I've been watching you, and you didn't even know it. I've sent my men to the Vanilla Club to keep an eye on you. Keeping an eye on both of you," he states, staring between Rosie and me.

"You even roughed up Joey here when he felt up your bitch at the club," Tony says, motioning to one of his henchmen who has a semi-automatic pistol pointing at my head. Joey touches his nose with his spare hand, clearly still feeling the pain.

"Lucky for you, he didn't kill you right then and there," Tony continues, and Rosie's eyes widen with realization.

I sneer in response. "He could have tried."

"Now drop your fucking weapons," Tony spits, grabbing Rosie from his man and pointing the pistol at her head.

"Everything is going to be all right, Rosie." I can feel my heart racing as the fear in Rosie's eyes continues to grow, and every passing second feels like a thousand wasps stinging my skin. The weight of the situation bears down on me, threatening to consume me, but I push through the fear.

"Okay, Tony. I'll do as you say," I reply, taking in the fear in her eyes.

He pulls her hair to his nose, and she closes her eyes. Fury runs through my veins, ice cold in its revenge.

I hear Justin whisper behind me. "No, Vin. We're as good as dead."

"Fucking do it," I yell back at Justin, my voice shaking with anger and desperation as I watch him with his hands on Rosie. Justin and his partner drop their guns behind me, but I know I can't risk a firefight with Rosie so close to Tony.

"Slowly, Vincent," Tony sneers, relishing his control over the situation. I can see the fear in Rosie's eyes as I slowly lower my gun to the concrete floor, knowing that surrendering is our only option for now. She shakes her head, understanding what this means for us, and I nod, trying to reassure and calm her as best as I can.

Tony shoves Rosie to the side, and I watch as she stumbles, then runs toward me. My heart races with relief and fear as I sprint up to meet her, catching her in my arms and holding her tightly as if she might disappear if I let go. I remove the gag from her mouth, and she takes a deep breath, tears streaming down her face.

"I'm so sorry, Vin," she says through tears. I take her in, and my heart aches at the sight of her.

"No, I'm the one who's sorry."

"Oh, how fuckin sweet," Tony mocks us.

The tension in the air is palpable, and I know that

anything could happen at any moment. Despite my efforts to remain focused on Rosie, I can feel the weight of his stare on me.

"Rosie, go outside," I command, my gaze locked on her glossy eyes.

"No, Vincent," she protests.

"Listen to your man, sweetheart. It might be the last time," Tony warns, causing terror to lace her hazel eyes.

My fury intensifies as I face him, but then I turn back to her. "Go now." I press her arm hard, urging her to leave. She reluctantly walks away, and I watch her exit as the door shuts behind her.

My focus drifts back to Tony, where he points his rifle at my head.

"I just have one question," I state.

"Oh yeah, what's that?" he asks as he smirks at the power he wields over us in our surrender.

"Does Domenic Gambino know you've switched sides?"

He stops suddenly and tilts his gun to the side. "What the fuck you talking about?"

"You're working with the rival, Angelinos. Why?"

As Tony's eyes narrow, his thin lips twist into a sinister grin, revealing a row of yellowing teeth. "This cat knows some shit, hey?" He snorts before adding, "Well, may as let you in before I blast you away."

Laughter erupts around him. He silences them with a firm hand as he stares at me with sinister eyes. "Domenic is as good as fucking dead." He spits on the floor next to him, his eyes narrowing as if to emphasize his contempt for the man.

"His father has always made me pay for the hit on your family. Always fucking punishing me for it. But if he wasn't man enough to put two holes into your old man, then I was.

Nobody disrespects the Gambino name like your old man did. He knew we'd lose millions of fucking dollars in the deal he brokered. But Gaetano blames me for it. Always has. Since then, he's been inching me out of the family, bit by fucking bit. Well, I know exactly how to hurt him. His fucking son, Domenic. He's not going to know what's coming once the Angelinos are through with him." His laugh echoes through the empty warehouse, a sound that chills me to the bone.

"You're one sick son of a bitch," I say, barely holding it together.

"And now it's time for you to meet your dead brother." He laughs and then aims the gun squarely at my head.

"You've gotta have a plan B, Tony," I say, and he pauses as he stares at me over the barrel of the gun.

The side door creaks open, and Domenic Gambino, son of the mafia boss, Gateano, marches inside. He wears an expensive black suit and a gold Rolex, giving the impression of a respectable businessman rather than a mobster.

As Domenic approaches, tension rises in the air. His eyes are dark and calculating, and his movements are deliberate and controlled. He's been trained for this, and it shows in the way he carries himself.

Tony's men shift uneasily, sensing that something is about to happen. But Domenic remains calm, like a predator stalking its prey.

"Domenic? What are you doing here?" The surprise in Tony's voice is evident as he asks.

I echo, "Plan B."

Tony's beady eyes reach mine, then dart back to Domenic's. He seethes as the realization dawns on him.

"You've been working with Slater?" he growls out in disbelief.

It turns out Gabriel, Rosie's brother, was indebted to the Angelino Mafia, who owns all the loan sharks in Silverton. When I paid off Gabriel's debt, I met with August Angelino to ensure that his entire debt was paid and squared up. However, I overheard a private phone conversation between August and Tony Gambino, during which they were planning a hit on Gambino's own family member, Domenic. I was tempted to kill Gambino then and there, but he wasn't present, and I still didn't know his whereabouts. All I knew was that he had betrayed his own family. At the time, the information was useless, but when Justin informed me they had Rosie, I knew what had to be done.

In a desperate bid to rescue Rosie, I called Domenic Gambino himself, using the only leverage I had left, even if it meant collaborating with the enemy.

"It doesn't matter, you piece of shit. You went against us with the Slater hit, and you've been screwing us ever since. My father has put up with you because of your family. But you've gone too far now."

"I don't know what you're talking about," Tony says, facing Domenic.

By now, at least fifteen men are inside the warehouse, and fear is evident on Tony and his men's faces. Like an errant dog, Tony is jerky in his movements, realizing the game is up.

"Dom, we go way back. Don't do this," Tony pleads with a shaky voice.

I slowly turn and see Justin signaling toward the door to our right, but I can't leave, not until I know the son of a bitch is dead.

Domenic draws his pistol slowly, with deadly precision, and I'm glad he's on my side.

"Get the hell out of here, Slater," he barks as he points his gun toward Tony.

"That wasn't the deal," I snap, and his nostrils flare.

He nods, acknowledging the phone conversation we had an hour earlier when I was driving out here. He gets Tony only if I get to see him put a bullet in him.

Tony looks from me, then back to Domenic. His weight shifts on each foot as he erratically shifts from side to side.

"Dom, you... you don't know what you're talking about," he stammers. Fear spreads into the air like urine seeping from a desperate man. He knows his time is up.

"You damn bastard, Tony. We were family. You don't order a hit on me and get to live."

"Dome—" Tony attempts to fire, but Domenic expertly dodges the shot and swiftly retaliates, delivering two precise shots straight into Tony's chest, causing him to collapse onto the ground, lifeless. The sound of gunfire fills the air, bodies falling, and screams echoing through the building.

Justin grabs my arm, pulling me toward the door, but my eyes remain fixed on Tony's lifeless body. I can feel the relief inside me, knowing that justice has been served.

More of Gambino's men rush inside the abandoned warehouse, creating a flurry of chaos and bullets whizzing past our ears.

"Dammit, Vincent! Now," Justin yells, grabbing my arm and pulling me toward the door. My heart races as we make a run for it, the sound of gunfire echoing in our ears

The sun outside beats down, and I squint, looking for Rosie.

She sees me and comes running toward me. She bursts into my arms, and relief hits me immediately. Her body trembles as she clings to me, her heart racing against mine.

I run my fingers through her hair, pulling her closer as I whisper in her ear, "I've got you, Rosie. You're safe now."

I kiss her and pull her in, wrapping my arms around her. I taste the blood in her mouth, but I don't care. I need her, all of her. She pulls back, and I take her in.

"Did they hurt you?" I ask, taking in her scratches. Dried blood lines the side of her face, and her mascara is smeared.

"No, I'm okay," she says as tears flood down her cheeks. "Is he dead?" she asks in a whisper.

Chaos ensues in the background as more of Gambino's men rush inside the abandoned warehouse. I know we need to leave, but I can't help but hold onto Rosie a little longer, savoring the feeling of having her back in my arms. But the sound of bullets continues to ring in my ears, reminding me of the danger we're still in.

"Retreat, Alpha one," Justin says into his comms unit. "We have to go now, Vincent!"

"We have to go, Rosie," I say, taking her hand and pulling her toward the car.

It's been over two hours since we left the abandoned warehouse and returned to my apartment. After Rosie was checked over by my physician and given the all-clear, she walked into the living room, where I was going over the events of the day, trying to make sense of it all.

I notice she's holding her overnight bag tightly in her hands, ready to leave. I pause, unsure of what to say or do next.

"Is he dead?" she repeats, but this time with more force.

I get up and walk over to her, and when she steps back, a pain hits my chest.

"Yes, but not by my hand," I reply, trying to placate her.

"I see," she responds, but there's no emotion in her voice.

"Where are you going, Rosie?"

"I told you, I'm leaving. None of this changes anything."

I blink. Am I missing something here?

"How can you say that? I didn't kill him!" I urge out.

She lets out a sigh. "It doesn't matter, Vincent. You and I, we'd never work. You're going back to London. I'm finishing college and starting a career in a few months."

"Maybe I don't have to go back to London," I say because she's slipping through my fingers. And it's true. I'm over London.

Maybe I could stay here with her, and we could make this work.

She shakes her head. "You let me go."

I'm confused. "What are you talking about?"

She slides her hand into the bag and pulls out her phone. "Justin's men found my phone. There's a message from you wishing me my best life."

"That's because I thought you weren't coming home!"

"I've never been in love. That was before you came along. I have always had to take care of myself, Vincent. That's just how I am and how I always will be. I will not be with someone who one day decides they can't be in this and casts me aside. There is no room for me with vengeance in your heart. You have to let him go."

Her words sting as I realize that she's right. I've let my desire for revenge consume me, and in doing so, I've pushed away the one person who means everything to me. I know I need to let my brother go and move on with my life.

"Rosie, wait, please," I say, reaching out to grab her hand.

But she pulls back, tears streaming down her face. "I'm sorry, Vincent. I can't do this anymore," she whispers before turning and walking out the door, leaving me standing there, alone and empty.

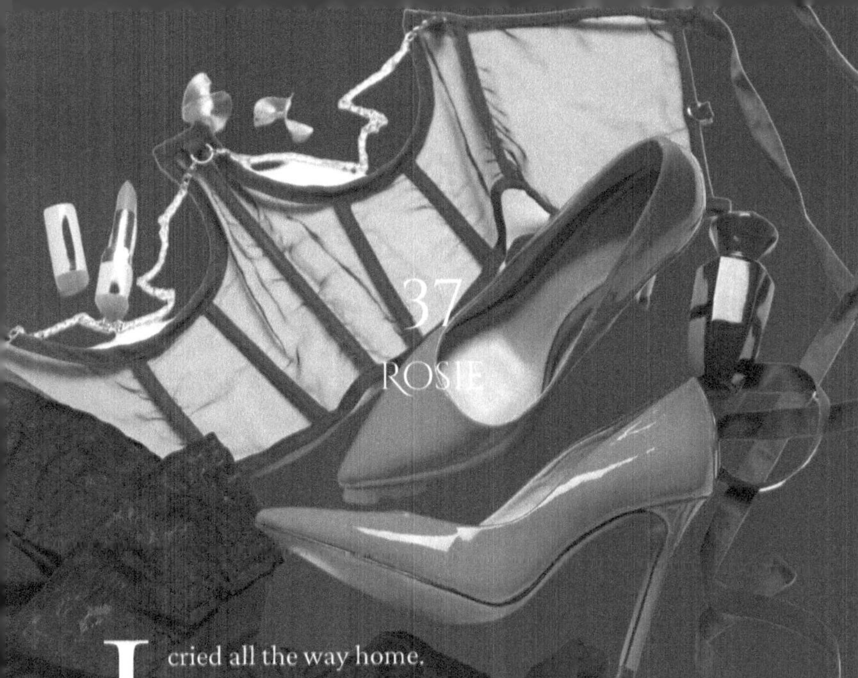

I cried all the way home.

Now that I'm here, the tears haven't stopped flowing. Thankfully, neither Sara nor Ethan are home to witness my breakdown, but they'll be back soon.

I was terrified for my life earlier, but what scared me even more was the thought of Vincent laying down his weapon and dying in front of me. It felt like yet another person special to me was being ripped away instantly, like my brother and mother before him.

I read the message in the shower at his place, where he had easily given up on me when he thought I wasn't coming back after my shift. He let me go without a fight, and I can't be with a man like that.

I need to be more to someone.

I need to be special to someone.

I thought that was him.

I saw it and felt it in his touch when we made love.

∼

It's after midnight, and I'm hopelessly drunk, drowning myself in a bottle of tequila while Sara and Freddie dance to a Groove Armada track in my living room.

I plant my head in my hands and wonder if Vincent ever truly had a chance, given how fiercely guarded I am.

My phone pings, and I quickly reach for it, already knowing it's not him. He's the type to be done with me the moment I give him an inch.

"Shit," I mutter when I see Angela's name on the screen. I haven't replied to her three phone calls and countless texts. Today was the last day of the internship program, and with everything that's happened, I completely forgot about it and never got back to her.

I thumb out a quick reply.

Me: *Hey, sorry, wasn't feeling too good today to come in.*

I see the dots quickly flash on the screen as she types a reply.

Angela: *Well, you didn't miss much. He wasn't here for most of it anyway. Let's catch up when you're feeling better, okay?*

Of course, he wasn't there. He was in a shootout with me as a hostage. I choose different words.

Me: *Love to.*

· · ·

I press my head into my hands, feeling hazy from the buzz of the alcohol.

"Come on, Rosie! Don't let your fall down the stairs stop you from dancing!" I pause suddenly at his words, then remember that was the story I fabricated to hide my injuries. Freddie pulls me upright, and my legs follow behind me.

I move halfheartedly to the beat when Sara calls out, "Come on! Forget about him. You've finished your internship. We're on spring break. You should be cheering!"

Sara grabs my hands and twirls me around. I let out a slip of laughter.

She's right. I need to forget about him.

A hangover as big as the Grand Canyon wracks through me when I wake and lurch over the toilet bowl, everything in my stomach leaving me. It's only after lunch that I start to feel somewhat normal again. And by 'normal,' I mean my heart still feels like it's been ripped from my chest, knowing I'll never be with Vincent Slater again.

Sara brings me a cup of peppermint tea, saying it's apparently good for nausea, and takes a seat across from me on the couch. Freddie and Ethan are at the other end, chatting about New York Fashion Week, and Freddie knows all things fashion by the sounds of it.

Ethan has come clean to Sara about his family's mega wealth and textile empire, and by the looks of it, they couldn't be closer.

"Thanks," I say, sipping on the hot tea. It's heavenly as it slides down my throat.

"So, now's definitely not the time to tell you I told you

so." She purses her lips together and tilts her head to the side.

"But you'll say it anyway?" I roll my eyes.

Her hand sits atop mine on the armchair. "Listen, I'm here for you. We all are."

"We?" I ask disbelievingly as I look at Ethan.

"Me too," Ethan says, plopping on the couch beside Sara, throwing his arm over her, and pulling her into the crook of his neck.

I stare at Sara. "What? I love him. We tell each other everything. I'm sorry."

I let out an audible sigh.

"Love you too, babes." Ethan plants a kiss on her head, and it's the sweetest thing.

No. I hate love. I hate anything to do with happily ever afters. Freddie looks at me, and I flare my nostrils, and he sniggers.

"I can't believe you fell for him, Rosie," Ethan says with a scowl.

"Hang on a minute, what's not to fall for?" Freddie adds. "And he is smitten with our Rosie here. I've seen it in his eyes."

"Yeah, well, sometimes love isn't enough," I say into my teacup.

"Do you love him?" Sara leans forward, dragging my eyes up to hers. It's so quiet you could hear a pin drop as I feel the weight of their stares.

"I did, but love isn't enough," I admit, defeated.

Sara frowns.

"I'm sure Brent, Darcy, or whoever you're reading might argue with you there," Freddie counters.

I shake my head. "Brontë, not Brent, and not even she could."

"What happened? You blurted out a bunch of gibberish last night, then collapsed in a heap of tears where we couldn't get anything out of you. We had to put you to bed," Sara explains, placing her hand on my knee.

"He has a lot going on. He lives in London for a start. And I am two months out from graduating. We're just at different timelines in our lives."

"Yeah, no. None of that seems like a reasonable excuse. Two people who love each other should be with one another," Sara says.

"Maybe he doesn't love her?" Ethan says, and Sara punches his arm hard, and he flinches.

"You know, maybe that's exactly it, Ethan." I stand and walk into the kitchen, hearing Sara scold her boyfriend over his remark.

"Now, who wants bacon and eggs? I'm cooking," I say, putting a stop to any more conversation.

Freddie jumps up excitedly. "I'll take some bacon and eggs any day of the week!" Sara and Ethan nod in agreement as I begin to prepare breakfast.

As the bacon sizzles on the pan, I try to push away thoughts of Vincent and what could have been. But Ethan's right. Maybe he didn't love me at all. If he loved me, he would have fought for me.

For us.

But he's not here.

He's probably halfway to London by now, forgetting we ever existed.

38

VINCENT

The knowledge that Tony Gambino is dead should make me feel content. It's been a week, and it should have helped me forget the vengeance in my heart, knowing that the soul sucker is now a corpse. And to some extent, it does.

However, losing Rosie is a another story.

I've spent most of my life searching for Edgar's real murderer, and not only did I find him, but he's now gone. I should be happy, and the police have no clue about my involvement in his demise. Domenic Gambino took care of everything and even destroyed the building, along with any evidence.

The media reported the killing as a gang-related incident, and thanks to Justin and Domenic, Rosie's and my name are not in the news. Justin got rid of the snitch feeding Tony information, which led us to Tony and the trap we found ourselves in.

The snitch has met his maker thanks to an inmate, which is a small consolation while Montero still rots away for his part.

But none of this can bring Rosie back. She's gone, and I can't stop thinking about her. It's not regret about Tony's death that keeps me up at night, but rather the regret of losing the one woman I ever loved.

The pain is so visceral that it tears at the outer edges of my chest like a stabbing pain. I throw back the rest of my scotch and the burn from the half bottle I consumed before it disappears. But even with the alcohol numbing my senses, I can't find any comfort. The penthouse has been so much emptier since she left. It's an empty hive in need of its queen.

I close my eyes, and the image of her looking up at me with desire fills my mind. Her hazel eyes stare deep inside me, her touch lingers on my skin, and we move together rhythmically, making love with our arms wrapped around one another. My mind goes hazy, and I lean into it, trying to forget the ache of her absence.

I just need to pass out.

It's been nearly two months since she left, and I'm still in New York, surviving on a diet of whisky and double-shot macchiatos. My brother is dealing with his own set of problems, so I'm stuck here, trying to fill his shoes and keep everything running smoothly. But in doing so, I've reverted to my old ways, the ruthless version of myself that I thought I had left behind. I hate this version of me, but I don't know how to shake him off.

Rosie was the only one who could bring out my softer side, and without her, I feel lost.

I'm running late for my weekly catchup with Harry and Caleb, but I need a quick drink to steady my nerves. So I pour a whisky and down it quickly, then grab my wallet and phone and head to the elevator.

The doorman holds the door open for me as I step out onto the bustling Manhattan street. The heat wave gripping the city is palpable.

Summer should be a time for laughter and good times, but I have none of that. And by the looks of Rosie, neither does she. Maybe I've waited outside her house a few times to make sure she's okay. Or maybe I've called Trinity University to find out when her final exams are so I can shadow her. Those moments are the only times in my week when my head isn't full of noise, and everything feels right because she's in my life.

But she's not. She doesn't even see me lurking in the shadows. Sometimes when I see her, she appears to be crying, and all I want to do is run to her and tell her everything will be okay. But she's right. I gave up on us too easily, and I don't know how to fix it. My hollow heart isn't mended like I thought it would be after seeking vengeance. If anything, I feel emptier. The pain is visceral, tearing at the edges of my chest like a stabbing pain.

As usual, I'm the last to arrive at Sojos. Julius, Caleb, and Harry are already seated at our regular corner table. The waitress greets me with a smile, as she always does when we come here. I nod back, feeling as though my ability to connect with anyone has been sucked out of me. Only when I think about Rosie does my desire come to life, pulsing like a defibrillator.

Even when she was being stubborn and not submissive, I still wanted her.

"Over here," Harry calls out, pulling out my chair.

"You look like shit," Julius remarks, sipping his beer.

"Could you come up with something more original than that?" I respond, annoyed at his lack of creativity.

I tune out as they begin discussing the game on the screen. Even Julius, who is usually quite talkative, seems lost in thought and glances up at me from time to time.

Dinner comes and goes, and I've lost count of how many whiskeys I've consumed.

"Are you really going back to London?" Harry asks, flagging down the waitress for the check.

"Of course," I reply.

"Are you sure about that?" Julius chimes in. "I think there's someone here who's keeping you from leaving, and you don't have the guts to do anything about it."

"Oh, straight in for the kill," Harry comments, amused. I glare at him before turning to my brother. "I'm here because the business is sinking while you're off doing God knows what."

Julius stares at me but doesn't say anything.

"What's going on with you, man? You've been weird lately," Caleb chimes in.

"I'm fine. Don't change the subject," I snap back, taking a swig of whisky.

"You can't just fire everyone," Harry says, trying to reason with me.

"Fucking watch me," I retort, feeling the anger bubble inside me.

"Come on, guys," Caleb intervenes, attempting to defuse the situation.

Julius holds up his hands in surrender. "You're right. We're all here for you, Vin. If you need us, we're here. We know how much she meant to you."

I feel a pang in my chest at the mention of *her.* "Thank

you. And maybe I have been a bit of a dick lately," I admit begrudgingly.

"Did I just hear him correctly?" Harry jokes, chuckling.

"No, what? Say it again," Caleb teases.

"I'm sorry, all right?" I say.

"What?" Caleb says.

"He said sorry," Harry adds.

"Come on, one more time," Julius joins in.

"Don't push it," I warn, but we all laugh nonetheless.

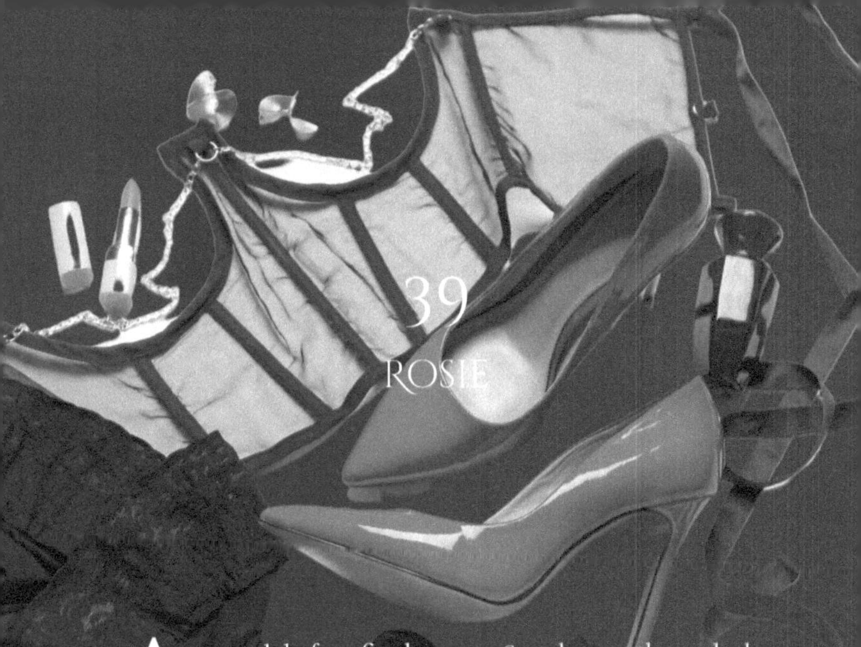

Aweek before final exams, Sara bursts through the door with a pile of mail in her hands. "This came for you. It's embossed with the Slater Corp brand," she exclaims.

Oh God.

The past eight weeks have flown by in a blur. I've been going through the motions of school, applying for jobs, and working. I'm no longer working at the Vanilla Club. Instead, I've taken a respectable job as a first-year student tutor on campus. It's enough to get me by until I graduate and move on to a new position.

I've been offered several roles, including one at Slater Corp. Julius even reached out personally to offer me a position, but I haven't decided yet which one to take. They are all offering above-average salaries, but I know the money will come. I'm finally confident enough to realize that I can do this.

Graduation is just around the corner, but I won't admit to Sara that I cry myself to sleep most nights. My willpower and strong veneer have been chipping away ever since I walked out of Vincent's penthouse. I'm tired of being strong all the time. It's draining. I want to go back to how Vincent cared for me, made me feel special, and took away all my decision-making. There was a power in that that made me feel so free.

Sara hands me the letter, and I recognize his handwriting immediately. "Come on, open it, or I will," she urges.

"All right, calm down," I reply.

I run my hand over the embossed letters of his name, swallowing down all the memories wrapping themselves around my heart. As I tear open the letter, something slips from the paper and falls to the ground.

Dearest Rosie,

It was my intention to take you away to St. Barts after you graduated, but maybe you can enjoy it with your friends instead.

The best thing that happened to me was you, Rosie.

Vin

I hear Sara scoop up the papers from the floor.

"Oh my God. These are tickets and accommodation to St. Barts," she exclaims.

I'm moved by the gesture, but I can't seem to move from the spot where my feet hit the floor. My fingers glide over the thick penmanship of his cursive letters, yearning to reconnect with him through his words, but my mind pushes away the emotions that choke my throat like quicksand. *God, I miss him so much.*

"You know we have to go, right?" Sara interrupts my thoughts of Vincent and reminds me of the trip to St. Barts he sent us. Reluctantly I pull away from his perfect penmanship and find Sara staring at me wide-eyed and full of excitement.

"Sara, I don't know if I can," I say, my voice heavy with reluctance.

She pulls me in for a crushing hug, and I let my head fall onto her shoulder, seeking her comfort.

"I know it's hard. I know you're tough, and you keep it all to yourself, but I also know you deserve this trip. Everything that's happened this year is enough proof that of all people, you need this trip."

I know she's right, as much as I hate to admit it. A vacation is what I need, and I've been longing to visit St. Barts or anywhere that's not in Jersey or New York. "Fine," I concede in a soft voice.

She pulls away, clutching my shoulders and staring at me in disbelief. "Fine?" she repeats incredulously.

"You're right. I need to stop being miserable and start living again. Vincent gave me this gift, and I should take it, right?"

"Oh my God, we're going to have the best time ever," Sara exclaims with excitement. "Do you think we should invite Ethan?" She considers before quickly changing her mind. "Actually, let's make it a girls' trip only."

"Yes, no men allowed," I agree.

"Absolutely."

~

As the graduation ceremony draws to a close, I'm hit with a wave of melancholy. Another chapter of my life is over, and I'm left standing here alone, surrounded by happy families and smiling graduates. Their joy feels so foreign to me like I'm a ghost watching from afar. It's time to move on with my life and forget him, but I know that's easier said than done.

Just as I'm lost in my thoughts, my phone vibrates in my purse. I glance at the screen to see Julius Slater's name and let out a resigned sigh. He's probably calling to check if I've made a decision about the job offer.

Again.

I'm graduating with honors and just have to choose what job I want. I've narrowed it down to two—Slater Corp and Solomon Capitalist, their competitor. I know Slater Corp really wants me, with the weekly calls from their recruitment manager. But part of me wants to go with Solomon Capitalist, just to prove to myself that I can make it on my own without relying on the Slater name. It's a tough decision to make, and I feel like no matter what I choose, I'll always wonder if I made the right choice.

As I stare at the call from Julius Slater, I debate whether to answer or not. I know what he wants to talk about, and I'm not sure I'm ready to decide yet. But my curiosity gets the best of me, so I answer the call.

"Hello, Julius."

"Rosie, how are you?"

"I'm good, thanks. Just finished up with graduation," I say, feigning my own happiness yet again.

"I know. Congratulations."

How does he know?

Vincent.

"So tell me, is Slater Corp lucky enough to have you here working for us?"

I let out a sigh. "Julius, as much as I want to say yes, I'm not sure if it's a good idea with all that's happened."

"I see."

"You know we didn't offer you the job because of your relationship with Vincent, right?"

"I know," I say. "I'm going away tomorrow, and I'll be back in a week. Can I let you know then?"

"Of course."

"Julius?"

"Yes."

"How is he?" I ask in a moment of weakness.

He lets out a bark of laughter.

"Rosie, Vincent, at the best of times, is a grumpy prick. And now that you're not in his life, he's on a fucking warpath."

"Oh," I whisper.

"How are you, Rosie, really?"

"I'm fine," I say, and I'm greeted with silence.

"Well, enjoy your vacation. Where are you going anyway?"

"St. Barts."

"St. Barts?" he parrots, and I wonder if he just didn't hear me.

"Yes." I leave out the part where Vincent gifted me the trip because it's unnecessary.

"Well, have the best time, and I'll hear from you upon your return."

~

As the plane descends into St. Barts' airport, memories of the destructive version of Vincent flood my mind. It's hard to reconcile that version of him with the caring, thoughtful man I fell in love with. The memories of our time together still haunt me, and I wonder if I'll ever truly be able to move on.

Sara snores beside me, the result of too many cocktails at dinner. I know this trip will be a turning point, a chance to escape the never-ending cycle of work and study and finally make a decision. I haven't had a moment to breathe, let alone process my feelings for Vincent.

But at night, my dreams are consumed by him, a constant reminder of the love I can't seem to let go of.

40

VINCENT

Since I sent Rosie the letter and tickets, I haven't received a single word. It's not surprising, given her fierce streak, but it confirms my fears that she's done with me. We're done. The realization is too much to bear.

I'm staring at my computer screen, but the emails might as well be in a foreign language. The sky might as well be made of neon lights, and the air might as well be suffocating. I can't stop thinking about her.

I keep checking the time. It's after nine, and I know she's already landed in St. Barts.

Without me.

The crushing pain bores down on my chest when a knock pulls me from my downward spiral.

"Come in, Julius," I say because no one else would be here this late.

He pushes open the door and steps inside my office.

"Still here?" My brother looks more tired lately, and I wonder what has happened to make him this way. I make a note to ask him, just not today.

"Looks that way," I reply flatly.

"I thought you'd be in St. Barts by now."

What?

"You spoke to Rosie?"

"Yes, we've been speaking. I want her to work here. In case you haven't noticed, she hasn't accepted our position yet."

"Of course, I've noticed. Tell me, what did she say?"

"She said she graduated today and that she is going on a trip to St. Barts and needs time to think about whether she wants the job."

I let out a sigh. "And that's it," I say with finality in my tone.

"Not exactly."

My eyes snap up to his. "Julius, spit it out."

"She asked how you are."

The edges of my heart soften. She still cares.

He sits down on the armchair opposite and leans forward in his chair.

"Vincent, I never questioned you when a building burned down, killing Tony Gambino a few months ago. I never asked why you were missing that day because I know you had to finish what you started. But you're still empty. You love her, yet I've doubted you've even told her."

"I do love her," I say, admitting to myself aloud what I've known for months.

"Then fucking open your heart and let her in. You deserve to be happy. Our brother would have wanted that. We all want that for you."

I swallow the thick mountain of sand in my throat as I listen to my brother's wise words.

"I might be too late," I admit painfully.

"You're a Slater. Impossibility is our possibility."

I close my eyes and take a deep breath, trying to push aside the fear and doubt that has been gnawing at me for so long. I know what I have to do. I have to find Rosie, tell her how I feel, and hope against hope that she will take me back. The thought of facing her rejection is unbearable, but the thought of never trying is even worse.

I raise my head, determination coursing through my veins. I have to take a chance. I have to fight for what I want. And what I want is her.

"Now go and get her," Julius says with a resolute nod.

We stand up in unison, fueled by a fiery determination that burns in my veins the next thing I know, I'm on the company jet with a singular purpose to get my queen back.

Thanks to my assistant, who packed a bag for me and met me on the tarmac, I arrive in St. Barts early in the morning. I'm dressed in comfortable clothes, feeling more relaxed than I have in months. For once, I slept because I wanted to, not because I was trying to numb the pain of losing my brother.

Julius' words cleared a path in my mind, allowing me to believe I'm capable of letting go of the past and living the life I deserve. But I can't do it alone. I need her to meet me halfway, push past her fears and barriers, and fight for us like I'm willing to do.

When I arrive at the hotel, the Olympic-size pool is teeming with the hotel's exclusive clientele, surrounded by dark gray tiles and dotted with blue and white umbrellas. The air is filled with laughter and splashing water as the bar staff in crisp white uniforms flit about, taking orders from vacationers lounging on the poolside chairs.

The luxurious surroundings are framed by lush palm trees and vibrant greenery, and the sparkling water of the pool seems to merge with the sapphire blue of the sky. But despite the idyllic setting, my mind is fixated on one thing.

Finding her.

I scan the area, hoping to catch a glimpse of her, but she's nowhere to be seen.

She's likely at her private pool or accessing the nearby beach, and the thought of having to search for her sends a shiver down my spine. But then, a familiar brunette catches my eye.

Rosie.

She approaches the south side of the pool, and I steel myself with determination.

I won't leave this island without her.

She's dressed in a lilac bikini, her brown hair cascading in tight waves from being wet earlier. As my eyes scan over her toned legs, I can feel my body reacting in a way that makes me tightly grip my hands around the tumbler of ice-cold water. But I know I really need to calm down and wait for her next move, painful as it may be.

She doesn't see me, but she's looking around for someone. Maybe her roommate, Sara, but I doubt it.

I've watched her from afar before, and I feel her sensing me. She takes her hand up to her throat, rubbing the column of her neck as she continues to look around. Like magnets, I know we're drawn to each other, and it's me she senses.

As I sit at the bar, my gaze never leaving her, a feeling of hope surges through my chest. I can feel Edgar's presence, silently urging me on and giving me the courage to face the woman I love without a clear plan.

I don't have a clear plan, which is foreign as I thrive on control and organization. In the past, I exerted my control over her, which she craved.

I can't help but think of how she surrendered to me, letting me take charge of her needs and desires. But I can't let myself get lost in those thoughts right now. I need to be fully present for this moment. My life may depend on it.

She's reading a book, and my impatience is growing. I can't wait any longer. I leave my spot at the bar and weave my way through the crowds of people, determined to reach her.

As I approach, her eyes lift from her book, and our gazes lock.

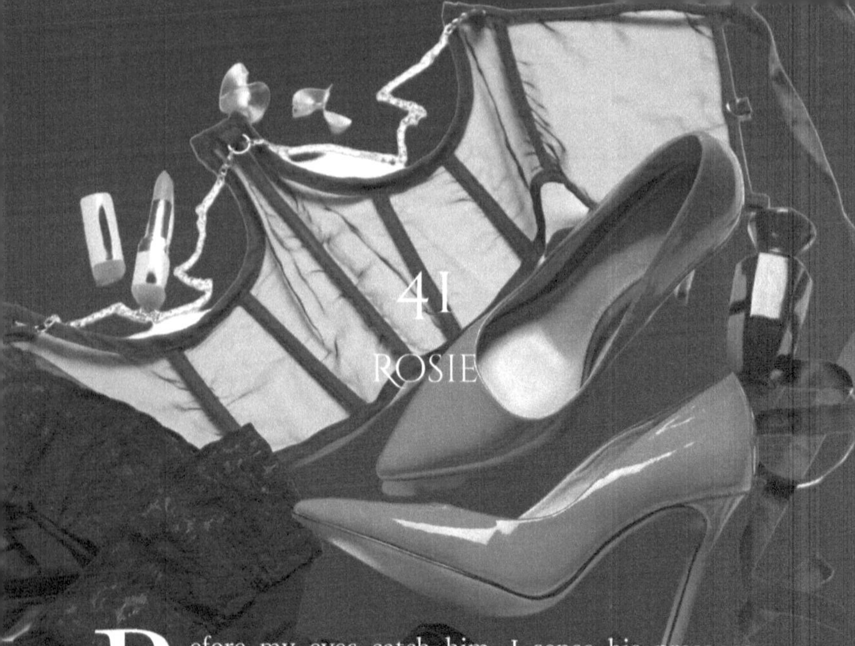

41

ROSIE

Before my eyes catch him, I sense his presence. Lying in my chair, a warmth envelops me and spreads to my chest. It's foolish to think he's here until he materializes before me.

As he approaches, I can't help but notice how time has treated him well. His loose black button-down shirt, with the sleeves rolled up, highlights his toned and tanned skin, bringing back memories of his dominant presence. His hair is longer, swept to the side in an unruly manner, and I fight the urge to run my hands through it. His forest-green eyes catch the sunlight and lighten, their integrity halting my heart and taking my breath away.

I've spent every night crying myself to sleep and every day burying myself in studying and tutoring just to forget him, and now he's here.

He takes the seat beside me and greets me with a smile. "Hello, Rosie."

I reply breathlessly, "Vincent."

We stare at each other in silence before I ask, "What are

you doing here? Aren't you supposed to be in London?" I sit up straight, facing him directly.

"I've been here all along, little one," he says, and his words hit me like a ton of bricks. I push away the memories of our past sexual encounters. I can't let them cloud my judgment right now.

His gaze wanders to my lips, then back to my eyes.

"Vincent, thank you for the tickets, but—" I start, but he cuts me off.

"I wanted you to think I was in London. But all along, I was here. I needed to be close to you even though you didn't want to see me. Do you know how hard it was to watch you, to see how beautiful you are, and not be near you? Not to breathe the scent of your hair or glide my hand over your skin and feel your warmth. It was like a pain that had no expiration date, enduring and soul-crushing, until I realized something. I may be a coward for not chasing after you, but so are you," he continues, and his words catch me off guard.

"What?" I recoil in confusion. "I am not," I protest.

He leans in, and his hand runs along my wrist, wrapping his thumb across my hand. Flames of desire ignite within me, but I quench them almost immediately.

"But I can't blame you because that's what I love about you, Rosie," he declares. I am left stunned and speechless. "Since a young age, you've always had to fend for yourself due to being abandoned by your father, losing your mother, and having a difficult brother. It has made you fiercely independent," Vincent says.

I feel a heat rise within me that isn't solely due to St. Barts' sun. "And what's wrong with that?" I ask.

"Nothing," he concedes. "But I also know you relished

the pleasure you deserved when you allowed me to take control. You felt free and liberated in those moments because you let me take care of you. You want that, Rosie. You need that."

My mind is racing, trying to process the truth behind his words. He pulls his hand away, and I feel the loss of his touch.

"But I'm not the only coward here," he adds. "You gave up on us too, just as easily, Rosie."

"Excuse me?" I swallow the lump in my throat.

"Everyone you've ever loved has died or abandoned you. I don't think you ever truly let me in for fear of losing me, so you decided to walk away first. Make a clean break."

I feel the weight of his words settling in my chest like a boulder, heavy and unyielding. The emotions that have been simmering beneath the surface of my carefully constructed walls threaten to spill over, but I hold them in check with a trembling breath.

I meet his gaze, trying to convey the jumbled mess of emotions swirling within me.

"I'm here for one reason only." He stares at me with intensity, his voice low and measured as he confesses, "To tell you that I'm completely and unequivocally in love with you. But the next move is yours."

As I look up at him, I struggle to comprehend everything he's telling me. I try to piece together the last few months we spent apart and the six months since I met this man and threw a drink on him.

"Vincent, it could never work," I confess. Maybe I should have given us a chance and been brave enough to take a risk on love. But the thought of letting my guard down and potentially getting hurt terrifies me.

He lets out a wistful sigh and leans in to plant a kiss on my cheek.

"Goodbye, Rosie. It's time for me to let you go," he says. As his lips touch my skin, a rush of emotions floods through me.

Memories of our past together come rushing back, each one more vivid than the last—the way he used to hold me, the sound of his voice as he whispered sweet nothings into my ear, the taste of his lips on mine. I close my eyes and try to hold on to the feeling and the memory of what we once had. But as he pulls away and leaves me, I know that I have to make a choice.

I sit here in shock, watching him leave with a heavy heart. My mind is racing with thoughts and regrets as I try to make sense of everything that just happened. The realization hits me like a ton of bricks.

I need him.

I need Vincent Slater, the ruthless CEO, the man who takes care of me and loves me like no one else ever has. He disappears into the hotel, and a fire ignites within me.

I know what I want, and I won't let him go again.

I burst forward without caring how it looks, my heart pounding with adrenaline as I try to catch the closing elevator doors. My eyes lock onto the broad back of the man I love disappearing inside, and I feel a desperate surge of emotion welling up inside me. The doors slide shut before I can reach them, and for a moment, I'm paralyzed with fear and regret. But then, with a burst of determination, I run toward the elevator and push the button repeatedly until the doors slide open again.

His finger is on the elevator button holding the door open.

"Vin, wait," I say breathlessly, stepping into the elevator. My heart hammers as blood pumps through my ears.

I feel his fingers wrap around my chin, tilting my head to meet his gaze. It's a possessive grip, commanding my body with his touch. He doesn't say anything, but the intensity in his eyes speaks volumes. I feel my heart racing in my chest as he holds me captive at that moment. "What is it, Rosie."

"I'm so scared," I admit. "But that's because I love you so much, and the pain of losing..."

A subtle smirk curls his lips as he pulls me closer and presses his lips against mine. His kiss is like a drug, filling every inch of my body with need and desire. This man is everything to me. My heart and soul belong to him alone.

A deep groan escapes my lips as I feel his growing arousal against my thigh. He pulls back, a knowing smirk still playing on his lips.

"You played me, didn't you, Vin?"

He leans in and sinks his teeth into my neck, and I pull him closer, letting out a breathy moan. "Sometimes we all need a little push in the right direction," he whispers in my ear.

"Is that right?" I let out a chuckle, and his eyes turn dark with need.

He reaches out, pushing the red emergency button in the elevator. I gasp as the elevator jerks to a stop, and I know there's no going back now.

Vincent's eyes meet mine, and my body erupts in a flurry of goose bumps, the intensity of his stare leaving me breathless and electrified. He steps forward, pressing me against the elevator wall, his breath hot against my neck. I bite my lip to stifle a moan, but it escapes anyway as his hand travels down my body, igniting every nerve in its path.

"The title is Sir, little one, or have you forgotten?"

My core clenches with a pent-up need that I can no longer ignore.

"No, Sir, I haven't forgotten."

EPILOGUE
ONE MONTH LATER...

Have you ever felt that warm, tingly sensation that washes over you when you listen to your favorite song or watch your favorite movie?

It's the moment when emotion takes over your senses, and you're left with a scattering of goose bumps splintering across your skin or a deep exhalation after holding your breath without even knowing. Sometimes it's a fluttery sensation in the depths of your stomach or a slash of heat across your chest. It's a feeling that permeates through you, transcending worries or fears, exciting you while also cloaking you with an unexplainable sense of calm. And at that moment, nothing else seems to matter. Even as the world around you crumbles to ashes, your focus remains solely on that *one* feeling.

That's what love is.

I sit at my desk and no longer have to imagine what love is because I am living proof that happy endings do exist, even for someone like me, who was once afraid to open up for fear of losing love again. And even for someone like Vin, whose hungry heart only ever had an appetite for vengeance and hate.

My phone pings, pulling me from my thoughts. I smile, already knowing it's Vin before I even check the message. It's nearly time to go home, so he's either organizing dinner at home or at a fancy restaurant or sending me another naughty message like he does throughout the day.

Damn, I can't get enough of those. The man never fails to make my heart race.

Since St. Barts, we have been inseparable. Vin and I have moved in together in his palatial penthouse, and he even calls me wifey. Not that we are engaged or anything, but the future is all we can talk about, and damn, I already know my answer when that day comes.

I swipe the message.

Vin: *Meet me downstairs now.*

I grin, totally craving his bossy demeanor. Then I sigh as I respond, aware that I still need to complete some tasks before I can call it a day and head home.

Me: *I'm still working. Give me thirty mins?*

A reply quickly lights up my screen.

Vin: *I am your boss's boss. Get that foxy ass down here right this minute.*

. . .

I burst into laughter but swiftly regain composure as I craft a reply.

Me: *Thirty mins, my love x*

I set the phone aside, yet the smile on my face remains unstoppable.

Working at Slater Corp has been everything I ever wanted. I'm at the start of my career at a global company, with a rock by my side every step of the way. Vincent doesn't baby me, nor does he favor me. And when I do ask him something related to work, his intellect and fresh perspective are such a turn-on that it's hard to remain focused.

Angela glances up from her computer and gives me a goofy look.

"It's him again, isn't it?" she asks.

Accepting the internship with Slater Corp was a no-brainer. But when they also hired Angela, I was ecstatic. We meet for lunch most days, except when Vin gives me mind-blowing orgasms on his desk.

I shrug, trying to play it cool. "Shh."

She rolls her eyes. "Girl, you're on the cover of *Hello Magazine* with the Boss Dog, and you're telling me to shh?"

I let out a burst of giggles that I can't seem to contain. Debra walks in from the office nearby, holding the phone to her ear. "Excuse me, Rosie?"

I lift my head. "Yes, Deb."

"Vincent is requesting you downstairs immediately."

Oh, dear God.

I blush from my scalp to the soles of my feet.

"Of course." I hear Angela snort, and I shoot her daggers while I collect my things, shoving them into my backpack before rising.

"Sorry!" I mouth to Deb.

"You're one of the hardest working here, Rosie. Go enjoy yourself."

Smiling at her, I throw my bag on my shoulder and wave at Angela, who is grinning from ear to ear.

Vincent is leaning against the car, looking as dashing as a prince in a fairy tale. His steel-gray suit molds perfectly to his biceps, and his green eyes have this hold on me. I feel my body immediately reacting to him.

"Hello, beautiful." He lowers himself to my height and plants a kiss on my lips.

"Mr. Slater, you're so bossy," I respond, relishing the feeling of his lips against mine, and as he laughs, I accept his extended hand.

We slide into the back seat, and he nods to his driver to move on.

His hand rests high up on my thigh. "Damn, I love it when you wear this skirt. I'm going to have to set you up with an office on the top floor just so I can see you every minute of the day."

I let out a laugh and take his hand in mine. "Then we wouldn't get any work done," I say, interlocking our fingers.

The warmth of his touch sends a wave of contentment through my body.

He runs his tongue across his lower lip. "I think I can live with that, Ms. West," he says, his voice low and husky as he caresses my thigh.

I briefly shut my eyes, savoring his touch, and upon

reopening them, I notice that his driver has strayed from our typical route home. "Where are we headed?" I ask, glancing around to gain some sense of direction.

"Somewhere." I glance at Vincent, seeking a hint.

He gently sweeps a loose strand of hair from my face, then asks, "Why didn't you tell me it was your birthday?"

I'm taken aback that he's aware. "I didn't think it was worth making a fuss over," I answer.

"Why wouldn't it be worth celebrating? You're worth celebrating every day, Rosie," he declares with a soft smile, his thumb stroking my cheek.

"Ever since Mom died, I guess I haven't found anyone special to celebrate it with," I say wistfully.

His hands tenderly cup my face. "You have me now. I'm yours, Rosie. I'm all in, and I promise to take care of you forever. So, celebrating your birthday is non-negotiable, all right?"

My heart squeezes at his heartfelt words. "All right." I kiss him passionately, and he pulls me into his strong chest, allowing me to lose myself in the moment.

When the car comes to a halt, I recognize the oversized front door at the Vanilla Club. Turning to Vin, surprise fills my eyes. A mischievous smirk graces his stunning face, and his gaze challenges me with a playful dare.

"Come with me," he says, taking my hand.

We slide out and walk inside. The place is empty.

Where is everyone? What's happening?" I inquire, grasping his hand as we climb the staircase to the top floor together.

He tightens his grip on my hand, and as we reach the upper floor, I look at him expectantly. "The entire place is ours for the evening," he reveals, his smile brimming with mischief.

"Really?" I exclaim, astonished.

"I wanted to make your birthday unforgettable, and we never got to explore these rooms," he remarks, his eyes growing darker.

Arousal surges through me as he speaks.

He leads me to one of the red leather doors and pauses. Drawing me in for a kiss, goose bumps travel down my arms and settle between my thighs.

"Remember when I asked you to write down every single fantasy you've ever had?"

"Yes," I whisper, my hands trembling with anticipation. It was just a few weeks ago, and I had done as he asked, not giving it a second thought until now.

Vin retrieves a gold key from his pocket and glides it across my bottom lip. The cool metal makes my insides clench.

"Welcome to your fantasy," he says, his eyes growing darker.

I step inside.

I cross the threshold and gasp.

The room is blanketed in a million rose petals, their intoxicating fragrance filling the air. A four-poster bed with black satin sheets dominates the center of the room. The walls are adorned with an array of BDSM and fetish equipment, such as floggers, whips, and riding crops, each meticulously displayed to inspire submission. I imagine Vincent skillfully using each piece of equipment on me, my arousal intensifying by the second.

I step inside and run my hand over the leather cuffs and collars neatly arranged nearby, ready for use. A cushioned spanking bench occupies another corner, while mirrors are strategically placed around the room to enhance the sense of voyeurism and heighten the dominant-submissive dynamic.

Oh my God.

When he asked me to write down my fantasies, I listed one thing and one thing only. To be his submissive in every sense of the word. I wanted to relinquish all control to Vincent.

"I told you, Rosie, you're the best part of me. I promise to always take care of you. That includes not only your heart but your body too. I will never deprive you of what you need."

"Vin," I whisper, the sultry undertone revealing my mounting desire.

The door shuts with a thud, and Vincent's forceful gaze locks onto mine.

"Address me as *Sir*, little one."

THE END.

WANT MORE?

Want more of Rosie and Vincent's sizzling romance?
Visit the link below for a scorching bonus scene...
https://dl.bookfunnel.com/mfwhtuclyj

Interested in the next instalment of the Slater Siblings Series?
A steamy arranged marriage romance with a HEA. Get Julius' book 'Chained Heart' now!
www.authormissywalker.com

Also by Missy Walker

Elite mafia of New York series

Cruel Lust

Stolen Love

Finding Love

Slater siblings series

Hungry Heart

Chained Heart

Iron Heart

Elite Men of Manhattan Series

Forbidden Lust*

Forbidden Love*

Lost Love

Missing Love

Guarded Love

Infinite Love

Small town desires series

Trusting the Rockstar

Trusting the Ex

Trusting the Player

JOIN MISSY'S CLUB

Hear about exclusive book releases, teasers, discounts and book bundles before anyone else.

Sign up to Missy's newsletter here:
www.authormissywalker.com

Become part of Missy's Private Facebook Group where we chat all things books, releases and of course fun giveaways!

https://www.facebook.com/groups/
missywalkersbookbabes

Acknowledgments

There are a few people to thank for this mammoth book!

Danielle A - First, for your kind heart and friendship, and secondly for the low-down on college life in New York.

Chayde, aka @thequeenofbooks. Thank you for being by my side, helping me with all things PA-ish. You've been my ear throughout this entire book, and from the bottom of my heart, thank you!

My beta team, Elle, Chayde, Maria, Jennie, Gemma & Nicole B - your feedback, support, and insight into my characters are invaluable.

To my amazing editors, Chantell and Nicki, I couldn't do this without you!

To the fans, especially those who have followed me from the beginning. You have no idea how much it means to me that I get to do what I love to do, each and every day. It's all because of you. Thank you.

Missy xxx

About the Author

Missy is an Australian author who writes kissing books with equal parts angst and steam. She loves writing stories about billionaires, playboys & forbidden romance – just to name a few.

When she's not writing, she's taking care of her two daughters and doting husband and conjuring up her next saucy plot.

Inspired by the acreage she lives on, Missy regularly distracts herself by visiting her orchard, baking naughty but delicious foods, and socialising with her girl squad.

Then there's her overweight cat—Charlie, dog—Benji, chickens, and bees if she needed another excuse to pass the time.

If you like Missy Walker's books, consider leaving a review and following her here:

tiktok.com/@authormissywalker
instagram.com/missywalkerauthor
facebook.com/AuthorMissyWalker
Private Reader Group -
https://www.facebook.com/groups/
missywalkersbookbabes